A TIME TO HEAL

A NOVEL BY

CLAIRE RAYNER

SIMON AND SCHUSTER · NEW YORK

FOR
NAN POWYS-LYBBE
WITH GRATITUDE

To every thing there is a season, and a time to every purpose under the heaven:

A time to be born, and a time to die; a time to plant, and a time to pluck up that which is planted;

A time to kill, and a time to heal . . .

Ecclesiastes 3:1–3

1

SHE DROVE into the hospital car park at half past nine, though she knew the unit would not be ready for her until ten. But it had been impossible not to be early. She had woken at half past six, filled with a nervous excitement that had lifted her shoulders and thickened her throat so that she could only drink black coffee for breakfast. Which had made George behave in a more than usually tiresome way about his own breakfast.

"What's the matter with it, then?" he had said, his tremulous voice thin with suspicion as he peered sideways at the boiled egg and carefully trimmed bread and butter strips she had given him. "You have it. Make me another one."

"There's nothing the matter with it. Nothing at all. I'm just not hungry, that's all. Now, do for pity's sake eat your breakfast and stop nagging. Look, you can watch me open it for you—see? Not a crack in it. So there can't be anything wrong with it, can there?"

But it had been foolishly self-indulgent to so allow her edginess to spill over into her dealings with him, for he responded to the testy note in her voice with predictable sulks, and she had to spend almost fifteen minutes coaxing him back to some semblance of good humor, so that eventually he had eaten the egg but still pushed the bread and butter away with an ostentatious narrowing of his eyes. He rummaged in his cardigan pocket for a stale biscuit to mumble over, watching her all the time with watery malevolence while she drank her coffee and tried to contain her mounting irritation. These senile paranoid notions of his were getting worse; and the illogicality of them was almost worse than being suspected of feeding him poison. Why he should think the biscuits he filched from the larder were safer than the bread and butter he watched her prepare was beyond her. She relinquished him to the care of Mrs. Davies at nine o'clock with more than usual relief.

9

And all through the drive in the smoky October sunshine along the dull road that stretched itself past the flat burned-stubble fields, her nervousness and excitement had mounted. She tried to control it, thinking deliberately about Oscar's return tonight. Would the trials have been satisfying for him? Would he be expansive and affectionate, or sour with frustration again? Either way, it would be agreeable to see him. She had to admit that though she had not missed his company very much, she had been frequently aware of a need for his physical presence.

She grimaced a little at that thought, and let her mind slide away to Ferris. It was unscientific of her to be so sure. No, not sure. If she were really certain, she would not be so anxious this morning, would she? *Why* so anxious, damn it? His progress had been steady from the start.

She ran over in her mind the whole pattern of the trial. The man had been moribund, undoubtedly, the first time she had seen him. He had lain neatly in the center of the screened white bed, his body making hardly any bulk under the taut counterpane, his chin pointing at the ceiling, the bones so sharply defined under the gray skin that she had suddenly remembered one of the plays she had been in at school. "His nose was as sharp as a pen—"

But there had been nothing else Falstaffian about him. Sunken temples and eye sockets, hands so thin that each joint showed clearly between the bones. She had had no conscientious objection to using him for the trial, none at all. Sister Hornett had said—and she had more experience of death than the rest of them put together—that the man would be lucky if he lasted another month.

"Well, hardly lucky," Sister Hornett had amended, snapping the file of notes closed. "I doubt he's a healthy organ left in his body, poor man. The only thing we can do for him now is to leave him to die decently. God disposes, as they say, Dr. Berry."

"Well, maybe he does, but I'm inclined to do some proposing," Harriet had said almost absently, reading his file. "I could use him for the human trial without any problems, looking at this history—"

10

"But Professor Bell's away!" Sister Hornett had said, her eyebrows curving up into immediate disapproval. "Wouldn't you be better waiting till—"

"I know perfectly well where Professor Bell is, thank you, Sister," Harriet had said tartly, once again leaning over to look at the thinly silent shape in the bed. "And since, as you pointed out yourself, this man will be well past taking part in anything by the time Professor Bell gets back, I'd hardly be better off waiting for him, would I? Any more than the patient would. We'll start immediately, if you please, Sister. I want him moved to the small side room in my unit. This afternoon."

And moved he had been, and she had started work without giving any more thought at all to Sister Hornett's misgivings. She had collected her specimens from the desiccated little body—and Ferris had seemed quite unaware of her activities, though with an almost embarrassed awareness of the way she was using him, she had talked to him as she worked, explaining what she was doing—and the tissue cultures had developed exactly as she had hoped they would, their action on the samples of tissue she had taken from neck glands being precisely as she had extrapolated.

And as the weeks went by, while the tissue cultures were prepared in sufficient bulk for the treatment, and Ferris had lingered on, her hopes had grown. And then, during the past six weeks, through the series of treatment sessions in the unit, she had watched him improve, saw his skin lose its dead color, watched the graph of his blood chemistry rise and then flatten out to normal levels, saw his body fill out as his appetite came back, above all saw the personality and mind inside the body become recognizable human attributes again, and her hopes had approached certainty. Successful animal trials were pleasing enough, but this—this was something quite different.

There was a controlled bustle about the unit when she came in, a tension that so accurately reflected her state of mind that she experienced a suddenly increased surge of anxiety that made her feel almost physically sick. She hadn't felt anything quite like it since the war. The war. David, her father—hell, this was ludicrous! She really must relax, treat this like any other morning; if she allowed memories of long-dead emotion to come bubbling up like this she'd be as much use as a sick headache.

"Good morning, Dr. Berry!" John Caister said from the console of gauges, where he was setting up for the treatment. He smiled at her brilliantly, his head a little on one side. "And how's our medical genius this morning? Speaking for myself, I'm in a *complete* tiz, I promise you."

"When aren't you?" Catherine Warne said acidly as she pinned a cardiograph on the board and nodded across at Harriet. "Good morning, Dr. Berry. I thought you'd like a full run this morning as well as last night's, under the circumstances. He seems very chipper this morning, I must say. You look a bit off yourself, though. Feeling all right?"

"Morning! I'm fine, thank you. Not precisely in a tiz, but—well . . ." Harriet smiled at John; impossible not to like him. Impossible not to like Catherine too, for all her acerbity. She was lucky to have so good a team on this project. "Ferris is in good spirits then? Good. Let's be grateful he didn't turn out to be a difficult type. Have we got this morning's pathology reports too? Splendid."

She slid into the pattern of work gratefully, and at last emotion settled, giving way to the comfort of shapely thought. She checked the results of the tests that had been run on Mr. Ferris, checked the injections lying ready on the covered tray beside the door that led to the hyperbaric oxygen chamber, and then, more to satisfy her need for order than because it was necessary, went to the microscope to look again at the series of histology slides.

The primary growth in the liver had undoubtedly gone; the difference between the biopsy taken the day they had started the treatment and yesterday's was extraordinary. And the lymph node slides too. Theo had assured her that there was complete remission when he had operated last week, but that had been simply a surgical opinion. Here was the microscopic evidence to confirm it.

It was still only ten minutes to ten, and with nothing more she could do until Ferris arrived from the ward at quarter past, she reached across the desk for the telephone and dialed.

"Theo? Good morning. Can you get away for a while? . . . I just thought you'd like to see how Ferris is. We're doing the last one this morning. What? . . . Mm. Bless you. Yes."

She hung up, and smiled across the desk at John. "I'm obviously showing the tension more than I realized. Anyway, Mr. Fowler seemed to notice it—he's coming to hold our hands, he said."

"Oh, that *is* nice!" John stood up and smiled his brilliant smile again. "Such a *perceptive* person, isn't he? I daresay a little coffee would come in handy. I'll make one of my special brews." And he flurried away.

"Gone to comb his hair and pretty himself, more like," Catherine said. "Are you sure you feel all right, Dr. Berry? You do seem a bit—you know."

"Oh, Catherine, do stop fussing over me! Of course I'm all right! But I'm—well, I'm edgy and I can't deny I'd have to be more than human not to feel a little strung out. Aren't you?"

"Not at all! When you get to my age, you know better. You've nothing to fret about, I'm certain. It's been obvious to me this past two weeks and more that you've made it. This'll be the biggest thing that ever came out of Brookbank. Could get you your Nobel. Should get it, if justice were to be done. You've earned it, as no one can know better than I do. I've seen how much work you've put into it. Anyway, high time another woman got some recognition. These men—so busy worrying about their own glory, they don't get down to any real effort."

"Oh, Catherine, for God's sake! I know you don't like Professor Bell, but it isn't true, and you know it. He does work hard—and he's had some nasty knocks, one way and another. The Ross-Craigie business, and—"

Catherine almost snorted. "Ross-Craigie! Best thing that ever happened to the place, losing *him* down the brain drain. If I'd had my way, I'd have washed him down a different sort. Just proves my

13

point! Cared more about his own glory than the job in hand. No, Dr. Berry, I'm right, you'll see. You've made it, you really have—oh, good morning, Mr. Fowler."

Harriet turned as the door closed behind Theo's square bulk, and she held her hands out toward him.

"Hello, Theo! You are good to come. I feel as stupid as a schoolgirl waiting to go in for her A-levels. John Caister calls it being in a tiz—"

"Caister? He would! Good morning, Mrs. Warne. Big day for the ladies of our august establishment! Though I don't imagine you need reminding of that fact."

"Indeed I don't. And if you'll excuse me, I must check the oxygen supplies. Caister calls himself a technician, but for my part . . ." and she went away, her back rigid.

"Lord, how that woman hates men! I wish you joy of her, Hattie. Such a tiresome lady! So, my dear, feeling the tension, are you? Your voice was vibrating like a zither on the phone—though I can understand it. Oscar coming home today too."

"Perceptive isn't the word! You can be positively clairvoyant. All right—yes. I *am* a bit anxious about Oscar. He sent me a couple of remarkably uncommunicative postcards, but—" she shrugged. "He must have met Ross-Craigie again."

Theo sat down in Caister's chair and, stretching his legs out in front of him, looked up at Harriet with a smile of pure pleasure on his heavy face. "Indeed he must! And dearly would I have liked to be there to see it. Little Willy, all dapper and puffed up with pride, hopping up and down in front of Oscar, glowering like—like I don't know what! Not precisely a confrontation of the gods, but pretty electric, all the same."

"Oscar has a right to be angry, though! Damn it, the man behaved abominably. We all know Oscar can be a little—well, ponderous in his approach, and wants every *t* crossed and every *i* dotted, but all the same, Ross-Craigie could have gone along with him. To march out with the whole scheme in his head and take it to the States was tantamount to daylight robbery."

"All's fair in love and science, my dear Hattie. And Oscar isn't

14

precisely fair in either department, is he? So I find a certain malicious pleasure in the situation. *Schadenfreude,* isn't that the word for it? Anyway, I feel it."

"Not that again, Theo, please. It—Oscar and I—it suits me well enough."

"Does it? Then why are you so nervous about seeing him tonight? You are, aren't you? You don't strike me as a woman glowing with pleasure at the thought of reunion with her lover."

"My God, Theo, why I let you talk to me as you do, I'll never know. I will *not* talk about Oscar. I asked you to come and see the last stage of the treatment, not to nag like an old woman. If you're in one of your disagreeable waspish moods, then you can go away and sting someone else. Why pick this morning to start all this again?"

"Because I love you, my dear Hattie. You're the best and most important friend I have. And more to the point, I'm the best and most important friend *you* have. And you don't please me this morning. You look positively haggard."

"With a friend like you, who needs enemies? If I look haggard it's because I'm a bit tense about this morning—I can't deny that. Or it could be due to the fact that I *am* a hag. I'm getting old! I've a right to look haggard."

"*Quelle blague!* You're not that far past forty! Bloom of your life, my dear Hattie. But you look ten years older today, and that's largely because of your anxiety about Oscar's return. Admit it! You're suffering a *crise de nerfs*—"

"If you're now going to start on your French grandee act, Theo, I'm not going to listen to you. Go away. I'll hold my own hand during the treatment—"

The door swung open and John Caister came in backward, carrying a tray of coffee mugs, and he turned toward Theo at the desk, his face pink with pleasure.

"I've made you some *splendid* coffee—just the thing to see us through the drama. How are you, Mr. Fowler? You *do* look comfortable there—no, please, don't move for little me! I'll have my coffee here by Dr. Berry's desk. You don't mind, Dr. Berry?"

15

Harriet took a mug from him and said sweetly, "Thank you, John. Theo was just saying how much he wanted some of your special coffee. He says you make the best in the unit," and she went and leaned against the oxygen chamber door, cradling the mug in her hands and smiling a little maliciously at Theo.

Catherine came back and took her own coffee from the tray, and for a few moments they drank in silence. Then Theo stirred and said, "Harriet, what are you doing about tomorrow?"

"Tomorrow? What?—Oh. At conference."

"Yes. Will you announce your success with Ferris?"

"Please—don't call it that yet," Harriet said swiftly. "There's still this morning's treatment—"

"Oh, really, my dear! Do spare me your feminine superstitions. Of course you have a success! There's not the least need to feel any doubt on that score."

"So I've already told her this morning," Catherine said. "No need for any anxiety at all. She's done it. In spite of Professor Bell's —well, never mind."

"I hadn't thought," Harriet said slowly. "I suppose so, if you're right and we've got a success. Why not?"

"Shall you tell Oscar first?" Theo was watching her under his thick eyebrows, and she looked back at him, puzzled.

"I told you—I haven't given any thought to the business of announcing it. I've been concentrating on the work."

"Dear Harriet! So like you!" Theo murmured. "You *should* give it some thought. Politics matter. You know that perfectly well!"

"Well, I know what I'd do in your shoes, Dr. Berry, that I do!" Catherine marched across to put her own and Harriet's empty mugs on the tray. "I'd slap it in front of him, I would, the whole thing, and let him put it in his pipe and smoke it. I remember, if you don't, the remarks he made about it all two years ago when you started. Thought it a lot of pie-in-the-sky compared with his precious jungle juice. But no matter what results he may have had in the States this time, he won't match what we've got here. And my word but I'll enjoy seeing all their faces when you do tell them!"

For a moment, Harriet let herself imagine the situation at conference tomorrow when she made the announcement—as indeed she would have to if this morning went well. Oscar had been undeniably lofty about the research she was doing, had made it fairly clear that he regarded it with a certain kindly condescension. That had been galling. To put in front of him her concrete results would be very satisfying; there was a relish to be found in the thought. Not very scientific, perhaps, but . . .

"Think about when to tell Oscar, Harriet," Theo said again softly as Catherine went into the oxygen chamber to prepare the table for Ferris and John took the coffee tray out. "Politics, you know! Oscar needs careful handling."

"Do stop talking about him as though he were a—a horse or something, Theo! Anyway, since I am—as you so carefully reminded me—his mistress, I hardly need any advice on *handling* Oscar."

He stood up and came to put an arm around her shoulders and kiss her cheek. "Hattie, I'm sorry. I didn't mean to bitch, believe me. I was simply upset to see you looking so . . ."

"Haggard."

"Tush! Worried would have been a better word. Forgive me?"

She looked at him for a moment, and then smiled. "Oh, of course! I should have more sense than to listen when you start griping about Oscar. If I didn't know better, I'd suspect jealousy."

"Dear heart! Sexual jealousy, thank God, will never complicate *us!* Unless, of course, you meant I might have a *tendre* for Oscar? Heaven forfend! I find my tastes to be quite other, I promise you. Even if I were foolish enough to involve myself with any member of the Establishment—which I would never do, since I am far too discreet—it would no more be with Oscar than that absurd Caister. Such an *obvious* young man! Nothing is more boring in any individual, of whatever sexual bent, than obviousness. My gem of wisdom for the day. Ah—your patient at last! May I examine him before you start?"

"I'd be glad if you would. Will you provide confirmation at conference if I decide to announce tomorrow?"

"Of course. Good morning, Mr. Ferris. And how are you?"

17

The man in the wheelchair, swathed in a heavy dressing gown and with his knees wrapped in a red rug, grinned up at them cheerfully. A small man, with a heavily scored face and very dark restless eyes under a crest of thick black hair, he had a simian look that made him appear very like the capuchin monkeys Harriet had used for her animal trials—a resemblance that had contributed to her decision to use him for the first human trial of her treatment.

"Right as ninepence, thanks, Mr. Fowler. Morning, Dr. Berry! Last date we've got, you and me, eh? Got to make the most of it, I have. My old woman swears if I don't stop talkin' about you, she'll give me the push! Not that she don't appreciate all you've done— my Gawd, she thinks you're an angel straight from Heaven, and that's a fact—but jealous! Well, you should hear 'er! I've told 'er, I've got a right to go on about you, seeing I really did hear the angels singin' loud and clear—though my old woman reckons I heard the devil, *and* had a right to—but you know what she says?" He grinned again and winked at Theo. "Says I'm disrespectful to a great woman, saying you've got a pretty face—the which you have —and a smashin' figure—the which you also have. She reckons ladies in science oughtn't to be talked about that way, but there, I said to her, a handsome woman's a handsome woman, and—"

"Mr. Ferris, have you always been as full of words as this?" Harriet said, smiling across him at Theo. "Or has the treatment done something unexpected to your tongue as well? I set out to treat your disease, not to turn on a cascade of chatter."

"Always was like this, before I got ill! Called me Polly when I was in the mob, they did. That's why my old woman married me, I reckon. She never got a chance to get a word in edgeways, not even to say no! Still, better than being dead from the neck up, 'n' it?"

The grin on his face slackened then and he added, "Or from the neck down. And I was, wasn't I? As near as you can get. I was having a bit of poke around myself this morning—seeing it was the last treatment. I knew before, you know. Knew what I had in there. Cancer—I knew all about it. I mean, I was thin as a bloody rail, and I could feel that great hard lump under my ribs"—he put

18

his hand on his right side—"and those up here, in my neck, not to mention in a couple other more personal places, and I tell you, not one can I feel. It's a bloody miracle, if you ask me. Injections, and a bit of a cookup in that there fancy oven of yours—and look at me! Believe me, Dr. Berry, I know what you've done for me, and never will I forget it. Anything I can ever do for you—"

"Mr. Ferris, you talk too much," Harriet said good-humoredly. "Now, can you get out of your chair yourself, and onto the table in the chamber? Mr. Fowler wants to have a bit of a poke around himself—not that we don't believe you, of course, but we want to be sure."

"Oh, can I! Just watch me!" And he got out of the chair and walked bouncily across to the oxygen chamber door, an absurd figure in his oversized dressing gown.

Theo examined him with great thoroughness, Harriet watching as his thick square fingers moved over the belly, felt the neck and armpits and groin, palpated the healed reddish scars of the several operations that had been performed to remove tissue for examination. And when he had finished, and they left Mr. Ferris to Catherine to be arranged comfortably on the table for the treatment, Harriet watched him write his short report in the case notes.

"Absolutely clear, clinically, Harriet. Indeed, I do congratulate you. I'm still not absolutely *au fait* with how the method works, but work it has for James Ferris." He smiled up at her. "This last treatment should confirm it then? Will you be able to be reasonably sure?"

She nodded. "Quite apart from the clinical evidence—not only the disappearance of masses but a normal biochemistry—there'll be the thermographs. Catherine's technique is remarkably delicate. She can accurately detect abnormal temperature areas that indicate even very small neoplasms, even in highly vascular tissue." She smiled a little wryly. "You were right before—I *am* being a little superstitious in refusing to say I've succeeded until after this morning. The last three weeks' thermograph results have been clear. I just wanted to run the full course as I'd planned. To be certain."

"Of course. You must be certain! Well, are you ready? I'd like to stay all through the treatment, but I've work of my own to do—"

"Yes. We're ready, I think—Catherine?"

The three of them, John and Catherine and herself, slid into the pattern of the treatment. As Harriet scrubbed her hands and put on sterilized gown and gloves in the small utility room, Catherine set the injections ready at the head of the table and connected the electroencephalogram leads to Ferris's skull before attaching the heating pads to his body, while he chivvied and teased her, she snapping back at his badinage without rancor. Even Catherine liked little James Ferris, and anyway, his ability to joke and chatter was very precious to all of them. John connected up the blood perfusion apparatus at the foot of the table, and checked, yet again, his oxygen gauges, and both were standing ready when Harriet came in. Theo perched himself on the table just outside the door and watched.

"I don't know about angels from Heaven, mind you, when it comes to this bit," Ferris said. "Feels more like the fires of Hell and that's a fact, once it starts."

"You don't really mind, though, do you?" Harriet said absently, as she uncovered her tray of equipment and clipped the sterile cannulas to the blood tubes leading from the perfusion apparatus.

"Nah, not really. Bit achy when it starts, like, but once I get a real hot sweat on, it's like floatin' away. Nice really—and a bloody sight cheaper than gettin' high on a skinful."

"That's all you know, ducky," John said. "I could keep myself in champers for a *year* on what one of these treatments costs, I promise you. . . . Blood temperature forty degrees centigrade, Dr. Berry. Body temp thirty-seven point two degrees centigrade—"

"That a fact? Well, get me! Always said I'd be worth a bomb if right was done—whoops—felt that, I did."

"Sorry—just another small prick." Harriet had eased the needle on the big syringe into a vein in the right ankle, and very slowly the colorless liquid began to drip into the bloodstream. "Right, John. The cannulae are all patent? You can start the blood flow—*now*—

that's it. Right, Catherine—blood pressure and pulse readings starting now . . ."

Almost twenty minutes ticked away, with only the reports from Catherine and John breaking the silence.

"BP one twenty over seventy. Pulse seventy."

"Blood temperature thirty-nine, body temp thirty-eight point eight—thirty-nine. Blood up to forty now—"

"BP steady—pulse ninety-eight, bounding a little—"

"Blood now forty-three. Body temperature equal. Shall I start the oxygen?"

"Yes." Harriet completed the injection and straightened up. "Well, Mr. Ferris? Feeling all right?"

"Bit achy, like I said," Ferris said, less ebullient now, his pointed, creased face glistening wetly. "But it'll go off in a minute, when it gets a bit 'otter—gettin' sleepy now—nice . . ."

"Good man. Just lie there and dream for a while. You can reach your bellpush? Remember, if you want us, just ring it."

They left him lying there on his table, the tubes gleaming redly as blood pulsed through them to and from the perfusion apparatus, and Catherine sealed the heavy door as John bustled over to his console. Then the four of them stood and watched as the gauges' needles swung, recording the buildup of oxygen pressure within the chamber, the temperature of the blood, the pulse and blood-pressure readings, and the electroencephalogram tracings.

Theo said, "How long, Harriet? And how hot can you safely get him?"

"He can take half an hour once we get him to forty degrees. No longer. He tolerates it very well indeed. Remarkably well. I could have used a generalized method, inducing fever by giving him some sort of toxin—I'd considered streptococcus erysipelas—but that isn't as easily controlled as this heated blood method, and I add to the effect with surface body heating. You notice I connected up a special link to the portal system. That way I get increased heat to the primary growth area in the liver, but he needs it generally, of course, for the lymph node deposits. And giving it in the presence of high-pressure oxygen enhances the effect. His blood pressure holds a remarkably satisfactory level, you see? Whether I could use the method on a patient with any other disorder in that area, of course, is a moot point."

"Hmm. Perhaps Ross-Craigie's work will link up with yours, then. His technique certainly seems to clear any atheroma problems."

Harriet looked startled for a moment. "I suppose so," she said slowly. "But would a patient with severe and widespread disease of this degree be able to tolerate his treatment? It would have to be done first, before my method could be applied, and I doubt if a patient as ill as Ferris was would have survived long enough for both approaches."

"But if this treatment has further trials that confirm it, my dear Hattie, surely there'll be no need to wait until the disease has reached a terminal stage before starting it? You used a terminal patient because you couldn't possibly experiment on a case in which orthodox proven methods had not already been tried and failed!"

She smiled then. "Oh Lord, Theo, I'm a pretty one-eyed scientist, aren't I? I've been so involved in treating this one case that I just haven't thought much about the future—about how and when the method will be applied if it does achieve success. You're right, I suppose! If this goes go into the armory of acceptable treatments, we'll get early-stage disease to work on, and more time to do it in. So Ross-Craigie's method may well fit in. Ye gods, what a thought!"

"What a thought indeed! Here's another one for you. Whither surgery?"

"What? How do you mean?"

"Dear Harriet! What do I spend most of my time doing? Providing surgical treatment for an assortment of cancerous conditions! If the treatment of tomorrow is to be the Berry treatment, what will I and my knife-happy colleagues do for our bread and butter?"

"Patch up the fools who smash themselves to jam on the roads,"

Catherine growled. "When Dr. Berry's work gets cancer out of the way, there'll be a hell of a lot more people looking for different ways to destroy themselves. They'll keep you busy enough."

"And you could go into the patchwork business in a big way, Mr. Fowler," John said. "Think of all those *lovely* transplants you could play around with!"

"Hmmph! You could be right. Anyway, Harriet, my dear, this method of yours is going to create a considerable stir in a great many ways you obviously hadn't thought of! I wonder if Oscar has? So much of the work that's going on here is tied up with cancer—what about his bread and butter if you've pipped him at the post with the Berry method? The Bell method goes right down the drain! Ah well, those are problems of the future, and right now I have a problem of my own. Such as the fact that I must go and wield my ironmongery on one of the patients in Geoffrey Cooper's series. What possible long-term results he can get in treating obesity with surgery I *cannot* imagine—but then, I'm just a simple surgeon, not a high-powered thinker like you research bods. Harriet, dear, when will you have completed?"

Harriet looked up at the clock. "Say twelve thirty. You'll have had time to check the thermograph by then, Catherine? He should be cool enough for it by what—eleven thirty?—yes. Half past twelve, Theo."

"I'll be in the theaters. Phone me, will you? I'll be waiting."

She phoned him at quarter to one.

"Theo? Well, we've finished. . . . Yes. Ferris is going home tomorrow morning. . . . Yes. He's clear. Quite clear."

2

SHE SAT with her elbows on the table, resting her chin on her hands and staring out of the dark window, and sighed softly with pleasure. An exciting day's work, and when she got home, George was in a more tractable mood than he had been for weeks, despite their breakfast-time argument, with only a few petulant complaints about Mrs. Davies's care of him. There was a letter from Gordon enclosing a new photograph of young Giles (absurd to think of herself as this child's grandmother, she had thought, looking at the small face squinting into the sunlight, and strange to see how like David he was growing, strange to think that Gordon himself had been younger than Giles when David had died). And now, one of Oscar's excellent dinners and a bottle of Oscar's excellent wine.

She looked across at him, then, and some of her contentment shriveled. He was twisting his glass on the table, staring into it, his head bent and his shoulders straight and tense.

Oscar had greeted her warmly enough, kissing the top of her head in the way he always did, behaving as though he hadn't been away more than a few hours. Despite his prolonged absence there had been no gift for her, not so much as a bottle of duty-free perfume bought hurriedly at the airport. But although this had hurt her a little, as such omissions always did, she had accepted it with the equanimity with which she always accepted his hurtful behavior—even found a certain comfort in it. He was always so, and it was as much a part of his attraction for her as the shape of his body and the smell of his skin.

He had fussed amusingly over his dinner preparations, still behaving very much as he always did, for he took a certain malicious pleasure in being so much more sophisticated a cook than she was. He had talked amusingly, too, about the "absurdly overdone" hospitality his American colleagues had provided, about some Middle Westerners who had enlivened the flight home with their "exaggerated touristy" behavior, and had asked with a careful display of kindliness after her family, wanting to know whether her father-in-law was any less difficult to handle, whether there was any news of Patty's latest emotional involvement ("Such an agreeable young woman, your Patricia—so like you"; typical of Oscar to offer her a compliment at remove).

But he had said nothing about what had actually happened while he had been in the States; asked no questions at all about the state of affairs at Brookbank. And although they had long ago made it a rule that they never talked shop when they were away from the Establishment, just as they never displayed any evidence that their relationship was other than a working one when they were there, she would have expected him to say something about his visit. To ask or not to ask? That, she told herself a little owlishly (for they had finished the bottle of wine between them, and were now drinking cognac), is the question.

He saved her the trouble of deciding.

"They're tipping him for this year's Nobel, Harriet," he said abruptly. "Apart from Müller in Switzerland and his metabolism work, there's nothing else that comes near it. And it's showy enough, God knows. He's made sure of that. The man's got a genius for personal publicity. I saw two television programs with him posturing like an organ-grinder's monkey—most embarrassing exhibition I've ever seen. But he has no grace, none at all. Not a mention of the work we did here, nor that I—we—put him on to it in the first place. None at all."

He stood up, and moved across to the Regency secretary in the corner to select a cigar, fussing with the handsome gold cutter and lighter; Oscar had a taste for the elegancies of life. "God knows I don't grudge the man his success—if he'd stayed at Brookbank and completed the job properly with us, he would have had his share of attention. It's the rank ingratitude that I find so distressing. Really distressing. I gave him every facility I could, worked very closely with him—even neglecting my own field of research to an extent, in order to help him. Then off he goes in a fit of pique because I wasn't prepared to tolerate any shoddiness in his work—and what Establishment head of any integrity would have acted otherwise?— and published in this helter-skelter fashion—oh, it's infuriating."

"Have you seen his reports? I've been too busy to read much. Do his findings really stand up?"

"Oh, they stand up," he said bleakly, going to the armchair by the fire, and stretching himself into it. "They stand up. They've developed a technique to apply the method in three hospitals—I saw it in action in Chicago. And they get impressive results. I saw three in vivo operations that were most impressive—virtually total removal of very large atheromatous (arteriosclerotic, they call them) plaques."

He turned his head to look at her then. "Do I sound peevish and jealous, Harriet? Objecting because the method works? Because, believe me, I'm not. I'm as excited as any one of the Americans about it. Damn it all, with coronary thrombosis the killer it is, not to mention the cerebral thromboses—Rosamund died of a stroke, remember, so I have a personal involvement—the fact that Ross-Craigie has published a method of preventing it is immensely exciting. No, my objection is that he made no mention whatsoever of the sources of so much of his success! I'm no chauvinist, but there's enough of the Englishman in me to regret bitterly that English efforts should be ignored this way. And he *is* a shoddy worker, God damn him!"

He stood up again, and began to move about the room, restlessly touching furniture and ornaments. "You know what happened! I just wasn't prepared to let him bypass what I regard as essential safeguards before he published, and he made it clear he thought me overcautious, not to say obstructive. Obstructive! Me! You know that's not true, Harriet!"

"It certainly wasn't as far as Ross-Craigie was concerned," Harriet said, a little absentmindedly, for she was beginning to find Oscar's tirade a shade wearing. And then, as she saw the expression on his face, she realized how foolish a remark she had made.

"You mean I *am* obstructive as far as other people's work is concerned? Is that what you mean?"

"Oh, Oscar, no! Not precisely. You can be a little . . . well, discouraging about a piece of work that doesn't fit your own ideas."

"That surely is what I'm there for, damn it all! What sort of Establishment would it be if I let every one of you rush off into whatever line of country you fancied? We haven't the resources, as you well know, and this is unjust coming from you, Harriet, really it is! How long have you been working on that auto-inoculation scheme of yours? Two years! And how much have you to show for it? Yet I've cooperated with you, haven't I?"

Harriet opened her mouth to speak; now was undoubtedly the time to tell him of her own news. But he gave her no opportunity.

"Have you—any of you—the least understanding of what my position involves? I control a meager enough budget, God knows, but it has to be accounted for—with *results*. Results that mean something to those bloody old women in Whitehall. And what results have any of you provided for me? Half a dozen tuppeny-ha'penny tests. At the risk of seeming as conceited as Ross-Craigie, let me remind you that the only worthwhile one was my own Bell's test. And when we do find a promising line of work, what happens? The man takes himself off with not only his own work done at Brookbank, but a hell of a lot of mine as well, and sells it to the highest bidder. My God, it makes me sick! I—"

He stopped sharply. "You must forgive me, Harriet. To rant on in this fashion like—indeed, I'm worse than Ross-Craigie!" He smiled thinly, and came to stand beside her at the table and put one hand on her shoulder. "Such a popinjay it is! He's got himself all tarted up in square glasses, and the most incredible clothes you ever saw—a complete caricature. I met him at some ghastly barbecue party, and he was wearing pink shorts—*pink*, so help me!—down to his knees, and anything less like a serious scientist you never saw. And when I ventured to suggest he'd been a little less than just in making no public mention of his Brookbank work—or of mine with him—my dear, he positively jiggled about with denials! I shouldn't let so ridiculous a creature annoy me so much."

27

He kissed the top of her head then, and his hand tightened on her shoulder.

"And it's outrageous of me to talk so to you after not seeing you for so long. I should be ashamed of myself, and I am. Put it down to fatigue. I slept yesterday afternoon in London after my plane got in and it was an easy drive up this morning, but it takes a while to get over the time switch."

"Shall I go, then? If you're so tired?" She looked up at him, not moving, and he smiled and shook his head.

"You know damned well I'm not that tired. Come to bed."

She stood up. "Yes. Bed. I think you need it."

He laughed a little. "You mean you don't? After the three months I've been away? Have you been comforting other sad widowers in my absence? Or even dear Theo?"

"Not kind, Oscar—and beneath your dignity, I should have thought, to dig at Theo. He's a damned good friend to both of us, and you know it. As for me—damn it, of course I've missed you! I'm past the age of playing the coquette, even if it would be believable, after almost twenty years. . . ."

He frowned fleetingly. "Not quite so long, surely. Rosamund died in—ye Gods, I suppose it is! Eighteen years. Very comfortable years, though. Mmm? Probably more comfortable than if you'd married me—though I've a clear conscience on that score. I did suggest it several times."

She began to clear the table. "Twice to be precise. And not with any notable enthusiasm at that. But I've no regrets. They *have* been comfortable years—"

She stopped. "Why are we talking as though they're over? Are they?" And she was a little startled at the stab of apprehension she felt.

"Good God, no! I sincerely hope not! I've no notion of dying for a good while yet, and you look in perfect health as usual! You were the one who started talking about how long it's been, not I. My dear Harriet, aren't you being a shade menopausal tonight? Flitting about in your conversation, and decidedly distracted. Half the evening I've had the feeling you weren't even listening to me. Not flattering. Such a welcome home for a wandering man!"

"I'm sorry! If I have been so, there is a reason—and it's not the state of my hormones, damn you! My God, why is everyone so determined to remind me of my antiquity today? No, there's a work thing—"

"Then not another word. Tomorrow is soon enough. Tell me then."

"Conference day tomorrow."

"God, is it? I suppose it must be. Six months goes bloody fast. Well, conference or not tomorrow, now, bed. You need it too."

"Look, let's stop deciding who is doing who a favor, shall we? I find it a little depressing, to say the least."

"I take your point. You can have the bathroom first."

Theo pushed a note across the table toward her, and she pulled herself out of her abstraction to read it.

"Harriet, dear," the highly stylized script ran. "Do try to look as though you are *pretending* to listen, at least! *I* know you are waiting to explode your own little bomb, but *they* don't. And your expression of patent boredom isn't too flattering to poor Geoffrey."

She smiled at him, crumpling the note into the ashtray, and obediently tried to listen. Geoffrey Cooper was reading lists of figures on his obesity work, the light glinting his glasses to a blankness that made him look like that cartoon character she used to enjoy when she was a child—who was it? Ah, yes. Little Annie Rooney . . .

Again, she had to wrench her attention back and started to look round the table, from place to place, at the neat way Oscar sat with his papers piled tidily in front of him; at Kidd and Chesterfield side by side, both industriously scribbling notes; at Catherine Warne doggedly smoking her way through a cigar ("Why shouldn't a woman use cigars?" she had said pugnaciously when Sam Lemesurier had wrinkled his nose at them. "They're a bloody sight safer than those cigarettes of yours, and anyway I like 'em." Poor Catherine. Aching for male approval and not knowing it. She should have married and had hordes of children; but that thought made her smile a little. Catherine, with children!). At Sam, fiddling as always with a box of matches, piling them into towers as he squinted over the smoke rising from the cigarette dangling from his lips; and young Rodney Ackermann, sitting with his hands carefully folded on the table, his head bent politely toward Geoffrey as he listened. So transparent his excitement at being a member of the Establishment, so hopeful in his just-down-from-university newness. He made her feel decidedly maternal.

Yet he was justified in finding research so exciting; even after so long in the field, she found it exhilarating, sitting here waiting to tell them of her own success. For she knew now, quite certainly, that she had succeeded. Yesterday's nervousness had quite gone. But she had had to wait a long time for this morning. Did Rodney realize that? she wondered. That she had been working here for more than a quarter of a century, God help her! and for the first time had come up with a piece of work that would really mean something? Would young Rodney last so long, going from tedious routine work to disappointment to more routine work to minor achievement, and back, yet again, to routine work?

Though perhaps he wouldn't have to wait so long. William Ross-Craigie hadn't. Wouldn't. She could in one way sympathize with the way he had refused to tolerate Oscar's ponderousness, with his decision to go where the speed of success was greater. But she could sympathize with Oscar, too. Sitting at the head of this rather mediocre research Establishment, and knowing there was less of his working life in front of him than behind him, he needed to exercise his authority.

With a start, she realized that Geoffrey Cooper had stopped talking. "Discussion?" Oscar was saying. "No." Well, I don't see there is much any of us can say. Clearly, you need at least another two series before you can make any real assessment of the method. I think we can budget for one more, at least, at this stage. But I hope you'll be able to give us a little more solid evidence—if you will forgive the pun!—next time. Er—Theo, you're prepared to go on working with Geoffrey on this?"

"I can't pretend I find it quite as interesting as Geoffrey does," Theo said lazily. "Paddling about in those enormously fat bellies you send me isn't precisely an aesthetic experience, dear boy. However! If it gets too depressing I can always close my eyes and think of England."

"As long as you don't close them for too long," Geoffrey said. "I have enough trouble getting patients to cooperate without losing them on the operating table, thank you very much."

"Trust me, Geoffrey, trust me! I haven't killed one yet, tempted though I may have been—"

Irritably, Oscar said, "Time is moving on, gentlemen. Now, what next? Harriet, I see you have a long report to give. Will there be much discussion, do you suppose? If so, perhaps I should get my own short report out of the way first."

"I think there might be," Harriet said. "I've made considerable progress."

"Indeed she has," Theo murmured, and Oscar looked at him sharply. "I know I'm merely the surgical member of this team, Oscar, but I want to talk a little about Harriet's report. I rather imagine everyone else will."

"Hmm. Very well then. My own report." He sat in silence for a moment staring down at his papers, and then said stiffly, "Not too good, I'm afraid. I ran trials on eighteen terminal cases, and on a series of twenty-seven medians. And although there would appear to be enough evidence to warrant continuing along the lines I planned, I can't pretend there is anything to get too excited about . . ."

He launched into an account of the results of his work in the States, and now Harriet listened carefully, making notes of the figures he gave. Indeed, not too hopeful, yet not so disappointing that they warranted abandoning the use of the drug. Every new derivative of the nitrogen mustard drugs behaved like this, she told herself. Some remissions of disease, occasional total remissions, but nothing that ever made a pattern, that offered the blanket treatment that Oscar was so obviously seeking.

For a brief moment she wondered how Oscar was going to react

31

to her own report. She had assumed, if she had thought about it at all, that he would be pleased, that he would share her own excitement, but if it meant—as it clearly would—that his own research project would lose its validity, would his pleasure be tempered by any other feeling? But there was no time to pursue that thought, for Oscar had stopped speaking, and was looking round the table, waiting for comments.

Geoffrey Cooper, more relaxed now that he knew his own work was assured for at least the next six months, spoke first.

"Well worth continuing, I would have thought, Dr. Bell. At least no one else, as far as we know, is working on the same lines—"

Oscar reddened, angrily, and Harriet bit her lip. Tactless idiot! Surely the man realized that Oscar was still smarting under Ross-Craigie's defection and success? Her uneasiness grew; was her report going to be tactless, too, in something of the same way?

"Thank you, Cooper. Does anyone feel I should take this off the budget, perhaps? I'm the first to admit these results aren't very striking. Kidd? Lemesurier? Chesterfield?"

The other men shook their heads, but it was young Ackermann who jumped in, his face a little pink.

"But of course it must go on, sir! There's as much value in disproving a method as proving one, isn't there? I mean, you took me on here because of disproving the Döpel theory on the enzyme action of copper, not because—I mean—well, I'd go on if I were you."

"Thank you, Dr. Ackermann," Oscar smiled fleetingly. "You all agree then? I continue with this—for the next six months, at any rate."

"Agreed," Kidd murmured.

And Oscar nodded, made a note, and leaned back in his chair.

"Thank you. Now, Harriet. We're ready for you. Perhaps you had better recap, for young Ackermann's benefit. He'll hardly have had the chance to find out yet what it is you're doing, and I want to be sure everyone's always clearly in the picture."

"By all means. In very brief and simple terms, I started two years ago on an idea involving the action of viruses in healthy cells. Reports from a number of sources—I'll give you the references later if you want to read them for yourself—indicated that new cancerous growths might be triggered by virus invasion of a cell, in which the virus RNA changed the cell structure into new RNA that resembled that of the virus. This theory I found very attractive. It accounts for the great numbers of types of tumor that occur, explains why so many different forms of treatment can be used for different forms of the disease. Some respond to radiation, some to cytotoxic drugs—like the one Oscar is now investigating—and so on. Well, it seemed to me that if an invading virus could change a human cell into a replica of itself, as it were, why shouldn't the cell be made able to change *back* by the action of another virus? I thought, if I could find a way of developing a new virus-type body that was the same as the healthy cell, and expose this to cancerous growths, to see if it could change the growth back into normal tissue—do you follow me?"

"A reversal of the neoplastic process, you mean?"

"Yes. In a way. So I started on a series of animal experiments— rats first and then capuchin monkeys. I have the results here if you want to see them—trying to grow healthy-cell-type viruses in specimens obtained from various types of tissue. Skin to start with, and then intestinal, and later respiratory system. It took a long time— there were a lot of false starts—but then I did start to get the cultures I wanted. I *could*, as it were, structure a virus-type body that would turn the key the other way. As long as I grew them on healthy tissue taken from the subject, I could reinject and grow them in the living animal, and—well, I got some very good results."

"A sort of auto-immunization method?" Ackermann asked.

"In a way. But not precisely like the methods a number of people are trying. I know, of course, about the several ways in which people are enhancing the production of interferon, which enables the body to reject foreign bodies, including cancerous growths, but this method doesn't work that way. This acts directly on the growth itself, changing cancerous cells back into normal ones. It doesn't leave great masses, however. If a growth has become very large, and I get a successful reversal started, the healthy cells seem able to recognize the presence of the excess cells, and they are reabsorbed. I've got a most interesting series of pictures—you can see cells joining together, diminishing in number. It's almost like watching a series of cell-division pictures run backward. It was this I reported at last conference, and I was given an extension to work further."

She looked at Oscar fleetingly. "I embarked on some massive animal trials at that point. I used over three hundred monkeys—a hell of a risk, I knew, because if I'd failed, the costs would be pretty grim. And the Establishment wouldn't have been very pleased with me." A faint ripple of laughter greeted that. "But I thought it justified on the grounds of my early results, and I'd refined the tissue culture technique considerably. The details are here if you want them. Anyway, I got a good result."

"Good!" Theo said. "There, my dear, is the understatement of all time. Only a hundred percent, that's all!"

"A hundred percent?" Ackermann almost squeaked it. "You got a proven positive result on every animal experiment?"

"Yes," Harriet said simply.

"Good God," Kidd murmured. "You kept very quiet about it, Harriet! I knew what you were trying, but—a hundred percent? Are you sure? What about spontaneous remissions? They do happen . . ."

"How often?" Theo said swiftly. "Even if you got a spontaneous remission in fifty percent—which you never do, as you know quite well—have you ever heard of any series that got this sort of total response? Believe me, if you can't believe Harriet. I've seen those animals. They're all alive and well and living at Brookbank, every damned one of them."

"I believe it!" Kidd protested. "I'm not making any snide cracks, Theo—I'm just shattered!"

34

"You didn't tell me," Oscar said sharply. "Why not, Harriet? I would have thought—"

"You weren't here when I made the final checks, Oscar," Harriet said quickly. "I could have cabled you, I suppose, but I thought—well, you were involved in your own work, and what point in telling you there in the States? I decided to wait until you came back. And then . . ." She hesitated.

"I took another hell of a risk, Oscar. I gave it a lot of thought, and I decided—well, you'd better hear it all."

And she launched into an account of Ferris's illness, describing as graphically as she could his almost dead state, the way the tissue cultures had developed, and then the way she had applied the treatment, and how he had responded.

"The last session was yesterday," she finished. "I have the thermograph readings here, and Theo examined him very carefully too, and you can see his clinical report here." She stood up and walked round the table to put the notes in front of Oscar.

"I think I've got a treatment," she said flatly. "Obviously, there'll have to be a great many more human trials, and we need to wait long enough to be sure we get no recurrences. But I've had no recurrences in any of my animals, not even the earliest ones I did over a year ago, so I see no reason to expect any different response in humans."

There was a long silence. Then Chesterfield said very softly, "Good Christ Almighty! She thinks she's got a treatment. I don't —Christ!"

And now they were all talking at once. Harriet stood beside Oscar, who alone sat silent reading the notes she had given him.

He looked up after a while, and said sharply, "Please—gentlemen—" and the talk faltered and stopped.

"Well done, Harriet," Oscar said, and stood up and held his hand out to her. "We must all congratulate you. I'll need time to digest all this, of course. It would have helped to have known something about it before this morning—but, however! You preferred to keep your own counsel so I—"

"That's not fair!" Harriet said quickly. "I wasn't trying to be secretive! I just saw no point in worrying you at a distance, that's all!"

"Worrying me! I'd hardly be worried by such important developments! However busy I was, I'd have had time for this. I might have asked you to wait for my return, so that I could have worked a little with you. As it is . . ."

"But in what way could you have worked with me, Oscar? We've been operating in totally different fields! Your drug methods are cytotoxic. Mine are anything but. I've worked on a cell regeneration scheme and—"

"Are you suggesting that my approach is simply destructive, Harriet? That yours has greater value because—"

"Oh, Oscar, for God's sake! Let's be honest! When I started this work you told me I had as slim a chance of getting anywhere as—as of finding a universal antibiotic! You told me I was leaping to absurd conclusions on the basis of very slender indications. Well, they *were* slender, I'm the first to admit that. But I saw a way it could be developed, so I wanted to do it. And now you're complaining I've been secretive about it, when for two years you've left me alone to get on with it and shown pretty clearly what you thought of my ideas. Well, all right! You were justified in dismissing it at the start, but to be angry now, when you must admit on the basis of this report I've given you today I've got somewhere—"

"While I've got nowhere? Oh, yes! I admit that! I'm not trying to denigrate your work, though I detect a certain amount of denigration of *mine* in your attitude."

"I deny that! I would never—Oscar, look. You're angry because I've thrown this at you as a surprise, and—"

"I'm angry, as you put it, because I've been kept in the dark! Because as head of this Establishment I'm supposed to keep checks on what you people do! I need to check your statistics, evaluate your methods—as a small example, have you verified your results against the figures on drug methods? Did you think to check against my own figures?"

36

"That wasn't necessary. You know that to check a totally differ-ent method's results against the figures collected on only one other set of observations would produce false statistics! I know I may go off half-cocked sometimes, but when it comes to my work I think *straight*—and I think thoroughly!"

He stiffened. "And I don't. Is that your suggestion?" he said, and his voice was thin and controlled.

"No! I said no such thing! But I do think you're angry not be-cause of being out of touch with what's been going on, but because of the effect on you personally. You don't really care at all about the fact that I think I've found a treatment. All you care about is the effect of it on *you*, and on *your* work, and *your* scientific name—"

"That is an . . . I try to perform my function as head of this Establishment, as the person who is supposed to know what is go-ing on here, and you imply that . . . that . . ." He floundered, and took a deep breath, and she could see the bitter anger and hurt in him, and felt a sudden sharp compunction; to have spoken to him so, knowing how badly he already felt about Ross-Craigie's behavior, and to have done it in so public a manner—it was unfor-givable of her. She should have told him last night, no matter how difficult the situation.

Impulsively she put her hand on his arm. "But you needn't be angry—it won't make any difference, Oscar! You'll still be part of my work! You *are* part of it! When we publish, it'll carry your name on it, and Brookbank's—"

He went very white, then, and she felt the muscles of his arm tense under her fingers, and she dropped her hand.

"Are you suggesting for one moment that I'm in any way *resent-ful* of your success? That is an outrageous assumption! All I ask of you—of any of you—is the common courtesy of being kept aware of what is going on! That I had to be away for three months hardly gave you the right to go head first into a human trial, and you ought to be the first to admit it! If anything had gone wrong and the man had died, who do you suppose would have been culpable

37

with you? Did you stop to think of that? Obviously you didn't! And I wouldn't have reminded you of the possible dangers of going headlong into work of this nature if you hadn't—"

"Oscar, please!" she said, now horribly aware of the stillness of the other people around them, feeling the tension in them. "Don't! Of course you're right. I did take a hell of a risk, but I did it in good faith, and I took every precaution that—"

"Precautions! What precautions could you have taken? None that—but this is all beside the point. What outrages me is your suggestion that I would ever—" he turned sharply then, and looked round at all of them.

"Can we get this clear, all of you? I do not, ever, want to stop any of you from your own work. I do not want to poach on your preserves. I know every bloody research worker there ever was thinks Establishment heads are no more than parasites who claim the glory of other people's work whenever they can. If I've given any of you any justification for such a belief about *me*, I'd like to know what it is. In the meantime, may I make it clear that when Dr. Berry publishes her work it will carry only the names of the people who actually worked on it, no others. I dissociate myself from it completely." And he turned and went, slamming the door behind him.

There was a long silence and then Theo said softly, "Oh dear. Oh dear, oh dear, oh dear. Harriet, my love, you may be a damned good research scientist, but you can be a bloody fool when you try."

3

"HE'S GIVEN you carte blanche, after all!" Theo said. "Witnesses, dear heart, the whole bit! 'When Dr. Berry publishes!' he said, and 'I dissociate myself from it completely,' he said. As I interpret that, it means do what you bloody well like, and he won't play in your yard, so there! It would be a piece of delicious justice if you took him at his word and went ahead."

"Would you like some more coffee, Theo? And there's still some Danish pastry left . . ."

"Trying to stop my mouth with vittles? Won't work, dear. Yes, I'll have some more coffee, *and* the Danish, *and* I'll talk with my mouth full. As I said, I—"

"I heard what you said, Theo. I've listened for what seems like hours to you saying and saying and saying. Do stop, if you have any affection for me. If you go on booming away much longer, George will wake up and that's all I'm short of—you must see it's totally out of the question. Quite apart from the fact that I couldn't do it to Oscar, there's the whole matter of the right *way* to publish to be thought about! One human trial, no matter how successful, isn't enough to publish on, and you ought to know that. I need more trials, with long-term follow-up, before I'm in any position to claim anything definite."

"Mere surgical oaf though I may be, Hattie dear, I know that perfectly well. I also know that the publishing of a preliminary report is normal practice—so balls to *that* for an excuse. No, my dear, the significant thing about your refusal is that you give as a main reason for it your inability to do such a thing to Oscar. Why? I never thought you nourished a great undying passion for him. Have I been wrong all these years in seeing your relationship as a vastly convenient one, but no more than that?"

She leaned back in her rocking chair, and let it sway a little, as she looked at him consideringly. "It's odd you should ask," she said eventually.

"Odd? Why? Give me the rest of that delicious cake, do. I'm feeling singularly greedy this evening. How odd?"

"Well, it's just that I've been wondering myself. About Oscar, I mean. For one not much given to introspection, I've been asking myself questions and charting my paths for all the world like a character in a television serial of the soppier sort." She grimaced. "Very yukky I've been."

"And what answers did you get? Did you discover why you can't bear to upset Oscar in any way? Did you discover you *are* nurturing a great flamelike adoration for the man? *There's* a thought . . ."

"I didn't discover anything. How could I, after all this time? Oscar is—well, he's like you. Part of me. He's been around so long, and we both satisfy something in each other, and how can I or anyone else say that's passion or not passion, or whatever? You tell me—"

"I'll tell you one thing, Hattie." Theo licked his fingers with catlike finesse, and drank the last of his coffee. "You're a damned clever lady, that's what you are. What's more, you're such an unde-vious person, you don't even know you're being clever, and that makes it *exceedingly* clever. You've equipped yourself with two men to play the husband's role for you. Oscar in bed, me every-where else. Very talented."

"Tell me something, Theo. What's in it for you? I know about Oscar. He needed a woman when Rosamund died, and there I was, and we'd always been very good friends anyway—he was incredibly good to me when David and my father were killed. I don't know what I'd have done if he hadn't come up with this job, and then—well, I know where I *am* with Oscar and what he wants of me. But you—since we've started talking about it, tell me about you. I lean on you, I use you outrageously for everything from arranging the lease on this cottage to the problems I have with George to chang-ing a fuse, and yet, as far as I can see, I give you nothing—tell me why?"

40

"Are you seeking compliments, Hattie? Want to be told how much I care for you, how enslaved by your charms I am?"

"Bitchy, Theo. You know damned well that—"

"Well, in a way it's true. I am enslaved by you. Does that make you feel better? Knowing that I'd rather be in your company than anyone else's that I can think of? That a Sunday evening spent here at your well-ordered fireside drinking your coffee is infinitely more pleasurable than the most amusing of places in someone else's company? I'd always thought, in my hopeful way, that you understood that it's possible for a man in my situation to care for a woman and to find expression of that care, and a reward for it, in nonphysical ways. Or have I been deluding myself all these years, and been consorting with a woman who is so obtuse she doesn't know there can be love without sex? Don't tell me that. It would cut me to the cuticle to think *I'd* been so obtuse."

She could feel anxiety seeping from behind the flippancy and for a moment wanted to lean over and touch him to reassure him. But she had learned long ago to control her need to communicate by touch when with Theo: he hated it so.

"No, of course I know. Know that there can be affection without sex—I mean, just as there can be sex without a great deal of affection. But I can't say I knew you liked my company quite so well. At the beginning, I thought it was a convenience."

He laughed. "Well, so it was, dear heart. As long as the Establishment gossips could link me with you I could get on dealing with my sexual needs in my own discreet way with no one to notice or care. And when there were functions at which I needed a woman to take my arm . . . well, you were always so splendid for the purpose! And there isn't any cheating in it, after all. Certainly I've since become so involved with you and yours that I can't imagine life without you. You and your children—even that unspeakable old man—are very important to me. Does that make up for my being a little less than honest in the early days?"

She smiled then. "Well, I was using you in the same way, I admit. Young widows are always prime gossip, and as long as they

41

thought you were having an affair with me, they didn't notice Oscar. You covered for him just as I knew quite well I did for you."

"But it's interesting, Hattie, isn't it, that right from the start you felt Oscar had to be covered? Why shouldn't it be known that you're his mistress? Why should it be less embarrassing for all of us to have you and me talked about as sleeping together, rather than you and Oscar? Have you always been afraid of him?"

"I'm not afraid of him! Not in that sense. I'm just practical. To have an Establishment head known to be so intimately involved with one of his staff would cause a good deal of politicking, you know that. I didn't fancy being cast for Pompadour. And as for you—come on, Theo! Better they should say you and I were having an affair than something a little nearer the reality? Even in these enlightened days, better to be labeled libertine than—"

"—than honest queer, hmm?" he cut in with a sudden bitterness." There's a nice moral point! Dirty old man better than clean-living homosexual—the whole thing makes me puke. But there, we should be grateful, I suppose! If that hadn't been the way of it, I'd no doubt have found some dreary gentleman with whom to build some sort of an establishment of my own, and I'd have missed a very gratifying friendship with you and your offspring. As things have turned out I can't complain. My lines, considering what tangled ones they are, have fallen in very pleasant places."

He lifted his head sharply then, as a thump and a creak came from above their heads, and Harriet sighed, and got up.

"I won't be long. Make some more coffee, there's a lamb. The kettle's still on—"

"Ye Gods, but this makes me furious, Hattie! Why should *you* have to deal with such disagreeable tasks—what about Mrs. Thing? Can't she deal with him?"

"She only sleeps here occasionally, when I'm away. And that can't be too often, because quite apart from the fact that he doesn't really like her all that much, I'd lose her altogether if I asked too much of her. Do stop nagging about it, Theo, and make the coffee. I won't be long."

42

As she helped George into the lavatory, and waited till he was ready to be cleaned up and taken back to bed, she let herself think, just for a moment, of the possibility of arranging for the old man to go to a home and, as always, dismissed the idea. He couldn't help being old and half-senile, and dealing with his lavatory needs and the rest of it wasn't so very different from dealing with those of a child, and she'd done that for long enough, Heaven knew. Though there had been an end in sight during those days, and there didn't seem to be any end to this. Except his death of course, and in all conscience, she could not bring herself to look forward to that.

Mercifully, Theo said no more about George when she rejoined him and the coffee cups, choosing instead to return to the attack on the subject of publishing her results. For another hour they talked about it, and Harriet became more and more confused about what she should do. Oscar had undoubtedly given her a sort of permission to publish, and whatever he had said in the heat of the moment about dissociating himself from her work, she knew perfectly well that he would gain credit from it. Brookbank needed a success, needed to be regarded by other Establishments, as well as by their Whitehall employers, as a place from which exciting work emerged, and this report of hers would undoubtedly bring Brookbank's name into the public eye. So why not publish her preliminary report? Why be so squeamish about Oscar's possibly unhappy reactions when he would in fact gain so much?

When Theo left at half past ten, and she had locked the cottage door behind him and washed up the dinner dishes, she sat for a while in front of the dying fire, feeling too edgy and alert to go to bed, though she was in fact very tired. And then, on an impulse, she decided to write to Patty, and ask her to come down for the weekend as soon as she could.

"I've some interesting work to talk to you about, and I'd be grateful for some of your ideas on what to do about it. Talking to you often helps me to sort out my own ideas, so if you can possibly get away, I'd appreciate it. Anyway, I miss you! Perhaps we could

43

get Gordon and Jean to come too, though when small Giles is here, no one actually gets much chance to talk, do they? But it would be agreeable to see you all . . ."

Then she wrote to Gordon, suggesting dates for a visit, and went to bed feeling a little more tranquil with the necessity to make a final decision thus shelved. She would now have time to get on with planning her next trials, and soothing Oscar, she promised herself next morning as she drove to Brookbank. She'd tell him she had no intention of publishing just yet and that should help. A little.

But neither that day nor the next would he see her. She tried to arrange a time with Miss Manton, his secretary, who hid a formidable personality and an inflexible determination to protect Oscar against all comers behind a vague fluttery manner that deceived no one, but which was remarkably effective.

"I can't get him to listen, he's so busy," she murmured when Harriet tried again to pass her and go into Oscar's office. "And I wouldn't go in now, really I wouldn't, Dr. Berry. He really is so *very* busy—he did say absolutely no one was to go in, really he did—so sorry." And he didn't appear at lunch on either day, and the following morning took himself off to London for " 'Discussions,' I think—" Miss Manton said vaguely, blinking at Harriet behind her spectacles.

"You'd think we had smallpox or something," Harriet said bitterly to Theo, at lunch. "The way he's avoiding all of us. No one's seen him since conference. He really is being very juvenile."

"He's ashamed of himself," Theo said sapiently. "He knows he behaved like a peevish baby, and he wants us all to forget it before he comes amongst us again in his Senior Seer's garb. He'll be around next week, I promise you. You'll see. How are you getting on with your paper for the journals? You are, of course, publishing? Hmm?"

"I am not," Harriet said sharply. "Not till I've talked to Oscar. So stop asking me about it. I've made my decision, so that's all there is to it—"

44

But it wasn't. The decision was taken from her hands.

She went back to her unit after lunch, humming a little below her breath as she always did when she was thinking about new work, to find Catherine sitting grimly on the edge of her desk, her arms folded as she stared at a man sitting neatly in Harriet's chair, his legs crossed and his hands folded on a briefcase on his lap.

"This is a Mr. Monks. J. D. Monks. Says he's got to see you, and won't say why. But he's been asking some odd questions. About Mr. Ferris."

Harriet frowned sharply. "Oh? What about Mr. Ferris? Is he a relation of yours, Mr. Monks?"

"Ah, no. No, not at all." Mr. Monks stood up, and held out his hand. "How do you do, Dr. Berry. I would of course have known you even if this very . . . er . . . helpful lady hadn't indicated who you were. Mr. Ferris described you very accurately, I must say! A most delightful man, isn't he?"

"What can I do for you, Mr. Monks? I am rather busy this afternoon, so if you could—"

"Ah, well. This is a somewhat private matter, Dr. Berry. Perhaps we could find somewhere to talk?" He slid his eyes sideways at Catherine who sat firm and stared at him challengingly.

"Until I know why, I don't see much point in—"

"I am from the *Echo*, Dr. Berry," he cut in smoothly. "I've been asked to see you on a private matter by Sir Daniel Sefton, our proprietor. I really think you would prefer we discussed this quietly at this stage."

She frowned again, and then said, "I see. I suppose—oh, well. Would you mind, Catherine? It'll obviously be quicker if I agree. You were going to do the ward checks for me, anyway, this afternoon, so perhaps you could do them now rather than later. Thanks. . . ."

"Well, Mr. Monks?" she said, when Catherine had gone, snapping the door closed behind her. "What is all this?"

"It really is very simple, Dr. Berry," Mr. Monks said, leaning back in his chair and recrossing his legs. "I'll be as brief as I can,

45

since obviously your time is exceedingly precious. Simply, then, we received a call from a Mr. James Ferris a couple of days ago, and he told us a remarkable story: about how desperately ill he had been, how he had been undoubtedly dying of widespread cancer until you started a new treatment on him. He described the treatment in some detail, and it was fascinating—quite fascinating. We—Sir Daniel, you know—were sufficiently impressed by him to investigate further. We've talked to his G.P., and to his relations and neighbors, and there is no doubt in our minds that he was a cancer patient. Yet he looks so remarkably well now! So Sir Daniel arranged for him to be examined by his own Harley Street man, Lord Broster—you know his name, of course—who confirms that Mr. Ferris is totally free of disease. So, of course, we find ourselves in a dilemma! Mr. Ferris—or to be absolutely accurate, *Mrs.* Ferris—is offering us his story at a fairly stiff fee. But we are ethical people on the *Echo*, Dr. Berry. We would hesitate to rush into print with so incredible and wonderful a story without first ascertaining not only its truth but the facts about the treatment. We know you have not yet published anything about it in the usual journals. Our researchers have been very busy these past days, I promise you! So, we'd like to know about the treatment, why it is being kept a secret when it is clearly so effective, why other poor sufferers are not being offered it—you must understand our interest, I'm sure! When promises of cancer cures appear, they ought to be made known. Widely known. Often, of course, we find a degree of . . . what shall I say? Doubt. You will, I'm sure, recall what happened when there was news from that German doctor about his treatment. Of the doubts people expressed? We would . . . hesitate . . . to publish information about your treatment if we thought for one moment that there was any such medical uncertainty about its validity, as there was in that case."

"I'm very glad to hear it!" Harriet said vigorously. "Uninformed public comment about unproven treatments is always disastrous—always! The last thing anyone wants is to wake unjustified hopes in very ill people. Of course you can't use this information Mr. Ferris has given you! I should have warned him, damn it. I—"

46

"Why?" Monks raised his eyebrows. "Isn't what he says true? Didn't you treat him and cure him?"

"We never use the word cure," Harriet said sharply. "And certainly not at this stage. When a patient has survived therapy for five years or more, and there are other patients on whom the treatment has been used who also show long survival periods, we may be prepared to talk very cautiously about the *possibility* of cure, but no more than that. If you knew anything at all about the subject, Mr. Monks, you'd know that! You really can't—"

"Please, Dr. Berry! Let's not say *can't*. Newspapers *can*, if they feel it right to do so, publish what they believe should be published, however much individuals may object. That is our ethical duty. . . . Oh, please don't look so skeptical at the word ethical! We do have an ethic, I assure you! That's why I'm here. The thing that so interests us and makes us believe you may in fact have a real answer to this scourge of our times is the fact that *you* are displaying such very ethical behavior. You have made no money from your method. You treated Mr. Ferris for nothing, and in a Government Establishment. One not noted, if you'll forgive my saying so, for such remarkable work as yours appears to be. As I say, our researchers have been very busy! But this brings up another point. In a Government Establishment, maintained by public funds, i.e., by our readers, there is hardly a place for undue secrecy! You take my point, I'm sure."

"There isn't any undue secrecy!" Harriet said angrily. "That is a most unjustified accusation! I'm trying to behave in the recognized scientific manner. I can't rush into popular print with a single case, for God's sake! And an unproven one at that! Come back in five years and I may be able to—"

"Oh, come, Dr. Berry!" Mr. Monks laughed gently. "You must see that is out of the question. We have been fortunate enough to be the newspaper Mr. Ferris approached! We must use our good fortune intelligently, after all! People will want to know about this now, not in five years' time—"

He stopped and then smiled slowly.

"I find it significant that you haven't at any point denied that

47

your treatment, as far as Mr. Ferris is concerned, has been most effective. Putting aside the scientific caution you so admirably display—of course!—you do agree he is now free of disease?"

There was a short silence, then Harriet said unwillingly, "Well, I can't deny a fact, I suppose. At the moment—and only at this moment—Mr. Ferris appears to be free of disease, yes. But you must understand that time is part of the measure of effectiveness. If Mr. Ferris survives another five years . . ."

"Indeed, your point is taken, Dr. Berry. But he is *at the moment* a healthy man. That is what interests me. What interests us. What interests Mr. Ferris! And what will undoubtedly interest our many millions of readers." He stood up, and hitched his jacket more neatly across his shoulders before holding out his hand toward her.

"Thank you, Dr. Berry. I am indeed most grateful to you. I will now return to Sir Daniel and advise him that in my estimation we should buy Mr. Ferris's story and—"

"But you can't! It would be quite wrong to—"

"Dr. Berry! You are not suggesting, surely, that Mr. Ferris has no right to tell us his own story in his own way! His life, whether he owes it to you or not, is his own property! He has an inalienable right to sell the story and we have an inalienable right to buy it! You wouldn't dispute that?"

"Well, no. Of course I can't say that he isn't free to do as he chooses. But when it involves a matter so important—"

"Precisely. So important, to so many people! Believe me, Dr. Berry, I respect and admire your scruples. They do you immense credit. I hope you will agree, despite them, however, to talk to our scientific reporter in due course. We would hate to have to publish only Mr. Ferris's account of the method. We might make mistakes, and that would never do, would it? We must get the facts straight, and we can only get them from you, after all! We'll be in touch, Dr. Berry, and I hope you will see how worthwhile it will be to talk to us honestly and fearlessly. Indeed, you have *nothing* to fear at our hands. As long as there is no hint that you are seeking personal gain from your treatment, no one will ever doubt your scientific integrity—as long as you talk to us and make sure we report only accurate material. Good morning, Dr. Berry. Talking with you has indeed been a rare privilege, believe me."

She sat still for a long time after he had gone, and then, as she so often did in a dilemma, went to look for Theo.

But he was operating that afternoon, and she had to wait until after six o'clock to tell him. She went into the operating theater changing room as soon as he had showered and was half-dressed, and he listened carefully as she told him of the conversation with Monks.

"To put it at its mildest, this is bloody," he said, knotting his tie, and reaching for his jacket. "We'd better try and reach Oscar at once. Where is he, do you know?"

"In London. Discussing," Harriet said bitterly. "But that blasted Manton woman won't say where, not if I beg her—"

"She'll tell me," Theo said shortly. "Wait for me in my car, will you, Hattie? I'll get the number from her, and we'll call him from your place."

But by the time Theo had convinced Miss Manton that it was her bounden duty to part with the telephone number of Oscar's hotel, and they reached the cottage, it was past seven thirty, and a call to the hotel produced the information that Professor Bell had gone out for the evening to dine with friends, and no, they didn't know where, and yes, they would leave a message for him, though he was not expected in for some hours.

"Which means that unless we're very fortunate and he does get the message tonight that we've been trying to reach him, the first he'll know about it all will be tomorrow's headlines. Hell and damnation!" Theo said, as he hung up.

"They surely won't publish anything tomorrow, Theo? They won't have time, will they?"

"Oh, don't be naïve, Hattie! Of course they will! You don't believe what that man told you this afternoon? They've already bought Ferris, believe me. They'd never have sent a man down here to see you if they hadn't. No, they'll publish something to-

49

morrow, come hell or high water, and—God damn it, I wish we could have got hold of Oscar tonight. He's going to be put in the bloodiest of spots by this."

"And you were trying to persuade me to publish in spite of him, and at once." Harriet said furiously. "This is one hell of a reversal!"

"Oh, be your age, Hattie! Publishing a straightforward paper in *Nature* or whatever is one thing. It'd be months before the thing came out, what with all their checks and the rest of it. Oscar would have had fair warning. But this! All sorts of emotional dramatic stuff plastered all over the tabloids—he'll have a hell of a job explaining that away in Whitehall! Really, Harriet, I *am* angry with you! You must have been out of your mind to say as much as you did. This Monks man is going to use all sorts of quotes, you realize that? You should have stonewalled with the old 'No comment' business. Surely—"

"Theo, shut up! I've had as much as I can stand. Of course I know, *now*. But anyone would have been manipulated into talking by that man. He was as smooth as—oh, it's easy to be as wise as you are *after* an event."

"I suppose so. I'm sorry, Hattie." He smiled at her then. "But it's you I'm thinking of, and that's what made me angry. You really aren't going to enjoy what all this will lead to any more than poor old Oscar will, I promise you. Oh well, we'll cope somehow. But looking after you can be a very wearing business. Come on. Make me some dinner, and we'll try to phone Oscar again later."

4

"BUT, HARRIET, what possessed you? Surely you realized what would happen if you admitted that you had treated Ferris? And why the hell you didn't warn Ferris to keep quiet—"

"Oscar, we've already been over that. I know, now, just what I should have done. But I didn't think at the time, so I didn't do it, so what's the point of going on? Mea Culpa. What more can I say or do? Wear sackcloth and ashes? The important question now is what do we do about it all?"

"Let's take another look at what they actually wrote, Oscar," Theo said. "Perhaps it isn't as bad as it appears at first sight—"

"If it were only half as bad as it looked when I saw the paper this morning, it'd still be pretty horrible," Oscar grunted, and pushed the newspaper across his desk. Theo pulled his chair closer to Harriet's, and together they looked bleakly at the front page.

It was dominated by a picture of James Ferris, grinning cockily out at them, two fingers raised in the old-fashioned victory sign over a great black caption that read "THE LIVING PROOF OF A GREAT BRITISH BREAKTHROUGH." Below that, the story splashed itself right across the page, and Theo began to read it aloud:

"James Ferris—Polly to his friends—is a miracle man. A bare few weeks ago, his family and friends were waiting hourly for news of his death from the cancer that had invaded almost every part of his body. He weighed a meager five and a half stone, then, and as he says himself, 'I could hear the angels singing.' But today, he is back at work, fit and healthy and free of his disease, a sturdy eight stone, eating well, and wondering if he might get fat enough to go on a diet. Why? Because of a miraculous treatment developed in a remote Government Research Establishment in East Anglia. Yesterday, we talked to the remarkable scientist who discovered the treatment, still beautiful forty-eight-year-old widowed Dr. Harriet Berry"—Harriet grimaced—"although she was very unwilling to talk about her lifesaving work. Unwilling because she has not yet tried the treatment on other sufferers, and as a good scientist, she will not make claims of success until she is absolutely sure. But we feel Mr. Ferris is enough of a miracle for her success to be obvious. Especially when we know, from other sources, that no less than three hundred laboratory monkeys have also had the Berry treatment with outstanding success. Every animal treated has been cured of the cancer it had undoubtedly been suffering from."

"And I'd like to know who the hell the 'other sources' are," Oscar said.

"So would I," Harriet said bitterly. "I suppose I ought to feel a little better knowing it wasn't just my fault it all got out—but I don't."

The newspaper story continued:

"Just what is the treatment? We will be bringing you, every day next week, a detailed account written by *Echo* ace science reporter James McClarrie. Order Monday's *Echo* now, for the demand for copies will be enormous, so that you can discover for yourselves what British science has done and is still doing to restore the hope of life to the many millions of people dying of cancer today. Tomorrow, we will give you James 'Polly' Ferris's own thrilling account of his experiences . . ."

Theo put the paper down distastefully. "Was it McClarrie who tried to talk to you this morning, Hattie?"

"I don't know. I didn't stop to find out. He was sitting there at the front lodge waiting for me, and as soon as I saw him I bolted for the unit. He didn't particularly look like a newspaperman— whatever it is newspapermen look like—I'm not sure I know. But he obviously wanted me, and I wasn't taking any more risks, after yesterday."

"Let's think about this intelligently." Oscar stood up and began to prowl about the room in his characteristic fashion. "Obviously you can't keep them off forever. They won't give up that easily.

And now it is out, the only thing to do is to handle it properly. The question is, how is that? I've had Blumer on already from Whitehall this morning. And I must say that though he isn't particularly impressed with the fact that I didn't mention anything about this work to him when I saw him yesterday—which I would, of course, have done had I known publication was so imminent— yes, Harriet—I *know* how you feel about that—still, I detected a certain degree of warmth in him. Not precisely approbation, mark you, but at least a cautious something. They need some results to justify expenditure, of course, and God knows we do too."

He stopped his pacing, and looked across the room at Harriet. "Harriet, let me clear the air a little at this point. Forgive us, Theo, if we talk a little in front of you—but you know us both well enough. Harriet, I owe you an apology. I was unnecessarily brusque with you at conference, and I can only plead surprise as an excuse. You threw something at me I was not prepared for, and what with everything else, I found it difficult to react . . . well, as I would hope I normally do in such circumstances. But of course I am, I really am, immensely pleased with your work, and appreciate perfectly well what sort of effect this news is going to have on Brookbank. All right?"

She looked at him, and felt relief filling her with warmth; here at least was one complication cleared up.

"All right," she said, and smiled and he nodded at her, and started his pacing again.

"So what do we do? I can only suggest we handle the whole thing as though we were cooperating fully, in order to keep some control over what is published. We've already seen what they can do without cooperation, so let's for God's sake be sensible, and get some of the situation back under our own thumbs. You see the sense of that?"

Theo was watching Oscar's pacing, his eyes half-closed, and Harriet, glancing at him, wondered briefly about the expression on his face. Not precisely angry, but . . .

"Harriet—I suggest you agree to see this man McClarrie. I'll sit in on the interview, if you don't mind. Just to extricate you from any awkwardnesses that might come up. Does that sound reasonable to you?"

"If you think the best thing would be to talk to him, then of course I will. You're in charge, after all!"

Theo stood up sharply. "I must go," he said, and Harriet looked up at him, surprised by the clipped note in his voice. He *was* angry, but why? He wouldn't look at her, and went to the door.

"I'll be in theaters, Hattie," he said, not turning. "Until six or so. Come and see me, will you, before you leave? Good afternoon, Oscar."

"Now what on earth—?" she began as the door snapped behind him, but Oscar shrugged and came to stand beside her.

"Theo and his moods always bore me. I can't think why you pay any attention to them. Now, we'll call the front lodge and see if McClarrie is still hanging about—and I suspect he is—and get them to send him here." He leaned over and kissed her cheek briefly. "And tonight, we'll have dinner at the flat, hmm?"

She laughed at that. "Kiss and make up? Of course. I'd like that. I'll phone Mrs. Davies and see if she can stay the night with George. I'm sure she will. She usually doesn't mind on Thursdays."

"Splendid," he said, a little absently, for he was already dialing. "Foster? Is there a newspaperman—hmm? . . . Yes, that's the one. Ask him his name and paper, will you? . . . Yes, that's it. Tell him Dr. Berry will see him, and send him to my office, will you? . . . Thank you." He reached for his intercom. "Miss Manton, tea for three, please, with sandwiches and biscuits and the like. Make it look attractive, will you?"

"Fatted-calf treatment?"

"Why not? It works like a charm, in my experience. Now, listen, Harriet. If there are any difficult questions, let me handle them, will you? I've had a good deal of experience of these newspaper wallahs, over the years, so—"

"With the greatest of pleasure," she said fervently. "I hate the whole business, believe me. Look, let me go and tidy up, will you? There are times when a woman needs a little extra lipstick."

54

When she came back, with not only a freshly made-up face and well-brushed hair, but a crisply clean white coat, she found Oscar and a tall thin bearded man sitting in a haze of cigar smoke, a tea tray adorned with food and a small vase of dahlias in front of them on the desk.

They both stood up to greet her, and the tall man shook hands with her in response to Oscar's introduction and looked at her closely.

"How do you do, Dr. Berry? I feel I might well be shaking hands with our next Nobel prizewinner. It's a privilege to meet you, and I'm most grateful to you for agreeing to this interview."

A little flustered, Harriet looked beyond him to Oscar, but he showed no expression at all, leaning over his desk to pick up her teacup and offer it to her.

"That sounds rather exaggerated to me, Mr. McClarrie. But it's kind of you—thank you, Oscar. No, no sugar. Well, Mr. McClarrie? Where do you want to begin?"

He held her chair for her as she sat down, and then returned to his own. "At the beginning, please," he said promptly. "I'll try to make it easy for you, though. I have a modest degree in physics, so I do speak a little of the language, if not as much as I might." He smiled a professionally brilliant smile. "I sometimes suspect that the culture gap doesn't exist only between arts and sciences, but in an interdisciplinary way within the sciences themselves. It's surprising how little biology a physics man gets. But I'll do my best."

"In very basic terms, then, Mr. McClarrie, I used on Mr. Ferris —following a very large series of successful animal experiments of which I believe you know—a method of inducing growth regression. I exhibited to him a culture of RNA-virus-type bodies grown on his own normal body cells, under special conditions designed to enhance the speed of their action. I used heat and I used hyperbaric oxygen—"

"Hyperbaric oxygen? One of the high-pressure chambers they sometimes use for radiotherapy?"

"That's it. A highly oxygenated cell is more vulnerable. There is a good deal of evidence that the use of hyperbaric oxygen enhances

55

treatment effects. I daresay I might have got results without it, but I thought it important to use as much speed as I safely could in so ill a man. It was a risk—but he was at risk of dying anyway, so I felt it justified."

"In the event you were right," McClarrie said and smiled gently, "there's no need to be on the defensive about that, Dr. Berry."

"I wasn't on the defensive!"

"No? Forgive me. I thought—however. You applied the treatment. May I just ask a few questions about the details of the method? Of the way you developed your vaccine? Because that is in effect what it is. . . ."

He launched into a series of extremely intelligent questions, and Harriet found herself beginning to enjoy the interview. To talk shop in depth with a person who really understood her subject had always been a pleasure to her, and she became more and more animated, letting her tea cool as she talked eagerly about her hypothesis, and not noticing Oscar's silence until he cut in suddenly after one of McClarrie's questions.

"How about the costings on this, Dr. Berry? It sounds to me—"

"Ah, Mr. McClarrie," Oscar said quickly, "this, I suspect, is where I must join in. Budgeting and so on is my department. Not nearly as interesting, of course, as the grass-roots work, but very vital, all the same."

"Oh, indeed, Professor Bell! And it must be very tedious for you to have to cope with all this administrative side. I know how distinguished a scientist you are in your own right, of course. Bell's test—"

Oscar smiled thinly. "And I still work at the lab bench, I can assure you, Mr. McClarrie. The only reason I am not completely au fait with every detail of Dr. Berry's recent project work is that I have just returned from the States where I was conducting a series of trials of my own. However, that is by-the-by. You were asking about costings. I can assure you that this method that Dr. Berry has developed is in fact an extremely expensive one. I have a breakdown here . . ."

56

He opened a folder on his desk and took from it a sheet of folded blue foolscap, carefully ruled into columns of figures.

"The cost of Mr. Ferris's total treatment, including full hospital inpatient care, of course, is in the region of three and a half thousand pounds. I haven't, of course, included costs of preliminary work, animal trials, and the like, which have been going on under my direction here since Dr. Berry started work on this project— when was it, Harriet? Two years ago? Yes, two years ago—which would have vastly increased the bill, of course. Quadrupled it at the very least."

"Three and a half thousand. Is that what it would cost today to treat another patient in the same condition?"

"Oh, probably far more, far more! We have the equipment here, in use, and I didn't account for that in my costings. If a general hospital wanted to apply the treatment, Mr. McClarrie, they would first have to install the extra pathological laboratory equipment, then the hyperbaric oxygen unit, improve staff/patient ratios considerably—say, the cost of treating one patient would be approaching, say, five thousand pounds, and you'll be pretty accurate."

"A lot of money."

"A great deal of money indeed. And I have in operation at this Establishment a number of extremely important investigations into dangerous—in the sense of life-threatening—conditions, all of which must be financed on a very meager budget indeed. Frankly, Mr. McClarrie, if you could, in your account of today's interview, make mention of the fact that we here at Brookbank are doing the work we do on a veritable shoestring, and if you could suggest that we should be given more realistic—not generous, but *realistic*— sums of money, I for one would be very grateful. And I imagine my staff would . . . hmm, Harriet? They must all be tired to death of listening to me preach economy at them."

"We know why you have to," Harriet said. "Look, I'm sorry, but I hadn't realized we'd been talking so long. I really must go—there are some things I must do before I leave tonight, and I—er—I don't want to leave too late if I can avoid it." She let her eyes slide a little wickedly across Oscar. "Will you forgive me? I'm sure there's no more I can usefully add."

McClarrie stood up at once, and held out his hand to her.

"Of course, Dr. Berry, and I am immensely grateful to you, immensely. May I perhaps talk to you again if by any chance there should be any extra details I want to sort out when I write my copy?"

"As far as I'm concerned, by all means. But you'd better check with Os—Professor Bell."

"Of course. And thank you again."

It was past six, but she went at once to the operating theaters, and she found Theo sitting in theater sister's office drinking tea while he wrote his notes of the day's operations.

"Well? How did the great confrontation go?" he asked without looking up.

"Oh, it was fine. He's a nice chap, McClarrie, and mercifully bright. Knows enough about biology to be able to ask intelligent questions. I'll look forward to seeing the articles he writes out of it all. Theo,"—she came and perched on the desk beside him, and put her hand over the notes he was writing—"stop a minute, will you? I want to know. Why did you leave in such a huff?"

"A huff? A *huff?* Good God, woman, I was raging! I couldn't trust myself to speak! And you call it a huff? Look, my dear benighted creature, when will you see that Oscar uses you as though you were his doormat? He stamps around on you, uses you outrageously, and you smile and simper and say 'yes sir, no sir, three bags full sir'—"

"What the hell are you talking about?"

"I'm talking about that sickly apology stunt he pulled. You've drifted into the ludicrous habit of treating Oscar and his sensibilities as though they were the rarest porcelain, but even you must surely see that you're being manipulated in the most outrageous fashion!"

Harriet felt her own anger rising. "I most surely do not! You're getting as paranoid as George with these delusions of persecution of yours! Except that for some extraordinary reason you choose to believe it's me who's being persecuted rather than yourself! You sometimes make me wonder, Theo, whether you oughtn't to go away for awhile and do some straight thinking about yourself, believe me you do—"

"And I begin to wonder if your brain is softening, believe *me*. You think he apologized for the sake of a tender glance from your *beaux yeux*? Not a bit of it, my dear sweet, naïve half-wit! He knows as well as he knows his own name that now the Ferris story is out, you're going to get a hell of a lot of glory. And he wants in on it. It's as simple as that, and *you* are as simple as that if you haven't the wit to see it! Either simple or addled by some sort of absurd passion for the man even if you don't know it. Now do you see why I'm furious?"

She sat and stared at him for a moment, her own anger draining away, for he looked far more unhappy now than furious, and clearly totally believed in the truth of what he was saying.

And it had to be admitted that Oscar had apologized with what was for him an unusual alacrity. Over the many years they had had their disagreements, but usually it was a matter of weeks rather than days before an episode was forgotten, and rarely indeed had one ended with an actual apology. Oscar had always tended to behave as though the argument had never happened, and that therefore no apology was needed. Yet this time he had apologized. Perhaps Theo had some justification for what he was saying.

She closed her eyes for a moment. "Theo, I'm so tired I could drop. Look, forget it, will you? I take your point, and I'll think about it. But please, right now, stop being so disagreeable. I really don't feel I can cope with any more alarums and excursions today. I've had enough."

He was immediately transformed. "Dear Hattie! I am sorry! You're quite right, of course. It's too bad of me to be so thoughtless and harangue you in this fashion. Shall we drive into King's Lynn tomorrow and have ourselves a fancy lunch, and talk quietly then? Mmm? Oysters and a steak tartare, and some very ancient claret? How does that sound? You go home and have a peaceful evening, and we'll talk tomorrow. I'd drive you, but I've promised to do a case for Geoffrey at nine. Will you be all right?"

"I'll be fine, of course. And thank you, lunch would be lovely. Bless you. Good night, Theo."

And she went, feeling a little guilty at not admitting she was spending the evening with Oscar, but there seemed little value in irritating Theo any further.

But it was not as pleasant an evening as it should have been. Oscar prepared as delectable a meal as he ever had and, refusing to talk about work in any way whatsoever, was an amusing companion, talking about theater and books, both subjects he knew she enjoyed. And later, in bed, he was particularly tender, making considerable efforts to please her; not that he was a particularly selfish lover, but he did not always give her the sort of caresses she most enjoyed. Tonight, his very willingness to provide the stimulation she wanted added to her sometimes-felt embarrassment about her sexuality. She had always recognized in herself a certain distaste for her own desires, and could never be quite sure what disturbed her most—wanting extended loveplay and not receiving it, or receiving it and being swept away by the violence of response it woke in her.

So, long after he was asleep, lying close to her with one hand carelessly thrown over her breasts, she wondered. Did he behave so to please her, or because he really wanted to? That had always been something she wondered about, his response. Certainly he seemed at times to need her body as much as she needed his, but even when he appeared most absorbed in their lovemaking she felt a certain remoteness in him, as though a small part of his mind were standing by, watching. But that could be, she told herself as she had done so often over the years, because of her own still lingering guilts about their relationship. No matter how emancipated a woman she might seem to be in some ways, she was still the middle-class daughter of a middle-class puritan G.P., still felt not only guilt about a sexual relationship outside marriage but a faint disloyalty to the long-dead David.

And tonight, added to her layers of often experienced doubts and questionings, there was a new dimension. Was Theo right in his anger? Was Oscar manipulating her for his own ends? If he was, could it not be simply that this was part of him, an inevitable result of the day's events? He *was* a somewhat devious man; it was one of the aspects of his personality she had long since recognized and accepted. No one could become head of such an Establishment as Brookbank without a gift for and a decided taste for intrigue, nor could it be run efficiently without an ability to manipulate people and events. She had always rather admired this in him, knowing she could never herself be capable of the complexities of his position. C. P. Snowery, Theo had once called it, watching the way Oscar had rid himself of an unwanted man and obtained the cooperation of another he had been angling after. "You've got to admire it," Theo had said, "even as you despise it."

But she didn't despise it, and she didn't despise Oscar either. She moved gently, turning to look at him in the thin light thrown by the street light outside the window, and he stirred and moved closer to her, and his fingers flexed a little, moving over her skin. She felt it rising in her again, that well of sexual need that lay in a heavy pool deep in her pelvis, and reached for his body, using the skill of long familiarity to arouse him sexually enough to rouse him in fact. And not until they had made love again did she sleep, optimism about the future returning, as it usually did, to wash away the niggling doubts and foolish guilts.

But it proved to be an ill-founded optimism. She had hoped that the interview with McClarrie would lead merely to a few days of artificial newspaper excitement, which would then leak away to nothing, leaving her to go on with her work, the road neatly open to proper publication of her results. She said as much to Theo, when they lunched cozily together next day, but he laughed at her.

"You sound like a child, Hattie, sometimes: 'It won't rain tomorrow because it's my birthday and no one would let it rain on

61

my birthday.' This is out of your hands, dear heart, totally. This isn't anything nice and simple like a new fission bomb or something of that nature. That sort of thing people lose interest in because it can merely kill millions. You've come up with something quite other, something that really interests people in a big way. Joe Doakes couldn't care less about methods of killing millions, but he cares like hell about methods of keeping Joe Doakes and Mrs. Doakes and all the little Doakeses alive and well. Even if the newspapers laid off in a few days—and you could be right about that, depending what else happens in this delicious world of ours— you're going to find a lot more will happen yet."

"I don't see—"

"You never do, do you? Well, I won't make any more prognostications. I get very bored with being Cassandra. Marrons glacées, I think, yes? Outrageously juvenile to like those as much as you do. And then we must go. I've a list to get through this afternoon somehow—" And he refused to say any more.

She was able to accept that refusal with equanimity, for she found other things to think about when she returned to the unit.

"Your son Gordon phoned, Dr. Berry," John told her as she came into the unit, a little sleepy from the excellence of the lunch. "Just after you left. He said to tell you he'll be down tonight, about half past seven—in time for dinner, you see—but on his own. And I'd no sooner hung up and written it all down for you, but the phone rings again, and this time it's your daughter, and she's coming down tonight too, for the weekend, and she said she'll bring some extra food with her, seeing you're being invaded. I must say, they are a splendid pair, rallying round like this, aren't they?"

"I didn't think they'd both accept so quickly—and anyway I asked them for next weekend or the one after . . ." Harriet said, a little startled.

"They can read," Catherine growled. "Of course they're rushing down to see you. What did you expect?"

Harriet stared at her for a moment, and then laughed. "God, I'm a cretin. I'd completely forgotten that. The newspaper—of course. Thank God it's Friday. If ever anyone needed a peaceful weekend away from work, it's me."

"Well, enjoy it," Catherine said. "I doubt there'll be much peace for any of us once the *Echo* really gets going next week."

5

SHE LOOKED at them both with deep pleasure, sitting there as they had been used to years ago, Gordon tidy as ever in the big armchair, Patty lying flat on her back on the rug, staring at the shapes of shadows on the ceiling as they moved with the firelight. There was a stab of guilt in her pleasure that enhanced it; fond as she was of Jean and much as she loved small Giles, it was delightful to have just her own two to herself.

Then Patty turned her head and looked at Gordon, and Harriet sighed a little. They had always bickered, as brothers and sisters do, but the differences between them seemed more intense as they grew older. They had been on reasonably amiable terms so far this weekend, but she could see the look on Patty's face, and knew she wouldn't be able to avoid returning to the attack, even though she knew her mother disliked hearing them disagree.

"Tell me something, Gordon," Patty said abruptly. "Suppose this treatment turns out to have dangerous side effects. It could, you know! Is the press justified in publishing all this stuff before the possible risks are known?"

"Oh, for God's sake, Patty, do be practical! Of course there are risks. But that's what life is all about. If you risk nothing, you gain nothing. Even in your ivory tower you must see that."

"Oh, I see it all right! Scientists are taking risks the whole time. But they're calculated risks aimed at avoiding future ones. Above all, they're not aimed at making money. That's what makes me sick about your whole attitude. You only think in profit and loss terms. You don't give a damn about the ethics of—"

"And you make *me* sick! Who the hell do you think pays you, keeps you in your job where you can be so high-minded and ethical? People who take risks with money, that's who. The people who own and run the firm you work for. All this socialist nonsense

64

of yours—you should have grown out of it years ago, together with the braces on your teeth. Oh, I know what you want. You want to see all the research Establishments under Government control so that you can paddle about wasting taxpayers' money while you polish your ethics to a high gloss. Well, because you're working for a commercial setup, you've got all sorts of extra privileges—twice the sort of equipment and facilities Ma's got, twice the staff, and a bloody sight better pay packet, too. If you want that, then you can't expect the luxury of ignoring the rights of the people who pay for it all."

"It's got nothing to do with politics, though it strikes me you're pretty immature politically if you see a decent concern for the rights of other people as something you grow out of. But that isn't the point at issue. Don't try to drag this off into a left-right fight. The point is—"

"The point is that Ma ought to be getting a better deal out of all this than she is. I still say Ferris had a right to get what *he* could out of the whole thing—but what really interests me is what *Ma* will get out of it. If anyone ought to be paid by that paper, it isn't Ferris."

"Gordon, Patty, please. I really don't see any point in all this. I—"

"I know you don't," Gordon said forcefully. "That's why it's got to be talked about. With both of you white-hot idealists—though I must say, Patty, it's remarkable you work for a commercial firm, and not a Government Establishment like Brookbank, with your attitudes."

"Because I agree with you. It's the commercial firms that provide the best working conditions. The point on which we differ is that you think that's as it ought to be, and I think it's bloody immoral. But when you've got to make choices between two ethics the most important one must win—and the most important one for me is the quality of the work I can do, not where I do it."

"Well, that sounds very elegant, no doubt, and it pleases you, but from where I'm sitting it's a pretty specious argument. However, I want to get to the point about Ma. I've said it before this weekend and I'll go on saying it. You are seventeen kinds of a fool if you don't leave Brookbank and take your work with you to a commercial firm where you'll get some decent facilities and a decent return for your efforts. It's all wrong that you should sit here in this pokey cottage, stuck with old George and not enough money to get some decent help to look after him."

"I don't see you and Jean offering to take the old man off her back," Patty murmured.

"Why the hell you should expect Jean to cope with a small child *and* a senile grandfather-in-law, while you—"

"Oh, do stop, both of you," Harriet said. "You're ruining the weekend with all this niggling! It's time you both grew out of it. I am *not* complaining about looking after George, and I am *not* asking either of you to take him on. There's no reason why you should. All I wanted of you both was an opinion on what I should do about publishing. That's why I wrote to you. Well, as it happens the decision's been made for me, so we can forget it. I do appreciate your concern for my future, Gordon, but really—"

Patty sat up and stretched, and then gave Gordon an affectionate thrust with her foot.

"She's quite right, Gord. All this sibling rivalry bit—it must be very boring. I'll forgive you for being an accountant if you'll forgive me for having a conscience. Okay?"

"Go to hell," Gordon said, but without rancor. "You always were a half-witted narrow-minded idiot, considering the sort of I.Q. you've got. And you always will be. The sooner you marry one of those damp young men of yours and get yourself involved with kids and family responsibility, the sooner you'll grow up a bit."

"Isn't it marvelous!" Patty said, smiling wryly at Harriet. "According to paterfamilias here—all of two years in the parenthood business, and a full-time expert—every woman can be debrained with a basinful of sex and the bovine babymaking business that goes with it. Roll on liberation!"

"But, Ma, there is at least one thing we both agree on, and I do

66

wish you'd think about it! You ought to take a leaf out of Patty's book and go to a commercial setup."

"He's right, I'm afraid, Ma," Patty said. "I hate him for it, and I hate the system for it, but he's right. You need a hell of a lot better deal than you're getting at Brookbank, if you're to complete this work properly. You ought to be able to run great series of trials and you need five times the equipment and staff you've got to do it. You'll never get that at Brookbank."

"And if you go to a commercial firm big enough to get the vaccine going in a proper way, think how quickly the treatment will be available for general use, once it's proved! That ought to warm up your two ethical scientific hearts! I'm right, aren't I? If you wait until after you've completed your work, it'll be at least another year or even more before the stuff becomes freely available, because they'll have to start from scratch? Whereas if you're working with them from the start—"

"Don't ask me to look that far ahead! It'll be years before we're ready to consider applying the method to general use. To start thinking at this stage about mass production of the vaccine is like —like deciding which course at university a child should read on the day he's born!"

"That's not necessarily a bad thing to do. We've put Giles down for his school."

"You would," Patty jeered. "Which one? Eton?"

"You have to think foward, Ma, if you're ever to get anywhere! Surely you do it with your work? You don't just charge off in umpteen different directions. You plan a scheme and follow it. So I don't see why you can't apply the same methodology to your private affairs. Just as an example, if you'd have thought ahead years ago, you wouldn't have the problem of old George now. You'd have made other arrangements for him long since. God knows, he was difficult enough to live with when we were kids and he was normal then. Now he's senile, he's impossible. You can't pretend it's affection that keeps you looking after him."

"No, I can't pretend that. I never liked him, and I like him less

67

now, and I'd be a rotten liar if I said otherwise. But he was your father's father, so—" She shrugged.

"Did *he* like him?" Patty asked. "Father, I mean?"

"Oh, I don't know, love. It's all so long ago now, I can't remember. That's what depresses me most, sometimes. Not remembering. I know it happened, being married to David, and I've you two to prove it. But it's all so remote now, as though it happened to someone else."

"So why the hell lumber yourself with George?" Gordon said. "No feeling for him, no reason to be so damned dutiful—"

"I don't know why. And do stop nagging. You sound as bad as Theo!"

"Oh, darling old Theo! How is he? I should have asked. Will he be coming to lunch tomorrow?" Patty asked.

"Of course! He always does. He's a creature of habit, like you two. Still arguing, still nagging. Habit, all of it." She looked at them affectionately. "Still, I like you as you are. That's habit too, I suppose. Shall you go mushroom hunting tomorrow, Patty? The way you used to do? There should be a few left in the far field. With that splendid ham you brought with you and a few new mushrooms I could produce a very Sundayish breakfast—"

"Jesus!" Patty said. "Have you seen the papers yet, Ma? No—you couldn't have."

She stood beside the kitchen table, her scarlet woolen cap at the back of her head, her sheepskin coat hanging open, and her nose pink with the cold, and Harriet took the freshly picked mushrooms and began to wipe them on a paper towel, amused at the way Patty was already deep in the Sunday papers; from the day she had learned to read, she had swallowed print, any print, voraciously.

"No," she said. "I haven't even looked at the headlines. I just brought them in. Young Peter must be going on another of his motorcycle scrambles today. It's the only time we get the papers before lunch. How many slices of ham can you eat? And call Gordon and ask him, will you?"

68

"Ma, listen to this." Patty came and stood beside her. " 'It was announced yesterday that this year's Nobel prize for medicine is to be awarded to William Ross-Craigie for his work on—' "

"What's that? Here, let me see." Harriet dropped the mushrooms, and took the paper from Patty, to look at the picture of William Ross-Craigie simpering up at her, and read the couple of inches of newsprint swiftly.

"Has the other paper got anything? Let me see—"

Patty was already leafing through the other one, a more popular and vociferous sheet than the sober Sunday heavy Harriet was holding, and she nodded after a moment.

"Mmm. Here it is. Much more, too. Look—"

They read it together, and then Harriet said doubtfully, "Well, one thing ought to please Oscar, even though they don't mention him. At least they say Ross-Craigie was a Brookbank man. I wish they hadn't brought up my stuff as well, though."

"Oh, for God's sake! It was inevitable! But, Ma, this'll stir things up a bit, won't it? Atheroma—this seems to suggest they're already using the treatment quite a lot in the States."

"They are. Oscar told me—"

The telephone shrilled sharply, and she heard Gordon thumping down the stairs to answer it. "That'll be Theo, I imagine."

Theo sounded unusually strained, not a hint of his normal flippancy in his voice.

"Hattie? Look, there's a problem—"

"I know. We've seen. Oscar will be pretty upset. He knew it was coming, I think, but a fait accompli is—"

"Seen what? Oscar? What are you talking about?"

"Ross-Craigie, of course! The newspapers. Isn't that why you phoned?"

"No. What about Ross-Craigie?"

"He's got the Nobel for his atheroma work. And the papers we've seen—well, one of them, at any rate—say he was at Brookbank, but Oscar isn't mentioned. He'll be—"

"Yes, he'll be—but never mind that now. This is something else.

Look, Hattie, I'm at the hospital. Had to do an early morning round. And there was a man here looking for you. I've tried to head him off, but some bloody idiot's told him where you live, and he's on his way. I wanted to warn you—I'll come at once, but he'll be there before me. It won't be easy—try not to talk to him till I come, will you? Maybe I can—"

"Theo, what is all this? What man? What does he want? I don't know what you're talking about."

"He wants to talk to you about—it's going to be pretty nasty for you, Hattie. Look, I'm on my way. Just try to wait till I come."

She stared at the telephone buzzing in her hand after he had hung up, puzzled and with a chill of alarm spreading in her. It wasn't at all like Theo to sound so agitated.

"Hey, Ma, what about breakfast?" Gordon called from the kitchen. "I'm hollow."

"You'd better make some toast or something," she said absently, and pulled her dressing gown around her and went to the stairs. "And make something for George, would you? There's some sort of panic on, and I've got to get dressed."

They both came to the kitchen door to stare at her.

"What is it? Wasn't that Theo on the phone?" Patty asked.

"Yes. He sounded—apparently there's someone coming from Brookbank to see me, and Theo seems to think he means some sort of trouble. Theo sounded very odd. Told me to try not to talk much to the man till he got here. Look, I must get dressed. Can you cope with breakfast for yourselves and George? I'll get him up and dressed first—come up and get him for me when I call, will you, Gordon? I'll be as quick as I can."

George was, inevitably, in an obstructive mood as she tried to hurry him into his clothes, muttering at her malevolently as she stripped off his soaked pajamas and began to wash him. He smelled worse than ever this morning, and her gorge rose as she soaped the thin old legs and buttocks, and then dried him. The hell of Sundays, with no Mrs. Davies to turn to. She called Gordon with relief to come and take the old man downstairs to the kitchen, and as she washed herself and dressed, she tried to think about what Theo had said.

Clearly, he was rattled, but why? Because a man wanted to talk to her? What man? Talk about what? Her bewilderment grew.

As she was zipping her skirt, she heard a car stop outside, and went to the window to peer out. An elderly taxi was chugging in the road, and a man in a raincoat was paying the fare. He turned and looked at the cottage, and she stepped back a little, watching him.

He looked very ordinary, his rather thin fair hair blowing a little in the early morning wind, his narrow shoulders hunched against the cold. Then, he opened the gate and walked purposefully up the path, and she heard the bell, heard Patty's voice, muffled, and the slightly deeper tones of the man answering her.

She finished dressing, and was brushing her hair when Patty came in.

"Who is it, Ma? He says his name is Ryman, and he won't say what he wants. Just that he has to talk to you."

"I've no idea. Just that Theo said it'd be nasty, whatever he meant by that. I'll be down in a minute. Have you had breakfast?"

"Mmm? Oh, I did some toast, and there's some coffee for you when you come down—Gordon's getting dressed. Look, Ma, I think I know—oh, hell, now what?"

There was a sound of a raised voice outside, and she opened the door to find George climbing the stairs, his head poked forward, and his eyes narrowed with rage.

"I know what you're doing. I know, and I won't go, d'you hear me? I won't, and if you don't stop it, I'll get the police to you, d'you hear me? I'll get the police to stop you, that's what I'll do—" he shouted, his voice cracked and shrill and a little breathless.

"For heaven's sake, what's the matter?" Harriet said as soothingly as she could. "No one's doing anything, so do stop shouting. Have you had your breakfast? Patty—"

"I won't go. I'll kill myself first, that's what I'll do. Then you'll be happy, won't you, be rid of me then, won't you?" His face

71

twisted a little, and he slid his eyes sideways toward Gordon, who had come out of his room, and now there was a hint of pathos in his voice. "Then you'll all be glad, won't you? That's what you want, isn't it? You've tried all the other things, and I was too clever for you, and now you're going to get rid of me this way." His voice began to rise again. "Well, I won't go, and I won't kill myself, not to oblige you, I won't—"

"No one is trying to get rid of you, Grandfather," Patty said loudly. "Now, come downstairs and finish your breakfast, there's a dear. No one wants to get rid of you."

"What the hell's got into him?" Gordon asked.

"It's the man who's come to see Ma. Grandfather seems to think he's come for him—he hasn't, Grandfather, truly he hasn't. He's just come to see Ma, that's all. Now do come on."

"I know what he's come to see her about. I know—going to put me away, going to get rid of me, that's what she's doing. Well, I won't go—" But he let Patty lead him away, and she grimaced over her shoulder at Harriet as she led him down the stairs.

"God, Ma, you'll have to do something soon about him! Is he always as bad as this?" Gordon asked.

"No, not always," Harriet said wearily. "It's my own fault, I suppose. I rushed him, and upsetting his routine always does start him off. And a stranger turning up into the bargain, and both of you here—I should have expected it. He'll be tiresome all day now, damn it. Look, do something for me, will you? Go on down and try to keep him happy for a while, will you? He always had a soft spot for you, and you may be able to convince him I'm neither trying to poison him, nor trying to get rid of him—"

"You ought to. Get rid of him, I mean. I know it sounds cruel and all the rest of it, and if he seemed to get any pleasure out of living with you, it'd be different, but as it is . . ."

"Gordon, please?"

"Oh, all right!"

"I'm sorry you're having such a foul weekend," she said, as he started down the stairs, and he looked back at her and grinned.

"I'll forgive you," he said. "Seeing it's you. Don't be long, though. I'm liable to slosh him if I'm left with him for too long, I promise you."

She came down to the living room, trying to look calm and re- laxed, to find the raincoated man sitting on the edge of a chair beside the dead ashes of last night's fire. He stood up nervously as she came in.

"Er—Dr. Berry? My name's Ryman. Steven Ryman. I'm sorry to come and bother you on a Sunday like this, but it is urgent, as I think you'll understand when I explain. I—er—I hope I haven't disturbed your—er—family too much." He glanced at the closed kitchen door. "It is early, I know, but . . ." his voice died away.

"Not at all," she said, and held out her hand, and after a mo- ment he thrust his own forward and shook it, and his skin was cold and damp against hers.

"I am sorry my father-in-law made such a fuss," she said, embar- rassed as she always was when she had to explain about George. "I hope he didn't—er—bother you."

The man smiled fleetingly. "Well, I was a bit startled," he ad- mitted. "He seemed to think I was going to take him away some- where."

"I'm afraid he does get a little confused. He's over eighty, you see, and old people—they can be a little difficult. Er—do let me take your coat. And I'm sorry it's so cold in here. We haven't lit the fire yet."

She took his coat and put it on the sofa, and then with a bright- ness she wasn't feeling said, "I'll just light it, shall I? So cold this morning . . ."

She knelt before the fireplace, shoving a few sticks from the log basket into the wood ash, and thrusting the gas poker under them before piling a couple of logs on top, and he watched her as the gas roared softly and the flames began to leap against the brick of the fireplace.

"There, that's better," she said. "Old-fashioned, these big fire- places, I know, but so pleasant, don't you think? And quite easy to

73

look after. They really understood about fireplaces and chimneys when they built this place. It's quite old, you know. We can't be sure, but it was supposed to have been built about two hundred years ago. We had to knock three tiny rooms together to make this room. A little awkward, of course, having the stairs running straight out of the living room, and the kitchen running off it too, but we manage."

"It's very nice," he said woodenly, sitting on the edge of the chair, his shoulders very straight and his hands clasped on his lap. "Er—as I say, I'm so sorry to come so early on a Sunday morning, but I had to. There's so little time, you see, and—"

She looked at him and his face was flat with misery and, embarrassed, she looked away. The man was exuding distress; it hung between them, almost palpable.

"Er—do let me get you some coffee, won't you? I think there's some ready"—she began to move toward the kitchen.

But he stood up, and said desperately, "No—er, no. Please, don't bother. I really—I just have to talk to you. I went to the hospital, you see, and they—someone told me you were living here, and I thought—well, I had to. It's really urgent. Ever so urgent."

She turned and looked at him again, unwillingly, and he stood there, his hands held stiffly clasped in front of him, his head held so rigidly that she could see a fine tremor in the muscles of his neck.

"I came down as soon as I could. I had to get the children organized, you see, and I had to go and see her as usual, of course, so I couldn't leave till late last night—gone ten it was. And I've got to get back for two o'clock visiting hours, or she'll—she'll wonder—" He swallowed. "I come from Kendal. The Lake District, you know? And trains are so bad at weekends—and I've got to get back. Please, let me explain to you. It's really very urgent."

She nodded, and came back to the fireside and sat down. No matter what Theo had said, this clearly couldn't wait until he came.

"What is it?" she said, and put her hand out toward the other

74

chair and he sat down again and leaned forward, his hands still tightly clasped on his knees.

"My wife. It's my wife."

He looked at her, and his eyes seemed to swell and glisten, and he sniffed hard, and swallowed, and then went on in a rapid monotone. "She's had three operations. They couldn't take the breast off, you see, too far gone, they told me. So they did her ovaries, and then some other operation on her back—her glands, and then they did a brain operation. That was a month ago, but—there's nothing else they can do, you see. He told me, the surgeon, he said they'd done all they could, and if it wasn't for the children they'd have sent her home, but the youngest, he's not at school yet, and it wouldn't be right, though God knows I wanted her home. But not like she is, she's got to be well, hasn't she? She can't come home like she is. And then they said—anyway, I saw in the paper, Friday I saw it. That man. He was the same, wasn't he? Got thin and the rest of it? She's got like that. She used to be a great strapping sort of—anyway, now she's like he was. So I came to ask you. I tried to phone, but they wouldn't let me talk to anyone, so all I could do was come myself. And I've got to get back at two o'clock, no later. You've got to do it for her too. They've told me, the surgeon, and the sister, they said—a week or two maybe. No more. And the youngest hasn't started school yet, do you see? You will, won't you? Do it for her?"

He stopped and stared at her, and then, not moving, still sitting with his hands held on his lap and his shoulders straight, he began to cry, his eyes spilling tears and his nose running onto his twisted upper lip, and she sat and looked back at him, numb with the weight of his misery.

"I—Mr. Ryman, please." She managed to stand up then, and went quickly across the room to the sideboard and poured some brandy into a glass and brought it to him.

But he sat still, weeping and gulping, and she stood unhappily beside him holding out the glass, and said again, "Mr. Ryman—please."

He moved then, and slid forward in the chair until he was on his knees in front of her, and he held onto her skirt with both hands, weeping, knocking the brandy glass from her hands, and she leaned over and lifted him awkwardly to make him sit down again.

"You will—say you will, please. You've got to, and we can get there by two o'clock if you'll come now and start it."

She stood there beside him, and put one hand on his shoulder, pushing him gently until he leaned back in his chair, and then she bent and picked up the glass and refilled it and brought it to him, and this time he took it from her, and began to drink, staring at her over the rim of the glass.

She had hardly been aware of the sound of a car outside, of the footsteps on the path, until the door opened and Theo came in, his overcoat pulled high around his neck, and the draft of cold air he brought with him made her turn. She looked at him appealingly.

He grimaced, and closed the door behind him sharply, and came and stood beside the man's chair.

"Mr. Ryman—I tried to explain to you at the hospital. I imagine Dr. Berry has explained too. She can't do anything. I'm sorry, but there is nothing she can do. Nothing at all."

Ryman stood up sharply, and thrust his face at Theo, his eyes bright and glittering in their puffy red lids.

"Well, you're wrong. She can—she can and she will—won't you?" He turned to Harriet. "You *are* going to, aren't you? I knew if I could explain to you—you're a woman, you understand. I knew you would if I talked to you, no matter what he said. He tried to get me to go away, but I knew you would if I talked to you—"

"Mr. Ryman, please—" Harriet said desperately, and looked at him, and he stared back, and then she shook her head.

"I'm sorry, Mr. Ryman. I do sympathize, believe me. I wish I could help you, but—"

"You said you would—"

"I'm afraid I didn't. I've said nothing. I can't. The treatment I used for Mr. Ferris—that was just an experiment. It should never have been written about in the paper. I can't tell you how sorry I am, but I can't help you."

"You can! Of course you can if you want to! You helped him! Why not her? What's wrong with her that you can't help her? There's three kids—the youngest not at school yet! You've got to—"

"Mr. Ryman." Theo's voice came crisply. "Mr. Ryman, I've tried to explain to you already this morning. It isn't anything to do with personal desires on anyone's part. If your wife is as ill as you say, then there just isn't any chance of helping her. Mr. Ferris managed to survive for the weeks needed to prepare the vaccine. And he was here, where the equipment is. To treat your wife Dr. Berry would need not only time, but would need to have her here, at Brookbank. Even if the treatment were available in this way— which it isn't because Brookbank isn't a normal hospital but a research Establishment—from the history you give it just isn't possible. I'm sorry. Dr. Berry can't help you."

"Dr. Berry . . . ," he said, and moved toward her, but she shook her head.

"I'm sorry, Mr. Ryman. What Mr. Fowler says is quite true. I can't help you. I wish I could, believe me, but it isn't possible."

He stared at her for a long moment, and then lurched toward her, his hands outstretched, and swiftly Theo moved and grabbed him.

"You lousy rotten bitch!" Ryman's voice was high, shrilling at her so that she winced. "Lousy stinking rotten bitch! I'll kill you— I'll kill you—"

Behind her the kitchen door opened, and Patty and Gordon were there and then both Gordon and Theo were standing beside Ryman, who was still shouting his rage, as Patty came and stood beside Harriet, putting a protective arm about her shoulders.

And then the noise stopped, and Ryman was weeping, holding his hands over his face as Theo picked up his raincoat, and urged him gently toward the door.

"Come on, Mr. Ryman. I'll take you back to Brookbank, and see if we can organize some transport back to Kendal for you. Gordon, will you come with me, please? You can drive, and I'll look after Mr. Ryman. We'll be back by lunchtime, Harriet."

And they were gone, leaving Harriet sitting very still with Patty perched on the arm of her chair, in a silence underlined by the soft hissing of the gas poker and the crackle of burning wood, until it was broken by a thin cackling laugh from George, standing in the kitchen doorway, his face stretched into a huge grin.

"That's showing them! That's what happens when they come to take me away! Oh, I'm too clever for you lot! That got rid of him, didn't it, eh? Got rid of him? That'll show you—"

6

SHE SAT hunched into her coat collar, staring out at the rain sluicing itself into thick runnels down the windscreen, listening to the radio crackling over the heavy uneven swish of the wipers.

". . . his work is already being applied in the United States, but Dr. Ross-Craigie now feels that his future research should be done in Britain. At a press conference in New York yesterday, Dr. Ross-Craigie announced that he is currently considering a number of offers to work in Britain, and hopes to be able to reach a decision shortly. A Department of Health spokesman yesterday denied that there are at present any plans to provide the treatment on the National Health Service, since costings on this complex technique have yet to be discussed with the Treasury. . . . The threatened rail strike. In London last night, union officials . . ."

Theo reached across her to turn off the radio, and looked at her briefly before returning his attention to the road.

"Well? Now do you believe me? When it makes a seven A.M. BBC news bulletin, it's big news. And the significant thing is that the item about your work came *before* the stuff about little Willy and his magnanimous decision to bring his gifted little self back to our stricken shores. There'll be people waiting at Brookbank for you even at this unearthly hour, I promise you, and God knows what it would have been like if you'd got there at your usual time. Like running into the Olympic stadium with the light at the end of the marathon or whatever it is those dismal athletic types do."

"It's all so *ridiculous*," Harriet said a little querulously. "So much excitement over an unproven method! Why should people come hunting me in this fashion, when Ross-Craigie's work has been proven? Why don't they go to him?"

"Because he isn't here. Because cancer cures are so bloody dramatic. Because he's a man and you're a woman—oh, yes, don't look

79

like that! Even in these egalitarian days, it makes news when women do something special. It's not so much 'isn't it remarkable she thought of that' as 'isn't it remarkable the poor thing can think at all.' "

"I've heard that before somewhere. Theo, do you suppose there'll be many more like Ryman?"

"I've no doubt whatsoever that there will," he said somberly. "I'm sorry about that, Hattie. I'd have avoided it for you if I could—"

"I know. You did splendidly, and I'm still very grateful. I feel very stupid about it. I should have expected something of the sort, I suppose, once the popular rags get hold of the Ferris story, but even after you phoned me yesterday, it didn't really register. Oh, God, but it was horrible! I've never really stopped to think much about the effects of the work I do, not in those terms, anyway. I mean, there were the monkeys, and a puzzle to be worked out, and it was exhilarating, following each little line, making it all add up neatly. Satisfying, like algebra. And even with Ferris, I didn't think much about the outcome from his point of view. When he was at his worst, he wasn't quite a person and it wasn't difficult to think only about his disease. But Ryman, yesterday—I'd forgotten, you see."

"Forgotten?"

"About grief. How it feels, what it looks like. I knew it very well once, but it was so very long ago."

"My dear Hattie, you must learn, right now, not to become emotionally involved in such situations. The world is full of such little domestic tragedies as Ryman's. Full of widows and orphans and picayune disasters. If you sit and mourn for them you'll be wasting your time—no, I'm not being harsh. Not in the least. I'm speaking no more than the bald truth. You must *not* waste your time weeping for the dead and dying, because your time can be put to better use."

"Oh, do me a favor, Theo! Don't start on a Joan of Arc kick! I'm no great scientist set to save the world from disease and misery. All I've done is get involved with a field of research that—"

80

"—can save the world a lot of disease and misery. Why be scared of the idea?"

"Because it's terrifying! This is me, Harriet, remember? I'm not made of the stuff of a Marie Curie! It's all so damned *accidental*. If I hadn't happened to marry David I'd just be a G.P. somewhere. If he hadn't happened to be killed, so that I had to get some sort of job to keep me going while I looked after two babies, I'd just be a G.P.'s wife helping out in the practice. If Oscar hadn't *happened* to be at Brookbank, hadn't *happened* to offer me a job when I needed it—don't you see? I've never planned a damned thing in my whole life—it's always just worked out the way it has. And now I'm in the middle of a situation where I've got to plan, and I'm not made that way—you know that! If you hadn't suggested leaving as early as this, do you suppose it would have occurred to *me* that there'd be people to avoid at Brookbank this morning? I just don't fit into this role I've been cast for."

"You don't know anything at all about yourself, do you, Hattie?" Theo smiled sideways at her. "Poor Hattie! If only you could stand outside yourself and see what really is there in you."

"I know what's in me! I know as much about myself as is necessary. I just wish everyone else did."

"You're wrong. You have no idea at all. Dear heart, you are a very remarkable person. You are as gifted an individual as any I've ever been privileged to know. There are times when I'm grateful to know that I'm your friend, do you know that? People cast you in this role, as you put it, because you fit it. Your achievement in your work is something very remarkable—"

"It is *not!* I told you, it's all an accident. Good God, Theo, even the work itself has been partly accidental. Remember, a year ago? When I nearly went off on that tangent into interferon? Until I noticed that odd reaction in—"

"Accident my fanny! Can't you see that it takes a very special sort of mind to recognize that part of a pattern is out of kilter, and then to work out *why?* And how to use that observation, as you used yours? It was an accident that Newton sat under the apple tree— but millions of others had observed falling objects before he was

81

hit on the head, and they didn't see the significance in it that he saw! You wouldn't deny that he had a special mind? So why deny that you have?"

"Theo, don't! You *frighten* me. I'm an ordinary woman who just happens to be working in a field that—that throws up events like the one I'm caught up in now. That's all."

"Oh, yes, you're an ordinary woman. In many ways you're a very ordinary woman, and I thank God for it. It's your very ordinariness that makes me love you so well—but it also makes your own life horribly complicated. Because as part of your ordinariness you carry some extraordinary gifts. Don't be frightened of it, my dear. But do, for your own sake, admit you have them, and use them as wisely as you can."

He laughed then. "Oh, why do I bedevil you like this? If you could use them as they should be, you wouldn't be you, I suppose. And you wouldn't need me, and I'm selfish enough to be glad that you do. So ignore what I've said. Don't see yourself as a heroine. Leave that to me."

"Thank you! I'd feel a bloody fool as Joan of Arc, anyway . . ."

He laughed again. "You don't look much like a heroine at the moment, I must admit. So be an ordinary woman and tidy yourself, do, dear heart. There may be photographers, after all, and one wouldn't wish to launch Brookbank's answer to Ross-Craigie looking like a windswept—"

"Not my fault. Dragged out of bed at the crack of dawn!" Obediently she opened her bag, and hunted for comb and lipstick, and after a moment's hesitation, pulled out her mascara as well.

"Ah!" Theo murmured, "a gratifying sight. I do like to see a woman getting all feminine. No—do use it. Your first instincts were quite right. You need the defense of a good paint job. I'll try not to bump you too much."

He slowed the car a little, and she put on her makeup, comforted by his presence—the only person in the whole world with whom she could be totally herself in an intellectual sense, to whom she could say what she liked when she liked. Yet dearly as she cared

82

for him and needed him, still there was a flatness about their relationship, a missing level, and it was this that she obtained from Oscar. Only with Oscar could she be physically herself. How much more pleasant and uncomplicated life would be if these two needs could be satisfied by one person! For a moment or two she bathed in an agreeably warm wash of self-pity, before letting amusement dissipate it.

"How's that then? Does my armor look sufficiently strong?"

He glanced at her and smiled. "Formidable! *Trés formidable.* You'll be fine, my dear. Just keep your head and your tongue and your temper with Oscar, and you'll be fine."

"I won't lose my temper with Oscar. There's no need to. I think he's over the worst about Ross-Craigie. He faced up to that last week, when he got back from the States. He won't be too upset this morning—or am I just being hopeful? Poor Oscar—he's having a rough time of it, one way and another, you must admit."

"I wouldn't dream of denying it. Ross-Craigie has treated him abominably, and he's justified, totally justified, in feeling as he does. Whether he's quite as justified in his jealousy of you is something quite other, of course."

"Jealous! Of me? Don't be absurd!"

"I'm not. Just stating facts. Of course he's jealous, Hattie! Legitimately so, I suppose, when you consider that his own hope of scientific salvation lay in his precious jungle juice. Who'll care about Bell's drug research when they can use Berry's vaccine method?"

"Hmm. As and when the vaccine method becomes available, that is. Which can't be for years yet, and you know it. So maybe Bell's drugs will come into their own all the same—you were right, Theo. There's a lot of strange cars in the car park."

"I'll drop you at the stores entrance, I think. Then you can go through the kitchens and round by the chemicals store. And don't worry. Once you're in the unit, no one'll be able to get at you without your being warned. I've a ward round at nine, and a short list at eleven, but after that, I'm available if you want me."

83

"Isn't it all too exciting for *words?*" John Caister dropped his armful of newspapers on her desk. "I had to run a positive *gauntlet* of newspaper people to get in this morning, truly I did!—I do wish you could have seen Catherine, though! Laying about her with her tongue as though it were an umbrella. Some of them looked positively *stunned,* really they did.—Oh, good morning, Catherine! And how many did you manage to scalp? You were marvelous—"

"I've brought the post, Dr. Berry." Catherine put a thick pile of envelopes on top of the newspapers. "And Miss Manton stopped me on the way up. She says Professor Bell wants you in his office to meet someone at ten. I told her you were very busy, and you'd try to manage it. How are you this morning? Did you have trouble getting in?"

"No. Mr. Fowler brought me very early—oh, Lord, have you seen this?" Harriet looked with dismay at the tabloid she had opened, at the way her own name shrieked across the headline in huge type.

"That's the least of it. Most of it's made up out of whole cloth, mind you. There's nothing that wasn't in the *Echo* last week, anyway, and in yesterday's papers. There's a good deal about Ross-Craigie too. Three of them say he's coming back to Brookbank —had you heard that?"

"No. Just that he's coming back to England. Where's the *Echo?* I want to see McClarrie's article—"

There was a silence as they read newspapers, and then Harriet said, "Not bad. Pretty accurate, in fact. At least he makes a strong point about the treatment being very experimental yet. Maybe that'll help cool the others down a bit."

"I doubt it," Catherine said. "As far as I can tell, there's not one of 'em gives a damn about facts. Never saw so much guessing and wild nonsensical statements in my life. Shall I open the post?"

"Do—John, which one have you got there? Let me see—oh, Lord, this is one of the worst."

"If it's Caister's favorite paper, it's sure to be," Catherine said sourly. "Here, give me a hand with these, will you? There's enough

84

to sink a battleship. Most of them are marked 'Personal,' Dr. Berry."

Harriet began to read the letters, and as each succeeding one joined the pile of those she had seen, she felt more and more depressed. Long accounts of relations' illnesses, appeals for help with husbands and children; in several, signed blank checks accompanied by desperate appeals to give treatment, no matter what the cost.

"I can't," she said abruptly. "Catherine, I can't possibly cope with all this. What on earth am I to do with them?"

"I'll look after them," Catherine said roughly. "No, don't read any more. I'll deal with them this afternoon. Caister, you can help. I'll work out a form letter and you can type some—"

John Caister picked up one of the letters and read it, and then another, and then he grimaced. "Not so much fun after all, I suppose. When you think about it. Oh, dear, I do feel all nasty now, and I felt so lovely before! I think I'll make some coffee. Would you like some?"

There was a silence for a while after he'd gone, and then Harriet said awkwardly, "Did Miss Manton say who it is that Oscar wants me to meet?"

"No—not that she'd tell anyone the time of day if she could help it, that one. I'll check with the front lodge porter, if you like. He usually has a list of people who are expected."

"No, don't bother. I'll find out soon enough. Oh, God, Catherine, isn't all this hell?"

"Yes," said Catherine. "It is. But it's worth it. And you can cope. Just stick to your guns, make them put all they've got into pushing the work on, and then you'll be able to do something about all this." She jerked her head at the pile of letters. "What we need is a bigger unit, a lot more equipment, and a good deal more staff, and we could take on a dozen or more patients at a time. And that's what we ought to be doing. Pushing on the research and treating them at the same time. We could turn all of them into Ferrises, given the right sort of help. And then, next year, it'll be you getting the Nobel. Just you push, now, when you get in to Professor Bell this morning. Just you push—"

"He's rich," she thought, as she shook hands in response to Oscar's punctilious introduction, and then immediately wondered why the thought had leaped into her mind. He wasn't displaying any obvious signs of wealth, although his clothes were well cut and fitted with insolent perfection. Because he was Sir? That was an atavistic response, if ever there was one.

"How do you do, Sir Daniel," she murmured, and he held her hand for a moment longer than he needed to, and then stood back as she sat down in the chair Oscar held for her. She felt his eyes admiringly fixed on her, and was suddenly uncomfortable. But she lost that almost at once, for she knew perfectly well—without knowing how she knew—that the admiration was spurious, produced because this was the way he always behaved with women when he first met them. "I'm getting almost as perceptive as Theo," she thought with a spark of amusement.

"Sir Daniel is the proprietor of the *Echo*, Harriet," Oscar said, and she glanced at him quickly; his voice sounded flat and heavy, and then she saw the rigid set of his shoulders and recognized the anger in him, the control he was exercising over it, and understood.

"I know," she said. "Mr. Monks mentioned the fact when I met him. I—er—I'm sorry you have had to become so involved with the work I'm doing here, Sir Daniel."

"I'm not," Sir Daniel said promptly and produced a wide smile. "Indeed, I am not. Scientific endeavor has always fascinated me, man in the street though I may be. I was very gratified indeed that Mr. Ferris chose to come to us with his remarkable story. Gratified, but not unduly surprised. We are, after all, the country's leading newspaper. It's quite a responsibility, running so—how shall I put it?—so integral a part of our national life. But we take our responsibilities very seriously, which is why I am here this morning. And why I so much appreciate Professor Bell's and your generosity in giving me some of your valuable time."

86

Harriet blinked, a little stunned by the smoothness of the man, and Oscar moved sharply behind his desk, and cleared his throat.

"Not at all, Sir Daniel. To be quite candid, we have, of course, little choice. I know from previous experience that newspaper people, once they have their hands on a story, are unlikely to let go. And we would prefer to be involved with what is published for our own safety's sake and, of course, for the welfare of the people who read the stories. We too have a sense of responsibility."

"Ah, you're angry, Professor Bell!" Sir Daniel raised his eyebrows slightly. "I'm sorry about that. I hope it isn't because of the way my people handled the story? I sent down two of my very best men."

"They behaved as well as any journalist can in such cases," Oscar said. "Yes, I'm angry. I can't pretend I like the way popular journals handle scientific matters. At best they confuse the average man who reads their material; at worst they create anxiety, stir up hopes that can't be fulfilled"—he reached across his desk and pushed a wire basket full of letters toward the other man. "These —you should read these. People asking for treatment, wanting information about the vaccine, offering God knows what in exchange for a private supply. It's sickening stuff."

Sir Daniel didn't look at the tray, keeping his gaze fixed on Oscar. "Ah, yes. We too have had our share of those. Deeply distressing letters, many of them. My own secretary has wept over several of the most tragic." He leaned back in his chair and crossed his legs comfortably. "In a way, I must confess I am, shall we say, *grateful* that you have experienced a certain amount of public pressure. It will help you to see even more clearly how difficult it is for us, who receive so much more."

"But you invite it!" Oscar said, his voice sharpening. "Damn it all, you published the stuff that created the demand!"

"Ah, no. No. I must disagree with you there," Sir Daniel said gently. "I really must disagree. We merely publish news. No more and no less. *You* are the people who unleashed the demand by providing the means with which to satisfy it. Neither of us *created* the demand—it's always been there, hasn't it? Why did Dr. Berry embark on a search for a cancer cure if it wasn't because she recognized the need for such a thing existed? What we must do now is not try to dodge the responsibilities inherent in finding such a cure, but turn our attention to deciding the best way to fulfill them."

"Sir Daniel, you really must stop talking about cures," Harriet said quickly. "That's what's wrong with the whole situation! I told your Mr. Monks—"

Sir Daniel shook his head. "Indeed, Dr. Berry, I understand perfectly well! I know precisely what you mean about the word 'cure,' but you must accept that this is merely a semantic point. As far as Mr. Ferris is concerned, he *is* cured. He was almost dead, and now he's alive. He isn't interested in statistics and five-year survival rates —what interests him passionately is the here and now. I seem always to be telling scientists this, and I never seem able to make them understand! *You* plant trees for tomorrow—well and good. But the Mr. Ferrises of this world—and I include myself in those ranks—are interested in picking apples. You've given Mr. Ferris a bushel of apples to enjoy now, and much he or anyone else cares about the apple supply tomorrow! That's your problem, not his."

"So what are you suggesting, Sir Daniel?" Oscar said harshly. "That we should abandon all the principles by which we work, the whole edifice of careful investigation and verification, and leap into the marketplace with a half-completed superficial set of results? Forgive me if I find that—"

"Immoral? So it would be if I were suggesting such a thing. No, my ideas are quite different. I share with you a concern for tomorrow's apple supply, even while I identify very closely with those who are eating them now. Which is why I came here to discuss with you, with Dr. Berry"—he sketched a bow in her direction—"a scheme whereby both the public demand for treatment and your scientific demand for careful research could be satisfied."

There was a short silence, then Harriet said carefully, "You came to discuss a scheme?"

"Sir Daniel has already told me that he wants to make you an

88

offer, Harriet. He made it clear that he intended to behave with
. . . perfect propriety—wasn't that the term you used, Sir
Daniel?—and therefore approached you through me, as the head
of this Establishment. He'll explain it to you himself. Do you want
to discuss it, alone, and then let me know of your decision? You
may certainly do so, if you choose."

She looked at him, frowning slightly. "Oscar, I'm not sure I understand. Aren't you involved with this scheme, whatever it is?"

He shrugged. "I gather not. As I understood Sir Daniel, it's you
and your work that interest him, and he approached me in a spirit
of protocol, no more. You're perfectly free to discuss with him any
matter you choose, with no reference to me."

She rubbed her face irritably. "Oh, I must be particularly dense
this morning. I really don't know what you mean. Why should I
discuss any Establishment matter without you being involved?
You'll have to be more explicit, really—"

Sir Daniel moved then, and said easily, "I think Professor Bell is
being almost too punctilious, Dr. Berry. He is aware that I am
about to offer you the chance to work elsewhere, and though as
head of your Establishment he is intimately involved with your
work, he is giving you the chance to discuss the offer freely without
his presence, which I suspect he thinks may hamper you in some
way. It is, if I may say so, very refreshing to find people so—how
shall we put it?—so delicate about the rights and needs of others—
But there! I've embarrassed both of you! Suppose I tell you of my
offer, and then let you decide whether you want to discuss it with
me alone or with Professor Bell taking part, hmm?"

"Yes—do," Harriet said a little sharply, aware of the tension and
anger radiating from Oscar and sympathizing with it; this man was
undoubtedly the most smoothly devious she had ever listened to,
and his excessive politeness made her feel extremely uncomfortable.

"Well, then. Let me be very straightforward about this." Sir
Daniel's voice became thinner, crisper, losing the blandness that
had so irritated her; it was almost as though he had realized she

disliked his manner and was deliberately changing it for that reason. "From what I've gleaned of your work, I've understood that you've achieved a remarkable result not only with Mr. Ferris but with a large series of animal trials. It is clear to me, nonscientist though I am, that this work of yours is a remarkable breakthrough, but will need considerable resources poured into it to make it go forward at the rate it should—indeed, *must*. I've also realized—and I did so long before these pathetic letters appeared on our respective desks—that there are a great number of people who will gladly lend themselves to aid that research because of their personal involvement with the diseases it hopes to cure—treat, that is. As a straightforward man, it was clear to me that the answer was to put you and your work together with the people who have the resources and the people who want the treatment. I approached colleagues—I needn't bother you now with who they are, though if you accept our offer, you will of course be told if you want to know —and we have formed a consortium. We're prepared to provide and equip for you a research unit where you will have all the facilities you require, where there will be an adequate supply of beds, nursing staff, and so on, for you to treat patients while you continue your research, which of course will be furthered by your observations on the treatment you give. We will handle for you all financial considerations, handle all administrative problems, free you completely from the pressures of working on a tight budget as you must do here. Before we go any farther, it may help you to know that you won't be the only scientist we are prepared to back in this way. Indeed, no. We've already made a similar offer to a colleague of yours, and I'm happy to say—in confidence, of course, which I'm sure you'll respect—that he has virtually made his decision to accept."

"Another scientist?" Oscar's voice cut in sharply. "May I ask who?"

"Well, it will be public knowledge very soon, so—though it is a little premature—however. William Ross-Craigie is coming to us. This year's Nobel prizewinner, you know. Ah, of course you know! He was once on the staff here, was he not?"

90

7

THERE WAS a long silence, and then Harriet said stupidly, "But I thought he was coming to Brookbank!" and was immediately angry with herself, for she had in fact thought no such thing; only the newspapers' wild guesses had put the idea into her mind. But she had felt the need to say something, anything, that would break the painful silence that Oscar had wrapped around himself.

"An absurd idea!" he said, his voice expressionless. "Why on earth should he return here?"

"He ought to, God knows! Most of what he's done since he left was based on what he got from you here. I suppose I thought, if he's coming back to England, Brookbank would be where . . ." her voice dwindled away.

"To come back here, Harriet, he would need an invitation from me. And I haven't issued one. Nor would I."

"Now, I wonder why not?" Sir Daniel said softly. "Do you doubt the validity of his work?"

"Dear me, no," Oscar said. "How could I? The Nobel Committee accept it, so I could hardly doubt it. No, there are other reasons why I could not—would not—ask Dr. Ross-Craigie to return to Brookbank."

"Am I permitted to ask what they are? After all, I see myself as his future—er—employer. Grant me the privilege of asking a former employer for a reference. Is he a difficult man with whom to work? Or are there other facts about him I should know before going ahead with his contract?"

"I hardly feel that you need any reference from me. Surely his experience in the States is what concerns you. It was work that he —um—completed there that brought him his accolade."

"Oh, Oscar, stop being so damned honorable!" Harriet said sharply. "People ought to know how Ross-Craigie treated you— treated the Establishment! It was outrageous!"

"Oh?" Sir Daniel said softly, and he looked from one to the other of them with his head to one side, birdlike and watchful. "What was outrageous?"

"Ross-Craigie was very much Professor Bell's assistant, Sir Daniel—No, Oscar, I *will* say it! He took himself off to the States with a solid basis of work done largely by Professor Bell. His success derives at least as equally from another man's work as from his own, yet he's given no credit for it to either Professor Bell or the Establishment that gave him his start. I for one—well, all of us here are sick about it. Professor Bell has every right to be—"

"Really, Harriet, I see no point in this display of loyalty, much as I appreciate it. Ross-Craigie, is, frankly, no concern of mine, and I'll waste no further time in considering him. What is more to the point now is Sir Daniel's offer to you. I'm sure you wish now to discuss it with him." He stood up. "You have the use of this office for as long as you need it."

Harriet opened her mouth to speak, and then closed it again, looking up at Oscar with a sense of bafflement. His anger seemed to have gone, and he was smiling at her, relaxed and affable.

"That really is most kind of you, Professor Bell," Sir Daniel said, and stood up himself. "Perhaps we could meet again later and talk further? It really has been a privilege to have had so much of your time already this morning."

Oscar moved toward the door, and Harriet said urgently, "No—please, Oscar, don't go. I really don't see that—"

"Harriet, my dear, I must! It would be most improper of me to stay when Sir Daniel wants to talk to you—and you must let me match his perfect propriety, after all! You know where you can find me later if you want to talk it over, but you really must talk first to Sir Daniel. I'll send some coffee in to you." And he went, leaving Harriet confused and oddly shy as Sir Daniel sat down and smiled across the room at her.

"What a very pleasant man your Professor Bell is! Clearly, you have an excellent working relationship here. One feels it as one comes into the place." He sighed a little. "I wish I could say the same of the *Echo* staff. But, there, perhaps I lack Professor Bell's gifts of administration. However, I'm learning. I'm always learning." He smiled a little more widely. "But I mustn't waste your valuable time, must I? We're here for you to talk about my suggestion, and I mustn't trespass on Professor Bell's generosity. Well, Dr. Berry, how do you feel about the idea?"

She sat silent, biting her lower lip for a moment, and then frowned. "I'm sorry. It's difficult to think very clearly. It's come as rather a surprise, and really, I can't see much point in talking to you about it at all, not until I've had a chance to think about it, and talk to Oscar, that is. I—" she floundered. "Look, I'm not one of these high-powered women who are good at this sort of thing. I do a job I like doing, and I can cope with that, but this other sort of stuff—it's not my—not one of my skills. Damn it, I don't even cope with balancing my working budget! I leave all that to Oscar. And to be asked to make a decision about such a thing, to consider breaking away on my own— I've been here at Brookbank for a very long time, Sir Daniel. More years than I care to remember, and I've never once considered the possibility of working anywhere else. All my friends, my home—I'm part of Brookbank."

"Of course I understand! And your honesty does you credit. Not that I'd have expected you to be any different, of course. I know enough about scientists to know how many of you find difficulty in—er—dealing with considerations that are marginal to the field of your endeavor. But may I make a few points, in the hope that they will give you a basis on which to think about your decision?"

He leaned back in his chair and stared up at the ceiling and again his voice took on its crisp businesslike note. "I am not for one moment suggesting that you should take on, with this new post, anything other than the pure science with which you are so very capable. I assure you that if I needed a scientific administrator, I would seek elsewhere. No, what I want to offer you is the opportunity to do your work in the best possible surroundings, with the best possible facilities, in conditions that far outstrip anything the Government can provide in an Establishment of this nature. At the same time, I want to offer to sick people the chance to receive the benefits of your work—*now*. Perhaps you'll succeed, perhaps you'll fail, though I doubt that, but for ill people that element of chance doesn't matter. Their chances are already so heavily loaded against them that they can only gain from being experimental material for you. And there is another consideration."

He looked at her for a moment, and then again began to talk at the ceiling.

"Money, in this very complicated world of ours, is a very important matter. Now, I don't want to make any attempt to pry into your personal affairs, but let me just say that I would be very surprised to hear you were all that well provided for financially. I know you are a widow, that you depend entirely upon your own earning ability, and I know the sort of level at which Civil Service Establishments pay their staff. *Our* establishment proposes to pay salaries far in excess of anything the Government could possibly afford. We propose, just for a start, a salary for you of some ten thousand pounds per annum. But even that is open to negotiation. If you feel you need more, then more you shall have."

She blinked. Ten thousand? It didn't sound real. She thought quite suddenly of George, seeing him sitting at the breakfast table as he had been when she left that morning, mouthing his breakfast. Ten thousand!

"And, of course, you will have no problems about your working budget. There will be someone whose job it will be to control spending, but he will not be there to stop you from having what you need. Only to ensure that you get it as soon as you need it."

"I—yes. I see," was all she could manage to say.

"But, of course, knowing scientists as I do, I don't imagine you will place as much weight on the matter of your own salary as would the rest of us. You find your satisfactions in so many other ways. Not least, of course, in the value to others—the noncommercial value—of what you do. Apropos of which, I would like to say one more thing, before leaving you to think the matter over, and of course to talk to Professor Bell about it."

He stood up, and came across the room to lean against Oscar's desk.

"Loyalty is a very estimable quality, and I for one admire it

94

wholeheartedly. Your spirited comments on Dr. Ross-Craigie's—er
—actions warmed me, they did indeed."

She looked away, embarrassment washing over her again.

"But there is more than one form of loyalty, of course, as I'm
sure you realize. And whatever loyalty you owe to your principal
here, however close your friendship with him may be—"

She felt her cheeks redden. "Of course Oscar's my friend! I told
you, I've worked here for a great many years."

"Of course! As I say, the loyalty due to friends is of great importance. But there is another that may be of even greater importance.
The loyalty you owe to your own gifts. Yes, gifts. You are clearly a
scientist of immense ability—however much you may denigrate
your powers as a businesslike woman!—and ability of that order is a
great burden. A tremendous burden. In my own humble way, I am
very aware of that fact. My abilities, such as they are, lie in the field
of public—er—education, public welfare. And there are many
times when I must put my personal feelings to one side because I
owe a greater debt of loyalty to the public I must serve with my
small talents than I can ever give to even the dearest of friends and
colleagues. You follow me?"

"I'm not sure that I do."

"Simply, my dear Dr. Berry, you must consider in which way you
can best use your talents to the greatest good. To remain here at
Brookbank, under the aegis of the Government, even if that Government is represented by a great and good friend, would mean
you are limited in the application of those talents. You would in
effect be depriving the society to which we all owe so much loyalty
the fruits of your efforts—fruits that only you can provide. My consortium can enable you to work to the best of your abilities. Brookbank cannot. I think you must, in all fairness, take this into account when you make your decision. Ah—coffee! How very
agreeable. Thank you Miss—er?—Manton? Ah, yes. How d'you do.
Well, now, Dr. Berry, will you allow me to pour a cup for you?"

"I can't understand him, Theo! I'm tired, and confused, and I
don't understand him. It's a total *volte-face!* He was furious when

95

we started to talk to this Sefton man. Fit to be tied. And then quite suddenly, he changed. I tried to talk to him about this offer, and all he'd say is, 'It's up to you. I can't influence you. You've got to decide for yourself,' over and over again."

She prowled restlessly from one side of the small room to the other, and he sat there, his green theater cap pushed back so that the grizzled hairline showed, his mask dangling beneath his chin, and watched her.

"Frankly, I thought when Sefton said Ross-Craigie was going to work for him that Oscar would really explode—but no! He just went off the boil, and if you can understand it, I'm damned if I can. And now this other thing—what about *this?* What would *you* have expected him to say?"

"I'd have expected him to say, 'Do as you think best, Harriet. I have no objections.' Precisely what did he say, in fact?"

"What?" she stopped her pacing, and stared at him. "You expected—oh, Theo, for Christ's sake! Am I totally idiotic? Totally out of touch? I've known this man for half a lifetime, and I expected him to clamp down at the merest hint of a television program! He's always refused to join in these discussion things himself. So why the hell does he want me to do it now? *Why* aren't you surprised? Why don't I understand what's going on in his mind?"

"Because you are my dear undevious Hattie, and because I have an evil twisted mind of my own that makes Oscar's virtually an open book to my reading. Do think, dear heart! When did Oscar go off the boil, as you so elegantly phrased it? When Sefton announced he was taking on Ross-Craigie, and you launched into a great statement about the appalling behavior toward Oscar the man had displayed. Who is going to be on this program at the weekend? Little Willy Ross-Craigie! And *who* can be trusted to tell the world in no uncertain terms of the underhanded way said little Willy behaved toward her dear Oscar? Think it out for yourself, dear heart, think it out for yourself!"

"Oh! Oh, I see. At least, I think"—she stopped and rubbed her face wearily. "Oh, Theo, isn't it all bloody complicated? I wish I'd gone into research on flatworms or something. I just never saw anything like all this could happen."

"Well, you should have. I've been telling you for years that Oscar uses you, but you never listen. I don't suppose you're really listening now. Are you?"

"What?"

"Really thinking about what Oscar's doing? Of course you aren't! You've agreed to go onto the program, haven't you? Why?"

"Why? Because—oh, I don't know! It's easier than saying no, I suppose, and as long as Oscar doesn't object, there's no real reason why I shouldn't, is there? Theo, tell me what to do! I'm so sick of floundering in all this—I need someone to tell me what to *do*."

"Do what's best for *you*," Theo said vigorously. "Think of Hattie, first, middle and last. Not what you want to do, because what you most want is to crawl back into a cozy past where you enjoy your work, and Oscar's happy, and everything in the garden's lovely. Well that you can't do, so opt for what will be of the greatest personal benefit to *you*. It's really as simple as that."

"Take this job, you mean? Certainly it'll give me a lot of money, and that'd be very nice, but I'm not sure . . ."

"I'm not either. You've never cared much about money per se, and it could be more of an embarrassment to you than a pleasure. Take it into account, by all means, but not first. No, there are other forms of benefit. Would you be happier in your work away from Brookbank? Get more satisfaction from it? Find your relationships easier to deal with? I can't tell you the answers, though I daresay I could make a pretty shrewd guess—"

"Then make it."

"No. No, my dear. Of course I could tell you what to do. Nothing would be easier. But it wouldn't help, because even though you're asking for direction, you don't really want it. No—don't look at me like that. You don't, however much you think you do. Whatever I or anyone else says, you go your own way. Damn it all, Hattie, how long have I been telling you to do something about

97

George? How long has Gordon been telling you? You know we're right, but still you go your way, even though I suspect that at heart you'd like to do as we say. But you can't because we've told you to. You're not devious, Hattie, but you're a woman, and that means by definition that in some ways you're totally absurd in your reactions —from a man's point of view, that is. So I'm not about to confuse the issue by giving you instructions to follow. It would only tire and bewilder you further. But poor dear Hattie, I do feel for you! Believe me, my own life would be a great deal less complicated if I didn't. You're the only woman I've ever known who's made me regret that I am as I am. I've even found myself fantasizing, wondering if I could marry you. God knows you need marrying! But there, love you I do, but—"

He shook his head and sat and looked at her, his face filled with affection for her, and for a moment she wanted to weep, wanted to go to him and touch him and say, "Yes—marry me. It would be all right—we could be happy, and sex wouldn't matter—" but even as the thought came to her she knew she was wrong. The desire to touch him proved that, with its reminder of that pool of need that lay so deeply inside her, yet was so alarmingly easy to tap.

"Dear Theo," she said. "I love you too. I can't imagine what I'd do if I couldn't find you when I needed to."

They sat in silence for a while, and then Theo moved and said briskly, "Hattie, go away. I really must write up my notes, and let Sister clear the theaters, and she won't do a thing while I'm still hanging about. Her protocol forbids it, silly bitch. So go away. And I'll take you down to London on Friday for this wretched 'Probe' program. I've no list tomorrow, and Geoffrey can deal with the ward rounds himself, for a change. Do the lazy object good. I'll pick you up at the cottage at nine, so be ready. And wear that green dress—the one with the leather. It should look good even in BBC color."

Curiously enough, she was enjoying herself. The drive down had been delightful, through the smokiness of a flaming late October, with trees gleaming gold across the heavy rich brownness of plowed fields, and the stop in Cambridge had had a timeless quality about it, a peacefulness that still lingered inside her. They had lunched at a hotel so laden with wooden beams, open log fires and polished brass that Theo swore it had been built the week before by a film company and staffed with extras; the waiter who served them with their pea soup and saddle of lamb was so exceedingly bent, so absurdly snowy-haired, and produced such a great deal of chat in a heavy East Anglican accent that he sounded as though he had been written by Surtees on an off day. They had giggled over blackberry pie and thick cream and coffee at the brace of horsey women at the next table, discussing at the top of their not inconsiderable voices a mare they had taken to stud that morning, and had been enchanted by the luscious barmaid who rested her splendid bust on the counter and shared equally loud confidences with a very burly red-faced farmer ("who, of course, probably isn't a farmer at all, but a shop assistant or a ladies' hairdresser," Theo had hissed).

And then, driving on through the dwindling winter afternoon, until they swept into London, through Edgeware and Hendon's tidy suburban strings of lights, and shopping centers filled with pram-pushers and uniformed schoolchildren, she had felt comfortable and at peace with herself. For good or ill, she was going to do this television program, so she might as well enjoy it and worry about the consequences when they happened.

And the decision to enjoy it seemed to have been enough to ensure that she did. They had been greeted at the reception desk with flattering respect, flurried about with offers of drinks and sandwiches and dressing rooms in a most agreeable manner, and when they had come to take her away to be made up, Theo had been asked by the very young and handsome but studiedly casual studio director if he would care to sit in; they could certainly find him a seat in the audience, and "if you find yourself filled with an urge to join in discussion later, please don't control it—"

Sitting now perched in the high chair with a plastic cape about her neck, she smiled at the thought of Theo being instructed not to control his urges, and the girl beside her said, "*Could* you just keep quite still—eyes closed, eyebrows raised—*that's* it. Fine—now the other one. Yes. Would you like me to do your hair for you? I have heated rollers here, so it won't be too difficult—"

She looked at herself in the mirror as the girl went to work with rollers and comb and hairspray, and marveled; the lines painted on her lids, the smudges of white on her cheekbones and below her eyes; they made her look quite extraordinary. Pleasantly extraordinary, she decided. I really must try to see if I can do that myself sometime.

Someone came into the room behind her, and she tried to peer sideways at the sound of her name being called, but the makeup girl held her head firmly, and the speaker came to stand behind her and talk to her in the mirror.

"Dr. Berry?" he said, and looking at his fair head and bright gaze, Harriet was reminded immediately of John Caister, and had a sudden vision of him, with Catherine, sitting in front of the television set in the staff common room at Brookbank, waiting to watch her, and for the first time felt a thick chill of apprehension seeping into her.

"Dr. Berry, I'm *so* sorry to bother you—I'm the floor manager, Jerry, remember? We met in the hospitality room a while back—*so* sorry, but *could* I just verify? There's a young lady—very charming, and that—at reception. Says she's your daughter, and wants to come in to the program—she and her young man with her. And really, much as we'd like to accommodate everyone who walks in off the street, you know how it is! Space, you see, *so* limited! But of course if she is, then of course we can find room for both of them. *Did* you arrange for her to come along?"

"I didn't precisely arrange—well, I told her about it, of course, but it never occurred to me that—oh, dear, it's just the sort of thing she'd do! She's fairly tall, dark curly hair? Looks a bit like me, they say. Oh, and she's probably wearing a sheepskin coat—"

"That's it—oh, well, that's settled then. I'll tell them both they can come in." He turned to go, and Harriet called, "Er—just a moment—the young man with her—what's he like?"

"Ah, well, yes. Hard to say. Wears his hair *very* long and has the most *enormous* quantity of beard spreading about. Too beautiful to be true, I assure you! To tell you the truth, Dr. Berry, it was because of that the reception people were so cagy and asked me to check. Ever since that time we had a young invasion on the program our doorman's been positively *allergic* to hairy young men. Makes his life very difficult—most of the staff go for the hairy look themselves, to be honest! However! I'll go and see they have a couple of seats near the front. We'll be on in fifteen minutes, girls, so move it, will you? J.J. been in yet, Dodie?"

"Not yet," a girl on the far side of the big room said. "If you see him, try and rush him in, will you, Jerry? I hate a last-minute push—"

The room seemed to take on an air of greater purpose now, as more people came in to perch on the barber's-type chairs, and Harriet felt a little flustered as her own girl took off the cape, and said coolly, "I think that should look fine. I haven't seen you on the monitors, of course, but if there's anything wrong I'll have time to come down before the off. Oh, Dr. Ross-Craigie? Could you come and sit here, please?"

Harriet turned and raised her eyebrows in recognition.

"Well, William! Hello! And my congratulations."

"Harriet Berry! They told me you'd be here, and I can't tell you how delighted I was to hear it. It's so much pleasanter having old familiar faces about on these occasions, don't you agree?"

He was wearing a very pale gray suit and a vivid pink shirt with a tie to match, and very carefully arranged the plastic cape to cover every bit of his collar before taking off his heavy square-rimmed glasses and leaning back in the chair. "No, don't go, Harriet. I'm dying to ask you some questions—ah, no—no, my dear girl, *not* that color. I know from bitter experience I look quite green without a good deal of brown in the foundation. Try this—"

As he fiddled among the sticks of makeup on the girl's table, Harriet looked at him, and took stock. He'd put on a little weight, had a sleek well-fed look that was quite new. In his Brookbank days he had always looked as though his clothes were a size too large for him, well cared for and neat though they had been; he had been considered a dapper young man even then. Now he was positively glowing with good health, good grooming and good taste.

"Now, Harriet, do tell me. How is Oscar? I thought the poor guy looked far from well when I saw him a little while back. We met in the States, you know? I was really concerned for him when I saw him at a party—no, honey, a little more highlighter there, if you'll allow me to say so. I've done so much television these past few months, I feel I could almost do my own makeup—"

It hasn't taken him long to pick up an American accent, Harriet thought, amused. Not much, but enough to be just noticeable.

"—so I wondered if he was sick, when he behaved so—well, even for Oscar, and we all know how short a fuse he has—he behaved very oddly. But I guess I managed to cover up for him, and so many Americans expect Englishmen to be oddballs that he got away with it. But I worried, I must say."

"Oscar is very well, thank you, William. Overworked, of course, and underpaid like the rest of us, but he's used to it."

He slid his eyes sideways at her and produced a wicked little grin. "There—I'd forgotten. You and Oscar—I should have known better than to go shooting my mouth off about him to you, hmm? But there was no criticism meant, believe me, Harriet. Just normal concern, I promise you—"

Harriet opened her mouth to speak but he went on, watching the girl's hands in the mirror as they moved busily across his face.

"As for being underpaid—well, not much longer for you, from all I hear."

"How do you mean?" Harriet knew she sounded guarded and could do nothing about it.

"Oh, oh, oh! Sorry! The last thing I want to do is go off before the gun's fired! Not a word more. What I'm not supposed to know about, I don't know about. Yes—thank you, dear. Very nice. It's a tough job making up a man whose tan has begun to fade, hmm? That's one thing I know I'll miss by coming back to the U.K. Those American summers! Too much . . ."

102

There was a flurry at the door, and the people in the room moved and swayed as though a wind had blown over them, and J. J. Gerrard, the anchorman of "Probe," came in followed by a man with a clipboard in one hand and a coffee mug in the other.

"You've got three minutes flat to perform your usual miracle, Dodie, my darling, so get to it—my coffee! Where the hell is my coffee? Ah, there it is—bless you, Tony. What would I do without you to follow me about with my drug—ah! Dr. Ross-Craigie. William—here, take this bloody mug, somebody"—he thrust the mug back at Tony, who fielded it with the obvious ease of long practice, and advanced toward Harriet and Ross-Craigie, his hand outstretched.

"Hi, J.J. Good to see you again. Seems barely a day since we did this for your New York program, doesn't it? Have you met Dr. Berry yet, J.J.? I can't tell you how good it was to see her again. Old friends, you know, old friends—"

"Dr. Berry, I am really grateful to you for agreeing to come on the program. I know how shy you scientists are—well, most of you, anyway"—he thumped Ross-Craigie on the shoulder, and Ross-Craigie grinned—"and my researchers told me they had quite a job persuading you. But I know you won't be sorry—sure of it. You'll do nothing but good, you'll see, coming here to tell people about your marvelous work. Marvelous. This time next year, you'll be the new Nobel, of that I'm sure. Our William here'll be as passé as last year's Miss World, what do you say, William?"

"Miss World! I should be so lucky," Ross-Craigie said promptly, and J. J. Gerrard threw his head back and laughed, and Tony and Dodie laughed and looked up at the clock on the wall, and moved in to urge J. J. Gerrard toward a makeup chair.

"Don't worry about a thing, Dr. Berry," he called over his shoulder, as the girl wrapped him in his cape. "I've done my homework very well, and I've got all the right questions lined up. William will tell you—he's done a couple of shows with me in the States, he'll tell you it's all easy. Real cool and easy—I'm the one that does all the work! You just have to follow my lead. So have fun! See you on the green—okay, okay, so get on with it instead of nagging, Dodie! Where's that bloody coffee—?"

She was beginning to feel a numbness creeping into her, quite destroying the sense of peace and comfort the day had built up. Someone took her arm, and led her out of the makeup room, and she was aware of Ross-Craigie chattering busily as he followed her out along the corridors toward a heavy door at the far end. Someone pushed the door open, and then another inner door, and she went through to find herself in a vast studio, with lights blazing at her from all directions, wires and cables strewing the floor at her feet, and a confused impression of heat and noise and the smell of people. Suddenly, she felt very frightened.

8

THE MAN who was holding her elbow so firmly urged her forward, up onto a dais, and settled her in a swivel chair, chattering busily all the time.

"Comfortable? Fine—now, just ignore this—it's only a mike. If you could just hang it round your neck and fasten it, so—shall I? I'm used to it—that's it—just like a necklace, hmm? We like to use a neck mike for people on the dais—releases the others—the ones on the booms, see? Up there—we keep those for people who have to move about, like J.J., and then of course we need a couple for the audience. We always get lots of great audience participation, though I'm sure you know that."

"I'm sorry—I don't see the program very often, actually, though I think I've managed it a few times—" she murmured.

"Don't you? Oh, good for you! So much intrusion, isn't there, with that great box brooding over one's living room? Never watch myself, I promise you, except in the line of duty, of course. Now, just relax, hmm? Nothing to worry about at all. The shape's pretty easy, pretty easy."

He peered at a clipboard he was holding. "There's just you and J.J. and Dr. Ross-Craigie here on the platform"—William leaned forward from his chair on the other side of the dais, and smiled brilliantly at her—"and an assortment of people in the audience who will probably join in later." He moved then from his position in front of her to go away toward the camera on her right, and now she could see the audience clearly.

They were perched in a dozen or so rows, raked steeply toward the back, with a small flight of steps separating them into two blocks. At first she had only a confused impression of color and movement, but then as she concentrated faces came out of the blur to be recognized.

Theo was sitting foursquare and calm in the second row, his arms folded, and as she caught his eye, he grimaced faintly, raising his eyebrows, and involuntarily she smiled. He moved his chin slightly forward, and following this indication, she let her gaze move along the front row. Patty was sitting there, looking curiously remote, and she thought, "How odd! She looks so different sitting there. So separate—" and was puzzled at the reaction.

Of course she was separate. Ever since going up to university eight years ago, she had lived her own life, only visiting the cottage occasionally, yet now, as though for the first time, Harriet could see her as a unique person, someone who existed and operated on her own level without any real reference to her family, to Harriet and Gordon and George. But then, as Patty caught her glance and smiled widely at her mother, the strangeness went away, and there was her own Patty again, looking just as she always did, always had since she had been a bouncy infant and a lumpy schoolgirl; a vigorous and rather large young woman full of ideas and ideals and immense and exhausting energy. "Dear Patty," Harriet thought gratefully, "come to hold my hand—nice child."

Patty leaned forward and mouthed something at her, and Harriet, her head to one side and a frown on her face, tried to understand. "I brought Ben. *Ben*—" and she turned to the man beside her, and he too leaned forward.

Squinting a little at the hair-encircled face and the very dark eyes that were looking solemnly at her, Harriet remembered. Ben— what was it?—Shoeman. The Canadian boy Patty had brought home in the summer. Was that still going on? Was Patty going to marry at last? And Harriet was amused at this very maternal response and smiled at Ben, who immediately responded with a wide grin of his own that lifted his beard so that the strong nose seemed almost to disappear. A pleasant boy, she thought, and was again amused at the pattern of her thoughts—thinking of him as a boy simply because he was a couple of years younger than Patty, when he was so very much a man in his heavy solidity.

Then she remembered the fiery way he had of talking, the violent enthusiasms and antagonisms he had displayed, particularly when talking to Gordon and his gentle little Jean; that had been very boyish. And that had been quite a summer weekend, when they had all sat in the garden, and Ben had shocked Gordon so profoundly with his exposition of his Marxist revolutionary principles, and Patty had so heatedly defended him.

Looking at them now, sitting so close together yet not actually touching each other, she realized why the thought of marriage had come into her mind. They were wrapped in the same aura, somehow, seemed to be intertwined.

"They're sleeping together," she thought, and felt bleak for a moment. It was sad to think of Patty starting her life with the sort of semidetached relationship she herself had with Oscar and for which she had settled as a second best: why couldn't she recognize the need for emotional security that marriage, and only marriage, could satisfy?

"Oh, God," she thought. "This is a hell of a time to get overtaken by maternal concern and my blasted puritanism—" and smiled and nodded at them both, and looked away.

She frowned then, as she saw a little farther along the row the neat and elegant Sir Daniel Sefton. "What the hell is he doing here?" she wondered, and glanced swiftly at Ross-Craigie. But he was sitting with his head bent, reading with an almost ostentatious concentration a little wad of paper covered with typescript. Yet she knew he was very aware of the people in front of him, could recognize the tension in him, and again felt it rising in her, felt apprehension swim into her belly, and she wanted to get up and run. Too many people, too much noise, too much heat, too much tension everywhere. It was almost intolerable.

She moved in her chair, almost stood up, and then a man broke away from the knot of people clustered round the cameras on her right and came into the big pool of light that spilled across the front of the dais. He signaled toward the back, and a microphone boom high in the roof swooped and swung, and came to stop just above him.

"Good evening, ladies, gentlemen, and assorted whatever the rest of you may be—" he called loudly, and there was a ripple of giggles, and faces turned forward, and she felt the weight of their attention as an almost tangible thing.

"I'm Peter Lister, general dogsbody on 'Probe,' and I'm here to tell you it's great to have you all here tonight. And I hope you've all brought plenty of intelligence and anger and involvement and the rest of it with you. We're here to hear *you*, to hear what *you* think about the big issues we bring out on this program. Not that I have to tell you—do I?—that the J. J. Gerrard program isn't the great J.J. himself, but *you*, the audience, the people who really matter, because you're here to put the point of view of the millions who watch this show every Friday night—mind you, don't tell J.J., will you?"

He looked from side to side of the studio with exaggerated caution, and then, in a careful caricature of a conspirator, hissed, "—he thinks *he's* the most important person on this program—"

Again, the ripple of laughter slid through the audience, and Peter Lister grinned and said, "And to tell you the truth, we, the program staff, we think so quite a lot of the time, much as we know how much the real success of the show depends on all of you. He's a great guy, our J.J. So let's hear it for J.J.! Come on, let's see just what you think of our peripatetic polemicist—traveling gasbag to you ignorant lot." Again the laughter rose, more sure this time. "—Let's see what you can do to show what you think of the man himself—J. J. Gerrard—let's hear it—" And he began to clap his hands with wide expansive gestures, and the audience took it up, and the applause grew, doubled and redoubled as the man in front of them made wide rotary gestures with his arms. And then, he held up both hands and abruptly the clapping stopped, and there was an attentive silence again.

"Oh, boy!" Lister cried admiringly. "Oh, boy—we've done it again! Who *are* you lot? Rent-an-audience? Trained to the last inch, that's what you are! That was just beautiful! But prove it wasn't a fluke. Try it again—start when I do, build as I wind you

108

up like this"—again the rotary movements—"and kill it as **soon** as I put my hands up like this—"

Obediently, the audience responded, and again and once again he put them through the routine, and then stood there, shaking his head from side to side in a sketch of amazed approval.

"You are the greatest we've had yet, take it from me. The *ger*eatest! Just sing out and chip in with the same sort of spontaneous spirit, and I tell you, we'll have the greatest 'Probe' program of the season. Okay—Jerry?—"

He peered into the shadows round the camera, and someone there waved, looked at his watch and held up two fingers. "Okay, then. In about a minute and a half, we'll start the music. Don't, *per*lease, try to watch the monitors—those screens above your heads—too much. You'll hate seeing yourselves anyway. People always do! And when I give you all the go, start the applause, just like we've rehearsed it. Okay? And keep it going until I give you the sign—and after that it's up to you and J.J. Enjoy, enjoy, and join in!" And waving widely at the audience, a few of whom waved perkily back, he moved back toward the camera group, wiping his forehead with a big handkerchief as he conferred with Jerry, the floor manager.

The studio slid into an uneasy hissing of talk, of barely concealed impatience, and the apprehension that had gone away as Harriet had watched Lister play with the audience as though it were his yo-yo (and it had pleased her to see that neither Theo nor Ben had joined in the applause, perturbed her a little that Patty had at first and only stopped responding when she noticed that Ben wasn't)— that apprehension returned, but now she could tolerate it. It sat inside her like a heavy cold wetness, but it was familiar now, and no longer quite so disagreeable. Indeed, there was an almost sensuous enjoyment to be had out of this feeling that was so very physical, and she thought suddenly, "Adrenalin. That's what it is. I wish I knew how it worked, how it made these specific sensations. Now, there's an interesting idea. I wonder if I could mount an experiment to monitor the effects of adrenalin—" and then irritated at herself, tried to pull her mind back to the here and now.

She looked at Theo, who produced the ghost of a wink; at Patty and Ben, talking softly to each other; at Sir Daniel Sefton, sitting with his crossed feet outstretched, and his gaze fixed on the shining toecaps of his shoes as he rhythmically and very slowly rocked them to and fro; at the audience sitting perched in their rows—"Like a lot of silly hens," she thought suddenly—and then, sideways, at Ross-Craigie, who was now sitting, arms folded in a positively Napoleonic pose, staring seriously at the audience.

From somewhere behind her she heard the thin tinny sound of music, and it rose and spread, and the audience heard it too, and stopped its soft chatter and looked expectantly up at the monitors, and she looked up too, to see words rolling up from the bottom of the screen, swelling and then shrinking as they disappeared at the top. Behind the words, she saw the audience in its rows, looking somehow much more vast than it actually was, and then saw, very small and neat, the dais with Ross-Craigie brooding on one side of the central chair, and a squarish rigid figure on the other. "Me," she thought, in wonderment. "How absolutely ridiculous, sitting up there like that."

For a moment she felt like a child again, a child who had played a private and rather frightening game of being two people, one the real Harriet sitting on the floor painting or brickbuilding or doll-dressing, the other a small nasty cruel Harriet who sat up in a corner of the room, on the little jutty shelf where the picture rails met beside the window, watching and jeering and disapproving. It had been a difficult game to control then, and now it was much harder, but she made herself pull her staring gaze away from the screen, and made herself look instead at the audience in front of her, all seeming like those drawings of Christmas angels that appear on calendars and cards, with the upward-thrown monitor-worshipping expression repeated on face after face.

From behind the camera group came a movement that split the cluster of men in two, and he came through the little aisle they made, his face relaxed and bearing an expression that cried isn'tall-this-amusing? The audience began to clap in response to Lister's violent gesturing, and J. J. Gerrard ran lightly up the steps to the dais, threw himself into the central chair, and turned and smiled at Ross-Craigie, who stared back at him somberly, responding only with a serious nod; and then he turned and leaned toward Harriet and murmured, "Butterflies inside? I have, I swear it—always do! But it makes for a good program—" And then he was holding up both hands as he looked at the audience and they stopped the clapping and sat up straight and expectantly as he looked around with his so-familiar lopsided smile.

"Well, good evening, and welcome to all of you, both here and at home, welcome as always to 'Probe.' I am your regular guest, grateful to be admitted to your living rooms once again, J. J. Gerrard! Thank you for inviting me, all of you at home, thank you for coming to the studio all of you here. Right, now, and what have we on the agenda for this last Friday evening in October? Let's see now—next week, as you may know, the witches and warlocks ride, come Hallowe'en, and in the second half of the program we are going to introduce to you one of *the* most way-out witches you ever saw! Oh boy, there'll be some spells cast here, I promise you, tonight! But right now we are going to concern ourselves with something very different . . ."

His voice changed, and the bantering note was replaced by a slightly ponderous solemnity.

"Tonight, we are privileged to have with us in the studio two very remarkable people. Both are British. Both are scientists. Both have been responsible for remarkable breakthroughs in medical practice. One of them, I am quite confident, will be next year's Nobel prizewinner. The other, I am happy to tell you, is *this* year's Nobel prizewinner. And we'll talk to him first, if our lady guest will forgive us. Ladies and gentlemen, may I introduce Dr. William Ross-Craigie!"

Applause, brisk, staccato and perfunctory, when compared with that with which J. J. Gerrard had been welcomed. Questions from J. J. Gerrard, crisp, simple, seeming to cry, "I'm-as-bright-as-the-next-man-but-you'll-have-to-explain-in-honest-language," with every syllable. Then, William Ross-Craigie's voice, with its mid-Atlantic flat classlessness, talking, talking, talking.

To Harriet, it all had a dreamlike quality at first, an air of absurdity; what was she, Harriet Berry, doing sitting up here like a monkey on a stick, listening to men with painted faces talking in such lumpy phrases, sentences, paragraphs, not at all as men normally spoke?

But then, arch and ridiculous though Ross-Craigie sounded to her ears, she began to be aware of the content of what he was saying. She began to listen to the sense of his speech, rather than the sound of his voice and the shape of his sentences, and relaxed, grateful for the comfort of things known, the sort of ideas she herself used as part of her stock in trade.

". . . the theories about fat in the diet, about exercise, stress, all of that, though it kept the popular press happy for years, and made a bonanza for manufacturers of low-fat foods and exercise machines and the like, still had all too little effect on the basic disease —atheroma."

"Ah, now Dr. Ross-Craigie, here you must forgive me if I interrupt. Atheroma? Can you explain to us precisely what that is?" J. J. Gerrard said brightly.

"By all means. Well, now, the word derives from a Greek word meaning gruel. Groats—as in hominy grits—er—porridge, you know?" Gerrard and Ross-Craigie exchanged a knowing cosmopolitan smile. "And it describes a condition in which plaques—that is to say, *layers* of this gooey sticky substance are laid down on artery walls. Now, just imagine the underground system here in London, or the subway in New York, or the metro in Paris or wherever, with the walls coated with great slabs of thick sticky gruel-like material. Every time a train went by—a train, by the by, loaded with more of the same sticky substance—what would happen? I can tell you what would happen. The layers would get thicker and thicker, and finally the trains wouldn't get through the tunnels! It is this that happens in the disease of atheroma. The arteries are the tunnels, and they silt up, and silt up, and eventually—no blood supply to vital organs! Coronary thrombosis! Heart attack! In some cases, cerebral thrombosis, which could be called a brain attack. Popularly known as stroke, or by some old-fashioned people as apoplexy. Now, I have always been very interested in this matter of atheroma. I looked at the literature all the time, I watched what other researchers were doing, I listened to the theories about diet, about the effects of cholesterol on atheroma plaque formation, and I thought—well, I just didn't find those ideas jelled with me, they just didn't jell one little bit."

"And when did you first start thinking along the lines that led you to your final breakthrough, Dr. Ross-Craigie? Can you remember a day when you said, 'Wow—that's it—here I go,' or is that too much to expect?"

"Ah, well now, J.J. that's one of the great myths of science, you know? Like a Hollywood B feature of the thirties era, that idea. I spent years—would you believe?—many *many* years thinking about the possibilities of finding an answer to the problem, long before I actually started practical work. No, no one can say, ever, that the great breakthrough comes like a flash of lightning. Believe me, I wish it did." He smiled wryly. "That would be so easy! As it is, I have had to work very hard, very hard indeed, to give a shape to the ideas I formulated."

"Well, at this point, Dr. Ross-Craigie, can you tell us how your revolutionary treatment operates?"

"With pleasure. Well, now, in brief and simple terms, I link up a patient to a special machine, a little like the well-known kidney machines used to extract unwanted toxins—ah—poisons—from the blood of people with kidney failure. Then, I pass his blood through special chambers which contain a solvent material. I won't go into the highly complex chemical structure of the solvent at this time; I'm sure your audience would be very bored by such highly technical stuff, but I can tell you that it derives from a radioactive isotope, which is very precious and costly, incidentally, and has the effect of actually attaching the blood substance that causes atheroma to the special membranes over which the blood containing the solvent passes. Are you with me? Yes? Great—great. Right. The patient lies there, and his blood passes over the membrane, and the solvent draws out the atheroma-causing substance, and deposits it on the membrane. And we keep changing the membranes, cleaning them, putting them back in the machine. Then, we do the next step, a more complicated one. We actually inject the solvent into the body to get at the really heavy layers. Oh, boy, but this is a difficult step indeed, indeed! We have to watch that patient like a hawk, on account of big pieces of atheroma plaque might break off, get jammed up in the heart or the brain somewhere—and then we're in trouble. That stage took a lot of planning, but we solved it. We track the atheroma in the vessels by using very sensitive Geiger counters and a new very sensitive stethoscope, which can actually *hear* where arteries are clogged, and if we find a big piece traveling—why we just go in after it."

"You mean, you perform an operation?"

"We surely do. We've had to do it only a few times, but we always—believe me, *always*—manage to find the piece and extract it. You see, with a Geiger counter chasing a radioactive substance, it's as good as being able to walk along a person's arteries with a torch! You can actually see what you're doing!"

"I imagine this is why the treatment can only be given in special centers? Where you can operate in a hurry if need be?"

"Yes, indeed. I require not only a specially prepared laboratory where I can carry out my researches—and I'm now seeking a way to avoid having to use surgery to catch drifting pieces of atheroma. I'll dissolve those wicked little pieces away yet, I promise you—but a well-equipped ward for patients to be in, an operating theater, a follow-up clinic, as well as, of course, the actual treatment room with its machine for using the solvent."

"So this is an expensive treatment?"

"Ah, yes. Yes, that is so. Pretty darned expensive. But—" he shrugged—"how do you evaluate the cost of a life? For myself, I'd reckon to spend a lot of money on my life if I had to. Wouldn't you?"

114

"Well, now that's a question, a very long question, we will consider later. But right now, I'd like to ask you this. This treatment—can it work for everyone and anyone? Can any patient, however ill, be helped?"

There was a brief silence, and then Ross-Craigie said heavily, "No doctor, no scientist, would ever dream of claiming a hundred percent success with any treatment. Having an appendix out is a very commonplace operation these days, very safe, very curative, but still, some people—a *very* few, but some—die of the illness every year. But I will say this about my treatment. So far, every patient I've used it for has done very well. I've treated a man with a heart so clogged up—well, I can tell you, he'd had seven, would you believe, *seven* coronary attacks, and survived them, but there could be little doubt the next would have killed him, and less doubt still that it could happen at any moment. He had his atheroma dissolved and extracted from his system, and he is just fine now—just fine."

A thin splatter of applause started, thickened, and spread, and J.J. let it run for a moment before holding up one hand and speaking above it. "A remarkable achievement, Dr. Ross-Craigie—truly remarkable. And this treatment can be used for any patient?"

"Ah—within reason, yes. That is, any patient who can be got into a special unit where the treatment is *available*. It can't be applied in the G.P.'s surgery, that's for sure!"

"Well, now, that brings up a whole new set of questions, but with your permission, I'd like to leave you for a moment and turn instead to our other honored guest tonight, a lady who has in her way done something equally remarkable in another field of medical endeavor. Ladies and gentlemen, Dr. Harriet—Berry!"

She sat stunned for a moment, for she had almost forgotten what she was sitting here for, so absorbed had she been in Ross-Craigie, so busily trying to work out what lay behind the bald oversimplified statements he was offering his listeners. Now she sat and blinked a little at J.J.'s face smiling happily at her, and said, a little brusque in her embarrassment, "Good evening."

"And good evening to you!" he said as the applause, obediently rising and falling in response to the signals Lister was industriously producing in his corner, frittered away. "May I thank you for coming here tonight, Dr. Berry? I know you weren't very keen to come. May I ask you first of all why this was so? Why you would have preferred, as you told us when we first asked you to be here, to keep the news of your breakthrough a secret just yet?"

"I don't think I said anything about secrets," Harriet said, a little hoarse with nervousness. "I agree I didn't want to talk about it. But as for secrets—well, it'll all be published in the professional journals in due course, so it will hardly be a *secret*."

"Ah, yes. No doubt. But not many of us read the professional journals, hmm?" He swept a bright blue gaze over the audience which immediately produced the required trickle of laughter. "But you *were* unwilling to talk. Why? When what you have done is so remarkable?"

Wearily, she began to explain, haltingly at first but then with greater assurance, the difference between a proven and attested treatment and/or cure, and a single success with a human patient, even though that human success followed animal trials of much greater success. She felt as though she had used the same words over and over again, as indeed she had, with Mr. Monks, with James McClarrie, with Sir Daniel Sefton. Surely they're bored, hearing it all again? a corner of her mind asked her, but she plodded on, explaining, explaining, explaining.

When she stopped, J. J. Gerrard nodded heavily, and turned back to his audience.

"Well, ladies and gentlemen, you don't have to take only my word for it that all Dr. Berry has told us about her treatment is true. That she has succeeded in curing—I'm sorry, Dr. Berry"—he turned back to her and bowed slightly—"that she has succeeded in the *care* of one human patient. You don't even have to take only Dr. Berry's word for it, transparent as it may be to all of us that what she is telling us is no more than the bare truth. No, use your own eyes, ladies and gentlemen. Let me introduce to all of you"— he stood up and stepped forward, off the dais, and ran with lithe youthfulness up the center steps between the rows of audience, while people turned and peered after him and the camera swooped its black eye in his trail, to the very back of the studio where shadows lay thicker. A sweeping spotlight followed him, outlined his broad back as he leaned over someone sitting at the very end of the back row. Then, he turned and came down the steps leading before him the small and rather shabby figure of James Ferris, who almost hopped from step to step in his delight, grinning hugely at everyone he passed, and nodding and becking like a mechanical bird.

"Ladies and gentlemen, let me introduce—James Ferris, the man who *didn't* die of cancer!" J. J. Gerrard cried, and Ferris jumped up onto the dais, almost tripping over his own feet in his hurry, and the camera turned and bowed to follow him, and then he hurried across the orange carpet to Harriet's chair, to seize her hand and shake it furiously.

"'Allo, Dr. Berry! It's good to see you, I can tell you! Best bloody woman in the 'ole world, that's what you are, and I don't care 'oo knows I said so—" And awkwardly, he lifted her hand in both of his and held it to his cheek, while behind him the audience clapped and cheered its approval.

9

THE EFFECT he had on her was quite extraordinary. She was filled with a compound of amusement and embarrassment, anger and affection, and an almost desperate desire to protect him. He looked so absurd standing there holding her hand to his cheek and she wanted to pull her hand away, to smack him with it, and then to scold him and take him away and tuck him safely in bed at Brookbank again; but threading through all that was the heavy black ribbon of anger. How dared he behave so, how dared he posture about in this witless beady-eyed fashion, holding himself up for the entertainment of these gawping stupid people? She had a sudden vivid memory of herself standing beside a small Gordon and Patty at the zoo, watching a monkey handle its genitals while it stared at them with the same sort of unwinking beadiness, and felt the same hot shame she had felt then, not because of what the monkey was doing, but because it had made her party to it, involved her in its behavior so intimately; and she pulled her hand away almost roughly.

The applause thinned as J. J. Gerrard led Ferris to a chair that one of the studio staff had pushed onto the dais, and sat down again himself.

"Well, now, Mr. Ferris, how do you feel about Dr. Berry and her work? Are you worried about the difference between a proven cure that has to wait years to get the seal of approval and—"

"Am I worried?" Ferris cried perkily. "Worried? Me? That's a laugh! What've I got to worry about? If I die tomorrow, I tell you I've no complaints, none at all. Bunce, that's what I'm havin' now, bunce! Lots o' profit. Every day I live now, feelin' great, is one Dr. Berry's given me, and I don't care who knows how I think about her. A right bloody marvel, that's what she is." And the audience laughed, and clapped and rustled with pleasure.

118

Ferris leaned toward her, and said very seriously, "I tell you what, Dr. Berry. I've talked to a lot o' people since I left the 'ospital, and there's not one doesn't say the selfsame thing I do. No matter what the scientific rights of it might be, it's now as matters —and right now I'm large as life and twice as natural, and I just wish the same was true for all those other poor bugg—poor devils as is lyin' in 'ospitals all over the place right now. I mean, what if it does turn out not to last for always, this cure o' yours—none of us is goin' to last for always anyway! Could be run over tomorrer, couldn't we? As I see it—and no one should know better'n me— it's a cure you've discovered and that's all about it. And I'm as grateful as—"

Suddenly her control snapped; she could feel the heat of temper rising in her and almost luxuriously let it go.

"If you were half as grateful as you profess to be, you wouldn't have done so stupid a thing as to go and talk your head off in this nitwit fashion! Did it never occur to you—just once—that in common courtesy if nothing else you should have told me what you were up to?"

She could feel the silent startled audience as a weight across her back, but she no longer cared about them, no longer cared about anything but letting her anger vent itself into the relief of words, and she heard her own voice going on and on. "Just for the sake of a few miserable pounds you go and expose me to all this wretched nagging and chasing—not to mention the sort of fuss you've started at Brookbank. I tell you, as far as I'm concerned you've behaved *abominably!* You've been selfish and greedy while professing this great concern for other ill people—"

" 'Ere, 'ang about a bit, Dr. Berry! There's no call for you to go on at me like that! What've I done to make you so—I mean, it's not right! I did it out of gratitude, talkin' to the paper. I knew you was too modest and that to blow your own trumpet, so I reckoned as I'd blow it for you and get other patients helped like me. As for the money—" His monkey face creased even more into a ludicrous expression of anxiety. "I felt bad about that, I really did, and I told my—well, I decided, last week it was, I decided what was to be done with that money, and it's gone already—well, most of it—gone to that relief society, the one that's always advertising to buy comforts for cancer patients. So you've got no call to—"

The applause crashed out, and he turned and blinked at the audience, and his face lifted into a tentative grin, and he made a half-hearted V-for-victory gesture, but almost immediately turned his head back to look at her again, his eyes dark and questioning.

"Oh, all right. So it wasn't just done for money," she snapped, not waiting for the sound in the studio to die away. "All the same, if you'd stopped to think for just one moment you'd surely have realized what would happen when you got yourself—and me—splashed over every newspaper there is! You said you just wanted to blow my trumpet for me, and help other patients, but for God's sake, Mr. Ferris, how could you *possibly* think all this would help other patients? Here I am, wasting time here and dealing with all this flap instead of getting on with my job. And I'm not the only person who's been seriously held up by it all! There are other pieces of research going on at Brookbank, and people I work with are having to waste their time too, with all the—"

"Oh, come, Dr. Berry, I do think, if you'll forgive my saying so, that you're being less than fair to Mr. Ferris here!"

She blinked and looked up and beyond Ferris to see William Ross-Craigie leaning forward, his hands between his knees, and as she did so was aware of J. J. Gerrard sitting back, his arms folded as he regarded her with an expression of almost eager amusement on his face, and she wondered fleetingly why he should look at her so.

"I mean . . ." Ross-Craigie went on, his voice filled with a sweet reasonableness. "Mr. Ferris here isn't as aware as you and I of the—er—the intricacies of laboratory life. He wasn't to know that the—er—there might be people with whom you work who would be jealous and resentful of your successful endeavors and who would make your working life—um—uncomfortable because of it. I believe Mr. Ferris genuinely did think he was acting for the best. I believe he truly does care a great deal for your work and—"

"I'm not going to talk to *you* about such matters as loyalty to working colleagues," she said hotly. "You, of all people! After the way *you* behaved at Brookbank—" J. J. Gerrard leaned forward, and now there was no hint of a smile on his face but a greedily inquisitorial look.

"Dr. Berry, you must let me come in at this point. Why should you feel so very strongly about Mr. Ferris's action? He's told you he didn't do as he did just for money. Is it perhaps true, and Dr. Ross-Craigie has suggested, that there are—er—other pressures being put on you?"

"Of course not! Complete nonsense. I can surely show a decent concern about the people with whom I work without it being suggested there are—that I'm motivated by anything *but* decent concern!"

"Yet, if you'll forgive me, Dr. Berry, what comes across to me from your displeasure with Mr. Ferris is not so much a concern about the work itself as about these colleagues. From your response to Dr. Ross-Craigie's remarks it's pretty clear that there have been —er—internal problems, shall we say?—at your Establishment. You and Dr. Ross-Craigie worked together there some time ago, as we all know, and—well, one cannot help wondering." He looked at her with his head on one side, his eyebrows raised in interrogation.

She stared back at him, and sharply became again aware of the audience, of the weight of their disapproval, and with the surge of her anger now dissipated by speech, felt the chill ripples of anxiety come seeping back. She had made a fool of herself, and she knew why, was aware that there at the back of her mind had been throughout the image of Oscar, hurt and embittered by the treatment he had received from Ross-Craigie, and the knowledge that he had wanted her to tell everyone about it. And she realized with equal clarity that her attempts to satisfy this unspoken demand of Oscar's had not only failed but rebounded on her own head.

"Oh, there's nothing wrong at Brookbank," she said wearily. "Nothing at all. But surely you can understand that one needs peace and quiet in order to work well! All the commentary there's been on my work—everyone seems very concerned that the treatment should be used, now, for patients. Well, I've told you why it can't be yet. I've told you there's a lot more research to be done. And I'm trying to tell all of you now that the more fuss there is, the longer it's going to take to do it. When you come right down to it, I have to say it *again*, I'm most particularly upset by the premature publication of this work. That's the real point for me. . . ."

J. J. Gerrard looked at her, as the audience moved and rustled in its rows, and then glanced at Ross-Craigie on his other side, sitting in arm-crossed sulkiness and clearly very put out by Harriet's attack on him; and then at Ferris who sat shifting his gaze from one face to the other as he tried to understand what had gone wrong.

"Now, come on, Dr. Berry!" J. J. Gerrard said, and there was a very sharp edge to his voice. "While that sounds very—uh—public-spirited, full of scientific conscience and all that, I have to say that from *my* seat in the stalls what really comes over is your anxiety about the reactions of the people with whom you are working. That was quite an—uh—accusation you hurled at Dr. Ross-Craigie's head there! Now let's really get down to the nitty-gritty, hmm? Like most ordinary men-in-the-street, I always reckoned the doctors, the researchers, the lifesavers if you like, were above the sort of pettiness that most of us get involved with—the jockeying for position, the—uh—keeping up with the Joneses bit. But now, listening to you here tonight, I have a distinct impression that all is not as ivory as it might be in the ivory towers—"

His eyes, which had been fixed on her face all the time he was speaking, seemed to shift and glaze slightly, and she realized he was looking at something over her shoulder, and automatically turned her head. Lister was waving furiously, one hand making tight rotary movements in the air, the other cupped over his ear. She turned back to J. J. Gerrard as he turned his swivel chair to face the camera.

"But that is something we'll have to come back to in the next part of the program. Stay tuned, won't you, and we'll be back with you in a few momentary moments—"

There was a second or two of immobility and then Lister was hurrying across the cable-cluttered floor to clamber on to the platform, his face creased with anxiety.

"J.J.! For Christ's sake, cool it, will you? The front office are going spare—they've had Monty himself on the line, not to mention the bloody ITA. And you're to cool it. I tell you if the break hadn't come as it did they'd have blacked you."

"What the hell are you talking about?" J. J. Gerrard looked genuinely startled, and Harriet realized almost with amusement that this was the first time she had been sure that his face was accurately expressing what he felt. "What the bloody hell do they want me to cool it for? We've got a great thing going here, got onto something that's really news, bloody marvelous television, and they wanted to *black* it? Why, for crying out loud? What's bugging them?"

"It's Monty, I think—you know what he's like about medical stories. You've *got* to be straight up—no probing on the medical stuff unless you know there's a quack to get at—and there's someone at the ITA too, I tell you, who just isn't happy about it—"

He stopped, and squinted a little, staring into space as he listened to the thin clacking coming from the single earphone strapped to his ear, and then he nodded and said, "Okay, Dave . . . J.J., David said we can fight it out afterward, but cool it *now*—we're back on the air under the thirty, so get off this laboratory politics stuff and back to the running order we'd planned. He wants Sefton next . . . okay, Dave . . . ten seconds, studio . . . let's hear it for J. J. Gerrard." And he was off, scurrying off the platform, his shoulders hunched and his head well down as he ducked under the camera that barred his way.

Now Harriet could see the monitors again, with the audience clapping furiously, and then a shot of the platform with herself and J. J. Gerrard and Ferris and Ross-Craigie in their waxworks row.

"Welcome back to the program that really digs deep—" J.J.

cried but he sounded almost perfunctory, with a hint of sulkiness underlying his words. "Back to discussion of the problems involved in medical research. For viewers who may have just joined us, we were talking about the—uh—communication problems of the scientists who work in this rarefied field of endeavor, as well as the problems of making the new treatments devised by our special guests tonight, Dr. William Ross-Craigie and Dr. Harriet Berry, as available as possible to as many people as possible. Dr. Ross-Craigie's treatment is already sufficiently developed for practical use right now. Dr. Berry feels her treatment has received—uh—premature publication, and is concerned about the effects of this. Right, now read on! What we must go on to discuss is the search for ways of making this premature publication anything but. In other words, how is Dr. Berry's treatment to be made—uh—available *now*? And how is Dr. Ross-Craigie's treatment to be made available to all the people who need it? Let me ask you both something. Isn't the main problem basically one very simple factor? Money? Isn't that the only bar to helping hundreds of thousands of sick people?"

Ross-Craigie nodded heavily. "Of course it is. Money always is the biggest hangup we have—"

"And time." Harriet cut in irritably. "Time—that's what I need."

"And time is money," J. J. Gerrard said smoothly. "Money can provide time just as it provides everything else. So let's get down to the real nitty-gritty, what do you say? Let's look at this whole problem of providing money and time to work on these new lifesaving treatments, of making them available to everyone who needs them —how are we going to find that money, hmm? I have to tell you I invited representatives of the Government, Treasury and Health officials, to come here tonight and tell us what provision the State is prepared to make. I have to tell you that they couldn't quite manage to accept. And I have to tell you that I for one wasn't a bit surprised."

Laughter rose and spread and someone at the back of the audience yelled, "Too busy voting themselves a rise in their pay!" And there was a spatter of clapping mixed with the laughter.

"No comment!" J. J. Gerrard called good-naturedly. "Still, I didn't see much joy in settling for that! I made a few inquiries of my own, and as a result of them, I want to introduce to all of you somebody else—somebody who *can* give us some information even if the Treasury can't. Ladies and gentlemen, may I present the man you meet every morning over your cornflakes and marmalade —Sir Daniel Sefton of the *Echo*—can we have a spotlight on Sir Daniel, please?"

The audience craned and stretched its composite neck as a light sprang up round Sir Daniel Sefton in the front row, and J. J. Gerrard leaned forward and smiled at him.

"Well, Sir Daniel? Would you care to comment?"

"Thank you, Mr. Gerrard. I'll be glad to." His voice was fairly quiet, but it carried an authoritative note that silenced the hiss of whispers moving through the rows of seats and that made it easy to hear every syllable.

"I of course share your concern that these treatments should be available as soon as possible. And on the basis of experience, I knew that the Government was hardly likely to provide much impetus. So, being a practical man, I set about finding some impetus. I am happy to tell you I met with some success. I now represent a consortium of people—financiers, businessmen, industrialists and the like—who regard these medical breakthroughs as of prime importance. We have established a sum of money—a very large sum indeed—and have already found suitable premises in which to establish a major research organization, where patients can be treated while at the same time research goes forward. Dr. Ross-Craigie is coming to us, and we wait only for a final decision from Dr. Berry to join us and work at our establishment in order to admit the first patients to the clinical unit."

There was a short silence, and then a roar of approval came with a violence that made Harriet feel momentarily breathless, almost flattening her fresh wave of anger, this time directed at Sir Daniel.

125

To have announced in so public a way that she had been invited to join him was outrageous, and for a moment she wanted to jump up and shriek at him, "I won't—I won't—leave me alone—I won't!"

J. J. Gerrard held up his hands, but the noise went on, yet despite it Harriet became sharply aware of another sound rising above it—of a single voice calling insistently. She peered into the dimness of the audience, puzzled, and then saw him, a tall middle-aged man standing up and shouting at the top of his voice. The audience seemed to become aware of him at the same moment, and stopped their noise, and J. J. Gerrard saw him too and called, "You have something to say, sir?"

The man nodded eagerly, and shouted, "Indeed I have—my God, I have. I want to say that this country needs people like Sir Daniel as much as—more than—it needs scientists—and I want to say that though I may be no industrialist or banker, just an ordinary bloke, I want to show how much I care about what he's trying to do. Like Mr. Ferris up there, I want to take *my* share—and I offer a regular five percent of my pay packet to help in the work—"

There was a sudden hush, and J. J. Gerrard looked at him for a long moment. "Well, that is the most . . . I really can't say . . ." He shook his head and bit his lower lip, so that the audience could clearly see how moved he was. "I don't know what to say . . ."

"And I will too—" came a sharp call from the other side of the studio, and after a very brief pause, three more people jumped to their feet and shouted, and then it seemed as though almost all of them were on their feet, all waving and shouting; and looking at the faces she could see as spotlights swung to pick out sections of the audience, Harriet felt a sudden chill of fear. They looked so blank, so brightly blank, and it was as though she weren't in a real place at all, as though these were shadows of real people whose substance had been left somewhere else.

Sir Daniel stood up, and moving forward spoke quietly to J. J. Gerrard, and then jumped onto the dais, and turned to face the audience, holding his hands up to them in exactly the same controlling gesture the other man had used, that J. J. Gerrard himself had used, fingers spread wide, the palms downward, moving his

126

arms up and down. "Like a marionette operator," Harriet thought, almost seeing the fine threads running from each finger to the people in the rows before him.

They stopped, gradually, and sat down, and Sir Daniel waited for an impressive moment before speaking.

"I've always known the people of this country are the most responsive and responsible in the world. And tonight has proved it. So spontaneous and wholeheartedly a generosity is humbling to see. It makes me feel a deep gratitude and pride in being an Englishman.—No, please—wait. Hear what I have to say. Much as we—and I know I speak for my colleagues in the consortium— much as we are touched and moved by your warm response, much as we would like to let you all feel that you too have a part in forwarding this particular work, I have to tell you that we can't, we simply can't, accept your splendid offers. And for a very simple reason. We are a business consortium, not a registered charity. We cannot legally accept charitable gifts of money. To do so, we would have to be licensed, as it were, by the Government, and the wheels of Government grind so slowly—indeed, that is why we set up our scheme in the first place—that we just saw no sense in wasting time applying to make the scheme operate on money collected from the great-hearted public of which you are all such splendid examples. May I ask you, if you want to give so generously to research, to send your money to those bodies which do exist as charities? I will see to it that the *Echo* publishes a list of them in the next day or two, so that you here tonight, and those among the watching millions who I know share your great-heartedness, can know where to send their donations—"

"Just a minute," the voice wasn't very loud, but it had a considerable depth, and people turned their heads to look toward it, and Harriet looked too and saw Ben Shoeman leaning forward in his seat, one hand up like a schoolboy signaling his teacher. "I want to ask a question."

"By all means," Sir Daniel said, and smiled affably. "By all means."

"If your setup isn't a charity, what is it?"

127

"A consortium, sir. I had thought I'd explained—"

"As I understand it, the word consortium means a partnership, an association. Is that right?"

"Well, yes. I suppose that is a definition."

"A partnership or association entered into for profit? I want to ask you and your—*colleagues*—a very blunt question, Sir Daniel. What's in this plan for you? I for one never yet heard of businessmen putting up money for anything but business. If they want to make philanthropic gestures, they don't form themselves into consortia. They philanthropize as individuals and get the glory for it. So what's in it for *you?*"

Sir Daniel stood and stared at him for some moments, and his face looked thinner as his upper lip rose very slightly and his nostrils pinched.

"I find your question a very unpleasant one, sir. A downright slur—" There was a scatter of shouts of "Hear, hear" and "Pipe down, you slob!" and "Shut up!" from the audience, but Shoeman went on as though he had heard nothing.

"I hope it is a slur, Sir Daniel. But the only way you'll convince me is by answering my questions. How is the money to be handled? What sort of return will your businessmen and financiers and industrialists get on their investment?"

"I decline to answer so insulting a question, sir. I do not need to. We are not a public company—"

"Ah! So you don't deny you've formed a company? That the thing's organized like any other business scheme?"

"Why should I deny it? There's nothing wrong with running things in a businesslike way, surely? If more of this country were run as efficiently as my colleagues and I run our concerns, we'd all be a lot better off—"

Once again, the roar of approval leaped up, and seeming to gain strength from it, Sir Daniel thrust his hands into his trousers pockets, and rocked gently on his heels, a faint smile on his face as he stared at Ben Shoeman. "Altogether, sir, I venture to suggest there are a damned sight too many grubby, pie-in-the-sky unshaven—

begging your presence!—halfwits around already, all a damned sight too ready to knock down the good solid institutions on which this country's greatness was founded, and offering nothing—nothing—to put in its place. No, sir, don't you try to dirty us with your nasty little mind and your nasty little slurs! We are not interested in the views of those who cannot observe a generous gesture without assuming some evil lies behind it. We are ashamed of nothing we are planning, and if you think otherwise—well, sir, all I can say is that that tells us more about you than about us!"

From the far side of the dais there was a wave of movement, and Harriet saw the man called Peter Lister gesticulating furiously and J. J. Gerrard cried quickly, "Thank you, Sir Daniel Sefton! And just before the close, let me give our lady guest—who else?—the chance of the last word! Dr. Berry! How do you feel about the great offers that have been made here tonight?"

Irritation overcame her again, and once more she allowed herself the luxury of speaking without thinking first.

"Frankly, Mr. Gerrard, I couldn't be less interested in all this posturing about and fussing over money! I'm a woman with a job to do, and if some people want to enjoy themselves playing the philanthropist, that's their concern. For my part, I just want to be left in peace to get on with my job—"

The audience rustled ominously with a sussuration of whispers, and someone shouted, "Shame!—Who bloody pays you then, but the ones that find the money?" She closed her eyes in sudden weariness, and then, gratefully, heard the tinny music again, rising over the audience's audible irritation with her, heard J. J. Gerrard cry, "Well, folks, time has defeated us on this issue at any rate—stay tuned and we'll be back in a few momentary moments with more probing in 'Probe'—"

The images on the monitor screens shivered and rolled and then blackened, and Harriet sat for a brief second, unbelieving. Was it all over? And then someone was standing beside her, speaking, and she blinked up at him. "I'm sorry—what did you say? I wasn't listening."

129

"Would you care to take a seat in the audience for the third half? We could find a place for you there toward the back, and—"

"Oh, no—no thank you. Really, I'd—all I want is to go somewhere quiet and cool."

"Well, of course! I know just how it is! Look, I'll get young Sue to take you to the hospitality room—we'll have to move a bit fast though—we've only a couple of minutes before we're back on the air."

He signaled a tall girl in very tight trousers and an even tighter shirt, who was leading in another woman, a small blonde in a very shiny purple dress, trailing necklaces and chains, her fingers stiff with rings.

"Sue—hello, Miss Ascole!—would you just sit here please, and I'll be right with you—Sue, be a lamb and take Dr. Berry back to the hospitality room, will you? Then come back fast—I'll need you. Right, now, Miss Ascole—we've got your props over there on that little table, and your cat is in his cage just underneath it. He's been a bit fractious, I believe, but I daresay we'll cope with him—can't expect a witch's cat to be exactly of bundle of purrs, can we?"

And the little blonde woman giggled and the chains round her neck clashed softly, and Harriet, suddenly feeling quite desperately tired, followed the lanky Sue out of the heat and noise of the studio to the cooler quieter corridors beyond.

They gave her sausages on little sticks and a plate with a curly crustless ham sandwich on it, and a few sad olives, and thrust a very large glass of gin and tonic into her hand, and she stood there bemused by the sound and the smokiness and let it all happen around her. She could see Theo on the other side of the room, talking to the little witch woman, Miss Ascole, who clashed her chains at him and sparkled while Theo gave his celebrated impression of an extremely sexually responsive man ("But I *am* extremely responsive, Hattie," he had protested when she had told him mildly that it wasn't kind in him to treat women at parties so. "Maybe," she had said. "But not, in my experience, to the sort of women you turn it on for"; "Not to any sort of woman, dear heart. But I do enjoy getting my own back on the breed, sometimes. If there were more women like you I wouldn't have to.") Beyond him she could see J. J. Gerrard talking very animatedly to an incredibly handsome girl wearing clothes so fashionable that she hardly looked real, and then she saw Ross-Craigie push through the crowd toward them, a glass in each hand, to stand very close to the girl with a proprietorial air, and, amused, she thought, "All the trappings of success—they suit him—like his glasses."

She played with the idea of Ross-Craigie in glasses of assorted shapes, oval and David-Hockney-round, and harlequin-spangled-upswept, and wanted to giggle into her gin. She knew she was too tired to drink at all, really, but it made her feel better, not relaxed so much as removed. In her present state, she could stand and look at the scene about her, at the overcrowded hospitality room crammed with people all desperately working at impressing each other, much as an ornithologist sits in a hide and observes the absurdity of mating rituals.

She must have been spoken to twice at least before she realized she was not in a hide, and turned her head to answer. Patty was standing there, with Ben Shoeman towering over even her five-foot-eight inches, her hands in the pocket of her sheepskin coat, smiling and a little flushed with embarrassment.

"Ma, you look half-pickled—glazed and definitely not of this world. Was it so awful? I did feel for you, really I did."

"It was horrible. Darling, you must be cooked in that coat. Do take it off."

"Now I know she's been drinking. It's the only time she comes the motherly bit—you didn't mind me bringing Ben, Ma?"

"It's the only time I dare come the motherly bit. Hello, Ben. How are you? Mind? There wouldn't be much point in saying so if I had, would there? Fait accompli and all that. Though in fact I'm almost grateful to you, Ben. While you were talking, they couldn't expect me to, and that was a comfort."

"But you did agree with him, Ma, didn't you? You can see that

131

horrible Sefton creature's jumping on your back to make himself money? Look, what was all that about your joining his precious new establishment? You aren't going to, are you? After what you said at the weekend, though, I don't suppose . . ."

Harriet laughed suddenly into her glass, and that made her cough, and Ben thumped her back with a genial ferocity that almost stunned her. "My dear Patty!" she managed to say eventually. "Last time I saw you you were solemnly advising me to find myself a commercial establishment where I could carry on my research without any of the pennypinching we have at Brookbank, and now you say that! It's enough to make anyone choke"—and she coughed again and wiped her eyes, and thought with a moment of intense longing of her bedroom at the cottage. So *tired*.

"Patty, you didn't! What the hell were you thinking of?" Ben said.

"Oh, for God's sake, Ben, I wasn't thinking of defecting to the bourgeoisie or whatever, so stop glaring at me! All I said to Ma was that Gordon had a point in urging her to leave Brookbank and go somewhere else. Only *he* said it to encourage her to make a lot of money for herself, and *I* said it because I knew bloody well she'd never get much chance to get anywhere with her work at that tatty setup she's with—"

"Ha—Gordon! Forgive me, both of you, but *Gordon*—"

"Dr. Berry, is there anything I can get for you?"

She turned her head to find Sir Daniel Sefton standing behind her and looking very directly at Ben.

"What? Oh, no. Thank you, nothing."

"Ah. Well, perhaps you'd care to sit down somewhere? This place gets incredibly crowded after a program. So many hangers-on come freeloading, you know. It happens every time—I've appeared on several of these programs now. I must say they've never before allowed the audience in for drinks, however—" And he put a hand on her elbow and tried to lead her away.

"Er—no, thank you, Sir Daniel. I'm fine here. May I introduce my daughter? Patty, this is Sir Daniel Sefton, of—"

"How d'y do," Patty said, redfaced, and raised one eyebrow a little at her mother, but Harriet hurried on, "—and—er—Ben Shoeman, Sir Daniel Sefton—"

"We have spoken, of course," Sir Daniel said frostily, after a moment. "And frankly, sir, I'm not a little amazed that you have the effrontery to come in here after the exhibition you made of yourself."

"Oh, don't be amazed, Sir Daniel," Ben said and smiled down with considered impudence at the older man. "Not effrontery at all. I kind of have a right to be here, you know? Like, I'm one of the family."

"Ben, shut up," Patty said, her face reddening more. "There's no need to—"

"Well, what's need got to do with anything? He wants to know what right a representative of the hoi polloi, like me, has to be here, so I'm telling him. Like, *Sir* Daniel, Dr. Berry here is my common-law mother-in-law on account Patty is my common-law wife. I guess you like labels, so there's a couple for you."

"Oh. Oh. I see. I'm sorry, Dr. Berry—"

"Sorry you were rude to us, or sorry she's my common-law mother-in-law, Sefton? Forgive me if I can't go on with this 'Sir' business. It kind of sticks in my craw."

"And *you*—" Sir Daniel stopped, and Harriet could see him literally bite back his anger, and then he smiled thinly. "You must forgive me. When I was brought up I was taught to apologize when I had unwittingly offended a lady, and old habits die hard." He turned to Harriet. "Tell me, Dr. Berry, did you find the program interesting? A pity we couldn't explore the issues raised a little further, but time, you know, and this audience participation thing J.J. is so keen on—it does limit one rather."

"It didn't seem to limit you any, Sefton. And you were one of the audience, or so I thought. Or was that just one of the phony plants they go in for on this program, the sort people like you relish?" Ben said offensively.

"Mr.—Mr. Shoeman. I am trying very hard not to pay any atten-

133

tion to your somewhat juvenile exhibitionism." Sir Daniel spoke softly but his voice carried, and some of the people standing near the little group stopped their own talk and turned to look curiously at them.

"But you seem determined to turn this private social occasion into some sort of—of Speaker's Corner. This is hardly the time or place to indulge in such half-baked heckling, and hardly courteous to your—er—to Dr. Berry or her daughter. If you wish to have an argument with me, you are at liberty to do so, but not here and not now. I will be happy to give you an appointment if you contact my secretary tomorrow morning. Dr. Berry, may I ask you to spare me a few moments of your time? Social occasion though this may be, it does have certain professional overtones, and I would—"

"Oh, no you don't, Sefton," Ben said loudly, and now almost everyone in the room was listening, and Harriet felt rather than saw Theo start to push his way through the crowd toward her. "No, you don't. I want to tell you something in a *professional* way. I'm by way of being a person who takes a professional interest in matters that affect ordinary people. The hoi polloi, you know? And I want to tell you that I am not about to sit down and let you and your crew of money-grabbers get your greedy hands onto the work of people like Dr. Berry. I'm telling you that I have every intention of finding out one hell of a lot more about your plans, about how you intend to make hay for yourself out of your precious new establishment, and when I do find out, I am going to tell the world, loud and clear, just what it is that—"

"Hey, hey, so what gives here?" J.J.'s voice cut in with a heavy joviality, and he came to stand beside Sir Daniel and look at Ben with his eyes narrowed. "Is this a private fight, or can anyone join in?"

"The more people join in, the better I'll like it," Ben said, and grinned again, clearly enjoying himself hugely. "I was just telling your co-performer here—sorry, this member of your audience— that my nasty little mind is ticking over in its nasty little way, and that I'm going to investigate his consortium. Simple as that! Me,

I'm one of your straight-up types. I don't go about things sideways. I reckon this consortium idea stinks, and I'm about to show the world why. Okay? So are you joining in, or dropping out?"

"Ben, please, will you stop this at once?" Harriet heard her own voice almost with surprise. "I for one am finding all this very tiring, not to say irritating, and as your—your common-law mother-in-law, I'm asking you—I'm *telling* you, that I want no more discussion of this now. Is that clear?"

He looked at her for a moment, and then lifted his head and laughed loudly, and leaned forward and kissed her cheek noisily. "Well, for you, Harriet, for you, what else can I do? You're the greatest, and I want you to know I really dig you, mother-in-law or not. Okay, Patty, let's go, huh?" And he turned and pushed his way toward the door, smiling cheerfully at people he passed, several of whom looked away in embarrassment.

"God, Ma, I'm sorry. He's not always so—hell, I'll phone you at home, tomorrow, all right? Goodnight, love, and you were great." And Patty kissed Harriet swiftly and followed Ben out of the room. After a moment the talk started again, louder than ever.

Behind her, Theo put a hand on her arm, and she turned to him with enormous gratitude. "Theo, take me away, now. I must be back soon anyway, to let Mrs. Davies get away—good night, Sir Daniel—Mr. Gerrard. I'm sorry about—oh, well. Good night."

10

"CANCER DOCTOR in TV Punchup!" Theo said, his voice thick with disgust. "How these people can face themselves over their own breakfast tables is beyond me. How could *anyone*—even the veriest idiot, write such crap? Punchup, indeed!"

"It might just as well have been," Harriet said, tiredly. "This morning, I really feel as though I've been pummeled. Have you read all the papers? Most of them seem to be going for me, don't they? It's a horrible sensation . . ." She shrugged her shoulders to cover the faint shiver of distaste that had run across her back.

"What is?"

"Being so thoroughly hated—some of these reports make me feel like the Borgias' tutor. But I didn't *do* anything to make these people quite so furious, did I, Theo? I hadn't thought so!"

"You showed you were yourself, that's all. Didn't conform to the stereotype. And nothing is more likely to infuriate people, even induce their hate, than damaging their fantasies. They're the most precious possessions anyone has. Not the reality of their lives, but their vision of it. *That's* your sin. That's why they're howling for your blood this morning."

"Theo, what are you talking about? When you get metaphysical or whatever it is, you lose me—"

"Metaphysical! Dear heart, you obviously don't even know what the word means! You asked me why people—the papers—are pillorying you, and I'm trying to tell you. Look, the stereotype of the scientist—what is it? Sexless, certainly. A scientist can have gender, but no sex. This creature, this impossible creature, is supposed to be way above the ordinary concerns of mere mortals. This identikit scientist is devout and devoted, forever immolating him-herself on the altar of science, a science that is, of course, in existence *only* for the benefit of mankind. You must have seen it yourself umpteen times! There they are, those TV doctors, those filmic researchers,

136

those novelish discoverers, selflessly struggling and suffering away, all to save the life of dear little Nell in the last reel or chapter or whatever. And what did you do last night? Instead of sitting there all be-haloed with your devotion to pure science, and looking with desperate anxiety over your figurative surgical mask at the agonies of dear little Nell and all her friends and relations, you sat there being Harriet Berry. Fed up with being nagged, and lashing out at the person who started the nagging going. My dear, you did a *dreadful* thing in the eyes of the Great British Public! Instead of laying your hand on Ferris's fevered brow, or holding his wrist as you frowned over his pulse, or even sitting back and accepting your just dues, his gratitude, you lashed into that little man as though you were an ordinary woman. You complained about having your time wasted! And not content with that you made your scorn of their bandwagon charitableness painfully clear. Dear Harriet, *real* scientists never complain or sneer like that—unless they're the other sort, of course."

"The other sort?"

"Ah, yes. The Bad Scientist stereotype. The one that cackles evilly over bubbling retorts and Bunsen burners and foaming test-tubes—I'd love to know where they get those from. I've certainly never seen such equipment in any lab I've ever been in—while he plots the destruction of mankind. The transplanters and the genetic engineers and test-tube-baby people—they're supposed to be that sort. But you—you're supposed to be your actual discoverer of a cure for the scourge of mankind! Come on, Hattie—after the way you kicked out at Ferris last night, and cocked a snook at the offered donations, and had a go at Ross-Craigie, who's the most stereotyped character ever—cut out of cardboard, I swear it, with plywood struts to hold him up at the back—what did you expect? Red roses?"

She laughed then, feeling her face relax and soften, and grateful to him for it. "I must be tireder than I realized. Yes, of course you're right! Papers don't really express what people are thinking any more than those stereotypes you talk about really have any resemblance to people like me. So I shouldn't care what these

headlines scream"—she flicked a finger and thumb at the pile of
newspapers in front of them on her desk with a dismissive gesture—"any more than I care about last night's stupidity." There
was a pause and she felt her face and shoulders settle back into
some of their original tenseness. "I shouldn't, but I'm afraid I do.
Call it the human bit again. I'm too anxious to be liked. Like most
people, I suppose."

"Most women, you mean! That's the real difference between the
sexes. Men very often couldn't care less about other people's re-
sponses to them personally. Oscar almost certainly knows he's
heartily loathed by most of the people here and revels in it—sees it
as a proof of his administrative ability, probably. Or it makes him
feel powerful—like flexing muscles and admiring the ugly bumps
they make. And plenty of people dislike me, and much I care! But
women—no, they want to be *loved*. They want to be seen to be
nice and friendly and basically very-good-sorts-don't-you-know:
whatever extraordinary things they do—like discovering cancer
treatments. And when some of them get together and manage to
rid themselves of that particular hangup and set out to get what
they want the way men would, and to hell with other people's
opinions, they find themselves getting a double share of oppro-
brium and anger from the world at large. Remember the suffra-
gettes and think of the Women's Lib lot now!"

"Theo, dear, whenever you start talking in this cascade fashion, I
have the distinct impression you're soothing me. You're like a
mother dishing out cocoa and biscuits and saying, 'There, there,
dear—don't you upset yourself—Mummy's on your side, so forget
the nasty boys at school—' "

"Holed in one," Theo said equably. "It works, though, doesn't
it? You sat there a while ago looking like a half-melted wax doll
with the flesh falling off your bones, all tense and creased, all because a few tabloid papers of the dingier sort use you to make their
headlines on an otherwise dull day! A few minutes listening to me
pontificate and look at you. Solidifying nicely!"

"Not a very flattering turn of phrase, but I'll take it kindly.
Look, Theo, are you busy today?"

"I am, believe it or not. I have a list in"—he glanced at his watch—"about three quarters of an hour. Why?"

"Oh. I hoped you'd be fairly free, as it's Saturday. I've sweet damn all to do here. Can't get on with another trial until Oscar gives me the go-ahead on another patient—not that there's anyone suitable in the hospital unit, anyway—and there's only the animals to worry about. I've got a small series started on a half dozen of the new monkeys, but frankly, John and Catherine could run those alone. The vaccines they're using are the ones I prepared before all this flap started—all I have to do is to collate the observations and graph them against the results of the last seven series I did before starting Ferris. I just thought, if you weren't too busy, we could— oh well, never mind!" She got up and started to pace the room, restless and irritable.

"Bored, love?" Theo watched her, his eyebrows raised gently. "Is that why you're so edgy?"

"Oh, I don't know! Yes, I suppose I am! If only I could get on with some work! If Oscar could stop the series we're doing, I swear he would—he's maddening—"

"See it his way, Hattie, if you can. He's under considerable pressure from Whitehall, you know that. I don't often defend the man against you, but—"

"Oh, I *know!* Do you imagine I'm blaming him personally? Of course I'm not! If I could it'd all be less frustrating. As it is—I'm aching to get on with some real work. I feel so *useless*, prowling around stupid television shows and wasting my time with newspapers—"

The phone on her desk shrilled, and she jumped slightly. "You see what's happening to me? Edgy as a cat! Hello, Dr. Berry's unit. . . . Who? . . . Oh. Hold on a moment—"

She put her hand over the telephone mouthpiece and said softly, "It's Sefton—wanting a personal call. Shall I tell them I'm not here? I don't think I could talk to him without chewing his ears off, after this morning's papers, on top of last night's performance—"

"Um. Let me think for a moment." He sat and looked at her,

139

consideringly, and then nodded decisively. "Talk to him. The man's entitled to an answer one way or the other. You haven't told him yet what you intend to do about his offer, after all."

She grimaced, but obediently uncovered the telephone mouthpiece. "Dr. Berry speaking. . . . Yes. . . . Good morning, Sir Daniel. . . . Hmm? No, I can't say I *am* feeling particularly well this morning. Would you, in my shoes?"

Theo got up, and came to perch beside her on the desk, his head bent toward her, and obligingly she shifted the earpiece slightly so that they could both hear the thin clacking tones of Sir Daniel's voice.

"No, I have no doubt I would not. I am truly very sympathetic, Dr. Berry—I would have protected you from—er—this journalistic onslaught this morning had I been able. Unfortunately, my night editor took it into his head to make a certain amount of—er—shall we say, editorial capital, out of last night's program. And inevitably, as the *Echo* leads, so do other papers follow. Once our first edition was out, every other paper naturally picked up the direction and started their own witch hunt—if you'll forgive the expression!"

"I'm not feeling particularly forgiving about anything this morning, Sir Daniel," Harriet said icily, and Theo grinned broadly at her and nodded his head in violent approbation. "I don't enjoy being made a public exhibition—"

"Oh, now, dear lady!" the distorted little voice said. "You can hardly blame the *Echo* for that. After all, you accepted the 'Probe' invitation—"

"Yes, I know that, but—"

"And really, one does need a good deal of experience to be able to handle such—um—so very sophisticated a public platform!"

"Well, of course, I'm well aware that no one would be likely to call me sophisticated."

"Oh, please, I meant no judgment on you personally! I was merely making a statement of fact—political fact. I can assure you that you are in good company if you feel chagrin at the—er—errors of judgment in your performance last night. I well remember what the Chancellor of the Exchequer said to me the day after *he* had suffered at the 'Probe' program's hands! So please, do stop blaming yourself. Also don't blame yourself for this morning's newspaper headlines. The only person to blame for those is myself! Had I not been a little—er—wearied, shall we say, by the—*discussion*—with your daughter's friend, I dare say—however! That is all by the by. What I would like to ask you, Dr. Berry, is whether or not you have yet reached a decision about joining us at Whyborne? Once you do join us, I think I can assure—indeed, I can *promise* you that there will be no more public complaining about you of the sort you have unfortunately suffered today."

"That sounds like a—shall we say, a bribe, Sir Daniel?"

Theo grinned more widely than ever, if that were possible, and patted her shoulder in encouragement. Harriet was beginning to enjoy herself; it was extraordinary how different she felt, talking to this man on the telephone, from the way she had felt when facing him beside Oscar's desk the week before. Then she had felt stupid, and rather helpless. Now, she felt almost powerful, and certainly in control of the conversation. Last time she had been more like a piece of wood swept by the opposing river currents that were Oscar and Sir Daniel. This time, she was a rock unmoved by the pressure. She liked the simile as it came into her head, and grinned back at Theo.

"A bribe? My dear Dr. Berry, you almost insult me! I am not in any way trying to bring pressure to bear on you! I merely made a statement of fact. No more!"

"Well, Sir Daniel, *I* am going to make a statement of fact," Harriet said. "A very definite statement. I am not interested in being part of a—a business consortium, now or ever. I am not interested in being made use of, as though I and my work were no more than—than mere commodities. I am sick and tired of all the fuss, all the interminable and exceedingly boring public discussion that's been going on. In short, Sir Daniel, I am not accepting the offer of a post at your establishment. Thank you for the invitation, but—no. Good morning, Sir Daniel!"

141

Very gently, she recradled the telephone, and looked up at Theo. "There!" she said, with her voice filled with satisfaction. "Now I feel a *lot* better!"

"Oh, no! *No*. Not again," Harriet said, staring at the newspaper in Catherine's hand. "I really don't think I could stand it. Please, don't expect me to read it—"

"You'll have to," Catherine said firmly and put the paper on the desk in front of her on top of the graph she had been working on. "It's no good trying to pretend it isn't happening, because it is. And not knowing what everybody's saying'll make it worse for you, not easier."

"It can't be worse," Harriet said irritably and pushed the paper away and stood up to begin moving restlessly about the room, her hands thrust into the pockets of her white coat. Catherine leaned against the desk, her arms folded, and watched her.

"Damn it all to hell!" Harriet said after a moment. "What more *can* they say? I've made up my mind—I'm not leaving here, and that's all about it. So the treatment won't be available for a long time yet, if ever, and they might as well forget about it and leave me in peace—"

She stopped by the door to the oxygen chamber and stared at it for a moment, and then turned toward Catherine and threw her hands out with what she knew was a faintly melodramatic gesture. "Look at us! Instead of being able to get on with another trial we've got to sit here, wasting what little facility we've got, because Oscar won't let me have another patient until the fuss dies down. If the papers are starting again, how much longer must I—"

"If you'd read the paper, you'd see that it isn't just the same old hooha all over again," Catherine said calmly. "Like I said, not knowing what everyone's saying makes it worse, not better." She reached behind her and picked up the paper and opened it and refolded it to a center spread to show the heavy black print of the headline.

"ARE YOU RICH ENOUGH TO BE ALLOWED TO

LIVE?" It trumpeted across the room, and Harriet peered at it but made no move to come and take it from Catherine's hand. So Catherine shrugged slightly, and began to read aloud.

" 'The new Research Treatment Establishment for Atheroma and Cancer at Whyborne in Buckinghamshire which accepted its first heart attack patients this week, is only to be used for people who can afford to pay the massive fees demanded by the Board of Management appointed by the consortium which set it up. This fact was revealed yesterday in an exclusive *Clarion* interview with Dr. Ben Shoeman, the young Canadian biologist who first suggested, on the J. J. Gerrard "Probe" program two weeks ago, that the establishment was to be a profit-making organization. "I now have conclusive proof that these people are planning to make money out of the heartbreak of desperate illness," he told—' "

"Ben?" Harriet said. "Ben told them—let me see—" And she took the paper from Catherine's hands and read it rapidly. "The five members of the consortium including Sir Daniel Sefton, the newspaper magnate, and Mr. Lewis Pirrie, the shipping millionaire, hold A shares in the private company that is registered as the owner of Whyborne. Dr. Shoeman said, 'Fees for treatment are not as far as I can discover set out in any official schedule, but I have firm evidence that at least one of the heart patients, a wealthy Cheshire farmer, is paying £200 a week as a basic charge, and his family expects to pay far more for additional expenses as his treatment gets under way. Clearly, only the rich are to be able to make use of these great medical breakthroughs.' "

"There's more on the leader page," Catherine said. "And it's even—well, look for yourself."

Harriet looked. "UNTO THEM THAT HATH" it was headed, and went on, "and that means not only material possessions but the gift of life itself, if you can use the word gift for what will be so very costly. Until today, disease and death have been the great levelers, striking the rich man at his table and the beggar at his gate with equal ferocity. But no longer is that true. There have been what might be termed straws in the wind; for some time now, the

143

lifesaving technique of treatment on a kidney machine has been hard to get for some poor patients, easier to get for those who could pay, but now we have a situation in which *only* the rich can be treated. The diseases of heart attack and cancer will no longer deal their painful death to a very small section of our society—the *rich* section. That this is immoral in the extreme is self-evident. What must be discussed now is what we, the bulk of society who cannot afford to buy health and life so dearly, are going to do about it. Are we going to sit quietly by and watch our mothers, our wives and our children die of cancer, our husbands and fathers succumb to the agony of coronary thrombosis? And make no mistake about it; this sort of heart disease is not confined to the rich, as some people think. The incidence among working-class people, such as bus drivers, is very high. We at the *Clarion* are committed to a campaign to bring these treatments within the reach of every patient who needs it, whatever his creed, his color *and his income*. Several unions and particularly those representing young people, such as university students, are holding a joint mass meeting tomorrow afternoon in London's Trafalgar Square to decide what they are going to do about it. The question we ask now is what are *you* going to do about it?"

There was a short silence, and then Catherine said, "You see what I mean? You've got to know what people are saying. And they aren't saying that your treatment isn't available, are they? Anything but."

"Ben must know I've refused to go to Whyborne! What the hell does he think he's—I *told* Patty the day after that TV business that I'd made up my mind to stay here at Brookbank and that I'd told Sir Daniel so. So why didn't Ben say so?"

"Kills half his story if he does, doesn't it?" Catherine said.

"What?"

"If he let on he knew that you weren't going to work for this Whyborne lot, there wouldn't be so much to hold a meeting about, would there? Not so much to sound off in the papers about? A treatment for heart disease matters, of course, but cancer—that gets everybody where they live, always has. So he doesn't bother to mention you one way or the other, and lets the *Clarion* people think you're going there—and why shouldn't they think it, seeing that Sefton man said loud and clear that you were, and hasn't murmured a word about your saying no to him?—and leaves them to write what they want. It makes a bigger noise that way. Sells more papers."

"But Ben doesn't care about selling papers, Catherine! Anything but. He's a great crusading Communist, and—"

"Exactly. And what do Communists want all the time? Revolutions, that's what. And believe me, this Ben is using you and your work for his own ends just as much as he says these other people are doing. I hate the whole bloody lot of them, Communists and Capitalists. For my part, they can all go and—" She produced a thick sound in her throat, part snort and part growl, and shrugged. "Ah, what's the good of anything? All we want to do is get on with a job, and all this—it's enough to make you spit."

They sat in silence for a while, and then Harriet said, "I think I've got to do something about all this. Haven't I, Catherine? I can't let it all just go on and on, can I?"

"I'm not the person to ask! How can I say? All I want is to see you get on with the work. It's—as far as I'm concerned, it's the most important thing in the world. My mother died of cancer of the uterus, and I looked after her the last three months. She just rotted away, and she wasn't fifty. And you've got—well, I'm only a technical assistant, but I'm not as stupid as some might think. And I'm as sure as I'm standing here that you've got the cure in your hands, that you're the only scientist working in the field who has, and it's wicked, *wicked* that all these rotten politicians and money grubbers can stop you from getting on with it, that—that great stupid idiot Bell can—" she stopped sharply, red-faced and breathless, and shook her head, and Harriet stared at her, amazed. "Catherine! I've never known you so—"

"I'm sorry. But even I have my feelings and sometimes—Look, don't ask *me* what to do. Ask Mr. Fowler, or—"

"I'm not asking you. I'm not asking anyone. I'm sick and tired of asking other people what I should do. The more I try to do the easy thing, the quiet thing, the more I try to keep everyone happy, the worse it gets. I'll manage on my own."

Catherine smiled faintly. "Well, good for you. I never could see why you consult other people ever, the way you do. You never do when you're working on a project, do you? You just think it out for yourself and get on with it. But whenever it's anything else, you— well, forgive me for saying it, but if we're being honest, I might as well—you flap around like a wet hen very often. I'm glad I never had any family."

"What's that got to do with anything?"

"A lot. All these emotional things—ruins a woman. I saw the way my mother was ruined by the stupidities of my father. And the way she got when my brother—anyway, I made up my mind then, years ago, I wasn't going to be torn into strips of useless rubbish by other people. Once my mother died, I stopped caring about any-one. Miller of Dee, that's me. I care for nobody and nobody cares for me. And I was right to choose that way, and you're the proof. A mind like yours, and you let yourself be pulled one way by Mr. Fowler and another way by that Bell man, and then your son and daughter—"

"For someone who cares for nobody you seem to have given a lot of thought to *my* affairs!" Harriet said a little sharply.

Catherine's face became suddenly scarlet, and then the redness drained away and she looked white and pinched.

"It's your work I care about. Not you. Not personally," she said stiffly.

There was an embarrassed silence, and then Harriet said gently, "I'm sorry. Of course you have every right to say what you please. We've worked together a very long time, after all. And you're right —I do flap about sometimes, and I need to be told. And I do let Theo and Oscar—well, I can't help it. They're my friends, both of them, and I need them. What else can I do?"

"Stop caring," Catherine said. "Don't have friends, don't get involved with people, and life runs a lot smoother."

146

"That's easily said. But I do care, and I can't turn it off like a tap. Emotional things—they don't work that way. You got emotional a moment ago. Could you have turned that off like a tap?"

Catherine stood very still, in her characteristic stance of arm-folded stolidity, staring at the floor, and after a moment looked up and her face was as closed and wooden as it usually was.

"So what *are* you going to do? I won't advise but I'm interested."

There was a pause, and then Harriet smiled faintly and nodded.

"What am I going to do? I'm not quite sure—let me think."

She began to prowl about the room again, her hands back in her pockets, and her chin tucked into her neck.

"I could try to contact Ben and ask him what the hell he's trying to do and ask him to stop meddling, but knowing the little of him that I do, I doubt that'd have much effect. And you could be right about his political motives, and if you are, he's even less likely to— no, forget Ben. I could call the *Clarion* and tell them there won't be any cancer treatment being sold to the highest bidder as far as I'm concerned—but you know what that will do, don't you? They'll start howling for the treatment to be made available here, and I'll have to say—again—that it can't, and we'll be no better off. All my instincts tell me to lay low and say nothing. To just sit tight and hope they'll forget all about me. They've got Ross-Craigie to play with, and he loves the publicity bit. Am I being specious, Catherine? Looking for the easy way out again, instead of really thinking it through properly?"

Catherine looked back at her, her face expressionless. And Harriet grimaced slightly and shook her head.

"Oh, all *right*. So I am! But I can't be doing with getting any more embroiled with these bloody papers than I have to. So I'll let them get on with it, and I won't have anything to do with it. There! I've decided."

"Shall you go to this mass meeting in London tomorrow?"

"Go to—? Good God, why on earth should I?" Harriet said in amazement.

"Might be informative. And you might just as well go as sit here

147

twiddling your thumbs. There's no work you can do, not until the powers-that-be stop being so stupid and let you start a new patient. I'm nearly driven mad with it—as you've seen—having so little to do like this. I'll go with you, if you like. Caister'll be here to hold the fort and look after the animals. It'd be interesting, at the very least, to see what they get up to. If we go down by train, first thing in the morning, we could be there well before two o'clock."

11

SHE STOOD with her coat collar pulled high around her cold-reddened ears, her hair blown irritatingly in her eyes by the biting November wind, staring up at the back view of Nelson on his column and wondering bleakly why she had agreed to come. What good would it do? She should have stayed at home, and no doubt seen what there was to be seen on the television news.

She could see the Outside Broadcast cameras below her in the Square, stolid islands in the middle of the swirling mass of humanity, and a little farther along the pavement edged by the stone balustrade against which she and Catherine were leaning another camera van was setting down its load.

The Square was filling fast now; so was the pavement on which they were standing, but up here were people like themselves who preferred the clear view offered by this higher vantage point in front of the National Gallery to the more immediate excitement but limited vistas of the Square itself.

"So young," she thought as the color and sound and smell of the people all about her filled her senses. "So stupidly young—" and then was irritated by her own dreary middle-aged reaction; why assume that they're stupid just because they're young? she asked herself.

Because they're part of all this stupid interference I'm having to put up with. Part of all this time-wasting, pointless nonsense.

"But it isn't their fault," her mind whispered back. "Is it? It's newspapers and television programs and the rest of it."

And then as a tall boy with a scrappy little beard struggling to cover the spottiness of his thin cheeks, and wearing an old army captain's greatcoat, squeezed himself into the small space beside her she realized why she had made so blanket a judgment of the crowds in the Square.

149

"It's Ben I'm really angry with," she told herself. "Ben who's being stupid—no, not stupid. Selfish and impulsive and ridiculous —oh, Patty, why did you have to get involved with such a tiresome creature? Why not find someone sensible and realistic and practical, like Gordon, to fall in love with?"

"Because Gordon's so dull," the silent voice that was herself whispered back. "Be honest. You love him—he's your son, and you love him, but he's dull, dull, *dull*. Patty couldn't have chosen a man like Gordon, any more than Gordon's dreary little Jean could have chosen a man like Ben." Harriet had to admit that angry as she now was with Ben, she liked him. He had a great deal of— something—charm? magnetism? personality? The words were banal, but there were no others she could think of.

Irritably she pulled her attention back to the here and now, and stamped her feet a little to restore some warmth to their numbness, and smiled encouragingly at Catherine, who had turned to look at her.

"Wish you hadn't come, Catherine?"

"They do make you feel a bit like God's grandmother, don't they?" Catherine said grudgingly. "There can't be many here who're over twenty-five. Most of them look as though they're only here for the beer—silly giggling schoolgirls over there—see them? If they aren't just here to pick up boys, I'm a green parrot. Mad, every one of them! Nothing in their bird brains but sex and boy-friends and yearnings for a lifetime spent up to their elbows in scum at the kitchen sink. Don't tell me they give a tuppenny damn about the uses of medical research."

"Oh, I don't know," Harriet said mildly. "Some of them look quite serious to me. Look at those there—see? The boys with the placards. Can you read what they say?"

"Not quite—just a minute—" Catherine rooted in her pocket, and produced a pair of mother-of-pearl-encased opera glasses, which looked absurdly incongruous in her sensible green woolen-gloved hands, and peered through them at the knot of banner-carrying people far across the Square. They were clustered very close to the plinth of Nelson's column, and some of their placards were almost hidden by the haughty upraised head of one of Landseer's huge lions.

"Move, you silly ass—" she muttered. "Ah, that's better. Hmmph! Pretty predictable stuff. 'The Third World Wants Food Not Miracle Cures for the Rich.' A debatable point, that, though the sentiment's worthy I suppose. And—there's another—just a minute—ah, *there* it is. 'Population Policy Should Come First.' First before what, I wonder? And—"

"May I borrow those for a moment, Catherine? I think I've spotted Ben—see? Up there on the platform, by the microphone?"

Catherine gave her the glasses, and Harriet focused and peered and there, neatly framed in the circle of her vision, was Ben, his face split by that characteristic wide grin as he stared upward. She swept the glasses upward, too, and saw just above him a long streamer being unfurled and stretched from one lion to the other. The words were big enough to be seen easily without the glasses.

"WE WANT MORE ROOM AT THE TOP!" they cried in huge red letters. And below it, in only slightly smaller black letters, "Get the Dead Wood Off Our Backs. They Are Killing the Young Generation."

"I don't quite see what that means," Catherine said. "I thought this was all about the evils of money and the rest of it. Didn't you?"

"I think they're starting. By God, Catherine, how many people are there here, do you suppose?"

"Only God could count them. Twenty thousand? Thirty thousand? Who can say? It's a hell of a lot, anyway—and noisy, too."

Someone had started to play an electric guitar up on the platform, and four people—their gender quite indistinguishable, for all wore fringed dungarees, heavy sweaters and long matted hair that obscured their faces—clustered around the microphones and began to shout or chant or sing; it was hard to be quite sure which.

Below them, in a straight line across the front of the platform, Harriet could now see the bobbing blue helmets of policemen, and seeing them remembered the storybooks she used to read to the children when they were small, with their pictures of Toytown policemen with square wooden heads and stiff wooden bodies; but there was no coziness about those policemen down there; *they* didn't laugh fatly in exchange for half crowns.

Some of the crowd below and around them joined in the singing, and some sections were swaying from side to side, like lumbering circus elephants decked in gay colors and tinsel; it felt to Harriet like the moment just before the curtain went up in a theater; an atmosphere tense and expectant, but with an underlay of emotion that could become either approbation or hostility. Which it was to be would be determined not by the people who were to feel it but by the show they would see when the curtain rose.

The singers and the guitar player at the microphones stepped back, and Ben moved forward to fiddle with the mouthpiece in an effort to raise it high enough for his great height, but still had to stoop to get his lips near enough.

"People," he shouted, and the amplifiers shrieked, and a huge laugh went up, and Ben grinned and fiddled again, and shouted once more, "People! Friends! You know why we're here today—"

Again his voice was drowned out, this time by a rapidly developing roar as an airplane swept close in overhead, looking like a cardboard cutout against the gray sky, and the pigeons swooped indignantly at the noise, and then settled again on the surrounding buildings, to huddle patiently and wait for the crowds to go away and give them back their Square.

"There's your bloody science for you," Ben boomed cheerfully into the microphone as the noise died away, and the crowd laughed, and swayed good-humoredly.

"Obviously a waste of time, all this," Harriet thought irritably. "It's more like an open-air pop concert than a genuine political meeting."

"You know why we're here!" Ben's voice echoed across the square. "All of us, young and healthy as most of us are, are here because of people who are old and ill. People who are dying. Old ill people always have died, always will. Jeez, they've got to! No one can live forever, and no one should! But we're here today on account of the way history's being changed under our eyes! On account of the way science is being used to stop old ill people dying. But only *some* old ill people—the *rich* ones. These capitalist spiders aren't content with robbing the workingman blind, stealing his bread and his labor and his health. Now they're using the money they're sitting on and clutching with their wrinkled grabby greedy claws to take life away! Not just to buy lives for themselves, but to steal it from the poor and the young—us! Because believe me, brothers and sisters, believe me, when one old rich man is saved from the death he is more than ripe for, he steals from one of us the right to live, to breathe, and eat, and *be*. They're shouting the odds about birth control, these slimy capitalist spiders, these stinking vultures, these useless dried-up hulks who've forgotten what life is about, they're telling *us* we have too many children, that the world is overrun with humanity, that we've got to control our young blood and let our genes die with us—but *they* are going to use the bread that they stole from us to make sure they go on living—and living—and living—until they and their kind have choked us all off the face of the earth! Now I tell you, science was never meant to be used for the old and greedy! It's for real people, the people who matter, the young ones with blood in their bones, and guts, and bellies! It's to make the world a better place, not to silt it up with dead wood! I speak to you as a scientist, as a biologist, who knows, really *knows*, what a danger is staring us in the face.

"For the first time in history, we've got the answer to one of the greatest killers of men, and almost got the answer to another. Science can now prevent the disease that leads to heart attacks and strokes, and very nearly can cure the diseases called cancer. The scientist who discovered this reckons the cure isn't sure yet, but I'm here to tell you that I believe it *is*. I know how cautious science is, and I tell you, *as* a scientist that that cure is within our reach. And what does that mean? What will it mean? I'll tell you—it

153

means no more and no less than the end of our species as we know it! Because of this lousy capitalist pig society we've inherited, that our parents complacently tolerated, and that we've got to put right —because of these capitalists, I say, this scientific leap isn't being used to save the young, the poor young who haven't yet had the chance to make their lives of any value, but for the perpetuation of the rotten—the old, the useless and the dried up! But you don't have to listen only to what I have to say about this. Here on this platform there are other people with other points of view—and you must hear them! First, there is Alfred Collins, who you all know—he's been a big man in more ways than one in the trades union movement for a long time! He'll put the point of view of the workingman, the *real* man. Then to prove to you we're not just one-eyed and intolerant, which they're always saying we are, we've got one of your actual capitalist spokesmen here—an economist, Angus Tirrell. Not himself a capitalist, but someone who really understands how money works, and what keeps the wheels of this society turning enough to crush us all under its weight! And then anyone else who wants to join in can have the use of our microphones— because this is a public meeting, a *real* public discussion, not one of your phony put-up television shows!"

He threw his arms up and stepped back, and the crowd shifted and roared, and Ben shook his hands together, boxer style, over his head, and moved to one side to make room for a big man, round and heavy-bellied and with his jacket buttons strained to such a degree that Harriet could clearly see the gaps between them, even from her place far across the Square. He too held his arms up high, and the crowd roared cheerfully back at him, and he stood there beaming at them in a very avuncular fashion until the sound dropped a little, and he could shout into the microphone.

"Brothers and sisters," he cried. "Brothers and sisters, you haven't heard the half of it yet! There's more and worse in all this science stuff that'll really make you sit up and think again, and think hard, you'll see! Brothers and sisters—"

"They're a damned fraternal lot!" Harriet muttered, and Catherine grinned briefly and nodded her agreement.

"—implications you've never imagined possible," the fat man across the Square was booming. "Even if these treatments was to be made available to the man in the street, you and me, and your mums and dads, do you reckon that'd be the end of the boss class's exploitation of the masses with them? Don't you believe it! I can tell you, if we don't watch it, don't keep a close control over the uses of these cures, we're goin' to be back in a state of life that hasn't been known since the industrial revolution shackled us all to the moneymakers! I've been doing a bit of investigating on my own part, doing some sums, and when you hear what answers I got, you're going to be very sick—very sick indeed! Just listen to this!"

He reached into his breast pocket and pulled out a sheaf of papers, and moving very deliberately took from another pocket a pair of glasses, and finally started to read into the microphone, but his voice sounded stilted now, with none of the free-rolling ease that had characterized it so far.

"Present life expectancy of the average man in this country, sixty-eight years, or thereabouts. Estimated on the basis of present death rate from coronary thrombosis—"

Catherine winced and tutted softly at his mispronunciation of the word. "—and strokes and all the diseases that come under the heading of cancer, if these treatments is used the estimated added life expectancy of the average man now aged thirty to forty is six years. This means, in real terms, that if the treatments are used for all of us, most people will live to the age of seventy-four or -five and a large proportion would have a very good chance of reaching eighty or more. Within the next twenty years, this would have the effect of greatly increasing the proportion of elderly people in the country to the ratio of about two and a half to one. That is to say, for every worker employed in industry and commerce and agriculture and other activities, there would be two and a half people of such age as to be nonproductive and in need of being supported. Some of these nonproductives will, of course, be children, and as such only temporarily in need of support, but this would account for only the half—that is, there would still be two old people to be supported by every one able-bodied worker."

He folded the papers and put them back in his pocket, and took the heavy glasses off his nose and stowed them away too, and looked impressively from one side of the Square to the other. Only the sound of traffic and the chatter and hiss of the birds perched high on the sills of the buildings around them came back; the crowd stood in a tight mass, no longer moving in swaying clumps, nor eddying and shifting as it had been doing from the very beginning of its formation, just listening.

"Are you beginning to see what all that means?" Collins cried. "I reckon you are! It's not so bloody marvelous to live to be over eighty, is it? Not if it means you're just a burden on other people's backs. I don't know about you young people down there, but speakin' as a man who won't see forty again, I can tell you this—I'd not want to go on in that fashion, being the sort of parasite that's been battening on me and my brothers and sisters in industry ever since I was fourteen and took my first job down a Kent mineshaft!"

The crowd cried back at him, and he held up his hands and bawled above their din, "But don't you fret, don't you worry yourselves! You don't think the bosses'd let things stay as they are, with workers damned near guaranteed to live to be eighty or thereabouts, do you? Not on your bloody nellies!"

Once more the crowd roared, and for a moment Harriet felt a tremor of fear, looking down on the vast animal in front of her with its octopus tendrils at the edges where, antlike, individual people joined in the mass or drifted away to the teashops of the Strand or up past St. Martins-in-the-Fields toward the penny arcades and cinemas and fried-onion-smelling hot-dog stalls of Leicester Square. It was made up of people, small fragile people, yet it had a terrifying shapeliness and cohesion as it rippled and responded down there on the stones of the Square, the fountains giving it its hugely glistening round eyes. But the fear subsided to lie low in her belly as the man on the platform between the bored black lions continued to shout and echo his anger at the animal he had leashed with his words.

"I'll tell you what the bosses'll do! They'll undo the legislation of years, the protective legislation we've fought so bloody hard for! They'll raise the age of retirement for a start! Make the lazy sods work till they're seventy, that's what they'll say. If a fella's goin' to live another fifteen years after sixty-five, then he'd be better off working than retiring, and he'd make a bit more profit for us! Why should we pay insurance and pensions and the rest of it to sixty-five-year-olds when they won't 'ave the decency to die and save us our good money? That's what they'll say. I tell you, cancer and heart disease—they're the best friends the boss class 'as got, always 'as been. Like my brother Ben Shoeman here said—the bosses, the capitalists, they'll use their money, the money we made for 'em, to keep their own lives going, and if they do give us a chance to get treatment, they'll make bloody sure as it's so that we can go on making the money for 'em—and I for one can tell you I won't put up with it! What we want out of all this is *our* chance of life—real *good* life, not just working hours—as well as them. What we want is a proper economic setup that'll make it possible for all of us to go on living comfortable and cared for but not a burden on anyone else, from the retirement age of sixty-five, as it is now. And until the Government can guarantee us that this can be done, these treatments shouldn't be made available to those as can pay for 'em, but only to those as is regarded as entitled to have 'em. People like us!"

A vast cry went up, and Catherine leaned close to Harriet and shouted, "That sounded very confused to me—did you understand it properly? Is he saying the use of curative treatments should be abandoned altogether, or just kept just for trade union members? Or what?"

"I'm not sure—" Harriet shouted back, and tried to move away a little, finding Catherine's closeness suddenly oppressive, but she was crushed on her other side by the thin young man with the beard, and couldn't move. But then, to her relief, another voice came shrilling at them from the big loudspeakers that were strung round the lions' necks and across the base of Nelson's column, and Catherine swayed away from her to lean over the parapet and stare

157

through her opera glasses at the new figure now standing in front of the microphone.

He was a tall thin man, wrapped in a heavy grayish-colored duffle coat, and his long hair blew in the wind as he stood, his shoulders hunched, both hands clutching the shaft of the microphone in a tight grip.

"I'm an economist. Left wing and not afraid to say so. I don't see how anyone with an understanding of the way economics operates in this society can be anything else. Only intelligent thing to be is a Socialist. Only the blind and the self-seeking can be reactionaries. By definition. I'll tell you what all this will mean in economic terms. Can't prove it, of course—I can only think forward and guess, but I make informed guesses, and I'm usually right. Not ashamed of that either! I'll tell you first that Alf Collins is quite right! The capitalist pattern is of exploitation of workingmen. Has to be to work at all! Right, then. Bosses don't want men to die before they reach retirement age—but don't want them to live much *after* that, either. A retired man is a drag, a waste of the gross national product, a useless nonproductive hulk. That's how capitalism sees the old. You've only got to look at this country's record of provision for the elderly to see that this is true! Inadequate pensions, half-hearted provision for the disabled—a mere nod toward humanitarianism, but no more than is absolutely necessary. So you can be sure that no Government in this country, or in any Western country for that matter, is going to put much effort or finance into medical research of this sort. They can't make any return on it, you see! Where's the profits in research that makes men live longer, to go on needing money and a roof over their heads and food and the rest of it, long after they ought to be out of the way? The sort of research that makes money for Governments is the sort that finds new armaments, that is said to be for defense—defense! That's a lot of rubbish! Armaments to sell to racist white people all over the world that want to kill off their black citizens! There's big money in that, big returns! But other countries aren't going to buy medical research results that'll keep those black citizens alive and well, are they? And this Government isn't going to spend real money on lifesaving for *you*, either! The money'll come from where it's coming from now—the private sector. And the patients'll come from where they're coming from now—the private sector! So what are you going to do about it? What I'd like to—"

Somewhere to the right of him, a section of the crowd had been moving and swaying more than any other, and almost gratefully Harriet began to watch it, and stopped listening to the man at the microphone, who was still shouting in his flat unemotional tones that made all he was saying seem so much more frightening.

Suddenly the crowd opened at the edge, near the platform, and a man shot out of the mass and started to climb awkwardly up toward the platform. Watching him, Harriet was reminded irresistibly of a film she had once watched of a human ovary shedding an egg. It had burst a bubble on its surface and ejected the tiny object in just such a peremptory fashion, and she giggled, almost hysterically, at the incongruity of the memory, and Catherine turned and looked at her, surprised. But Harriet shook her head, and stared down at the platform, at the man from the crowd who was now pushing at the duffle-coated figure by the microphone.

For a while there was a great deal of confused noise, as the microphone whooped and shrieked, and the figures on the platform gesticulated angrily at each other, and then Ben moved forward and picked up the overturned microphone and shouted, "We said it was a public meeting, and so it is—and there's a man here can't wait till our invited speakers are finished—so okay! So we'll treat him with a courtesy he didn't offer us, and give him the platform. Here you are, fella—go ahead—" and he shoved the microphone at the other man and stepped back.

There was a moment of silence, as the little man by the microphone stared at it, and Harriet could almost feel the fright that was in him, knew it had suddenly overcome the anger and urgent need to join in that had carried him from the anonymity of the crowd to the loneliness of the platform.

But then he seemed to find his anger again, and he pulled the

159

microphone closer, and spoke, and at first his voice was high and shrill and rather tremulous, but it strengthened as his anger rose higher, fed by his own words.

"Make me—sick—sick and tired. Sick and tired, all this high-flown rubbish! You kids—you think you're the only ones as ought to live? 'We Want More Room at the Top!'" He flung one arm up toward the streamer and its slogan that flapped lugubriously above his head. "What *you* mean is you want euthanasia for anyone over forty—you reckon we're all dead, all of us that aren't wet kids like you lot any more! Well, I'll tell you, it's some of *you* as ought to be cleared out of the way! Shoved into the army, like we was at your age! You wouldn't be here, all you greedy bastards, if it wasn't for the likes of me, and the poor sods as is your parents! You lot ought to be made to *work*, instead of being given our hard-earned money to sit around in your universities doing nothing, just dressing yourselves up and being immoral and making revolutions and trouble!—No, *you* bloody shut up! We've all listened to your socialist rubbish—now you lot listen to some common or garden sense for five minutes—"

Some of the crowd roared and shouted its approval, far more shrieked anger and jeered insults, but Ben and Collins waved their arms and gesticulated at them, and the sound dropped enough for the angry man at the microphone to be heard again.

"As for all this rubbish about old people and the rest of it—the trouble with everyone today is they want spoonfeeding! I don't see why old people shouldn't work if they're fit for it. I'm not asking for special treatment on account I'm fifty-five—and I won't when I'm sixty-five nor seventy-five, neither! If I can't fend for myself when I'm older, then I don't want no one else doing it for me. There's no reason why the Government should stop people as is careful and has a bit of cash from spending it as they want. If I or anyone of my family got one of these diseases, I'd reckon to pay my own way to treatment, not expecting to have it done for me—and there's plenty of people in this country that'll feel like I do! But I'll tell you this much—there'd be no problems about making this treatment cheap and easy to get for everyone if it wasn't for the money we have to waste on you students and your like! There you sit, fat and greedy and wicked, having sex all over the place in your colleges and the rest of it, eating up the money we've made to keep you there, we who left school at fourteen to earn our own livings— put you lot in the mines and the factories and the army and we'd have plenty of money for medical research and the old and—"

She stopped listening, stopped straining to pull the sense of the words out of the booming echoing roar, and leaned against the coping in front of her, feeling the sick beating of her own aorta as the ridge of stone pressed into her belly, and fixed her mind on that. It was all so crazy, so impossibly crazy. How could those men down there across the Square be saying all this to these thousands of people? How could *she* be any part of it, she with this heavy beating in her middle, she with her cold numb feet, she with her hair blowing so irritatingly in her eyes? How could the long tranquil unnoticed months of work in the shabby laboratories at Brookbank, in the odorous rooms full of animal pens, in little James Ferris's side ward, have led to all this? It was crazy, and she wanted to shout at them all and tell them so.

"Are you feeling all right?" Catherine said in her ear, and she turned and stared at her, and after a moment shook her head.

"I shouldn't have come," she cried above the noise.

"You've got to know what they're saying," Catherine shouted back. "Better to know than—"

"I don't *want* to know! It's all—I don't understand it all, and I don't want to. It's making it all so horribly complicated. I just did a job of work I wanted to do, that was all, and now—listen to them!"

A great roar had gone up, and the crowd below them shifted and eddied, and there was a sharp increase in the pressure against her back as the crowd behind them craned forward to see why, and she felt a sudden panic rise in her as the stone edging pushed harder into her belly and the weight at her back increased.

She bent her shoulders slightly, and shoved backward, and tried to turn, to push her way out of the crowd, oblivious of the individuals who made up the mass, aware only of the malevolent weight of bodies, and using her elbows and her knees almost viciously, managed to turn her back to the platform in the Square, to move toward the National Gallery.

"Here, 'old 'ard—who do you bloody think you're kicking? Clumsy great bitch—keep your bleedin' knees to yourself, or I'll—" He wasn't young, not one of the straggly thin boys in ridiculous clothes, but an ordinary middle-aged man, almost invisible in his mediocrity with a neatly knotted tie under the grayish collar of his shirt , his narrow shoulders encased in a dark brown suit, and his thin dull hair plastered against his skull by the wind. The violence of his speech seemed doubly menacing because he looked so meek; and she stared at him, at his face so very close to hers, and felt the hundreds of other faces pressing on her from each side; and the panic inside her rose and bubbled and spilled over.

"Let me out—I've got to get out—get away from me—" she shouted into the face, and with an immense effort moved her arms, now almost pinned to her side by the weight of the crowd, and brought one elbow up and thrust it at the narrow chest in front of her, and the shock of the impact ran up her arm and jarred her shoulder painfully.

"You stinking cow! I'll kill you for that—" The meek face split and the words came at her like pebbles that stung her skin, and she ducked her head, and then, suddenly, Catherine's hand was on her arm, hard and firm, and she could hear her shouting "Make way—please make way—she's ill—give us air—let us through, please—" And even as Harriet heard the words she knew it was true. She was ill, and she did need air, and she felt a wave of nausea rise in her and was grateful for it and let herself droop against Catherine's restraining hand.

She was moving forward now, propelled by Catherine, and the crowd shifted and swayed unwillingly in front of them, but it did open a narrow pathway, and they edged forward, Catherine repeating over and over again, "Let us through, please she's ill—let us through—ill—"

And then they were stopped, quite sharply, as a woman's face detached itself from the mass and peered closely at them both, and then more closely at Harriet, and she shrilled in a high eager voice, "She ought to feel bloody ill, she should. She's that scientist woman that was on the telly. It's her that started all this, with her cures for rich people!"

Harriet stared at her, at her red-faced excitement and narrow-eyed triumph and said, "What?" hearing the note of heavy stupidity in her own voice, and the woman turned her head from side to side eagerly collecting people to listen to her, and cried, "I never forget a face—never, not in all my life, and that's who she is, I'd take my dying oath. You're that doctor that found this cancer cure, aren't you? You are, course you are! I never forget a face, never have. I thought you was wonderful, I did, till I knew what you was up to. Making cures for those as can pay—people like you ought to be—"

"It is—she's bloody right—it is—take a look—"

"No—don't be daft—let the poor old thing through—you can see she's ill—let her through—"

"But it *is* her—I never forget a face. I tell you it *is*—ask her and see if I'm not right—"

Catherine was pushing her forward again, trying to get away, but once more the pressure built up before them as the woman who had recognized her pushed against them, bringing other people to push too, and they were pinned, totally helpless, caged in the heavy smell of human bodies.

Harriet closed her eyes and leaned back against Catherine, for one brief moment wondering whether to try to slide into unconsciousness, but she had never fainted in her life and knew that any attempt to pretend to do so would fail; and then the thought of actually fainting, of being even more helpless in the middle of this weight of people, so filled her with terror that she snapped her eyes open again.

Somewhere to her side she felt rather than saw someone pushing successfully through the crowd toward them, for people moved back, pressed against each other, turned their heads away, and stopped looking at her, stopped craning over each other's shoulders to see her.

"All right—all right—what's the trouble here? Someone ill? Make way there, if you please, make way—"

"Toytown," Harriet said stupidly, and giggled, and Catherine looked anxiously at her, and squeezed her arm, and then awkwardly raised her own arm to put it round Harriet's shoulders, and Harriet said gratefully, "Thanks—"

The policeman, looking just as wooden under his helmet as the row of distant policemen she had seen in front of the platform across the Square, was close beside her now, and he too put a protective arm across her shoulders so that she was wrapped in a shell of safety between the two of them, and again she giggled softly, because it was all so silly.

"All right, now—let's use a bit of common, shall we?" the policeman said good-humoredly. "Make a bit of a way through for an ill lady, now—come on, make a way—"

"It's her—" the wager woman shrilled. "Her that invented the cure—"

"Yes, I know," the policeman said cheerfully. "And badly in need of a cure for herself at the moment, so make way there—"

And then, at last, they were out, the three of them, there in the bustle at the edge of the pavement as curious faces peered at her and a self-important little man in the black and white uniform of the St. John's Ambulance Brigade who had appeared from out of the paving stones, or so it seemed to Harriet, was leading her away toward an ambulance across the road, officiously holding up one hand at the traffic as they went.

"I'm all right—" Harriet protested weakly. "Really, I'm all right —I just got a bit scared. The crowd was too much."

"Of course, of course," the policeman said soothingly, and she wanted to giggle again; he sounded exactly like one of the nurses at Brookbank coaxing a recalcitrant patient to submit to unwanted treatment. "But we'll just have the ambulance people check on you—just to be sure. Er—" he looked down at her, his face now less wooden as a ripple of curiosity moved across it. "Was she right, that woman back there? Are you the—er—?"

"Yes," Harriet said. "Yes, I'm Dr. Berry. I shouldn't have come."

"You're right there, madam. I don't think you should have, neither. Well, we'll get the boys to check you're okay, and then I'll see you well out of the way. Just to be on the safe side. They're stirring 'em up a bit back there—" And he jerked his head toward Nelson's column.

She stood at the steps leading to the ambulance door and listened to the booming voices, to the confused shouting, and felt as much as heard the anger and frustration and aggression that were there and nodded.

"I was frightened," she said. "That's all that was the matter with me. I was just frightened."

"You still are," Catherine said flatly. "I am too, now. But we had to know, didn't we?"

"Yes. I suppose so," Harriet said, and climbed wearily into the ambulance.

12

"FOR GOD'S SAKE, Patty, haven't you *any* influence with him? You're as good as married to him, and I would have thought—"

"Then you thought wrong," Patty said sulkily, and moved awkwardly on the lumpy old couch to sit hugging her knees and glowering across the room at her mother. "I don't own him any more than he owns me. We don't dig any of that sort of—people belong to themselves. No one else—except the state, of course. And what Ben wants to do and what Ben believes in are his affair. I can't try and make him be different just because—well, I can't."

"You mean you won't."

"Same difference."

Harriet stood up, partly because, as always when she was anxious, she felt the need to move about, and partly because of the extreme discomfort of the chair she had been sitting in; why did squalor and discomfort so often go hand in hand with left-wing thinking and advanced ideas? she wondered briefly, looking with distaste at the dirty floor, the unwashed dishes on the table, the general griminess of the big room, twilit now as the afternoon dwindled away.

"Look, Patty, I'm not asking all that much of you, am I? I'm not doing one of those 'I'm-your-mother-and-after-all-I've-done-for-you scenes,' but—"

"Aren't you?"

"No I'm not! Damn it, why are you so hostile? What's happened to you? You've always gone your own way and followed your own ideas, but you've never been quite so—"

"Oh—I'm sorry." Patty relaxed a little, and leaned back against the wall, shoving a pillow behind her back. "You could be right—in fact, to be honest, I know you are. I mean, I've—well, you might as well know. I've already tried."

"Tried?"

"Yes! Do you think I like seeing Ben stirring up trouble that involves you? I want him to stir up trouble, of course—I'm as revolutionary as he is—and I'm with him most of the time, but I don't want *you* to be involved! I know what it must be like for you, and I know how you must feel about it. But he just says—well, it doesn't matter."

"You might as well tell me."

Patty looked at her, miserably, and after a moment made a face and to Harriet it was as though she were a gawky eleven-year-old again; that was the way she had always looked when something got too complicated for her to handle.

"What is it, love? Isn't it working out properly for you? When I saw you together at that TV thing I thought—you looked right, you know? I certainly wasn't particularly surprised when Ben said you were living together. Has it gone sour already?"

"No—not really. Only because of you. All this."

Harriet frowned. "You're arguing over me? That's stupid! I never saw myself as the sort of mother who caused—"

"Oh, it's nothing to do with you *personally!* That's the whole thing! Ben—he's very advanced politically. Very. He's working hard for revolution and he's right of course—I know that. But I'm —I'm not as political an animal as I thought I was. I don't want him involving you and your work in his—in what he's doing. But he says that personalities don't come into it. Revolution and social change—they can't take notice of private feelings and bourgeois relationships, and—so that's why I'm here and not with him there in the middle of it all. I can't shout the odds about what you're doing, and the way your work'll be used. Not the way Ben's doing it."

"But how can he go on building his whole argument on what he knows isn't true? You did tell him I'd turned down Sefton?"

"Oh, of course I told him, but until it's public knowledge he's going to assume you *are* going to Whyborne. And there's nothing I can do to stop him." There was a pause. "Nothing I will do. He can't make me join in, but I'm not going to fight with him any more over you. You might as well know it, Ma. When you have to make choices—" she shrugged.

"What's he going to do after this? Are there going to be more of these meetings? More fuss in the *Clarion?*"

"I can't say," Patty slid off the couch to cross the room to the cluttered sink and cooker in the far corner. "Can I make something for you? Tea or something?"

"No thanks. Patty—"

"He'll be back fairly soon, I imagine. Are you—are you going to wait and talk to him yourself?" Patty said over her shoulder, with a studiedly casual air.

"You're asking me not to?"

Patty looked at her briefly, and then her glance slid away and she shrugged again. "It's up to you. I've told you, I've refused to have anything more to do with it. I won't argue with Ben about you."

"Or with me about him? Well, that's reasonable enough. And I don't suppose there'd be much point in it if I did talk to him, would there?"

There was a pause and then Patty said, "No. I don't think there would."

"Then I'll go. I don't particularly want to make things any more difficult for you than they are just for the sake of it. And I'm too tired for an argument. I'm just sorry that—oh, well. What's the use of talking? Where did I put my coat?"

"You'll be all right?" Patty crossed the room to take Harriet's coat from the back of the door. "You're sure you've got over it all? I hate to think of you—I mean, you're sure Catherine'll be waiting to see you home?"

"For God's sake, Patty, I know I'm your mother, but I'm hardly decrepit yet! Don't be so solicitous all of a sudden! It's insulting."

Patty laughed awkwardly. "Well, yes. Sorry again! All right, then. Er—we'll be in touch."

Harriet nodded, and Patty opened the door for her, and then followed her from the almost dark room to the head of the stairs, dingy with grimy paint, and smelling faintly of unwashed lavatories.

"Anyway, you know where you can reach me when you want me, don't you? You've got the laboratory number. I'm there most evenings till seven or so."

"Yes." Harriet started down the stairs.

"And there's Gordon, of course, he'll cope if you need anything."

"Stop apologizing!" Harriet said lightly and stopped and looked back at Patty, standing there in the dimness with her face almost hidden by the hair falling over her cheeks. "I told you, I'm not decrepit. And I know how it is."

"I suppose you do. We're very much alike in some ways, they say. Not in others, though. Look, Ma—"

"Yes?"

"Oh—nothing. Take care. The bottom step's a bit shaky. It's an old house—"

"Yes. I'll take care. Goodbye, Patty."

She sat beside Catherine in the rattling train, swaying with the movement and watching her own reflection in the black window, and tried not to be irritated by the knowledge that Catherine's anxious gaze was fixed on the back of her head. Catherine had always been strongly partisan toward Harriet in her absurdly feminist fashion, but now it seemed to have crystallized into an intensity of concern for her as a person rather than for her work that was embarrassing at best, alarming at worst. Life was complicated enough, heaven knew, without having to cope with doglike devotion from one of her staff. She moved irritably in her corner, and closed her eyes.

"Did it help, going to see Patty?" Catherine said.

Without opening her eyes Harriet said shortly, "No," and then felt guilty about being so peremptory and opened her eyes to look at Catherine and smile at her.

"No," she said more easily. "The poor girl's in love. What can she do? You were right, of course. He *is* a revolutionary and he's very thorough about it. So there's nothing Patty can do to persuade him to find another way to stir up trouble—foment unrest, isn't that what they call it when they're talking about strike leaders? Anyway, that's the way it is. This meeting won't be the last, by any manner of means. He's going to get all the mileage he can out of it all."

"So now what?"

"Oh, I don't know, Catherine! Why ask me? I should have stuck to my original decision and laid low and done nothing. What good has it done, going to that blasted meeting and then going to see Patty? None at all. So please don't ask me. I just don't know."

She reached home with a deep sense of gratitude that made her feel very old indeed. She stood just inside the front door hearing Catherine's car hiccuping away into the silence of the East Anglian winter's night, and looked at the last flickers of firelight crawling busily on the ceiling and furniture, listened to the hiss of the burning wood, absorbed the smell of floor polish and wood ash and coffee and almost wept with need of it all. Security and the comfort of known things—she had never before realized on so keen a conscious level just how much they meant to her.

Mrs. Davies was sitting sprawled in the armchair in front of the fire, her heavy legs stuck out awkwardly in front of her, fast asleep. As Harriet moved into the room and took off her coat to put it down on the big polished table, she stirred and then woke fully and jumped stiffly to her feet in alarm.

"Oh. Dr. Berry, you gave me that much of a fright! I didn't hear you come in, my dear. I must have been right out of this world, that I must! Not that I'm to be blamed for it if I was, I'll tell you that, my dear! A proper old devil he's been tonight and you might as well know it. Run me ragged he has. Worse nor any babe, but there, these old 'uns—all the same, aren't they? I remember my old aunty—she looked after her man's dad—must have been ninety, and he—"

"Oh dear, Mrs. Davies, has he been tiresome? I am sorry."

"Well, not altogether his fault, I daresay. Not feeling too proud,

170

I'd say, in hisself. Looked quite pale and peaky, he did for a while there. Not that he didn't work hisself up to it—I'd be a liar if I said otherwise. Got into a right paddy there, he did. Wanted you here, and was very put out when he heard you was up to London. Reckons you're plotting to put him away, you know, but I said to him, the doctor won't do no such wicked thing so you stop your soft talk—but it made no nevermind to him. Went on and on about it, he did, so by the time I got him up to his bed he wasn't feeling so proud in hisself. Anyways—"

"Well, you'd better be on your way, Mrs. Davies. I'll go up and take a quick look at him but I daresay he's all right. And thank you for waiting so late."

"That's all right, my dear. Makes no nevermind to me, not of a Saturday. By the time my old chap gets back from his darts and the rest of it, it's long gone midnight, so not to fret yourself. I'll see you on Monday, then, as usual. Good night to you—"

He was lying hunched up in his bed, the light on the bedside table still burning, and as soon as she opened his door, quiet as she was, his eyes snapped open and he stared at her malevolently.

"I'm not going!" he shrilled at her. "Not going, and you can't make me—do you hear me?"

"No one's going anywhere," she said wearily. "No one at all, so stop worrying. I just came in to see how you were. Mrs. Davies said you hadn't been too well."

"Had a pain, I did," he said, pathos immediately taking the place of his suspicious anger. "Nasty it was. But that old bitch—she don't care. I could die, here on my own with her, and she wouldn't care, and you'd be glad, wouldn't you? Rid of me then, you'd be."

"Oh, don't start that again now. Not tonight. I'm tired out—absolutely exhausted right the way through to my middle, and I can't face your damned—" She stopped and took a deep breath, seeing the narrowing of his eyes, the sideways look of suspicion that had crept across his face, and was immediately furious with herself. To treat the old man with anything that sounded like anger was asking

171

for trouble; it might be self-indulgent to let herself say what she really wanted to say to him, but it was a shortsighted self-indulgence. Inevitably such episodes led to hours, if not days, of difficulty with him.

"I'm sure Mrs. Davies meant no harm. She told me you got into a bit of a temper with her, and that upset you, but you know she means well, and she likes you—" she said carefully, and went to the bed to tuck the covers in on each side of him.

"No she doesn't! Wants me out of the way, like the rest of you." Petulantly he twitched the covers out of her hands, and his voice rose shrilly. "She's in league with you, and don't you think I don't know it—I'm not as daft as you think I am, and don't you think it. I may not have been a fancy doctor like you, but I made my son into a doctor, good enough to marry you, fancy though you may be. I told his mother at the time, I said to her, our David, only the best'd be good enough for him, and doctor she may be, but is she the best, that's what I want to know."

He grimaced suddenly, and raised his left shoulder awkwardly against the pillow, and his mouth opened wider as he gasped noisily, and arched his back slightly. Then, clumsily he lifted his right hand to reach for his other shoulder and arm and held on to it.

For a long moment they remained very still, he clutching his upper arm and breathing with obviously painful effort, his mouth stretched to a caricature of a grin, his eyes screwed so tightly closed that a tear was pushed out of one corner to slide across the bridge of his nose; and she, just standing and looking at him.

Her tiredness was so much a part of her now, so deeply bitten into her that her very bones ached, and she felt curiously remote from what was happening—aware of herself standing there, watching the old man in his pain, counting each painful breath he took, but not in any way involved with him.

And then, he relaxed, and his grip on his upper arm lessened so that his hand slid down the sleeve of his pajamas, incongruously gay in yellow and white stripes, and his head rolled a little to one side, and she thought, "Resuscitation—if he's stopped breathing I ought to do the kiss of life."

172

But even as she thought of it, her gorge rose, and she knew she couldn't. She could no more bend over that old body, no more open her mouth and fix her lips round his to breathe air into his lungs than she could lift her feet from the ground and fly around the room. She actually retched as she thought of it, as she looked at the flecks of spittle on the lax bluish lips, the wrinkled yellow skin around them.

And then he moved his head again and turned it on the pillow until he was looking up at her, his eyes blank with surprise, and after a moment he said hoarsely, "Pain. I told her . . . pain. Keeps coming . . ."

The reaction in her was so immediate and so sharp that her legs felt as though they weren't there, and she let herself fold a little at the knees and hips, not knowing how she was controlling her own muscles but letting it happen; and she was sitting on the bed beside him, staring down at him, one hand on his wrist as automatically she counted his pulse. She did not know how she had brought herself to put her hand on him, to actually touch him, didn't know how she had been able to control the wave of revulsion that had climbed into her throat, for she was still filled with a violence of feeling that she could not even name, could not fully recognize for what it was. And she did not want to name it, for she knew, somewhere deep inside the exhaustion that was coloring everything she did, that it was an emotion that she had always had but had always hidden from.

He was cold and clammy to the touch; his pallor had given way to a tightly localized flush, high on his cheeks, that looked as though it had been painted there. She felt his pulse chattering against her fingertips, noting the thin reediness of it, the uneven hurrying speed, and automatically estimated its rate; a hundred and forty or thereabouts. "He's in shock," she thought, staring down at him. "He's really ill."

He moved a little then, and again grimaced and his right hand moved a little and then relaxed.

"It hurts," he said, and it was like a whimper. "Pain, told her . . ."

And then, at last, she came back to herself, and the exhaustion was damped down as it had to be, and she stood up, almost briskly, and spoke in the special doctor's voice she had learned to use those long years ago when she had been in general practice; she rarely needed it now, at Brookbank, but when she did, there it was, ready to jump out of her mouth as though a button had been pressed somewhere.

"Now, listen to me. You aren't well, and I'm going to get some-one else to come and see you—another doctor, a specialist. Do you understand? I'm going down to telephone, and there'll be another doctor coming to see you soon. I want you to lie here *very* quietly until I come upstairs again. Do you understand? You're not to move at all."

He looked up at her, and the blankness shifted in his eyes, be-came a gleam of triumph and he said in the thick hoarse voice that had so revolted her, "Told you. Told her . . . said I was . . ."

"And you're not to talk. Complete rest, you hear?" She made herself lean over him, and smooth the sheet across his chest, and then she went to the door, and looked back for a moment at the narrow head on the pillow, the eyes thinned to a slit but still watching her, and nodded at him and went down to the telephone.

The next few hours were a confused and even more exhaustion-filled blur. Sam Lemesurier came up from Brookbank without de-mur, and she was intensely grateful to him; she should have called the G.P., a slovenly bumbling middle-aged man who served the village and the surrounding farms and cottages, but she had never used his services, knowing perfectly well how useless he really was. Sam could have objected strenuously to being hauled out to an old man who was nothing to do with him, in the middle of a bitterly cold night, but he just grinned at her when she opened the door to him and began to thank him, and pushed past her to dump a couple of heavy bags on the sitting room table.

"I brought the ECG machine, since you were so specific about the diagnosis. Though quite what we can do if—however—here, you look rough, Harriet! Christ, you could have had a coronary yourself from the look of you."

174

"I'm tired," she said, almost guiltily enjoying his concern and finding reassurance of her personal value in it. "I was up in Town all day and got back to this. I'll do a bit longer yet, though."

Sam spent almost an hour with the old man, fiddling with the leads from the machine, making his tracings, and checking the readings. From time to time, George slid into uneasy sleep, only to wake again with a grunt of pain after a short while, and Sam gave him some morphine, jabbing the needle into the skinny arm with cheerful callousness.

"I can get an ambulance to take him up to Brookbank tonight, Harriet. He ought to be monitored and we've got the gear there, of course—but we can't keep him long, you know that? We're research, not clinical, though we've got those few beds we can use for short-term things. Theo did Geraldine Cooper's varicose veins for her in one of Geoffrey's obesity beds, I know, but this—even for you, I doubt Oscar'd let the old boy stay with us above twenty-four hours or so."

"I'll worry about that in the morning," she said. "I'll talk to Oscar, or Theo maybe. But right now—if you can get him in, I'd be grateful. I couldn't trust myself to stay awake and watch him the way I am—and if he had another—"

"Well, of course! Christ, you don't think I'd leave you alone with him, do you? Even though it's not too bad, you know. It's almost certainly on the anterior aspect. I can't be sure till I get another tracing tomorrow, but it looks anterior at present. And if the clotting can be controlled he's got every chance of doing well. Mind you, he's pretty old for it—what is he? Seventy-seven? No stripling. Still, he could do well. We'll see more clearly tomorrow."

13

SHE SAT in the square-backed armchair in Sister Hornett's kitchen-cum-office, leaning back against the embroidered cover with its incredibly red and yellow and blue flowers and faceless poke-bonneted be-parasoled crinoline lady, all worked by Sister's own hands during slack times on the ward, and tried to feel like herself. It was a necessary exercise, because ever since she had got up that morning, she had felt strange, almost depersonalized, as though all the things that were happening to her and around her were only shadow events, projected onto a screen like a film or a television play.

Perhaps this sense of unreality was due to the fact that she had been alone in the cottage when she woke that morning? She explored the idea with an almost academic detachment and found it had some sense in it. For as long as she could remember, she had never been alone in a house. First as a child at home; then as a student living in college; then marriage to David, and the children. For a moment her mind tried to keep to thoughts of David, but she pulled herself away, almost violently. After that, the children and George and sometimes Oscar. How long since she had woken and known that she was totally alone, surrounded by empty rooms?

But that wasn't what had made her feel so odd this morning. She realized with shame that the solitude had given her intense pleasure; that the memory of the previous night's events, crawling into her sleep-sodden mind, had brought a wave of luxurious relief.

"Think of yesterday," her mind whispered. "Think of yesterday and the men who talked—"

Obediently, she tried to think of yesterday and the men who talked, but all she could do was re-create a set of jerky images of mouthing figures far away on a distant platform, none of which had any relevance for her.

There was a sound outside the half-open door, a rattling and a faint creaking as a trolley was wheeled along the corridor, and a voice cried irritably, "Mind that offside wheel, Joe—silly bastard 'oo left that there ought to be shot—" and the sounds dwindled away to culminate in a distant rattling of iron gates and the whine of a lift going away down to the bottom of the building.

And then as the sound died, she felt a movement of air, chill but stuffy, across her face, and smelled the pure breath of hospital—formaldehyde and disinfectant, flowers and floor polish, vegetables cooking and lavatories and carbolic-soapy bathrooms—and she knew why she felt as she did. And this time she gave up the attempt to push the memory and the thoughts away, but let them take her over completely.

She had sat, like this, in a hard-backed chair in a ward Sister's kitchen-office, waiting to be told what she already knew. She had listened to the business of hospital going mindlessly on, to trolleys and lifts and noisy porters, smelled the smell of hospital, and had tried to plan a future that didn't contain either David or her father. She had been ready for it, in a way; no one could live in London in wartime and not be ready for it, but the readiness had not been enough. Now it had happened, it was so much bigger, so much emptier, so much sillier than could ever have been foreseen.

And she had, at that moment in time, done the most positive thing she could. She had pulled the door shut, there inside her mind, and had hidden behind it, refusing to look out and beyond into the silly huge emptiness. So that when the young doctor came, with Sister hovering behind him, their eyes filled with a sick mixture of pity and macabre curiosity, and "thank-God-it's-not-me," to tell her in deep embarrassment that they were both dead, she had nodded composedly, and taken the death certificates and gone away to the babies and to George, leaving the door closed firmly on the future.

Now, sitting in that future in another ward Sister's office, separated from that day by twenty-five years, she knew she had never opened the door again, not for herself or even for the children. She

177

had lived a day at a time in everything personal, including her dealings with Oscar. Only where work was concerned had she ever planned forward. In a working context she could think not only of tomorrow but of next week, next month, next year, five years' time. But not otherwise.

So this morning she felt as she did because once again she had reaffirmed the existence of the closed door within her mind. It was comforting to have reached that understanding. Now she knew, she thought she felt a little better and almost experimentally opened her eyes to look round the room, at the old-fashioned scrubbed wooden dresser with its rows of thick white cups hanging on hooks, its stacks of plates and trays and biscuit tins, at the small urn hissing lackadaisically in the corner beside the sink. She ought, surely, to feel right now that she knew why she had felt so odd.

But it made no difference. The sensation of being split in half, of being partly nonexistent, was still there, and irritably she stood up and went to the window to stare out at the sprawl of buildings four floors below her, at the corrugated iron roofs of the pathology lab complex, the weather-stained felted flat roof of her own unit, with its little boiler house alongside that had to be constantly watched to make sure the temperature in the animals' rooms didn't drop to chill the monkeys to expensive death.

Somewhere in the very pit of her mind there was real knowledge, understanding that was trying to get out and scream at her, but even as she tried to reach it, she knew part of herself was still grimly hanging on to the knob of the door—

"Silly *bitch*," she said aloud, and turned round, moving with a heavy purposefulness. If she stayed here alone much longer, she would go screaming mad. High time someone came and told her what was happening.

But as she reached the door, it swung open wider, and Sam and Sister Hornett came in.

"Sorry to keep you, Harriet. You didn't need to come up here, you know, I'd have phoned you as soon as—"

"I know. But I had to," she said shortly. "Well?"

178

"Well—" Sam began, and then the door moved again, and Theo put his head round.

"Sister Hornett? What's all this I hear about—Harriet, *there* you are!" He came in, squeezing past Sister Hornett who primmed her mouth and looked offended, to stand in front of Harriet and peer into her face. "My dear girl! Have you been up all night? You should have called me!"

Sam laughed with a heavy and patently false jocularity. "I told her last night she looked a bloody mess—been cavorting around the metropolis all day, she told me." He grinned at her, his head on one side. "Come on, Harriet! Don't look so stricken! I know the old boy's ill, but he's not dead yet, is he? And even if he were—damn it, woman, he's old enough to tot up his accounts, after all!"

"How is he this morning?" she asked curtly. "Have you done the rest of the ECG's you wanted?"

"Yes, I've done them." Sam, embarrassed, became immediately businesslike. "And as I thought, he's had a couple of small anterior infarctions. I've done a little preliminary work into the state of his arteries, and they aren't too good. Not bad for his age, of course, but still, there seems evidence of a good deal of atheroma. So he needs anticoagulants and very careful nursing if he's not to have another serious go like last night's. If he does, he won't do, I'm afraid. But at present, he's not too bad. His heart is basically sound, considering the rest of the clinical picture. So there you are."

"Will you continue treating him here, Dr. Lemesurier?" Sister Hornett asked. "Because you know, the bed situation . . ."

"Um. I was coming to that," Sam said. He leaned back against the dresser and took a crumpled cigarette pack from his pocket to fuss with lighting one, not looking at Harriet. "I could ask Oscar to let me keep him, Harriet, but to be perfectly honest with you, I'm not all that keen. I was happy to come out to you last night—I mean, Christ, I wouldn't wish that slob from the village on my worst enemy—but I'm having enough trouble keeping my series going with useful patients, as Sister here could tell you, and there's nothing at all that—well, I know how you feel, Harriet. He's a relation of yours and all that, but from my point of view, a man of seventy-seven isn't much use either as research material or—" He shrugged. "I'd rather you got him in somewhere else, if you can. I'm sorry."

"I gather he's not fit to be looked after at home?" Theo said with a certain eagnerness in his voice.

"At home? Well—I suppose he could, eventually. But he needs some inpatient treatment, to get the anticoagulants stabilized, and, of course, until these infarctions heal. After that, with full-time nursing, maybe."

"Then it means a home," Theo said with decision, and looked at Harriet. "No, don't argue with me, Hattie. Not now, anyway. You can't possibly arrange to care for him full-time at home, so that's all there is—"

"Mr. Fowler, have you ever *tried* to find a place in an old-age home for an ill old person?" Sister Hornett said crisply. "Because if you had, as I did before my mother died last year, you'd not even mention the possibility. They're not interested in invalids. Not unless you can pay, that is." She looked at Harriet, her eyebrows raised a little. "Twenty pounds a week and more some of them ask—and the nursing they get—well!" she sniffed. "I wouldn't look after a cat the way they look after some of their old people, I can tell you. If Mr. Berry needs careful nursing, he'll not get it in any old-age home *I've* ever come across."

There was a silence, and then Sam said awkwardly, "I'm sorry, Harriet. But I don't see—look, I'll call Peders at the District General, if you like—"

"Thanks, Sam. You've been marvelous," Harriet spoke almost mechanically. "But I need time to think about this. Could I—how long can you keep him here, under treatment?"

"Oh, several days, easily, and to hell with Oscar," Sam said heartily. "Glad to oblige. But we'll have to do something right away about making other arrangements. It can take a lot of time to fix up."

180

He grinned at her and came across the cluttered room to pat her on the shoulder, spraying cigarette ash over his waistcoat as he moved, and she smiled at him and thanked him again, and he went away, Sister Hornett surging importantly behind him, leaving her alone with Theo.

He sat on the edge of the table in silence for a while, watching her as she went again to the armchair to lean wearily back against the crinoline lady.

"So what are you going to do, Hattie?" he asked gently. "You must see now that you'll *have* to do something. As for what Sister Hornett said—well, I daresay that was all a bit exaggerated. I've no doubt I could manage to find somewhere. Anyway, found it will have to be."

She shook her head, not opening her eyes. "No, Theo. Sister Hornett was right—about the sort of care there'd be, I mean." She looked at him then. "If I put him into a home, even supposing we find one that will take him, he won't get treatment. He'd just be left to die."

Theo looked back at her, his face expressionless, and then said carefully, "He is, of course, a very old man."

"Which means you think, like Sam, that the sooner he dies the better? Is that what you mean?" She could hear the note of hysteria in her own voice, and very deliberately damped it down, and said more coolly, "No, I'm sorry, Theo. Whatever you think, I've got to get him somewhere he'll get *treatment*. Not just a bed to lie and wait for death in. Treatment, proper nursing—"

"Hattie, may I suggest we don't discuss it right now? You're somewhat overwrought, I suspect, and I'm not sure you can give this the sort of thought it needs. Tell me, had you done anything about lunch before you left home to come here this morning?"

"Lunch?" she stared at him, and then laughed to cover her embarrassment. "Theo, I'm sorry. I'd forgotten it was Sunday. Will you forgive me if we miss out on the usual arrangement? Because frankly, I didn't—"

"Did you think I was asking for a meal, for God's sake?" he said

181

angrily. "Really, Harriet, you do me less than justice! There's something remarkably self-centered about someone who can produce an insult like *that*, under the—" He stopped, and then shook his head. "As I said, you're overwrought. And I'm not precisely myself at the moment either, come to that. Forget it. All I wanted to be sure about was that there would be no meal burning to a crisp at the cottage if I took you into King's Lynn for a pub lunch. That's all. You've obviously not eaten at all yet today, and you're green with fatigue. So come along. After lunch, we can talk about George and his future." He stood up and smiled at her. "Come along, now."

She shook her head. "I can't leave Brookbank, Theo. Gordon—I called him this morning. He's driving down this afternoon."

"Oh. Oh, of course. I'm sorry—I should have realized. And Patty?"

"Not Patty," she said stiffly. "There's no point in calling Patty." She looked up at him and saw the puzzlement in his face. "Because of Ben," she added. And then shook her head again. "You don't know about that, of course. I—later, I'll try to explain."

"Later, then. But you still need lunch, so come on. We'll have it here. Even Brookbank's roast lamb and boiled cabbage are better than starvation."

"Well, I must say, I can't think what you're being so stubborn about, Ma. You've got Theo's considered opinion on George's whatyamacallit—prognosis," Gordon said crisply. "If that's the word. Anyway, whatever your own medical opinion may be, it's clear to me that both Theo and Lemesurier feel the best answer would be some sort of home where nursing can be provided. Now *you* say you won't consider it. *Why?*"

Harriet was staring out of the common room window, watching the gate porter desultorily dragging a rake across the uneven gravel of the almost empty car park. "Do you know something?" she said abruptly. "I hadn't really thought about it until today. I haven't addressed him directly for—oh, years. I never *call* him anything. Isn't that extraordinary?"

"What?" Gordon said, a little irritably.

"George. I call him 'George' when I'm talking to you, Theo. I call him 'your grandfather' talking to you and Patty, but I never call *him* anything. Only 'you.' Are *You* all right? Do *You* want anything? You, you, you. Which makes him nobody at all."

"Really, Ma, I know you had a rough day yesterday and that last night—but do, please, let's stick to the point. I have to be back home tonight before eight. We've got people coming."

He caught Theo's glance. "Well, for heaven's sake, I couldn't suddenly cancel a business dinner party, could I? It's—anyway, Ma, could we please come to some sort of decision? Now? Because once we have, I can get on and—"

"I've come to a decision," she said, and came back to her chair, to sit in it rather straight, with her hands crossed in her lap. "I won't have him put in a home."

"Oh, for God's sake!" Gordon said disgustedly, and threw himself farther back in his own chair, and crossed his legs with a snapping energy that he could only just control. "Sometimes you talk as though you're getting senile too! What do you—?"

"And you've made another decision to go with that one," Theo said softly.

"Yes." Harriet looked down at her hands on her lap. "If it doesn't—if I can't arrange it, then I'll think again about your suggestion, both of you. But I must try first."

"Try what?" Gordon asked, and his voice was heavy with controlled irritation.

"William Ross-Craigie," she said, and for the first time looked directly at Gordon. "At Whyborne. This is his sort of case, and if he'll take him, I want him to go there."

"Are you out of your *mind*?" Gordon cried after a moment of stunned silence. "Have you the remotest idea how much that'd cost? Come on, Ma, be your normal intelligent self, do me a favor! Where does that sort of money come from?"

"He's got some of his own—not a great deal, but some. And I've a certain amount I could use. And—perhaps you would care to contribute, Gordon. He is your grandfather, after all."

Gordon stared at her, his face blank with astonishment. Then he shook his head, and stood up and began to move a little stiffly about the room.

"Now, look, Ma, I don't want to sound like some sort of ogre, but could we perhaps talk a little common sense about all this? My grandfather is a very old man. I won't ask you to consider at this point the fact that he's also a disagreeable and difficult old man. I'll just say—he's old, is no longer in full command of his faculties, and from my own observations, is getting very little pleasure from his own life. Would you agree with me so far?"

"Yes," she said, and her voice was quite flat and calm.

"All right then. Now, he's had a coronary, and the chances are he'll have more and, let's face it, die of it. He's got the disease that will end his life. It has to end sometime! Now where's the sense in trying to treat that disease? Where's the *logic* of it? Sure, Ross-Craigie could probably get rid of the problem—but what for? To leave a disagreeable difficult old man who isn't enjoying his life all that much, and who is one hell of a burden—no, Ma, I *will* say it—is one hell of a burden, to go on living! How long for? Where's the *sense* of it?"

"And if it were you, Gordon? You who had a disease like this? Would you want the people around you to add up the accounts as you're doing?" she asked in the same flat voice.

"But I'm young!" he cried. "I'm not thirty yet! That's the whole point of what I'm saying. God damn it, the man's almost *eighty!* Why waste money sending him to Whyborne? Why should every penny he's saved all these years be frittered down that drain? Why should your money be used up in such a stupid fashion?"

He was still walking about the room, and both Theo and Harriet followed him with their eyes as he went on, almost as though he were talking to himself rather than to them.

"I've got Giles to think of—and the next ones, whenever I decide there'll be next ones, and I can't go pouring money that by rights belongs to them into the life of a useless old man! And I don't see how you can suggest wasting your money that by rights belongs—where's the *sense* in it? It's bad enough to see you wasting your time here, earning a fraction of what you should, instead of making sure there'll be something to keep you going later on, without suggesting—"

He stopped quite sharply, and stared at Harriet, and she stared back, feeling the coldness inside her climbing and filling her throat with knowledge and the understanding that had been clamoring to escape all day.

"And what about Patty?" Gordon began to bluster. "I don't see her here being asked to *contribute!* Why not? She's earning too— *and* she seems to be being kept by that ghastly Shoeman, so if anyone has any spare cash it'll be her, not me, with a family of my own to support! So much for her so-called liberation ideas! Fine until she has to take a bit of responsibility—"

Looking at him, feeling the coldness and stillness inside her, she could see what she had never really noticed before, or perhaps had noticed but had refused to recognize. She was good at not recognizing things she didn't want to, she thought bleakly, watching his face as he went on and on, explaining, justifying, refusing and excusing. He and George—the same person. The same narrow inturned sort of person. Measuring every tiny value against every potential loss, and coolly calculating the answers.

"Gordon, you really needn't go on," she said with a sudden loud crispness, and he stopped in midbreath and looked at her, while Theo sat with his head drooped forward, his hands linked across his front, and not moving at all. "You can stop right there. I won't ask you for any help with the cost of this. I'm not going to steal from you anything that belongs to you. But I don't share your conviction that George's money is yours by right, any more than that the little I have belongs to you."

"I didn't say that!"

"Not in so many words. But you made it very clear that you think that way, so . . ." she shrugged.

"Look, Ma, is it so terrible to want to see you make some sort of financial arrangements for your own future? You're almost fifty, damn it! Still young, but not that young! By the time you retire, I'll still have a young family—and even if you worked and earned until you were *seventy*, I'd still have family at university, wouldn't I? So I'm taking the long view—is that so wicked? Of course I don't wish the old man dead, but I don't see any sense in spending money on—"

"It would cost money to put him in a home, Gordon," Theo's voice cut in quietly. "Perhaps as much as a thousand pounds a year. You would have been content to see money spent that way?"

"But the National Health Service—"

"It's getting more and more difficult to get elderly people cared for in NHS hospitals," Theo said, and his voice was still quiet, but a heavy anger lay beneath it, and Gordon shifted uncomfortably. "The only likely service the state could offer in such a case is some limited home help and the like, but it would be your mother who would carry the load. She'd have to do the nursing, she'd have to worry about his care. And, of course, she'd probably have to give up her own work to do all that nursing and worrying. How do you feel about that?"

"Oh, for God's sake!" Gordon exploded suddenly. "I don't *know*. And I haven't time to stand here talking about it interminably in this fashion. Look, Ma, I'm sorry, but I'll have to go. It's a long drive back, and Jean needs my help if—so do as you think best. You know my views, but do as you think best. I'll cooperate in anything you want to do. Just let me know about the bills, and I'll meet them to the best of my ability. All right? I can't say fairer than that. I must go."

He leaned over and kissed her cheek briefly. "I'll call you at the cottage tomorrow, for news, all right? Take care, now—"

And he was gone, with a crisp nod at Theo, leaving them sitting silent and uncomfortable in the diminishing gray light of the common room with its scattered shabby armchairs and overhanging smell of long-brewed coffee and damp pipe tobacco.

"I'm sorry, Hattie," Theo said at length.

"So am I. Very. I should have known, in a way. If I'd thought about it. He was the one who always made his sweets last longest,

186

when he was small." She smiled a little. "He used a pin to pull tiny bits of the inside out of chocolates, to make them last longer. Very ingenious."

"Why didn't you call Patty?" Theo asked abruptly after a moment.

"Because she's made her choices," Harriet said, "Poor Patty! She did try, very hard, I think, but she couldn't quite do it. I'm sad for Patty. But she's made her choices. I'll explain it all sometime."

"She chose Ben?"

"Yes. She chose Ben."

"So, apart from me, there's no one left for you to lean on?"

She laughed gently at that. "A little melodramatic, Theo, my dear, aren't you? I haven't exactly been abandoned in any sudden sense, you know! Gordon and Patty—they've lived their own lives for many years now. I'm quite sure we'll go on having the sort of friendly relationshp we've all three had all those years—nothing's really changed, you know! But thank you, all the same."

"Aren't you angry with him, Harriet? I know I am! I'm not precisely a physical person, but it was all I could do to keep my hands off him! Of all the jumped-up, cocky young—"

"No, I'm not angry. Not with Gordon. I should have seen it long ago. Perhaps I did, in a way. It's odd, you know, all that business in Trafalgar Square yesterday, the things they said." She stopped and grimaced. "But you weren't there. I forgot. You don't know what was said."

"It was very well reported this morning," Theo said dryly. "I know a good deal about it. Was it very grim, from your point of view?"

There was a pause. "Yes. It wasn't very—I got scared in the crowd. Frightened poor Catherine stupid. And then came home, to all this—"

He stood up and moved about the room, switching on the small table lights that were scattered about so that the window's grayness dwindled and flickered into a dark blueness, and she blinked a little in the glare.

"Yes—home to all this. Harriet, I suppose I shouldn't ask you.

I—perhaps the reason I got so furious with Gordon was because he was simply voicing my own feelings, though with a few more fiscal overtones than I had produced. I think it's unnecessary, shall we say, to seek the sort of treatment for George that you're suggesting. Just tell me—why? *Why* do you want to send George to Whyborne? Why are you prepared to spend that sort of money on an old man's disease? I just don't see the logic in it, any more than Gordon did."

She looked at him across the room, and shook her head slightly. She knew why now, knew why she had felt as she had all morning. It had come to her quite vividly, the answer she had been seeking, as she had listened to Gordon and watched him clutching eagerly at his own youth and future, watched him dismissing George's and her own. But knowing it and being able to say it, even to Theo . . .

He seemed to hear her thinking, and stood there smiling at her in his familiar heavy fashion. "You can tell me anything, you know, Hattie. I'm Theo, remember? Not Oscar. You can tell me anything."

"I—" she smiled too then, knowing it to be a glittering silly social smile that meant nothing but disguise. "I wanted him to die last night, when it started. When he had the attack I watched him and I hoped that he was dead. And this morning, when Sam—I was angry with him because he wasn't dead. That's why he's got to go to Whyborne. Hasn't he?"

14

"MY DEAR DR. BERRY! This is a very agreeable surprise! After we last spoke, I was sure that—well, I have no doubt you will understand why I should be so startled to see you this morning and will forgive me."

"Good morning, Sir Daniel," she said stiffly. "You know you owe me no apology. The reverse, in fact. I—er—I didn't know I would see you here today. I came to see William—Dr. Ross-Craigie."

He crinkled his eyes at her with great charm. "I do hope that doesn't mean you don't want to see me?"

She curled her toes inside her shoes in an effort to prevent herself from producing a facial grimace; she couldn't remember ever disliking a person quite as much as she disliked this man, and for so little cause. Apart from a certain smoothness that wasn't really to her taste, there was no real reason for such a reaction. He had, in fact, paid her the very genuine compliment of wanting her to work for his establishment, had offered her a great deal that was very tempting. It was she who had turned him down, she who had made herself a legitimate object of his dislike in refusing to be manipulated by him. So why should she feel as she did?

"Not at all." She knew the smile she produced was a false one. "I had simply assumed that you spent all your time in London, at your newspaper, rather than here. And it's just a professional matter I want to discuss with William."

"Oh, I spend a great deal of time here at present—still setting up, you know! As the administrative head of the establishment, I have to be around, poking my nose in a great deal, until the place is running smoothly, and I can lay my burden on the shoulders of the full-time administrator we've appointed. However, I mustn't talk about *my* problems! You want to see Dr. Ross-Craigie, and see him

189

you certainly shall. Let me take you along to his laboratory and office."

Harriet nodded toward the girl at the reception desk. "Someone's already trying to find him for me, thank you. He knew I was coming, of course. I telephoned him yesterday."

He smiled broadly at that. "Well, actually, I know. He told me." He looked at her with a faintly elephantine roguishness."Forgive me for showing surprise at seeing you? I couldn't resist it—you looked so startled to see *me!*"

He took her elbow in an intimate protective grip and nodded at the girl at the desk, who immediately put down the telephone she had been dialing and hurried to open a door at the far end of the foyer.

"So, shall we?—And we'll go the long way round, if you don't mind. I do so much want to show off our establishment to you. I'm really behaving just like a small boy with a new train set in his Christmas stocking. The reception area, here, now, you like it? We aimed at creating an atmosphere that was welcoming and unclinical. So many of the people who will pass through it will be desperately ill, so of course we would like them to have a favorable first impression."

She looked around at the bleached-wood low-slung furniture, at the brown hessian covered walls and their brightly colored abstract paintings which were in fact recognizable pictures of horses and ships and nudes, at the heavy black-painted iron and rough-stone compositions that alternated on the low coffee tables with carefully arranged bowls of chrysanthemums and ears of barley and polished-copper beech leaves, and nodded.

"It's very nice," she said in a colorless voice, hating all she saw. Like the sort of coffee bar where they give you watery instant muck at exorbitant prices, and offer you minute slabs of soapy cheesecake as though they were conferring the accolade—horrible! she thought viciously, and let him guide her through the heavy door still obsequiously held by the horsily elegant receptionist, who stared at her superciliously through her incredibly long eyelashes, and made her feel extremely middle-aged and dowdy.

190

"Now, we come to the more businesslike part of the establishment. Here are the admin offices—general secretary, you know, and accounts, and purchasing and so on—" he said, leading her firmly along the deeply carpeted corridor, past more wall decorations, this time of the exaggerated collage sort, with pieces of metal and wood and leather projecting out at assorted angles. "I hope you notice the color schemes? The browns and golds of the foyer giving way to the shades of purple we use here in the corridor. Each office has its own individual scheme, tailored to the personality of the occupant. My own, I must confess, is a rather austere black and white—ah, now! Here we come to the really important area, from your point of view."

He led her through a pair of transparent plastic double doors to a complex series of laboratories, all gleaming with chrome and ceramic and concealed lighting, filled with what she knew from her own yearning study of the catalogues to be equipment of the most recent and therefore most expensive design, into rest rooms and study rooms, conference rooms and libraries.

"We thought by providing three or four specialist libraries rather than one large one we would facilitate study for our staff . . ." he murmured as she stared at the fully laden and carefully labeled shelves, at the microfilm equipment in the corner, at the projection apparatus for slides. "One doesn't want to waste valuable scientific time simply for want of a few pounds intelligently spent, does one? Now, here we have something we're *very* proud of—"

He led her into another room, banked with television screens, that had a broad console almost covering one wall, and he began to fiddle with switches. "I'm not absolutely sure how all this works, I must confess."

One of the screens shivered, rolled and settled to show a view of a large laboratory, even more heavily equipped than those she had already seen. "Ah, I managed it! Splendid! That's the main cancer research laboratory. The one you would have had," he said, not looking at her. "This room is a great time-saver. Any one of the staff can come in here and see what's going on in any part of the establishment. Visiting students can sit and watch work in progress. If one really understands all this equipment, it's possible to get close-ups, to observe any corner of any laboratory or inpatient section—"

He flicked another switch, and a picture of a room with a bed, surrounded by a number of pieces of equipment, sprang onto another screen. "You see? We've tried to think of everything."

"It looks like a most efficient spying system," Harriet said with a touch of acerbity. "Heaven help the poor little technician who tried to put his feet up for a lazy half hour! He'd get short shrift, I imagine."

"The equipment, of course, was never intended to be used in such a fashion," he said, his urbanity thinning. "And I doubt it would ever need to be. I don't intend we should employ staff who would ever want to—*steal* time in the way you describe. We shall be paying top salaries and shall select our staff—even the lowliest of porters or typists—with rigorous care—most rigorous, I assure you."

"But you haven't any staff yet, have you? The labs and rooms I've seen are all empty."

"Ah!" His affability returned immediately. "What can I do? I have in fact a great deal of staff for this section on the payroll already. Technicians, statisticians, physicists, computer programmers—you haven't seen the computer yet, of course. A really outrageously expensive piece of equipment, that—but none of them are here yet for a very good reason. I've shown you the cancer research side of the establishment. The heart research side is already very busy, well staffed and active. But there, *that* division has its head of research, Dr. Ross-Craigie. This one hasn't."

He looked at her, his head on one side, and then smiled again and took her arm. "But there, I mustn't go on like this, must I? You'll accuse me of having an ulterior motive—which of course I have! This way, now."

He talked only of inconsequential things as they left the cancer research wing behind and moved across a paved courtyard, in the middle of which a ferociously modern brass fish vomited water into a broad green bowl surrounded by banks of very luxuriant plants, and into the heart research division. And she knew why he chat, tered on, giving her neither need nor opportunity to answer him. He wanted her to see all she could, to recognize the lavishness of his establishment, and marvel.

And of course she did; she couldn't fail to do otherwise. Everything she saw was so incredibly expensive; even the breath of deodorized warm air that occasionally made itself felt as they passed a corridor junction spoke eloquently of the most costly air-conditioning and heating systems. To have equipped so remarkable a place in so short a time—for even if he and his consortium had started work on it the moment they had heard the first rumors of Ross-Craigie's success, they had had only a few months in which to operate—was a remarkable achievement.

And though she didn't want to, she could not help comparing what she saw with the conditions under which she had worked at Brookbank for so long. The converted sheds that were her animal pens, the cobbled-up consoles and gauges she had to use to control her treatments in the oxygen chamber, the collection of antiquated calculating machines which was the nearest they had to a computer —it was pathetic compared with this lavishly flowing cornucopia of facilities.

And the staff, too; this part of the establishment was humming with activity, people bustling along corridors, doors swinging open to show heads bent industriously over lab benches, and uniformed nurses pushing wheelchaired and trolleyed patients from place to place. They had a cheerful purposeful look that again compared very favorably with the slightly weary ploddingness most of the Brookbank staff displayed. The only thing that was the same, she noticed with a spark of amusement, was the way they reacted to the sight of Sir Daniel. They showed the same wary, slightly scornful expressions of respect the Brookbank staff displayed when Oscar made his somewhat majestic way along the corridors.

"And here we are!" Sir Daniel said, opening a door and ushering her into an office that was decorated in vivid splashes of orange and lime green. "Dr. Ross-Craigie's sanctum. I'll let him know you're here. Do sit down and be comfortable, won't you?"

He crossed the room to a door on the far side to ring a bell that was fixed to the jamb and came back to help her out of her coat, bustling a little as he settled her in a chair.

The door opened, and William Ross-Craigie came in, his hair vigorously sleeked back across his scalp, his square glasses clamped to the bridge of his nose in a way that announced, as clearly as if he had worn a placard, "I-am-a-scientist-at-work!"

"Harriet, my dear!" He took his glasses off with a sharp twist of his wrist, shook hands with her with dispatch, replaced his glasses, and sat down in a straight-backed chair, all in one cohesive movement. "Splendid to see you! What can I do for you? You said a professional matter, so we won't waste any of our time with superficial chitchat, hmm? What's your problem? I'll do all I can to help, of course."

She blinked, and then stared at him, curiously tongue-tied. It had seemed the obvious and sensible thing to do, yesterday, when she had phoned him and asked to come here this morning. Why should she feel so uncomfortable now? Damn it, this young man had been her junior at Brookbank for a very long time, had deferred to her not only because of her seniority but because of her greater scientific ability, and she had accepted that as her due. Yet now, facing him sitting there in a laboratory coat that was almost insulting in its brilliant whiteness, its perfect crispness, she felt as though she were the one who ought to be humble before him. The realization of the effect his posturing had had on her made her angry, and she spoke with a sharpness she had not intended.

"I don't, of course, intend to waste your time, William. I came to offer you a patient. I hope you don't feel patients are too time-consuming to interest you."

"My dear Harriet! Did I give that impression? Do forgive me! I'm afraid we work at a much greater pace here, you know. Greater than you're used to, that is. It's one of its charms for me—so like the Stateside places I worked in. So invigorating, you know what I mean? Not a bit like dear old sleepy Brookbank!"

"Not that sleepy. I've managed to stay awake long enough to do some useful work there, anyway. For my part, the quality of work one does depends not so much on external conditions as on the inner equipment one started out with. You can't get that out of expensive catalogues."

"Oh, oh, oh!" Ross-Craigie beamed at her, and looked over her shoulder at Sir Daniel, and it was as though he'd winked at him. "Do I detect a note of green old jealousy there, Harriet? My dear, I *do* understand! The first time I was shown over an American laboratory, I *hated* them for having so much! And this place—my dear, Whyborne is twice, *three* times as good as any lab I ever saw there. But I'm sorry to have been so . . . well, you know how it is! Every place has its own special . . . ambiance, you could say, and I guess ours here is of pace and worthwhile effort and endeavor. You can't waste a second here, not one second. There's something in the very fabric that makes you give of your best the whole time, won't let you waste a thing."

"Then I won't waste your time. Simply, William—"

"If this is a professional matter, perhaps I had better go?" Sir Daniel said from behind her.

Ross-Craigie looked up at him, and his eyes narrowed slightly. "Mmm? Oh! I see!—er, no—no, please don't! I'm sure Harriet won't object. After all, you're heading this establishment, so you have a professional involvement with anything that happens here. And I'm sure you won't mind, Harriet, when I tell you that Sir Daniel sits in on a great many of our scientific discussions. He asked us to try to—er—help him learn as much as he could about research, and this is an excellent way to do it, isn't that so, Sir Daniel?"

She looked over her shoulder at the older man's face, and as he caught her eye he looked as near to embarrassed as she had ever seen him. Clearly Ross-Craigie's sledgehammer tactics were intolerable to him, in his guise of subtle manipulator, and she almost smiled. There was at least some humor to be found in this situation.

"I don't object in the least," she said. "How could I, after all? I'm in no position to do so."

There was a pause, and then she said baldly, "I want you to take a relation of mine, William. He had an infarct on Saturday night, late. Sam Lemesurier gave him emergency treatment, and he's in Brookbank now, but he can't stay there. I want him to come here for treatment by you. I've brought his notes. You'll find all you need there—cholesterol levels, ECG tracings, complete blood picture." She took the package of notes from her handbag, and gave them to William, who settled back, immediately surrounding himself with concentration, and began to read.

She watched him for a moment, and then shifted her gaze to stare out of the big picture window at the gentle Buckinghamshire countryside beyond. It was a gray and white day, with traces of frost still edging the stark black arms of trees, and trailing narrowly along grass verges and under hedges. She could see birds minutely wheeling and swooping far away, over a tractor absurdly small as a child's toy which was turning a yellowish stubbled field into a rich deep brown, and wished, quite violently, that she was a bird or a worm or a tractor driver, anything rather than herself sitting here listening to Ross-Craigie concentrating over George's notes.

"He seems to have done very well, considering," Ross-Craigie said eventually. "But he's an old man. And in my experience, I'm afraid, the older patients need more treatment. They haven't the stamina to tolerate concentrated effort, you see. One must tailor it to their individual needs. For him, I'd say at a guess, he'd need a couple of months here." He looked up at her, and then bent his head to fold up the notes and carefully replace them in the folder.

"I see. Well, if necessary. Will you take him?"

He frowned a little, and sat turning the notes in his hand, tapping each corner in turn on his knee. "Are you suggesting he come here as a normal patient, Harriet? That we book him a bed in the unit? I have a couple of beds to offer, but—" He looked up at her very directly. "Look, Harriet, forgive me for saying this, but I know your situation—goddammit all, I worked with you long enough. I know the sort of miserable money they pay Brookbank people, even the best of them. Can you afford to send a patient here? Or has he enough money of his own?"

"Afford? I don't know. I'll do my best. George has a little of his own, and I'll subsidize the rest."

Ross-Craigie looked up at Sir Daniel again, and raised his eyebrows. "Over to you, Sir Daniel. I really can't—Harriet, Sir Daniel is the person to talk to about this. Not me. I can only discuss the research side, the treatment side."

"Is Mr.—er—I don't know the name of the patient we're discussing?"

"Berry. My father-in-law."

"Ah, yes. Mr. Berry. Is he a—how shall I put it? Is he a worthwhile patient from your point of view, Dr. Ross-Craigie? Can you treat him successfully?"

Ross-Craigie nodded. "Oh, yes. Almost undoubtedly." He kept his eyes fixed on Sir Daniel who was still standing behind Harriet, out of her line of vision. "I must tell you, Harriet, that these notes, slender as they are, indicate a patient who would respond well to treatment as long as enough time was allowed, for his general frailty, that is. But as I said it would mean a good deal of time."

"How much?" Harriet said baldly. "Not time. How much money?"

There was silence, and then Sir Daniel moved across the room, to stand with his back to the window, so that his face was partially shadowed.

"The cost of a month's treatment of a coronary patient here averages out at somewhere between a thousand pounds and fifteen hundred. I imagine, from what Dr. Ross-Craigie says, that in this case it would be nearer the greater figure."

"Undoubtedly," Ross-Craigie murmured. "And as I said, a *couple* of months."

"And we do have a major problem here," Sir Daniel said smoothly. "Independent though we are of Government pressures, we are of course subject to the rules of—ah—our own making. We had to make a firm statement of intent at the very start if we weren't to jeopardize the very existence of this establishment. We knew, full well, that if we did not make such a rule, so sensitive are

197

we—our staff—to the needs of patients, that we would—um—shall we say, we would be likely to accept every patient who came for care, irrespective of his ability to contribute the cost of that care. And within a few months, generous as was our foundation sum, we would be bankrupt. This must not, of course, be allowed to happen. To destroy a potential power for good of the sort we have here at Whyborne, by misguided philanthropy aimed at individuals rather than at the mass of need, would be—"

"You're saying that people who cannot pay will never be treated here. That the *Clarion* was right, in saying that this place is to be used only for the very rich?" Harriet cut in. "Let's be direct and not waste any time!"

"Then, yes. That is what I am saying. I don't like to be put into a defensive position on this, but so many people hold such woolly sentimental views that totally ignore the real practicality of the situation, so many people show absurd and unthinking emotion when they hear that a medical establishment does not intend to become the sort of useless place a charity institution inevitably is—consider the National Health Service—that I find I *do* produce a defense, almost automatically. In fact, it is not so much a defense as a statement of good intent. However, that is not the point—"

She stood up and smoothed her skirt with both hands, and buttoned the jacket of her suit, keeping herself busy so that she need not look at either of them.

"Then there's no point in any further discussion," she said, and her voice sounded thin and flat in her own ears. "I can't, of course, afford to pay three thousand pounds. We just don't have anything approaching that sum available. So there it is. I'll have to find some other way of looking after my father-in-law."

"Well, now, let's not jump to conclusions!" Sir Daniel said, and there was a note of jocularity in his voice that made her look up sharply. He was smiling at her, his head on one side in what she was beginning to recognize as one of his most characteristic poses. "Do wait and hear the remaining content of our statement of intent. We wanted to attract the finest staff to our establishment.

Wanted to offer them the best we could, not only in working conditions, equipment, facilities and the rest, but in salaries, staff welfare, and—um—allied matters. So as part of our constitution it is laid down that treatment for members of staff and any one member of their family they nominate should be quite free of any charge."

15

SHE NEVER KNEW how she managed to drive back to Brookbank without smashing the car and herself with it; from time to
time she became aware of herself driving, noted road signs and
traffic lights; from time to time she was startled to find she had
reached a particular point on her route. But for most of the long
hours she was lost in a welter of thoughts that ran round and round
in her head like mad mice.

He had offered her lunch, offered a car to drive her to the nearest station, had done all he could to make her feel important to
him; it had reminded her of the way David's mother had behaved
when she had first visited their home; but that thought brought
back into her mind the core of her dilemma—George. What was
she to do about him? What could she do that would be right for
him, and right for her, and right for Oscar and—

And so it had gone on as she drove through the drooping twi-
light and early darkness, and by the time she reached the short
stretch of side road that led from the main highway down to the
driveway and the gates of Brookbank she was stiff and numb with
that sort of edgy fatigue that forbids sleep and relaxation but that
continually creates more exhaustion with its demands for conscious
attention. She wanted, quite desperately, to crawl into a hot bath,
to drink a great quantity of hot tea and then to creep into bed to
stay there for days on end. But she had to get back to the unit to
see how George was.

And, she remembered with sudden guilt, to check with Catherine and John on the day's work, and the state of the animals. Not
even when Patty had gone down with a severe attack of measles
and had had to be admitted to the local hospital, or when Gordon
had nearly killed himself on his bicycle and had needed half his
scalp sewn up in the casualty department, had she been so remiss
about work, so wrapped up in her personal concerns.

But then, she thought bleakly, I wanted them to get well. I did the best I could for them, and wanted them to get well, and got on with my work while I waited. But this time, it's different. This time I have to keep making decisions.

She swung the car into the short twisting driveway that led to the front gates, and braked sharply, peering ahead through the dimness, puzzled about something but unable to realize for a moment just what it was. And then she noticed that the lights that were strung along the curving old roadway were dark, and realized at the same time that they had been out on the other road as well. Ever since she had left the highway, she had been driving only by the car lights. She strained her head to one side, and listened, and was even more puzzled, for somewhere ahead of her there was noise and confusion and other lights that should not be there.

She got out of the car, moving awkwardly in her cold weariness, and stood still in the darkness, smelling the heaviness of rotting leaf mold and damp earth, and listened. The car engine chugged softly beside her, but above it she could hear confused shouts and a sort of high yet hoarse chanting, and she thought confusedly: it sounds like a lot of drunken monks playing about with their plainchant. And then, irritated at herself, she shook her head and got back into the car. Whatever it was, she'd never find out here, out in the darkness of the road.

She put the car into gear and slowly moved forward to curve around the last bend of the driveway; ahead of her should have been just the porter's lodge flanking the gates, the single light suspended from the arch of rather rusty iron which was all that still remained of the original design, put up by the Georgian petty squire who had built the house, burning above her. It should have been dim and quiet and peaceful, and for one brief moment she thought she was half-asleep and seeing things that weren't there, so startling was the sight before her.

The driveway seemed to be paved with a mass of people, seething and rolling and heaving under smokily bright lights that were blazing flames that seemed to leap out of the crowd. She blinked at their haloed brilliance, feeling the cruelly sharp light almost piercing her tired eyes, and then peered again, and saw the flames came from old-fashioned naked torches which were being waved about by a few people. There were probably no more than half a dozen of them, but in her tiredness they seemed multiplied many times over.

The sound was even less understandable here than it had been a hundred yards up the driveway; the chanting was louder but just as confused, the shouting angrier but no more comprehensible. Irritably she wound down the window, and put her head out and shouted, "Get out of the way! Let me through—" but her voice was lost in the din.

She tried shouting once more, and then angrily wound up the window. Whatever nonsense this was, she wasn't going to sit in a cold car in her weary state a moment longer than she had to; she was going in to see George, was then coming out to drive home, and she didn't give a damn one way or the other about all this, or what it all meant.

Once more she put the car into gear, and began to inch forward, at the same time putting one hand firmly on the horn so that it blared full-throatedly; and after a moment she kicked the switch beside the accelerator pedal to throw her headlights forward.

Before her the crowd shifted, and turned, and flowed backward to separate and then re-form behind her, and she realized with a sudden fear that she was surrounded by bodies again, just as she had been in Trafalgar Square; this time there was a shell of car between herself and them, but still they pressed sickeningly against her, and she could see faces peering in at the windows, and even as one of the torches was thrust so close to the windscreen that she flinched against its brightness, she felt the car rock as someone climbed onto the hood.

Panic rose in her, sharply and with a sick familiarity, and she put her hands up to her face and shouted, "Go away! Go away!" But the noise outside was so great that she could only just hear her own voice. The car began to rock again, and terrified, she shrank back even farther in her seat, and her foot slipped on the clutch, and the car, still in first gear, gave a convulsive jerk forward as the engine stalled, and she felt a sick thump and grinding under the wheels. And then, there was almost silence outside, though a few voices from the back of the crowd produced a desultory shout or two.

Suddenly a voice that came from very near her right ear, muffled by the closed window yet still clearly audible, shouted, "The fucking bitch—she's run 'im down—get 'im out, someone, get 'im out, and then we'll show 'er—"

The car rolled again, moved, and she sat in terrified rigidity as it was bodily lifted and then dropped a few feet farther back, to shake her like an egg in a box as it hit the ground with a jarring impact. All she could do was sit still and tense, her hands clawed into fists at each side of her face, her elbows held against her body so firmly that the muscles in her arms and across her shoulders trembled painfully.

Somewhere in front she could feel almost more than see activity, as a shape was lifted from the ground in front of her wheels, and carried away into the crowd, and then she saw the big gates open, and the crowd surged forward, and flowed through it. But then there was a shout from her right again, the same voice that had shouted before: "'Ere! Come back, you sods—we'll do this first—" and the crowd turned and shifted and came back toward her, torches leaping and flaming in her eyes.

It started almost gently, affectionately, a side-to-side rocking that was almost pleasant, and for a moment she relaxed her arms and shoulders, tried to put her hands down on the wheel to hold on, but then, quite sharply, the rocking accelerated, became vigorous, angry, vicious, and she was thrown from side to side of the car, helpless and feeling her gorge rise as terror took over. She couldn't hold on, couldn't tell where she was, where there was anything to hold on to, only fending off the walls of the car as they came, in strict turn-and-turn-about rotation, to hit her, to thrust at her, to stun her with their impersonal blows.

It seemed to stop almost as suddenly as it began; the car was still, and she was lying half-sprawled across the passenger seat, and then the door opened behind her, and she shrank against the crumpled smelly old leather under her cheek, terror rising higher in her.

"Move over, for Christ's sake," a voice said, and she turned her head and peered bewildered into the confusion of lights and darkness and said stupidly, "What?"

"Move over, you idiot! I'll drive you in—get out of the *way*—" And almost viciously, he shoved her hard, and she lifted her right leg awkwardly, flexed her knee, and dragged herself out of the driver's seat and across to the far side to sit crumpled against the window, her shoulders hunched and her hands up to cover her head.

"It's all right," he said, and she turned and peered again as the engine coughed and then started, and the car almost leaped forward. This time the crowd moved away, and let it pass, and looking at Oscar's face in the darkness, she thought, for one brief second, that he was sorry; he had wanted very much to hit someone with that furious thrust.

And then they were inside the gates, and the car was moving more quickly, swerving around corners, along the narrow ways between the buildings, the twisting ways around the Establishment that they all knew so well, but which always confused visitors. Behind them the sound thinned, became no more than a distant crying, and then the car stopped outside the stores entrance, and Oscar turned off the engine to sit with his head up, listening. But all they could hear was that remote calling, nothing nearer, and he nodded sharply, and got out, to come around the car and open her door to help her out.

"Not too bad," Theo grunted. "Bruises, of course—or there will be by tomorrow morning, but no more. How are you now?"

"Bloody," she said, and moved stiffly, wincing at the pain in her back, across her shoulders, down her sides.

"You're sure there's no real harm done?" Oscar's voice was sharp, and he turned away from the desk, putting the phone down with a clatter. "The police should get that lot cleared fairly quickly

—it wasn't as many as it looked. They're sending an ambulance from the District General for the injured man, and if Harriet needs any further care, she could go too. Sure you don't want any—"

"No," Theo said. "She's had a fright and a bit of a thumping. That's all."

"That's all?" she began to giggle, stupidly. "Theo, you are— you're the outside of enough. That's *all*? I feel like—"

"I know. But why the hell you didn't just reverse out of the driveway and head for home and phone in from there, I'll never know. To go and deliberately drive at an angry mob is asking for it!"

"I didn't know it was an angry mob," Harriet said, and now she felt some of the fatigue the excitement had kept battened down creeping up again, chilling her aching arms and legs, icing her belly to solid numbness. "I didn't know anything. I hooted and went forward and I suppose I thought they'd move, if I thought at all. The man—the one I hit—"

"Fractured femur and a few crushed ribs. No other damage I could see."

She breathed deeply and tremulously. "I thought I'd killed him."

"So did I. Watching from the lodge window, I thought—that's all I did. I thought." Theo raised his head, and looked across the room at Oscar, his eyebrows up. "There's your actual man of attack and action, you know. I was thinking, *now* what do we do, how do we get Hattie out of that bloody car and in here, and dear Oscar shoots out for all the world like a cross between Superman and Tarzan, and lo and behold, brings in the terrified maiden. Well, hardly maiden—"

She looked up at him, and could see the anger in his face, and pitied him; all the help he had ever given her, obviated in his own eyes by one action of Oscar's. She knew how he felt, and pitied him deeply because it had happened, and yet knew she despised him for it too, just a little. Had she ever foreseen such a situation, had she been asked to guess which of them would behave in so

205

physical a fashion to help her, she would have been certain it would be Theo. How dare Oscar behave so uncharacteristically? she thought with a spurt of anger. And then realized how stupid she was being, for wasn't Oscar the most physical man she had ever known? Was not her relationship with him on an entirely physical level, while that with Theo was based on thought, shared thought, planned thought? They had in fact behaved very characteristically, both of them. And she smiled up at Theo from the depths of the armchair in which she was stretched and said softly, "Not to fret . . ."

Oscar was moving restlessly about the office, his head thrust forward, and he said petulantly, "There's plenty to fret about. Of all the stupid—" Above him, the lights flickered, and he looked up. "For God's sake, is the emergency generator going now? I couldn't—"

"Changing over," Theo said. "They've probably managed to do something at the power station." He went to the window and, standing to one side of it, peered out carefully. "They've gone, I think," he said after a moment, and opened the window to lean out into the cold darkness and look toward the main road far away to his left. "Yes," he said. "Road lights are on again."

"Shut that bloody window. It's cold," Oscar said, and Theo pulled his head in and slammed the window shut with an angry snap of his shoulders.

"What is all this?" Harriet asked from her armchair, and she knew she sounded dreamy and a little remote, and was glad of it. The aching was easing now, and she felt warm and almost relaxed as the exhaustion that had been building all afternoon became a shell inside which she could hide.

"Oh, a lot of Communistic rubbish!" Oscar said. "That's all. But my God, they can—"

"Not entirely, Oscar," Theo said. "Not all those men are Communists by any manner of means. And I'm not so sure it'd be such a terrible thing if they were. I—"

"Look, Fowler, I'm in no mood for any of your needling and coat trailing and childish playacting, do you hear me? I've had a bastard of a day, and all I'm short of is—just stop it, will you? If you've anything to say that's constructive, then by all means, but do me a favor, and shut up otherwise. Right?"

From the edges of her dreamlike state, Harriet could see that Theo felt better, that his anger at himself and Oscar was lessened, now that Oscar had displayed his own anger, and she was puzzled. Because he showed his weakness, because he showed he's frightened of what's going on? That must be why, and smiled inside herself. I'm getting to be a very clear-seeing person, she thought with owlish satisfaction.

"Harriet wants to know what's been going on. Would it be suitably constructive to tell her that there has been—how do they put it—ah, industrial action, that's it, industrial action, *possibly* Communist-inspired, but by no means an entirely Communist affair, and that it's all because of her and her work?"

Now she felt herself fully awake and completely aware of what was going on around her. "Based on my work?" she asked sharply.

"Well, yes, since Fowler has—" Oscar breathed a heavy gust of annoyance. "It's all this bloody stuff that cheap tabloid paper—the same stuff as all that ridiculous haranguing in Trafalgar Square over the weekend."

"Ben," Harriet said dully.

"What?"

"Ben. My—Patty's—Ben Shoeman. He's—he finds what I'm doing useful for his revolutionary purposes." She produced a curious sound, half-snort, half-giggle. "Isn't that ridiculous? Me, rallying them to the ramparts—or is it the lampposts? I really don't know."

"You're dead on your feet, Harriet. I think you'd better get to bed. Look, you can't go home tonight—" Theo came to help her to her feet. "There's no guarantee they won't go there, and—well, you stay here. You can have one of the spare staff rooms, I imagine."

But she resisted his tug on her arm. "What happened? You'll have to tell me before you can get me to go—"

"The local power station," Oscar said impatiently. "They got a notion into their Neanderthal heads that we were treating what they're pleased to call 'stinking rich capitalists' here. So they pulled all the plugs out or whatever it is they do when they have a wildcat strike—"

"—effectively cutting off power to a large area of East Anglia as well as Brookbank, the real object of their fury, and marched up here to protest," Theo cut in with relish. "Getting stoned out of their minds on the way, as far as I could judge. There's the British workingman for you—always mixes business and pleasure."

"They went on strike because of—I don't believe it!" Harriet said.

"Then the sooner you suspend your disbelief the better," Oscar said shortly. "Because that is precisely what they did. I had a dozen of them in here—illiterate clods."

"They spoke with a countrified accent, in other words," Theo murmured.

"—and made what they pleased to call their demands. Demands! I never heard such impudence in my—"

"What demands?" Harriet was trying to concentrate. "What did they want? Me on a plate or something?" And again she made her curious sound.

"They wanted—oh, such absurdities—the animals let out, for a start. They've got some antivivisectionist notions mixed up in it too—the most stupid business. What sort of people are they who imagine you can release a few hundred capuchin monkeys, not to mention infected rats and mice and guinea pigs, into an East Anglian winter? That should give you some idea of their caliber."

"We've had to put a guard on the animal pens," Theo said soberly. "They're so scattered about—we couldn't be sure no one could get in and meddle, so"—he shrugged—"we've got a rota going until such time as the police can take over."

"But they're all right at the moment?" Now Harriet was fully awake again. "My God, my monkeys—are they all right?"

"John Caister's with them. He's staying the night. What this will do to the staff budget doesn't bear thinking about," Oscar said, and then, surprisingly, looked at her and smiled. "So there you are,

my dear. You've really been causing some excitement here tonight!
And then after we'd managed to shove them outside the gates and
locked them, making them paralytic with rage as a result, you
calmly drive into the middle of it all, and proceed to run down one
of their number. You must admit it has a certain piquancy, this
situation."

She smiled back, and let herself slip a little more deeply into the
comfort of her remote feeling. "It's nice of you not to be angrier.
In your shoes, I'd be—I don't know. Probably I'd want to give me
the boot, my marching orders, the sack, my stamped-up cards—"
Oscar looked up sharply at that, but it was Theo who looked
closely at her and then laughed suddenly.

"How much brandy did you give her when you brought her in
here, Oscar?"

"Mmm? Oh, I don't know . . . some . . ." he indicated the
glass on the desk with a vague gesture. "A glass—I didn't measure
it."

"Yes. And like an idiot, I gave her some too. My dear girl, you're
half-smashed, do you realize that?"

"Yes, I think I do," she said. "But I needed both lots of brandy,
so—" And she shrugged, and smiled up at Theo, who shook his
head at her.

"Well, what with a long drive and then what happened at the
end of it, and a positive cascade of brandy to follow on—come on.
We'll get one of the night nurses to nurse you to bed." He helped
her to her feet, and she winced again as the ache in her back and
sides returned, and leaned against him as he led her to the door.

"There's something I wanted to know," she said vaguely.
"Something else. Something important. I can't remember what it
is. Theo, I can't go yet . . . there's something else . . ."

"Dear heart, you're in no condition to—"

"That's it!" she said, and managed to pull away from Theo to
stand supporting herself on her own two feet. "George. I must go
and see George and find out how he is before I go to bed. Please,
Theo, I must."

Theo looked over her shoulder at Oscar, and after a moment

said, "No need, Hattie, I saw him myself not a couple of hours ago. He's fine. Just fine. And you can't go to see him now—he'll be asleep. It's getting fairly late, you know. Come on—let's get you to bed."

As obediently as a child, she went.

16

SHE FELT a great deal better than she would have thought possible, remembering the state in which she had gone to bed. She woke to the strangeness of the impersonal staff bedroom and lay very still for a while before moving experimentally; she would have expected to have a headache at the very least—brandy taken in excess was not one of her usual experiences—and to be bruised and sore most certainly. But her head was clear, and though there were some large and lurid bruises on her hips and arms, she was no more than a little stiff.

She drove herself to the cottage to bathe and change her clothes and eat some breakfast and to phone the District hospital to ask about the man who had been injured the night before. They told her he was "progressing satisfactorily," and she was startled by the wave of sheer relief that surged through her when she heard that.

It's not as though it was really my fault it happened, she thought defensively. They frightened me—But all the same it was comforting to know the man was in no danger.

It was past eleven by the time she walked into the unit. Catherine was sitting hunched over a pile of graphs, but jumped quickly to her feet as soon as she saw her.

"Dr. Berry! Are you all right? I couldn't find out anything about you this morning—I've been worried sick."

"Considering everything, I'm fine, thanks, Catherine. Where's John? In the animal pens? I think I'll go and see—"

"No, there's a policeman there now. John went to bed sometime in the small hours. I saw the monkeys early this morning, and they seemed to be perfectly all right. You've no need to worry, really. Come and sit down and—"

"I think I'll go and see for myself, all the same. I won't feel really sure until I have. Could you put out a call for Mr. Fowler for me? I'll be back in about fifteen minutes, and if he's free I'd like a word with him. And after that, Sam—but I'll call him myself when I get back."

The policeman, a large young man with a downy dark mustache, his helmet on the floor beside him, was sitting reading a newspaper in the little cubbyhole that served as an office to the main monkey room. He jumped up awkwardly as she came in, and put his helmet on.

"No one to come in here unauthorized, madam," he said a little breathlessly.

"Oh, that's all right. I'm very authorized. They're my monkeys. I'm Dr. Berry." And then, as he still looked suspiciously as though he were going to send her away, she fished in her pocket for something to identify herself. "Here—will this convince you? A letter addressed to me—see?"

He looked at the crumpled envelope, and then more closely at her face, and suddenly smiled, which made him look even younger.

"Sorry, madam. Of course. I recognize you now. Saw you on the J. J. Gerrard program, didn't I? Go right ahead, madam."

"Thank you," she said drily, and went into the main room, lined with its tall cages, and noisy with the activity of the monkeys who raised a great chatter as they saw her.

"Smelly little beasts, aren't they?" The policeman stood at the door, looking at the animals with an expression of distaste on his round polished pink face. "Can't be doing with animals myself. Dirty objects!"

"You probably smell unpleasant to them," she said shortly. "They don't smell as they do because they're dirty. Only because that's their natural scent. Could you close that door, please? Drafts are very bad for them; they're delicate little creatures and need a controlled temperature."

Pinker than ever the policeman went away, closing the door sharply behind him, and she pushed one hand deep into her pocket and began the tour of the room. She always followed the same route, starting at the far end and zigzagging from one side to the other, missing no cage, and finishing at the door. She took a handful of nuts from the bowl on the feed table to reward them with, and they chattered and shrilled at her, their alarmingly intelligent little faces, as expressive as always, pushed against the cage bars to greet her.

"There you are, funny face," she murmured as the largest monkey in the far pen reached through the bars with tiny perfect fingers, so veined and delicate that they looked like models for a Capo di Monte figurine. "Some for you. Are you fit and well, you lovely thing? Are you—?"

She always talked to them in this nursery fashion, and she was really rather ashamed of it; but it came to her so naturally and easily and it gave her some pleasure to do so, so she continued with the habit. Sometimes she had wondered whether she wasn't being thoroughly absurd, anthropomorphizing like some writer of nursery storybooks. Or perhaps she liked treating these elegant intelligent creatures as though they were her babies in an effort to deny their intelligence, to make herself feel less guilt about using them as she did.

For she did feel guilt, in a totally unscientific way, in a highly subjective emotional fashion. Whenever she saw them, with their beautiful liquid eyes, their shapely little heads, their arrogant curling tails, she wanted to look away, feeling herself to be a great ugly clodhopping soulless lump when compared to them. And when she had to make them diseased, in order to try her treatment, she suffered a good deal of distress; to deliberately damage such charming little humanoids demanded considerable efforts of will.

She felt soothed and more comfortable when she reached the door, her largesse of nuts disposed, and sure in her own mind of the health and vigor of each one of them. They had all had cancers of one form or another, and had survived her treatment. She felt a great affection for them all as she looked back at them squatting in their cages and chewing delicately at the food she had given out.

Theo was waiting in the unit when she got back, perched on the corner of Catherine's desk and watching her capable hands moving over the graphs. He looked up eagerly as she came in.

213

"Hattie, dear, how *are* you this morning? You look better than I'd hoped, I must say."

"Good morning, Theo. Please, don't fuss about me. I'm perfectly fit, thank you. Look, there's something I want to—can we go to the ward? I want to see George, and—"

"George. Mmm. Look, Hattie, I lied to you last night."

"What?" She had gone over to her own desk to make a note in the animal health book, and she looked up sharply at the heavy sound in Theo's voice. "Lied? About George?"

"Yes. You were in no condition to—"

"Never mind that. What about him? How is he?"

"Not too bad. But he had another small infarct yesterday—not too unexpected, after all! Sam did warn you. Fortunately Sam was in the ward when the monitor started bleeping, and got him out of fibrillation very quickly. He's not bad at all this morning, considering."

She put the book down on the desk. "Catherine, I'll be in the ward, Dr. Lemesurier's, if anyone wants me. Will you tell John Caister that I've checked the big animal room this morning, as soon as he comes on? I didn't check anything apart from temperature and humidity, though, so he'd better—or you could do it at the one o'clock round. All right? Theo, later, I want to talk to you."

"Now, if you like." He got to his feet. "I'm not operating this afternoon and I've done my morning rounds. So, at your service."

They went up in the lift to the ward in silence, however, for he looked at her face, closed and remote, and kept quiet. She was angry, obviously, but there was more than that in her preoccupation. She knew he was aware of her mood, and was catering to it, and that made her more tense; the sense of responsibility it forced on her was more than she wanted at this moment.

George was lying propped against his pillows, sleeping, his face looking narrower and more fragile than it had been when she last saw him. There was a high round flush on each cheek that looked absurd, almost as though he were a wooden doll. His pajama jacket was open, and she could see the monitoring pads strapped over his

214

ribs in the area of the heart's apex, and the delicate licorice rib-
bons that were the leads coiling away among the sparse grayish hair
toward the monitor screen. Automatically she raised her eyes to
look at it, and for almost a full minute, she and Theo stood there
watching the little yellow spark bouncing its cheerful way across
the screen, leaving fine traces behind it that disappeared even as
they were looked at.

As though in the depths of his sleep he became aware of their
presence, the old man moved his head, and grimaced so that his
mouth opened to show the flecked yellow teeth, and then his eyes
opened, and for a moment he looked blankly at them, uncompre-
hending and dull. Then recognition came, as obviously as if he had
been a hawk with transparent eyelids to roll back.

"Said you wanted—" he said hoarsely. "Got rid of me, didn't
you, got rid of me? Told 'em . . ." He closed his eyes again, and
seemed to have gone back to sleep, but then he opened them
again, and stared malevolently at Harriet, and she opened her
mouth to speak to him, but Theo was before her.

"You do talk a lot of old cobblers, George," he said, and his
voice carried a hearty friendliness. "Get rid of you, indeed! Believe
me, you're a lot more trouble here than you ever are at home. The
sooner they can get you better and out of here, the better everyone'll be pleased."

"Much you know," the old man muttered. "You don't know
nothing about her and what she does. Boyfriend . . ." He closed
his eyes again and then snapped them open, and said very loudly,
"Great pansy! Filthy poof—"

Harriet's face filled with a scarlet flush but she couldn't prevent
herself from looking sideways at Theo. For a moment she could see
humiliation in his expression but then he smiled, hugely, and
turned and looked at her, and the smile was in his eyes as well, and
didn't seem to be covering any less pleasant emotion; only amusement was there.

"Noticing old bastard!" he murmured. "Don't look so stricken,
dear heart! He's not the first to taunt me, and surely won't be the

215

last. Usually, you know, remarks like that bespeak a certain—shall we say, AC/DC temperament? But perhaps we can acquit George. At his age and in his state of health, who could do otherwise?"

He turned and looked at the old man again, once more sleeping with his mouth hanging lax and unattractive, and then took her arm and led her out of the ward toward the office-cum-kitchen.

"You wanted to talk to me," he said. "About George, I imagine? I'm sorry about misleading you last night, but you really weren't in any condition—"

"I know," she said abstractedly. "It doesn't matter, not now. I've sorted out what to do anyway. Do you suppose Sam'd let him be moved, Theo? After this new attack?"

"Ask him," Theo said. "He's in his office downstairs. You say you've definitely—what happened yesterday?"

She had started down the stairs, moving purposefully, and he had to hurry to keep up with her.

"Later—I'll tell you later. But I need to talk to Sam first. Ah— there he is. Sam! Just a moment—"

He looked back over his shoulder, and came back up the stairs, for he had been going on down to the next floor.

"Might have known it," he said equably. "Every time I go to get myself a bloody cup of coffee, someone comes between me and it. How're you, Harriet? Proper Boadicea stunt you pulled last night, I hear! I thought you'd be very hors de combat this morning."

"A little bruised, that's all. Sam, I want to talk to you about my father-in-law."

"I didn't think you wanted to proposition me. Come on—you too, Theo? Some Boadicea you're turning out to be—nurse-maided all the time by this surgical oaf—"

He chattered on, totally unoffending in spite of the things he was saying, as he led them into his untidy little office, heavy with the fustiness of stale cigarette smoke, and heaved a pile of books off the only armchair for Harriet.

"Now, about the old boy's heart," he began. "You've seen him this morning?"

216

"Yes. He looks—"

"Ropy. I know. But it's not as bad as he looks. It was a very small infarct, yesterday's, and his prognosis is about the same in spite of it. He just needs extra care at the moment. So things aren't all that different, really."

"There's one thing that's important to know, Sam," she said, and smiled at him. "And in asking this, I want you to know how grateful I am to you for looking after him as you have."

"Oh, listen, it's a pleasure, believe me," Sam said awkwardly. "I must say, I've been feeling a bit of a sod about saying he had to go, the way I did last Sunday. But, Christ—you know how it is here, Harriet! Oscar on our tails like some bloody hound dog, always sniffing about costs. And there just aren't the resources here for ordinary treatment! Just this handful of research beds, so—"

"I know Sam. So, how soon can he be moved safely?"

"How soon?" Sam turned the corners of his mouth downward as he thought about it. "Hard to say for sure—no less than a week, anyway, after yesterday's go. Say a couple of weeks. We'll keep him here that long, and sod Oscar if he starts his—"

"I'll deal with Oscar," she said. "Don't worry about that."

"Where have you arranged for him to go?" Sam asked, fishing in his pocket for a cigarette. "Got him into a home, have you?"

"Whyborne," she said after a moment, and Sam put down the cigarette unlit, and stared at her.

"Whyborne? Jesus! That'll cost you a fortune, won't it?"

"They treat staff and their families free of charge," she said flatly, and didn't look at either of them, keeping her eyes fixed on her hands crossed in her lap.

There was a long silence, and then Theo said carefully, "I see. Have you told Oscar?"

She looked at him then, "No. Not yet. I think—I'll have to tell him tonight. Not now. Tonight."

She was bewildered, totally bewildered, and for a while let him go on, without either resisting or cooperating. He was kissing her

217

with a controlled violence that was unusual in him, his hands moving against her body with an urgency that was beginning to excite her—more than just beginning, in fact—and now she pulled back, trying to hold his hands away from her and having to use a good deal of force.

"Oscar? For God's sake, Oscar, listen to me, will you? Did you hear what I said? I—"

"I heard you." He looked at her closely, his eyes a little narrowed. "I heard you." He took his hands away from her hold, and reached for her again, and this time she let him pull her brassiere off altogether, just as he had already pulled off her blouse, cooperated as he fumbled with the fastenings of her skirt and then tugged impatiently at her girdle.

It was all so ridiculous; she had started to tell him about her decision to go to Whyborne, and why, and he had listened, and then started making love to her, right there in the drawing room in front of the fire, pulling her down onto the heavy rug. She couldn't remember him doing that ever before; Oscar was a man of elegance and order and had always made it clear that he loathed what he defined as messiness, preferring to invest everything he did, even and perhaps particularly sex, with style and a certain panache. Usually before he made love to her he bathed and shaved, came to her wrapped in a handsome dressing gown over gleaming skin just faintly scented with one of the subtle body oils he so favored. And certainly he liked her to be bathed and powdered and scented for him; had once objected because she had come to bed too soon after brushing her teeth, so that she smelled of spearmint. "Very unerotic, my dear," he had murmured, and she had learned the lesson well.

Yet now, they were rolling on the rug like a pair of urgent children who had just discovered sex and thought they had invented it; certainly he was. He was kissing her body now, his head moving against the bare skin of her belly, and then he moved more sharply, and with a shock of pleasure so intense that it made her almost cry aloud, she realized that he was intending to provide her with all

218

the stimulus she most enjoyed and which made her most eagerly responsive.

There had been times during the past eighteen years when he had apparently gently but with unmistakable intent teased her about her "peasant earthiness—such very carnal tastes, yours, my dear. But there, women—so sensual—" Yet now he was being quite as sensual as she could ever wish him to be and she was lost, quite lost in the sea of sensation into which he had plunged her with such skill and dispatch. She no longer cared why he was behaving so, only how, and with the urgency rising in her reached for him, to try to pull him closer to her to make him move more quickly and directly, but he laughed softly and said, "Not yet— wait a little—not yet—" and again dipped his head toward her body so that this time she did cry out with her need and urgency.

And eventually, just when she thought she could bear it no longer, but would reach orgasm too soon so that it was a merely surface experience instead of the deep reality which she most urgently wanted it to be, he moved and plunged at her, hurting her marvelously over and over again.

And then they were lying still, damp and breathless, and he moved away from her slightly and whispered, "Good? Was it good?"

She laughed softly, deep in her throat. "Bloody marvelous. Bloody marvelous. As if you didn't know . . ."

"Twice?"

She yawned hugely, and then laughed her growling laugh again, and said, "Yes. Twice. Like the Queen of Aragon—"

He laughed too, but more loudly, and his lips were so close to her ear that she winced at the sound, and he rolled away from her, to lie on his back beside her, staring upward, and she lay there too in a haze of pleasure, watching the flames of the fire making patterns on the plastered cornice of the ceiling.

She dozed for a while, and woke sharply as the light struck her lids. He came from the lightswitch to sit down on the sofa, fully dressed and sleek, staring down at her, and she lay there looking up at him, blinking a little, and said uncertainly, "Oscar? I fell asleep—"

"Indeed you did," he said, and continued to look at her, quite unsmiling, and she became aware of the way she looked, of her tights still dangling from one leg, of the rest of her clothes littered about, and she sat up, stiff and awkward, suddenly very aware of her own body.

She could see all too clearly how it must look to him; quite apart from the ugly blue and purple bruises of yesterday's incident, there were the somewhat heavy sagging breasts, the crêpy pleated skin across her belly, legacy of two pregnancies, the gleaming white stretch marks across her hips. To be looked at by a fully dressed man, in very bright light and under such conditions was suddenly the most deeply embarrassing thing that had ever happened to her. She collected her clothes awkwardly, and with all the dignity she could muster, knowing it to be pitifully little, went to the bathroom to wash and dress and repair her self-esteem.

He was sitting beside the newly made-up fire, a pot of coffee and two cups ready on the small table, when she came back, and he looked at her and nodded toward the other armchair, and she went there, feeling almost like a gawky teen-ager again.

He gave her a cup of coffee, and she sipped it, and then put it down beside her. It was too hot, and somehow even that made her feel at a disadvantage.

"What happened to you, Oscar?" she said lightly, and smiled at him. "Such urgency! Really, if I'd been Mata Hari, you couldn't have been more . . ." she shrugged.

"But you aren't Mata Hari, are you, my dear?" He smiled at her for the first time, she realized with a faint surprise, since she had woken.

"No, I suppose not. But I've never pretended to be! I'm just Harriet, that's all."

He laughed a little. "And I know Harriet very well, don't I? 'Hmm? Do I know how to make you happy, my dear? Do I please you?"

"You know bloody well you do! You're as talented a lover as—oh, I don't know. I've never precisely set out to make a comparative study! Apart from you and David, I've no criteria. I just know that you . . . make me feel happy, yes. You please me, yes. Is that why you were so urgent, Oscar, because you were suddenly filled with the need to prove yourself a great lover?"

"Not to me, my dear. Not to me. But I was attempting to prove something. I suspect I've succeeded." He drank some coffee, and then refilled his cup. "The question now is, have I proved it to you? Because that was the object of the exercise."

"I'm not sure I understand what it is you're getting at, Oscar." She sat back in her chair, watching him closely, her arms resting heavily on the brocade covering, feeling in herself a weariness that contained as much of the memory of yesterday's aches as of this evening's sex.

"No, I don't suppose you do, my dear. For an intelligent woman —even brilliant in your own field—you can be remarkably obtuse."

"Thank you!"

"Neither compliment nor insult was intended, I assure you! Just a statement of fact." He looked at her, and laughed softly. "Poor Harriet! Shall I spell it out for you? Make abundantly clear what it was I was trying to prove? And for what purpose?"

She looked back at him, sitting there with his legs crossed, his trouser legs carefully pulled up to reveal smooth black socks and gleaming shoes, and for one moment hated him; and even as the knowledge of her hate moved into her mind she knew it was part of his attraction for her. His hatefulness, his deviousness, the fear he could create in her, the need to cater to his whims and desires— all that was intensely exciting. It made her body move in response as no amount of mere tenderness could do. And she thought for a confused moment of her childhood and her father's brusque voice, of her years tucked away in girls' boarding schools and girls' boarding houses in her student days, and knew why it was she felt so. And shut her eyes wearily and said, "Yes, tell me what it is."

"You told me you wanted to go to Whyborne."

"That I *intend* to go to Whyborne," she said, snapping her eyes open. "I didn't ask permission, Oscar. I told you of a decision."

"Ah. Yes. That is what you think you told me. I am suggesting you think again."

"Why?"

"Because I don't want you to go to Whyborne. Better perhaps to say I don't want you to leave Brookbank."

"Look, Oscar, I appreciate all you've done for me over the years. I know how you must feel about people leaving you—though I'm not doing a Ross-Craigie on you. You've never worked with me on my stuff, actively opposed it at the beginning, in fact—no, don't interrupt. I do understand. But try to understand it from my point of view. I've got responsibilities of my own—to George, to my own children—"

"Children? Those large young adults?"

"There's no need to be—however. Yes. To those large young adults. I must make the sort of provision for my own future, in a financial sense that will . . . relieve them of the burden of my care." She made a small face. "I don't intend ever to be to them what George is to me. So, I'm going to Whyborne. Please, try to understand and be civilized about it! We've been friends a long time, Oscar, very good friends, and I hope you can think about this in terms of friendship rather than as an employer."

He raised his eyebrows at her with great urbanity. "But that is precisely what I am doing, my dear Harriet! I too want to ensure our . . . *friendship* survives and continues to . . . ah . . . give us both the satisfactions it already does. Though, of course, one must be honest about this. I might perhaps—how shall I put it? I suspect I might recover more quickly from the loss of your friendship than you would the loss of mine."

She looked at him, feeling the chill of fear he could so easily arouse climbing into her throat. "I'm not sure I quite understand you," she said carefully.

"Oh, I think you do, somewhat obtuse though you can be in your sweet feminine fashion about these matters. But let me be blunt, just in case. If you leave for Whyborne, then you and I—that is the end. Our friendship ceases. I can't, in all conscience, go on with a—with such a close relationship with a member of another establishment's staff. It would simply not be possible, since to do so would put me in a highly equivocal position. But I daresay I would soon be able to find a . . . um, shall we say, a substitute for you?"

He stood up, and placed himself tidily in front of the fire, and she looked up at him standing there with his hands in his pockets, his belly flat and muscular between them, his sleek gray head poised above neat shoulders, and she knew he was parading himself for her benefit.

"You, on the other hand, Harriet, are not perhaps in so happy a situation. I know I am over fifty, but a man of fifty, you must admit, is still very much a man. And in my experience quite an interesting one in the eyes of quite a number of women. Including even very young ones."

He smiled down at her. "Nature is cruel to the female of the species, isn't it, Harriet? You at forty-nine are not—well, handsome though you are, interesting though you are, sexually—ah—adventurous as I know you to be, you must admit that to find a new relationship would be for you a great deal more difficult than it would for me."

She closed her eyes, and shook her head and said softly, "I don't believe it. I don't—not even you, Oscar. Not even you could do such a—"

He smiled again. "Come, my dear girl! You surely must know I can and, indeed, that I mean every word I say. Don't you?"

She looked at him again and nodded slowly. "Yes. I know."

There was a silence, and then Oscar threw his head back and laughed loudly. "So absurd, my dear, isn't it? Lysistrata was a woman, isn't that so? And here am I, a man, following that splendid example. There must be a message in there somewhere for the Women's Liberation movement!"

17

"DR. BERRY!" John Caister said again. "There's a man to talk to you. I really think you'd—"

"What is it?" she looked up, irritably, suddenly aware of the fact that she had been staring at the same graph quite unseeingly for a very long time, and that John had already spoken to her twice. "What did you say?"

"There's a man to see you. They've sent him up from front gate, so he's not one of those awful newspaper people. To tell you the truth—" he lowered his voice "—I think it's the fuzz. Smell them anywhere."

"Fuzz?"

"Plainclothes, but fuzz all the same. Will you see him?"

"Yes," she said heavily. "I might as well," and pushed the papers in front of her to the back of her desk. It was extraordinary how flat she felt, how drearily old, yet emotionally quite calm. I should be weeping, or howling for his blood, or being a woman scorned or something, she thought bleakly. I should be hating him.

But she knew she didn't, and knew she never would. Oscar's chilly deviousness, his selfish manipulation of others, even and especially herself, was one of the things about him that made him so intensely exciting a partner. There was nothing new, nothing surprising in what had happened last night; it was all of a piece with the man she had known and enjoyed all these years. Even used for my own selfish purposes, she thought. Maybe I'm as devious as he is, in my own way. But at that thought, she smiled a little wryly. Her own attempts at manipulation would bear as much comparison with Oscar's as a child's game of tiddlywinks would to a master's chess ploy.

"Good morning, Doctor."

She turned to look at the man standing just inside the door, a very ordinary-looking man with thinning red hair brushed neatly over his bumpy skull, a soft dark brown hat that almost exactly matched the color of his overcoat held in his hand.

"Oh—yes. Good morning," she said. "You wanted me?"

He came toward her, holding out his hand, and almost automatically she held out her own to shake hands with him, and then saw the identity card held in the palm, and dropped her arm to her side.

"I would appreciate just a few words with you, Doctor. If you don't mind. My name's Sydenham. Mr. Sydenham."

"I thought one usually addressed policemen by their rank. Even plainclothes ones."

"Well, so they do, in some branches of the service. But me— well, I prefer not to. Keeps things friendlier, doesn't it?"

"Then this is a friendly visit?"

"Of course! Shouldn't it be?"

He looked at her with a huge waggishness, and she said sharply, "Do sit down. No, no reason."

"You'd be surprised, Doctor," he said with an air of great confidentiality, as he sat down in the chair she had indicated, and put his hat on the floor beside him before crossing his legs comfortably. "Even the most respectable of citizens these days tend to react very nervously when they meet policemen. It's the motorcar, you know. Makes everyone feel like a criminal, doesn't it?"

"What can I do for you, Mr. Sydenham?" she said with all the crispness she could muster. "I really have a great deal of work on hand, and I would like to—"

"But of course. Of course. Well, first of all, let me tell you how sorry I am that you were so unfortunately involved in that little fracas at your gates the other night. Very nasty experience it must have been. Very nasty."

She made a small grimace, and unconsciously moved her shoulders, still a little stiff from the bruising. "Yes. It was rather. Though, I suppose, since it was my work they were complaining about—"

225

"Whatever their complaints, they should have put them through the proper channels," Sydenham said very firmly. "They had no right to go interrupting people in the normal course of their business—exposing people to danger and trouble—not to mention themselves." He looked at her sharply, with his eyes narrowed to a bright beadiness, and she flushed.

"I should have realized, of course," she said stiffly. "You've come to see me about the man I—I injured? I can assure you that I had no intention of—I just thought, if I moved forward slowly they'd get out of the way, but they didn't, and I got alarmed, and my foot slipped on the clutch and"—she bit her lip. "I didn't *try* to hurt him."

"Oh, we know that, Doctor, never fear! They set out to hurt *you* all right, but we know quite well that what happened to that bloke was his fault and no one else's—apart from the rest of the mob, of course. And he's doing all right, anyway. They'll have him tidily tucked up at the District General for several weeks with his broken leg, and a very good thing too. Give him time to cool down, won't it? No, it wasn't that little problem I came to see you about. You'll hear no more about what happened there—though I can't hide from you the fact he talked a bit wildly about bringing charges against you. But we soon convinced him he hadn't got a case."

"Thank you," she said, and felt the inadequacy of the words, and reddened again.

"No, I'm not here about that." He sat silently for a while and she looked sideways at him, feeling uneasiness move in her chest. "I'm from a rather specialized department of the force, Doctor," he said eventually. "I deal with what might be called immigration problems. Aliens and the like."

She frowned. "Oh? I don't see how—"

"No, I don't suppose you do," he smiled at her, his face creasing again into his schoolboy beam. "People never do think of—well, I ask you. When I say immigrant or alien, what's the first thing comes into your mind? People with black faces, and funny little men all wrapped up in big black coats and talking wiz zee vairy theek accent, hein, achtung, jawohl? Yes, of course. But no one ever thinks of Australians or New Zealanders. Or Canadians. Do they?"

"Canadians? You want to talk about? . . . Oh. I—" she stopped sharply. "Perhaps you'd better explain a little more."

"But you already understand a little, I think, don't you? Well, I won't beat about the bush, Doctor. I'm sorry to have to put you in any sort of invidious position, but—well, it's to your interest as well as ours to do something fast about this young man, isn't it? And since he's your daughter's, ah . . ." he paused delicately.

"Well?"

"I went to see him this morning." Suddenly his voice lost its faintly jocular note and became very businesslike. "We got a call from the local police a few days ago, actually. They realized what was going on, and since we'd been—how shall I put it?—we'd been looking for a way to persuade him that he wasn't precisely *persona grata*, as the lawbooks say, we've been keeping an eye on him. And this morning"—he shrugged—"he made no bones about it. Very straight he was, I must say. Told me exactly what he was up to, and listened to me very courteously. I'll grant him that. But I'm not sure he really took in what I said to him. And it would be a great help to me—to the Government, to be more accurate, if you'd—well, maybe he'd pay some attention to his—er—to his girl's mother, don't you know? So, I thought—"

"I may be particularly dense, Mr. Sydenham, but I don't really understand what it is you're talking about," she said sharply.

"Oh, now, Doctor Berry!" he said, looking a little hurt. "I thought you—well, I'm sorry. All right, I'll start at the beginning. For several weeks, we've been watching Dr. Ben Shoeman, on account of suspecting he was a subversive type, who could cause trouble. For a while he behaved very well, in a legal sense, that is. He's organized public meetings, used the papers to spread his efforts, but he's kept inside the law. But now he's been and gone and properly blotted his copybook, organizing those men into a wildcat strike, and he's said, before a witness—the local sergeant was with me—he's said that he intends to go on stirring up such strikes, so we've got him, haven't we? I was empowered to warn him that unless he voluntarily left the U.K. within the next thirty-six hours we would be forced to take legal steps against him. He didn't believe me at first—it's funny how often people think they've got special status, being Commonwealth citizens and that. But I think I got it across to him. Certainly I got it across to Miss Berry. She seemed very eager to go. But just in case—I thought I'd ask you, quietly, you know, to have a little word with him. He's not far away, after all, and if I could be sure he was booked onto a flight, I'd feel a lot better—"

"Ben's *here?*" she said. "With Patty? Are you sure?"

He smiled again, almost pityingly. "Yes, Doctor. They're staying in King's Lynn, at the Old Crown. They've been here well over a week. I understood from what Miss Berry said that she'd—er—left her job. They didn't like her—um—friendship with Dr. Shoeman, according to him, and gave her the push. Very sharp things he had to say about her ex-employers, I must say," he smiled reminiscently. "Yes. Very sharp."

There was a silence for a while, and then Harriet stirred and said stiffly, "Well, it was good of you to let me know. Thank you."

"You'll try to—er—persuade him of the wisdom of going home?" Sydenham said, and again his eyes were beadily bright. "For Miss Berry's sake as well as his own. I would have thought—"

"Thank you, Mr. Sydenham. You've made your point." She stood up, and moved over to the door to hold it open for him, but he sat still, and smiled at her, still looking comfortably relaxed in the hard straight-backed chair.

"Of course, once he has gone, you'll have no more trouble here. Those boys from the power station—not the brightest in the world, you know. Without Shoeman around to jolly them up and keep the ginger going, they'll be back to normal working in no time. Won't be hanging around the gates any more, impeding you all."

He stood up then, and came toward her, holding out one hand,

and almost against her will, she held out her own, and touched his briefly.

"Thank you, Doctor. I know you'll help the boy see sense. And I've no doubt he'll settle down in time. It's amazing how many of these young hotheads learn the errors of their ways, once they get a girl. That's a lovely daughter you've got, Dr. Berry. If she doesn't have him eating out of her hand in a cozy house somewhere in Toronto or wherever in a few months, I'll be very surprised."

He sat there, laughing hugely, and she wanted to smack him as though he were a silly child, yet still found a certain pleasure in watching his genuine enjoyment of the joke, even though she saw nothing particularly funny in it herself.

"But it *is* funny, Harriet!" he said when she told him as much. "Surely you can see that? Some greasy pig comes to tell you what a bad boy I am, and please will you trot along and tell me so, and make sure I do as I'm bid—and you go and do it! Come on, Harriet —you can't say you don't think it's funny? Really *sick* funny?"

"I didn't see it in those terms," she said. "But maybe I'm old-fashioned. I was told that a—that someone I know is in trouble, and—" she shrugged. "I wanted to help. In however ineffective a fashion, I wanted to help. And to find out what was going on."

"Ah, now, that's better!" Ben said, and leaned back in his chair to call over his shoulder. "Isn't that better, Patty?"

Patty was standing on the other side of the room, staring out of the bedroom window at the street below, and she didn't turn when Ben spoke to her, only hunching her shoulders.

"She's feeling a bit—" Ben grinned cheerfully at Harriet. "You should know. Your daughter!"

"Why was that better?"

"Eh? Oh, because you were honest! You wanted to find out what was going on. Great! What better than to want to know what's happening around you? Only making it different, that's all! Care for a beer, Harriet?"

He stood up and moved over to the stack of beer cans on the

dressing table, seeming to fill the blank little room to stifling over-crowdedness with his bigness. "No? Patty, you sure will. Here."

Patty came to take her tin of beer, and then sat on the bed, her legs pulled up under her, and she looked briefly at Harriet and said harshly, "I hear that George is ill. Gorden phoned and ranted some stuff at me. What's the score?"

"It's not important," Harriet said. "I've sorted things out. He's had a coronary, but he—I've arranged for his care."

"That your old gramps, Patty?" Ben came and sat beside her on the bed, throwing one arm across her shoulders, and Patty immediately relaxed, and curled her shoulders toward him so that she was almost cowering against his chest, and looked at her mother with a slightly challenging lift of her chin.

"Yes, George is Patty's grandfather. But you've nothing to worry about. He's—it's all under control."

"I'm not worrying, Harriet, believe me I'm not worrying! I'm not about to start fretting over an old man when I've got plenty else to fill my time with. Patty feels the same way, hmm?" And he looked down at her and tightened his grip on her shoulders.

"Yes," she said, and looked at Harriet again, but then her eyes slid away, and she drank some of her beer, but without much sign of enjoyment.

"So, you want to know what's going on, Harriet," Ben said. "Well, I'm here to tell you. Why not? You've asked me, so I'll tell you. The pigs have been watching me—I knew that. Pigs always watch me. I'm one of your interesting cats."

He laughed again, and finished his beer, and chucked the can in the general direction of the wastepaper basket, not bothering to turn his head to see whether he had missed or not.

"So, after that nice little do up at Brookbank, they come and they tell me they know, they have some real lovely evidence, none of your made-up stuff, some *real* evidence that I'm a nasty subver-sive whisper-it-not-in-Gath actual *Communist*. How's that, then? So like, I say to them, sure, I'm a Communist, want to see my party card? I'll show you. Is that such a terrible thing to be in this royal throne of kings, this sceptered isle and the rest of that crap? So they say, no, great, be what you like, as long as you don't do nothing naughty—like doing something practical about what you believe in."

"Do something for me, Ben," Harriet said. "Stop addressing me as though I were a public meeting. I'm getting bored."

"Oh! Oh! Sharp teeth, your lady Ma has got, Patty! Okay. Okay. They know I started the strike at the power station—pretty good result that, hmm?"

"Not particularly. I didn't enjoy it much."

"Who said anything about enjoying it? What sort of yardstick is that? I like you, Harriet, you're a great gas. And you're a bloody good scientist—got twice the brain I'll ever have. But you can be bloody stupid, just like the rest of—"

"Ben, shut up," Patty said softly, and he looked down at her, and after a moment, took his arm from her shoulders and leaned back against the head of the bed.

"Okay. So, I told 'em I'd organized the strike. That I'd plans for a few more such operations. So they said I'd better get out before I was thrown out. So I've decided to go. End of report. Anything else you want to know about what's happening?"

"You say you're *going?*" Harriet frowned. "But I thought—"

"You thought like the pig thought," Ben said, and now his voice was harsh. "You thought I'd stay here out of some crazy notion of—hell, I don't know what—honor or something. That I'd be ashamed to lose face by turning and belting the hell out of here before they pick me up. Fuck that for a—listen, Harriet, you may be bloody stupid, but you aren't moribund, are you? What the hell would any intelligent man do when he's told he's been tumbled, and that from here on any efforts he makes will be—I did the *intelligent* thing, on account of I'm a very intelligent guy. I booked a flight to Montreal. We go from Manchester, tonight. So you needn't have come, need you? You could have saved yourself the trouble of running pig errands." He was leaning forward now, red-faced and angry, and suddenly she smiled.

231

"Dear Ben. Poor dear Ben," she said softly. "You *do* feel unhappy about it, at that, don't you? For all your talk about bourgeois relationships and the expendability of people, and the rest of it, you feel unhappy about the way you treated me. Because you spent some time as a guest in my home, and because I'm Patty's mother, you don't like getting me mixed up in your politics and your revolutionizing. Isn't that true, Ben? Isn't that why you're going, as much as anything?"

He stared at her for a long moment, and then he shrugged and smiled again, and once more his face disappeared behind its mask of hair and laughter.

"There's a clever Freudian-type lady, then! Got it all worked out, all nice and tidy. Well, think as you like, Harriet, my dear common-law mother-in-law. Think what you damned like. I'll tell you I'm going because I am not about to waste my time getting mixed up in any legal argument, and because my work here is pretty well done, anyway. Your stupid pigs—they think the trouble'll stop just because they've got rid of me? They think the whole cozy rotten edifice you've got here on this precious island of yours'll be safe for another few hundred years on account of they got rid of Wicked Ben, the most revolutionary of men? Jesus, how filled with crap can people's heads be? It won't stop, because it *can't*. There's plenty of people left here like me, plenty I've taught, plenty who understand what's got to be done. And they'll do it, whether I'm here or not, and—what's the good of talking? Do me a favor, Harriet. Go home. Go home, and leave me to fight it out with Patty—yeah, don't look like that. You know we fight over you, don't you? You know we're going to go on fighting over you and—"

"I'm going with you," Patty said, and her voice was thin and ugly. "I've told you I'm going with you, so there's no more to say. You don't have to—"

"No, I don't have to. No one has to. Ah, shit! What the hell—do me a favor and go home. I've had it up to here—" And he threw himself back on the bed, and lay staring up at the ceiling, his beard thrusting sulkily upward.

Harriet stood up, and moving very slowly began to pull on her gloves. Then she looked up at Patty, still sitting in the same hunched position on the bed beside him. They looked at each other for a long moment, and then Patty moved petulantly.

"Do me a favor too, Ma. Go home, will you? I never could be doing with a lot of long-drawn-out farewells. We're going, and that's all there is to it. You know how it is. There's nothing else I can do, is there?"

"No," Harriet said, "there's nothing else you can do. But I told you I knew that in London, didn't I? You don't have to feel so unhappy about it. I'm putting no pressures on you—I never have."

"No, damn you!" Patty shouted. "You're not! That's what makes it so—oh, go *home*, will you?"

I should want to cry or I should try to beg her to stay here or something, Harriet thought, looking at the bleak misery on her daughter's face. I ought to, and I can't. It ought to feel like losing a child, but it doesn't because my children have been dead long since. Poor young woman. Poor young stranger. Poor dead children.

She turned at the door, just for a moment.

"Goodbye, Patty. Take care of yourself."

"You too," Patty said after a moment. "You take care of yourself. You'll be all right?"

"I told you before, I'm not decrepit. Not quite yet."

"But you'll be all right . . ."

"Yes. I'll be fine. Goodbye."

She sat staring into her glass, twisting it from side to side so that the muddy dregs of the wine swirled into patterns, so absorbed that she almost jumped when Theo put his hand out and touched her.

"Hattie, I know you have a certain amount of right to be abstracted, but try to remember I'm here, please! It's very dispiriting to speak twice to one's guest and still make no apparent impact."

"What? Oh, I'm sorry, Theo. I'm being quite abominably ill-mannered. What did you say?"

"I said—oh, whatever it was, even I've forgotten it now, so it couldn't have been all that important. Will you have some pudding or do you prefer cheese?"

"Hmm? Oh, neither, thank you. Just coffee. It was a splendid dinner, and I did appreciate—"

"Stop appreciating, and start being *with* me. I'd find your company rather than your palpable absence quite sufficient recompense for the provision of your dinner, I assure you."

She laughed then. "Oh, dear, you are being grand! But at least that proves you aren't really annoyed. I *am* sorry—I didn't mean to go off into a brown study."

"Deep purple, more like. Why, Hattie?" His voice took on a softer note, and she looked away from him, embarrassed, and he seemed to recognize it, and returned to raillery. "What can ail thee, Dame at arms, alone and palely loitering—it doesn't sound quite as euphonious as it might, somehow, but the mood is right. What the hell *does* ail thee? Apart from Patty's departure, that is. I know that you've come to terms with that business, so what else is bothering you? You've been walking around surrounded by your subfusc clouds for almost a week, and I for one am finding it exceedingly depressing. Hence, frankly, this expedition to the bright lights and wickednesses of King's Lynn. I thought perhaps a cordon bleu dinner amidst all this decadent society would unbutton you a little."

She looked round the small restaurant, at the chubby Norfolk farmers and their well-upholstered wives, the damply eager young men and their giggly girl friends, and laughed a little. "Anyone who really unbuttoned here would cause a riot," she said. "Try it. Climb on the table and dance a fandango and see what'd happen."

"Nothing, dear heart, nothing whatsoever. They'd look away, and order some more scampi and sauce tartare and murmur about the weather and the state of the crops, and if anyone did show such ill breeding as to make any direct comment, it'd be to dismiss me as a mere mountebank from Brookbank. And what can you expect from these scientist wallahs, and waiter, bring me another brandy and a pink gin for madam."

234

"Probably," she said, and looked down at her glass again.

But he said at once, "Oh, no you don't—you're not going off again. Now, tell me what the problem is. I've told you, I'm bored out of my mind by your drooping about the place, and I insist that you pay for your dinner by telling me what it is."

"There are times when I wonder how much of your interest is based on concern for me, and how much on mere curiosity," she said with a flash of sharpness. "You can't bear not to know everything that's going on around you, even if it's nothing to do with you, can you?"

"Oh, mere vulgar curiosity is all, I assure you," he said equably, and she reddened.

"You can make me feel like a complete bastard sometimes, Theo," she said after a moment. "Of course I know your interest is genuine. I had no right to—"

"Yes you did. Every right. I can't give you any other sort of emotional relief, can I? If I could, I would. But at least I know I can give you the chance to say what you want when you want to say it, and that can be extremely cathartic. Even more so than active sex, in my experience—defining sex as merely a way of discharging tension that is, rather than in the romantic creative guise. I'm not even sure that there is such a guise, anyway." He folded his hands on the table, and bent his head to stare at his interlocked fingers. "You could say I've been suffering a little this week, watching you getting more and more frustrated as you bottle up your—whatever it is you're bottling up—and wanting to give you the chance to pop your cork—elegant phrase!—but being kept at arms' length. I mayn't be precisely the sighing yearning lover, but my situation has its parallels."

There was a silence, and then she said, "I told Oscar. Last week, I told him I was going to Whyborne, and the reasons for my decision, and—" she grimaced. "I told him."

"And what was his reaction?" Theo asked softly.

She felt as though he knew the answer but was forcing her, for some reason of his own, to say it, and the anger that had been

235

simmering in her all week burst upward, and she said furiously, "He did for me what you could never do, and then said it was for the last time, all right?" and then, horror-struck, closed her eyes, feeling the hot color come flooding over her neck and face.

"You see what I mean?" he said after a moment. "That was very cathartic, wasn't it? Almost orgasmic, you might say. Really, my dear, you underestimate what I can do for you. I may not be precisely able to—um—offer the sort of service Oscar and some of our farming friends here would define as the service a man can and should give a woman, but I have my uses."

She opened her eyes to look at him, and he smiled at her and shook his head slightly as she opened her mouth to speak.

"Whatever you do, don't say you're sorry. If you did then I think I might indeed lose my temper. I might even be reduced to throwing a fit of classical homosexual hysterics, with lots of wrist flopping and head tossing and flouncing. And not only would I like to spare you so unedifying a sight—I'm not sure I'd know how to do it."

He raised his head and looked around for a waiter, and they sat silently as the man fluttered around them with coffee pots and offers of liqueurs. Then Theo leaned forward and patted her hand. "All right. That's over and done with. The embarrassment, I mean. You said it, I heard it, and now we can move into the peaceful post-tumescent phase, hmm? We'll relax and talk sensibly, and you'll feel much much better, I promise you."

"Thank you. I think—I hate to admit it, but I do already."

"You see? Theo's Therapy for Threatened—I can't finish it. Alliteration was never one of my skills."

"Threatened," she said. "You chose aptly, there. I am threatened. It's a—not a particularly agreeable feeling."

"You said the last time?" Theo said carefully. "Is that what you mean by a threat?"

"It's a very powerful one," she smiled at him, knowing it to be with a too bright falsity. "Either I stay here at Brookbank on his terms, or I go and . . ." she shrugged. "I go."

236

"A strange man, our Oscar. He seems to value himself very little."

"What?"

"Even in my pansy way, I'm capable of love. I value myself too well to offer less to the people with whom . . . I become involved. Yet Oscar seems able to turn off the taps of his affection very easily, if he can make so—um—suggest so commercial a basis for the continuation of your relationship. Good God, woman! Surely you must see it's the end of the road for you two? How can you go on with a man who tries so—?"

"You're suggesting I undervalue myself too. Maybe I do. Because I could go on with him, even now. Because value myself or not, I damned well understand myself. And I need him. Do you think I haven't thought about this? I've thought about it all week, until I'm stupid with thinking. I've thought about George and Gordon and—I've thought and thought and thought. And at the end of it, I'm no nearer a decision. I know what I need and I know what I want, but God help me, they're diametrically opposed to each other."

"You love him, then?"

"Love? Stupid word. Mawkish word for a mawkish feeling. I don't know what it is. I just know what I need in a man, and he's the only one who can provide it. So—" She smiled again, the same falsely bright rictus of a smile. "So!"

"Let's be logical about all this, Hattie. There must be—" He shook his head and pushed his coffee cup aside to begin making marks on the tablecloth with the tip of his coffee spoon. "Why is Oscar so hell-bent on keeping you at Brookbank that he'd—that he would behave as he has in order to do so? To use blackmail of this order he must be hard-pushed, hmm?"

"I don't know," she said wearily. "I just—"

"Rhetorical question, dear. I know why. It's because you're his only hope of getting any farther in his own career. Because he dare not lose another good worker as he lost Ross-Craigie. If he does, he'll find himself relegated in no uncertain terms. Without you, I may safely say, Professor Bell will become just a name on a door at the Department of Science and Technology in Whitehall. They'll change the Brookbank Establishment head and kick him upstairs into higher-paid uselessness, and well he knows it."

"Oh, for God's sake, Theo, don't be ridiculous! I'm not that important to him! The reverse in some ways. He's got his own interests that cut right across my lines of work, and well *you* know it. I'm damned if I'm going to be made into—into some sort of object for people to make deals with and—"

"You already are such an object, you silly creature!" Theo said with real irritation, "Do stop being so tiresomely modest, and use your bloody *brain*. In scientific terms Oscar's an also-ran, a second-stringer, and he knows it as well as he knows the sun will rise tomorrow. But with you at Brookbank, the Government will release money to cover your work—Jesus Christ, woman, didn't that strike business *register* with you? All that fuss at the Trafalgar Square meeting, the public meetings and screechings and television programs going on all over the place still? You're big—you're bloody enormous! And it's only because you won't face up to it that Oscar's able to manipulate you the way he does! If you stopped for one moment to think intelligently about yourself, instead of just about your work and your personal relationships, about *yourself* as a person, as a scientist, then you'd see just what—oh, why do I try? Look, let me spell it out for you. The Government want to settle all this unrest as fast as they can. They want people to feel that this great cancer treatment everyone keeps on about is available to *them*, not just to the people who can pay for it. The best way to settle the fuss is to pour money into Brookbank, to show the world and his wife that a beneficent British Government is busily arranging that the Berry process shall be used as soon as possible for anyone who needs it. Why do you think Oscar's been spending so much time in Whitehall since all this began? He's not getting his arse measured for a seat in a Department office, I promise you!"

"Are you sure? He hasn't said anything to me about more grant money—"

238

"I'm damned sure he hasn't! Why should he, when he's so certain he's got you firmly held between his finger and thumb? Look at the way you've been behaving all week—depressed as hell, and now I know why—Christ, Oscar must think he's home and dry. He must know that he just has to twitch the thread, and back you come dancing at the end of it. God, it makes me sick!"

"It makes me sick, too," she said and her voice was very low. "I don't enjoy being the way I am. I wish—oh, God, I wish I were totally sexless, just a mind that wanted to work. Then it'd all be so easy. I'd do my work, and to hell with everything else, with George and Oscar and Ben and Patty, the whole lot of them. I wish I were like Catherine."

"Do you?" He smiled a little. "No, you wouldn't enjoy being Catherine. She suffers, too, and don't think otherwise."

For a moment she saw a vision of Catherine's face, the morning before they had gone to London for the Trafalgar Square meeting, saw again the way she had looked at her, the expression on her craggy face, and knew what he meant.

"It would be good to work at Whyborne," she said after a moment. "It's an incredible place. Equipment, facilities—incredible."

He put his head to one side and looked at her consideringly. "Would it be so good? What about the—well, for want of a better word, what about the morality of it? Rich man's privilege and all that. Doesn't that come into it at all?"

She shrugged a little. "I can't pretend I've ever thought that much about it. Politics—I'm vaguely pink, I suppose—Patty used to call me a bourgeois liberal of the worst sort, but to be honest with you I've always found discussions of such things somewhat juvenile. Spotty young men and eager girls with bad cases of sex in the head sitting around in common rooms putting the world to rights with a few easy words. I've grown out of it."

"Oh, come on! This isn't politics of that sort! This is something far more fundamental. You can't tell me you've no views either way about the uses of your work—you can't be so stupid. One way or the other, you have to be involved. No scientist today can possi-

bly go on operating at any sort of worthwhile level without thinking out his own views—"

"Oh, come off it, Theo! Don't tell me Ross-Craigie's thought it
out!"

"Yes he has. He's a convinced self-seeker driven by cupidity,
mainly, with a desperate need to be on top of the heap no matter
how crappy a heap it may be, with all the underlying fascism that
goes with such an attitude. He's totally consistent in all he does.
He puts William Ross-Craigie first, last and in the middle, and
does what's more profitable for him, every time. But you—you
seem to operate in a vacuum sometimes! You're talking about
going to Whyborne just because of some—some misguided emo-
tionalism about George. And about Gordon and his attitude to the
future, I grant you that—I saw how deep that particular gibe went
—even at the cost of causing yourself all sorts of personal loss.
Look, Hattie, I'm not telling you you should stay at Brookbank—
far from it. I'm human enough and petty enough and mean
enough to want to see Oscar get his comeuppance, and get it he
will if you go. I'd also like to see you at Whyborne in order that
you get the chance to do the work you're capable of, and get the
rewards—in money and kudos—that you're entitled to. And I'm
not one of your pinkish lefties. I couldn't care less about the rich-
man, poor-man argument. But surely *you* have some ideas about
the morality of it all?"

She thought for a few moments. "Yes, I've got some ideas. Not
very well formed perhaps, but—God, but it's difficult to think
about that side of it! Whenever I try, I keep thinking of other
things. Of Patty and her damned Ben, and how they'll get by in
Montreal. Of George. He'll be fit to be moved in another week,
and that makes the decision—the *final* decision so bloody urgent,
and Oscar—"

"Try. It may help you to make the decision more easily," he said
and smiled at her encouragingly.

"You look like a schoolmaster when you do that. All right, I'll
try. Morality—well, this rich-man, poor-man thing—I'll tell you

this much," her voice took on a bitter note. "I can't be the only one who's lumbered with an old person they loathe, who's got to make decisions about the life of such a person. Well, if this treatment—and it applies to mine as much as to Ross-Craigie's—if it's limited only to people who can pay for it, it'll at least ensure that the only people who go on and on living into revolting old age are the ones with enough money to pay for the care they need. Rich old men aren't as heavy a burden as poor ones. God knows I'd rather die myself in my sixties than live to be an albatross like George in my eighties."

"A valid point," Theo said with a fine judicial air. "There's a case for selection for death, just as there's a case for selection for birth? Certainly, we'll soon be at the stage of having to license people to give birth, and it's logical to suppose that others will have to be hurried on their way a little to make room for the licensed newcomers. And money's as good a way of selection as any, I suppose. In these egalitarian times, the ones with money tend to be the most capable, the most energetic, so why not?"

"More schoolmasterish than ever, Theo. Take care or you'll be looking over the top of your glasses at me."

"A delightful thought—almost worth getting glasses for. So, your social conscience could stand up to working at Whyborne. Well—"

"And on a purely selfish note, it'd be pleasant at the very least to get away from all this trouble with the strikers. No one can enjoy running a gauntlet of pickets in and out of the place—and what it must be costing to run that generator every time they turn off the power—"

"They've only done it twice this week. It could be worse—and Hattie, you're naïve indeed if you think the striking and the rest of it will be escaped if you go to Whyborne, just as it was naïve of your Sydenham man to think it'd all stop when Ben went. For God's sake, once you go there, the place'll be bombarded, because you really *will* be doing what they merely think you're doing now. Much as I hate to admit it, I must tell you that any high-minded attempt on your part to cool down that situation will depend on your staying here at Brookbank. But my own feeling is to hell with that—go to Whyborne and sit it out. Sefton won't be the sort of man to be unduly worried by a few strikers. H'd cheerfully sit out a general strike as long as there was something in it for him."

"No doubt. So you think I should stick to my guns, Theo? Go to Whyborne, and forget Oscar?"

"You could, you know." He smiled at her with a great warmth. "You do yourself an injustice, you know, my dear. You've let Oscar —who you must know can be appallingly destructive when he tries —you've let him convince you that you're totally without attraction for anyone but him. But do be logical, Hattie. If you were so sexually repellent, would he be—would he have been prepared to continue the liaison as long as he has? Would he be so prepared to go on into the future, as he clearly is if you stay here?"

"Dear Theo, you are kind. But I know the power of habit. And that's what I am to him. A habit he can break if he needs to."

He shook his head. "Such a nonsense. You really are—my silly Hattie, even at your age—about which you seem to be quite ridiculously self-conscious—you're a handsome woman. You've obviously got a lot to offer any man, and you needn't have any fears that—"

He stopped sharply and leaned back in his chair, and his face seemed to close up suddenly.

"I'd better stop. Not only will I not convince you, I might even alarm you more. After all, who am I to assess any woman's sexual attractiveness?"

"Theo, please, don't . . ." she said, and put out her hand, and at once pulled it back.

"You see?" he said. "I can't help you, after all, can I?" He laughed lightly. "Why can't I face up to reality and see what I really am, hmm, Hattie? I should have a little boy running before me with a sign saying, 'Thou art but a surgical oaf,' so that I stop trying to behave like a great wise psychotherapist. I thought you'd feel better if you were encouraged to talk, but as it is—"

"I do feel better," she said. "Much better. And I've made my decision. Really made it. I'll go to Whyborne, and put up with—well, I'll get along without—on my own. The sky won't fall for want of Oscar. Will it?"

He smiled then, with an enormous relief. "I'm delighted, Hattie. Really I am. I think you're going for the wrong reasons, but I'm glad you are. And you'll see, I'm right. It won't be so—"

A waiter was standing hovering behind him, and a little irritably Theo looked up.

"Mr. Fowler, sir, is the lady with you Dr. Berry?"

"What? Yes—this is Dr. Berry. Why?"

"You're wanted on the telephone, madam. The caller said he was sorry to disturb you, but it *is* urgent."

"George—" she said and stood up, and Theo too pushed back his chair, and they hurried across the room together, watched by every other diner there, all obviously delighted to find so interesting a happening to exclaim and conjecture upon.

But it wasn't Sam Lemesurier's voice that came clacking out of the telephone.

"Dr. Berry? I'm *so* sorry to bother you in the middle of dinner like this, but I just didn't know what else to do. Catherine's not here and anyway—well, I think I'd be grateful if you'd come back tonight. I went to check the animal pens as usual, just before going off for the evening you know, and there was the policeman, all right and tight as usual, so no one could have got in—anyway, three of them—the capuchins, you know, not the rats or guinea pigs—three are ill and one of them is dead, poor little thing. And I—well, I know what I think it is, but I'm only a technician after all, so if you could—"

"I'll be there soon, John," she said sharply. "Go back to the pens and stay there, and check every animal that we used, do you understand? I'll be there as soon as I can."

18

THE YOUNG pink policeman put a beaker of tea in front of her, and said loudly, "It's half past five, Dr. Berry. You ought to drink that and then go to bed. If you'll forgive my saying so."

"You're very kind," she said absently, and obediently sipped the tea, which was very dark and very sweet, and then put the beaker down and forgot it at once.

"John—which one is that? Have you started the RJ series, or are you still on the QI's?"

Gently, John slid the syringe needle out of the elbow crook of the small arm strapped to the bench, and flipped over the identity tag that was almost lost in the fur of the animal's neck. It snapped at him as he moved, baring its teeth in a perfunctory grimace, and then lay quietly, staring up at him with unwinking black eyes.

"QI 26, this one. I'll start the RJ series as soon as I've got this lot of specimens ready to go back to the unit. Are you ready for this one?—stop it, you little brute. I'll bite you back, you do that to your John—can you take him from me? Mind yourself now. He's *very* put out at losing his beauty sleep—never a thought for poor tired old us, rotten little—over you go then—"

He moved the animal to her bench, scolding and nattering at it but holding it with a gentleness that it clearly approved of, because it tucked its head down into his neck, and scrabbled against his chest with feet and hands, its tail waving majestically so that it curled under John's nose and made him scold even more.

She took her own animal across the room to the far pens, trying not to count up the total, but finding it repeating itself over and over in her mind.

One dead, and clearly it must have been hit with a particularly virulent form of disease to have succumbed quite so quickly, and three very ill, lying lethargic and dull-eyed in their pens. All from the first series she had treated. And in the same series, seven doubt-fuls, some with masses in their abdomens, some with scattered glands in axillae and groins. It was an ominous total.

She stretched her back wearily as she shut the cage door on the animal she had slipped into its straw-covered sleeping box, and turned to stare across at the working area. On each side of her the cages stretched away into the warm dimness, and she could hear the sleepy chattering of the animals, and the rustling of their straw bedding as some of them rooted around, disturbed by the activity in the big room.

The working benches were vividly lit, a clearly defined pool of white light centered in front of each of the tall stools. John fin-ished fixing the restrainers on the monkey on her bench, and then turned to peer into the dimness, looking for her.

"All ready, Dr. Berry—and I don't think there's any trouble with *this* one. He's a great deal too cheeky altogether to have much wrong with him."

She came across the room into the light and smiled at him. "I hope not—my God, John, you look—what time did that man say it was? Your eyes look like—"

"Pissholes in the snow, as my old grandma used to say, dirty old thing that she was. Ooh, I'm sorry, Dr. Berry—what *was* I thinking of, talking to you like that? You must be thinking I'm terrible. But there, I'm a bit past it, one way and another, and it just slipped out, as the—there I go again! If I wasn't going to come out with something worse! It's getting on for six, since you asked. No point in going to bed now is there? Too early altogether. Another hour, and we'll have checked the lot. And I don't know about you, but I couldn't sleep till I'd got the whole lot of them finished."

He looked at her through his red-rimmed eyes, and then his gaze slid away, embarrassed, and she smiled at him, and said, "Thanks, John. I appreciate it. Try not to be too miserable. Not yet anyway."

"Well, I'm trying, that I am, but I tell you, I could cry, really I could. I was as sure as sure you'd done it. Really proud of you. Well, I still am, and I know it's just—I mean, I had such a nasty

245

shock, you see, coming over to feed the little buggers, and there it lay, all stretched out and nasty. Really turned me up, it did. I was so sure, you see, it came as a double shock."

"It's unscientific to be sure till you've got your long-term results. You ought to know that by now." She was examining the animal on the bench, her fingers moving across its belly, reaching into the fur under its outstretched arms, and it gibbered a little as she worked, turning its head from side to side as it tried to reach her restraining hold.

"Oh, I know that, but you can't deny, you were sure too, now weren't you?"

"I should have known better," she said, and with the skillful ease of long practice held the monkey's jaw so that it had to open its mouth in a wide gape, and she could see easily into the gleaming pink cavern with its wickedly white little teeth. "This one's all right—but I didn't expect otherwise. He's from the last series but two—all the recurrences we've found are in the first series only. Just over a year."

"They are recurrences, I suppose? Or is that a silly question?" John said, and began to make a list of blood test specimens on the laboratory requisition forms, clicking the crimson-filled glass bottles from one metal mesh rack to another as he counted them.

"Yes," she said shortly, and went to put the monkey back in its pen before opening the last cage to start on the most recent series, the RJ's—according to her own code, the series she had treated last spring. For a moment she stood still, remembering the smell of lilac coming in through the open windows of the unit as she and Catherine and John had put the little black creatures, strapped onto their trolleys, into the oxygen chamber, had checked over the results of all the previous series, and let hope and a secret sureness start building.

Yet hopefully almost sure as she had been she had always expected something like last night. Somewhere deep in her mind she knew the expectation of it had lain, as inevitable as the realization of the hopes had seemed to be.

246

She had stood there in the doorway, Theo beside her and the policeman peering over their shoulders looking at John sitting lugubriously on the tall stool and staring down at the small body of the monkey on its enameled white tray. It had lain there, it's fur looking springy with health in the light, its eyes half-open, and it was almost as though it were alive until she touched it, and felt the cool flaccidity under the fur, saw the head roll lazily, sickeningly, sideways.

They had put it into the cold room, waiting for daylight and a postmortem examination, and she had taken off her coat and reached for the plastic overall that was waiting beside the bench, tying it on over her black silk grosgrain dress with only a momentary awareness of its incongruity.

"You aren't, surely, going to work tonight, Hattie?" Theo standing there in the doorway with his coat collar still pulled up round his ears had seemed as irrelevant as a buzzing fly. "It's almost midnight!"

"I won't be long," she had said, already moving swiftly, getting out syringes and needles, biopsy trocars and cannulae, bottles of local anesthetic. "I really won't be long—" and for all she knew he had gone immediately or had stayed watching them work for hours, for she had at once forgotten him, had forgotten the policeman, been aware only of herself and John and the monkeys as living and important creatures.

And now, though she knew academically that some hours had passed, it was as though she had been here only a few minutes, either that or all her life. It was an odd sensation, to be working so smoothly and efficiently inside a body that tried to drag her down with its boring weariness and aching; that she was working well she knew with certainty as she watched her own smooth brown-rubber-gloved hands moving in front of her, saw them check animal after animal, take biopsy specimens from one after another; but that she was achingly desperately tired she knew just as well, for her eyes were hot and sandy, and no doubt looked as red-rimmed as John's.

She remembered what he had said about his eyes and giggled

suddenly, and he looked at her and said sympathetically, "Like that, is it? I *do* know—I could positively shriek with it, myself. But that's the last, Dr. Berry. I've got the bloods all ready to go over, so I think I'd better go and get them into the fridge as soon as soon— never do to have all this work wasted just by not getting them preserved right. Shall I come back?"

"What? Oh—oh, no. No, there's no more we can do now. We'll begin the tests on those as soon as we start in the morning."

"Catherine will, you mean. Willing and eager as I am, Dr. Berry, no sight nor sound of me does anybody have a *minute* before lunchtime. Two o'clock, I'd thought, in my hopeful way—"

"Oh, yes—yes, of course. Two o'clock will be fine. And—er— John."

He looked back at her from the door, his face crumpled with fatigue under his ruffled fair hair, and looking very much older with a tired and waxen expression replacing the pertly eager one he usually wore.

"I'm very grateful to you, John. You were absolutely right to call me back as you did, and it was bloody good of you to stay the night and help me like this. I didn't even ask you to, did I? Just took it for granted."

"Oh, it's a pleasure, I'm sure. Anytime . . ." he said, and ducked his head awkwardly, and smiled and then looked suddenly solemn. "Not that I mean that exactly, do I? I mean, I'm sorry it was necessary. I'll see you then, at two o'clock, shall I? Mind you sleep well, now. Then we'll be able to think about where we go from here, won't we? Right now, I couldn't think about a *thing*."

She slept only for a few hours, waking sharply at eleven o'clock when a cleaner, singing loudly, came clattering into the staff spare bedroom. The woman had apologized profusely before escaping from the room with exaggerated quietness, turning the handle of the door to close it with agonizing slowness, but by then Harriet was fully awake with no hope or desire to sleep again.

She showered and dressed, putting on the black silk dress with distaste, for it smelled musty and stuffy with overtones not only of cigar smoke and cooking from the restaurant (which was one much given to the use of exaggerated flambé dishes that impregnated the air with the smell of hot oil) but with her own sweat. It was very clear evidence that she had worked flat out the night before—not that she needed it, for her shoulders were stiff and she knew that came from too many hours bent over a lab bench.

Catherine was in the unit when she got there, her head down over her microscope, the racks of blood bottles beside her.

"I found your note, and I've done the first batch," she said brusquely. "What's the rest of the news? I haven't had a chance to go to the animal pens to check. Recurrences?"

"Recurrences," Harriet said heavily. "One dead, three definite, seven possibles. All in the first series. Then there's the batch you've got there. I'm not sure about them. There was a three-month lapse between each series, of course, so they may be—the most recent series are fine. The animals are lively, no clinical evidence at all of any disease."

She yawned suddenly, and then said apologetically, "I worked till gone six this morning. I feel positively hammered. But—"

Catherine looked at her over her shoulder and said dourly, "You'll feel better if you get out of that dress, I imagine. There's a skirt and blouse of mine in the locker room you can borrow if you like. Nothing fancy, but better than that—"

"Thank you. I'd be glad of a change. I need some breakfast too. It seems a long time since I ate last night—which is silly. It wasn't all that long ago."

"Well, go and change," Catherine grunted. "And get yourself a meal in the canteen. I'll have finished these by the time you get back. Oh, and there's a message for you. On the desk." She bent her head again to the microscope.

"My dear, do please, contact me as soon as you surface today," Theo had written. "I'll do all I can to help, but obviously I say not a word to anyone until I hear from you. Don't be too depressed; I've no doubt at all that this is a temporary setback of the ordinary

249

kind, and you'll sort it all out with your usual dispatch. As ever,
Theo."

She should have felt warmed by his solicitude, encouraged by his
staunch assurances, but all she found in herself as she crumpled the
note and dropped it into the waste bin was a mild irritation. He
was mothering her again, and today she found it annoying rather
than comforting. She was too busy to be bothered by his concern,
was too preoccupied with other matters to worry about him worrying about her; and she was talking as much to him as to Catherine
when she spoke.

"I've got to do the necropsy on the one that died. Not that I'll
do much of a job until I get my head a bit clearer. I'll go straight
over to the pens when I'm ready and start. Come over as soon as
you're ready, will you? And if John arrives, he can come too. I want
him to start the second round of checks. Christ, there's so much to
do—"

But a change of clothes, to Catherine's businesslike black skirt
and blue gingham blouse (which smelled faintly of coal-tar soap, a
fact that amused her out of all proportion to its intrinsic humor),
and coffee and hot toast did a great deal to restore her and to
further banish Theo to the back of her mind, and she went over to
the animal rooms in an almost buoyant mood; there was a piece of
important work to be done, and what mattered was the work itself,
not its possible outcome.

She had opened the little body and removed most of the major
organs to tagged jars by the time Catherine and John came to join
her. Catherine began at once the work of preparing histology slides
from the lymph node specimens Harriet had set ready, while John
stopped on his way to the cages to stand beside her for a moment
peering into the small cadaver with his hand held over his nose.

"Smells a bit more than usual, doesn't it?" he said, and Harriet
nodded, absorbed in her delicate dissection of the pancreas.

"Widespread disease," she said. "Miliary. See? The pancreas—
absolutely riddled. Most interesting. Catherine, come and look at
this—"

250

They slid into a familiar working pattern, and in some ways it was to Harriet as though time had turned itself backward. This could have been any time in the past two years with the three of them working together almost cozily, dovetailing information, plotting it on charts, and watching the facts fall into focus. Only when she caught sight of the policeman still sitting doggedly in the little office was she reminded of the events that had led to his stolid blue presence being there, and then the memory came only to be immediately dismissed.

It was surprising how little time it took them to organize the facts they had. They came, all three of them, back to the unit with their charts and graphs, to sit and eat the ham sandwiches and drink the coffee that John provided, talking and contradicting, comparing and criticizing, and as ever, Harriet found a great deal of help in Catherine's decisiveness. She was trained only as a laboratory technician, but she knew her job inside out, and had a considerable gift for cutting through unnecessary trimmings to the real heart of a piece of work.

"I've got ESR readings and blood chromatography here—I saw no point in doing any further work on the chemistry on those blood specimens. They were too sparse, anyway. But added to what you've got from the necropsy, and the first of the histology slides, I'd say—well, perhaps I shouldn't. Once is enough."

"Well, I'm going to say it," Harriet said firmly. "Because it's obvious to me, at any rate, it isn't as bad as it looked last night. Not nearly as bad. I won't know for certain for another week at least, but on present showing, there's no reason why we shouldn't be able to reverse it again. Damn it, I said long ago—you remember? I said then when we got the first clear series, that we'd have to watch for recurrences that needed a new course of treatment. The one thing I didn't expect was that the disease would be quite so virulent when it did recur."

"The one that died—it had a primary of lymph tissue, remember? Could that have anything to do with the rapid spread of it?"

"Mmm. Maybe. But whether it is or not, one thing's sure.

251

We've got to be prepared to reestablish treatment fast once we have evidence that a recurrence is possible. Obviously we can't start too soon—we'd be in danger of setting up exaggerated autoimmune reactions which in themselves could—Catherine, have you graphed the EW series, and the FX's? Because it seems to me logical to suppose we could plot a graph which would show the critical time area quite clearly. We'd know exactly when to start the next series of treatments to make sure not only that we get no recurrences but also that we get no prematures. Are you with me? Then, we'd—"

"Yes, I see—but I couldn't—look, I'll go over to Norwich tomorrow and see if I can use the university terminal to the big computer at Rothwell. Could I, do you suppose?"

"I'll have to ask Professor Bell's permission for that, of course, but I don't imagine—"

She stopped quite suddenly. In the rush of work, the almost exhilarating absorption in the problems presented to her, she had almost totally forgotten the situation she was in. Not Theo's note nor even the policeman sitting in the animal rooms had really reminded her, had made her fully aware of the complications she would now have to cope with. Oscar would have to be told. And if she were intending to go to Whyborne, they would have to be told there too.

She closed her eyes, trying to think logically, and through the mist of concentration Catherine's voice said insistently, "And as well as getting permission to use the Rothwell computer, won't Professor Bell have to be asked about Mr. Ferris? We *are* going to have to bring him back, aren't we?"

Oscar sat hunched over her pile of graphs, and she sat there in the armchair on the other side of his desk, her hands quietly folded on her lap and feeling rather more composed than she would have thought possible. This was the first time she had been alone with him since the night he had presented her with his ultimatum, and she had frankly expected to feel some confusion when she faced him. She had remained standing outside his office door this morning for several moments before she could comfortably walk in and face Miss Manton and then Oscar himself.

But he had said nothing whatsoever that could be construed as remotely personal, not even after Miss Manton had closed the door on them both and gone away with Oscar's instructions that he was not on any account to be disturbed.

"Well, Harriet? What can I do for you? Sorry I've not been around much to talk about Establishment problems these past few days—I've had to spend a lot of time in London. You said on the phone you wanted to discuss problems. Nothing too complicated, I hope?" And he had looked at her with a bland gaze that told her nothing of his thoughts or feelings.

"Rather complicated," she said crisply. "You'll find it all here," and she had put in front of him the graphs and charts and her carefully prepared report, which John Caister had typed at almost midnight not without some complaining, and sat back to wait.

Quite what he would say she couldn't imagine. As she sat there in the large shabby office, staring out at the grayness of the December morning, she wondered, vaguely, whether he would share her disappointment, or display anger, or show a triumphant if childish pleasure in her failure, and couldn't decide which was most likely. With Oscar, it was impossible to guess.

"I see," he said after a long silence broken only by the rustle of turning pages. "As you say, a rather complicated set of problems. But not so complicated that they can't be unraveled."

He smiled at her, a small wintry smile, and stood up to begin his characteristic pacing about the room, and she sat and watched him as she always did, and listened to him talking.

"As I understand it—and since I have had so little part in this piece of work, my understanding is of necessity a little limited—as I understand it, the first series of animals you treated successfully have shown severe recurrence of their original disease, in a particularly virulent and fulminating form. One animal is dead and—"

"Two are dead. Another died this morning," she said flatly.

253

"Two are dead and—ah—two very ill. And seven show definite disease but aren't yet too toxic. Of the next series, there are blood changes, some biochemical evidence of pre-disease processes, but no frank disease. Later series are still perfectly fit and well."

He paused, and looked at her expectantly. "Have I got the picture clear?"

"Yes," she said. "That's precisely the situation. But there is a little more to it than that—"

"I'm coming to that. Now you say, on the basis of your previous work, that if you can start a new preparation of your autovaccines on each of these animals, and start it on your second series at the right time, you can prevent recurrence. And if you can start new courses of treatment at once on your first series, you should, given sufficient resources, be able to have the same success with your treatment again. Have I got it right?"

"Yes," she said again.

"Hmm. And above all, the human series—Mr. Ferris, in other words—needs to be brought back here to have a new batch of vaccine prepared and a course of treatment recommenced."

"Not until we know that he's in need of it. We can't give the vaccine as a prophylactic. Only when we know he's showing precancerous cells. And to know that, we have to run daily investigations. I wouldn't feel justified in making the time lag any less."

"No need to be so belligerent, Harriet! I take your point, indeed I do, very precisely. You're asking me for a great deal of Brookbank's resources, a considerable sum of money, and additional technician and laboratory staff so that you can go ahead with dealing with—ah—the situation. Especially Mr. Ferris."

He was standing by the window now, and staring out into the dripping dismal garden that backed onto the main administrative building. He stood there for a long while, it seemed to Harriet, sitting as still as ever in her chair but feeling less true composure than she was displaying. She realized now that she had actually expected him to send her away with a flat refusal to spend more money on her project; had really thought he would be pleased by

254

the setback and would regard it as sufficient evidence of failure to warrant ending the work altogether. Yet clearly he was not going to react in any such way; and she began to feel tension rising in her, spreading through her shoulders to link her hands in a tight grip.

He turned sharply and came back to his desk to sit down. "Well, if that's what you need, that's what you need. Certainly there can be no question—Mr. Ferris must be brought back, as soon as possible. Can you arrange that?"

The tension began to ebb, leaving her shaking slightly, and she moved awkwardly, crossing her legs and forcing herself to relax before answering him.

"I imagine so. I'm afraid the last time we met, it was all a little . . . unfortunate . . ."

He raised his eyebrows in interrogation.

"The 'Probe' program."

"Oh. Yes, I'd forgotten that. Still, on such a matter as this—it won't be easy to persuade him to return, if he's feeling fit. Not without frightening him rather a lot."

She grimaced. "I know. But one way or another, he's got to come back. As long as you're sure I can have the resources."

"I've said so, haven't I? I won't back down, I promise you. I never back down on anything," and for the first time he let his glance slide across her, reminding her, repeating.

"I didn't think you would," she said dryly. "I was just making sure."

"Now you're sure. Right. I'll speak to Personnel and see you get some extra lab staff right away. I imagine Caister and Mrs.—what is it, Mrs.—Warne—could do with some rest. Not to speak of you. You look a little fatigued. Would you regard the offer of—ah—assistance from other personnel as an—um, as an attempt to remove from you some of your control over your own work?"

"I'm not sure I understand you," she said sharply, and he smiled.

"Oh, I'm not offering to work with you—far from it. It would never do, would it? Even though providing such assistance is part of my function here. However—no, I was wondering about young

Ackermann. He'd be useful, I imagine, and he's not precisely overworked at the moment."

"No thank you," she said immediately. "I've worked alone for too many years now to be happy with another researcher cluttering up my unit. I like my independence." She smiled then, a little wickedly. "Though I'd like to be able to ask Theo to help with some of the biopsies and so on. If there's no objection. He's a very good surgeon indeed, of course, and he's in total sympathy with my work."

"Oh, Fowler—by all means. I don't think of him as precisely one of the Establishment's researchers, I must confess. More in the nature of a superior—very superior—technician. After all, surgery . . ." he dismissed surgery with a flick of one eyebrow. "Now, if you would care to let me have a clear account of your needs, I'll put things in train. You'll have the additional equipment as soon as ever we can get it."

She stopped at the door, and turned back, and said a little awkwardly, "Oscar—" and he looked up and smiled at her.

"No, Harriet. Work, just work. Another time we can discuss other matters, hmm? Your most immediate concern is to go and find your Mr. Ferris. But just one word of warning. Be discreet in your approach to him. Do remember that your—er—that Sir Daniel Sefton has in effect bought him. You may not want Sir Daniel to know, just yet, that it's necessary for Ferris to return here. I'd keep that in mind if I were you."

19

"WHEN I GOT your letter, I said to the old woman, 'There, you see? I told you she wasn't the sort to bear no grudge.' She was sure you'd never want to have nothing to do with us again, after the way you told me where I got off that night." Mr. Ferris's eyes gleamed with memory. "That was a turn up for the book, that was. There was I thinking you'd be glad, and—but there—" He shook his head. "Old news, all that, old news. Anyway, here I am, large as life and twice as natural, and at your service. I told 'em at work— no matter if you sack me, I said, off I'm going because I know I'm needed. Not that they'll sack *me*, never fear. One of the sights, I am. They brings these delegations round the factory, from all over —Yugoslavia, Czechoslovakia, you name it, they come—and they point me out like Nelson's column! Oh, no, they'll keep my job open for me, while I'm 'ere, cooperating in your research. I told 'em that was what it was all about, cooperating in your research."

"Still talking the hind leg off that poor old donkey, Mr. Ferris? Give the old thing a rest and do yourself a favor," John Caister said, and Ferris grinned at him, and threw a droll glance at Harriet before rolling his eyes up and smoothing one eyebrow with a carefully licked little finger in an exaggerated sketch of camp behavior.

"I appreciate your generosity, Mr. Ferris, very much," Harriet said. "It's good of you to come so far from home and for—er—possibly for quite some time."

He looked at her sharply, the little black eyes snapping with intelligence under the crest of dark hair, and said, "A long time? How long?"

"It's hard to say at this stage," Harriet said carefully. "It depends a good deal on how the research goes. I may be able to tell you more in a few days."

"You would tell me if it was more than just research?"

257

"How do you mean, more than just research?"

"Now, come on, Dr. Berry! You know what I mean, as well as I know what *you* mean a lot of the time. I'm not so green as I'm cabbage looking, let me tell you. I may be just one of your common or garden working class, *and* proud of it, but that doesn't mean I'm daft, does it? And the way you're talking—" he shook his head. "You sounded funny."

"Well, charming!" John Caister said. "You'd sound funny too if you'd been working as hard as Dr. Berry has this past couple of days. Forgotten what her bed looks like, poor lady."

"John, be quiet. Mr. Ferris, I'm not—"

"Why?"

"Why what?" She was finding it difficult to meet his eyes, for he was looking at her with a directness that made her feel as though he were holding her by the arm.

"Why have you been working so hard?" He twisted about in his chair and looked round at them all, at Catherine sitting arm-crossed at her desk, at Theo standing leaning against the oxygen chamber door, at John Caister, his head bent over work he wasn't doing in an attempt to hide his pink embarrassed face, for he clearly knew he'd said too much. And turned back to Harriet again looking quite different. His eyes had lost their sharpness, and his face had settled into deeper lines that seemed to drag the flesh downward from the fine bones.

"It isn't just research, then. It's something to do with me, personal."

There was a silence, and then Theo said quietly, "Yes. You're quite right, Mr. Ferris. It *is* research, but something more than that, and it is very much to do with you."

The little man looked over his shoulder at him, and grinned a little, but with none of his usual perkiness.

"Ta, squire. Nice to 'ave someone doesn't think I need wet nursin'."

He turned back to Harriet. "Well, Dr. Berry? Seeing as how the game's been given away good and proper by loverboy 'ere"—he jerked his head toward John—"and Mr. Fowler's treated me like a grown man and been honest with me, 'ow about you coming clean, too? It's your game, after all, and it's you as ought to explain properly. If you don't mind, that is."

"I don't mind," Harriet said. "In some ways it will be easier for me if you're completely in the picture. I just wanted to protect you from—however. Briefly, Mr. Ferris, some of the animals on which I originally tested the treatment have become ill again. We're working hard to discover the reason why they should have become ill again, and we're checking on all the other animals we used to make sure we can spot any further onset of disease before it actually happens. On the series that followed the one that has shown signs of illness we *have* managed to spot it, and we're preparing new vaccines for them now, and for succeeding series. But—"

"It could 'appen to me too, is that it? I could start gettin' ill again."

"Yes. It could happen to you too. And we want you here so that—"

"Yes. So's you can spot it in time. Well."

He put his hands on his lap, and began twisting his fingers, turning them from side to side, closely watching each movement he made.

"It's a funny thought, 'n' it? You get to thinking about what it'd be like to be dead, and then you get better, and you reckon it'll never 'appen again, which is bloody stupid when you know it's going to eventual, one way or the other, and you said as how—five years—you know? And then when it does 'appen again—it's a funny thought."

"I'm sorry," she said gently, and he looked at her and laughed very loudly.

"Sorry! Oh, I go for that! That's rich, that is! Sorry! What d'you suppose I am? Tickled? Oh, gawd, I didn't mean that, but—well, you know! Here I am, feeling twice as nice, and you tell me as I'm goin' to get cancer again, and then you says *you're* sorry. Well, I ask you! How'd you be?"

259

"As angry as you are, Mr. Ferris. And not, perhaps, quite so well controlled," Theo said in the same quiet voice, and Mr. Ferris looked at him, and after a moment managed to grin again.

"Like I said, Ta, squire. No flies on you, is there? Yeah, I'm mad—bloody flamin' mad. 'Oo wouldn't be? I'd like to . . ." he closed his eyes. "I don't know. I don't know what I'd like to do."

Theo moved then and came across the room to put a hand on the little man's arm.

"Think about what you'll do when you get through this, Mr. Ferris," he said. "Because I'll tell you something. I believe you will. I have a great deal of faith in Dr. Berry's techniques, and I truly believe you'll get through this and out the other side feeling"—he smiled—"three times as nice."

Ferris looked up at him, his face very still, but his eyes were bright again, and he stared at Theo for a long time, and then nodded.

"Right, mate. If that's the way it is, that's the way it is. When do we start? On the *research?*"

It was as though the whole room had relaxed a little, as though the very fabric of the place had softened and spread and taken away with it some of the tension that had been pressing on all of them. Catherine bent her head to start work on her eternal charts, and John stood up and smiled hopefully at Mr. Ferris, and Harriet too stood up and moved across to the door.

"Right now, Mr. Ferris. We want to examine you very thoroughly—Mr. Fowler as well as myself and then start a great battery of blood tests. Boring for you, I'm afraid, but—"

"Oh, don't worry about that. Got as many 'oles in me as a colander already. Will there be any operations? That I would like to know."

"Yes," Theo said. "I want to take some biopsies—remember? Little samples of tissue from different organs. I'll use a local anesthetic for today's, but after that, you can have generals and we'll do as many at a time as we can. That'll be less tedious for you."

"Well, *que sera*, as they say. Lead on, Macduff!"

260

He stood up and bent to pick up his suitcase from beside his chair, and John immediately hurried across the room to take it for him, but with a sharp upward look that was so filled with scorn that John stepped back in confusion, Ferris took it himself and followed Harriet and Theo out of the room.

He lay there staring up at the ceiling as they examined him, and it was as though he had gone away somewhere, leaving his body behind on the red-blanketed couch for them to play with. She looked at his face once or twice as she worked, but he was quite expressionless, and gratefully she returned to what she was doing.

Ever since she had sent the express delivery letter she had been worried about how she would tell him, what she would tell him. The experience of grief was one she knew too well to gladly expose herself to a further onslaught. But he had taken the news remarkably well, she thought, as she stepped back from the couch to make way for Theo, and began to enter her notes in the chart.

Theo moved swiftly and easily, his hands exploring the belly inch by inch, moving under each arm, probing the groin, and Mr. Ferris let him move his arms and legs as though they were no part of him, was as relaxed and flaccid as though he were anesthetized. But when Theo had finished and pulled the blanket up over his nakedness, he turned his head to look at them both, and his eyes were wide and darker than ever, the pupils greatly dilated.

"I know what I'll do," Ferris said, and his voice was almost dreamy. "When it's all finished. I'll go back to Majorca, that's what I'll do." He smiled at Harriet. "Have you ever been there? After that business with the papers and all, we went there for two weeks, me and my old woman. They said, I'd been a cancer patient too, so why not 'ave something for meself out of it—anyway, we went there. To Camp de Mar. It's a lovely place."

"I've been there," Theo said. "It's a pretty island."

"It smells so different. Sort of dusty and hot, even in the winter, when we went. And there's the hotels and all that marble and the stuff they eat in the bars—all 'orrible when you think of it, octopus and that—but it's all right to eat as long as you don't know till after what it was. And the sun and those courtyards inside the 'ouses, and wood shops and the sitting on the pavements drinking that coffee, and all the people from all over the world walking about and talking, and the sun sort of licks your skin and makes your eyes go all lazy. It's a lovely place. I'd like to live there. I really would like to live there. I said to my old woman, 'How about it? Open a little caff, sell tea and that to the English—there's plenty of them goes.' But, there, she didn't fancy leavin' the neighbors, you know 'ow it is. But I'll tell you this much. If I gets through again, I don't take no for an answer. You don't get a second chance all that often."

He looked at Harriet very directly, his eyes still very dark but sharper now above the bright red of the blanket pulled under his chin. "And you'll see to it, will you? I'll have that caff in Majorca, will I?"

"If I have anything to do with it you will," she said, and managed to smile at him. "That's a promise."

He nodded, apparently content, and she looked at Theo, seeking his reassurance just as Ferris had sought hers. But he didn't look at her.

In a curious way, she enjoyed the next few days. There was the pall of anxiety that hung over Mr. Ferris to be negotiated every time she went into the treatment room for the daily tedious run of tests, but that apart, there was the excitement of the work, the sheer comfort of the patterns that each day's efforts created, the sense of power that filled her as she planned and organized, to give her satisfaction.

It was a cushion too, protecting her from the anxieties that had seemed to fill her so pressingly during the doldrum period when there had been no real work to do, and no urgency about the little there was. She managed to find time to slip into Sam Lemesurier's ward to see George each morning before starting the day's work, and though she cared still, very much indeed, about his progress, the edge had gone from her caring; and when on the third day he was released from the monitoring equipment and accused her of arranging it deliberately—"I'll have an attack and die of it and no one will know, and then you'll be glad"—she had simply laughed and reassured him as best she could without feeling any of the dull anger such comments usually aroused in her.

Another considerable source of comfort was the way the power station strike seemed to peter out. Sydenham's judgment, rather than Ben's, had been right after all, for the pickets disappeared from the gates of Brookbank. They just weren't there one morning when she arrived, and she was intensely grateful for that. For her it was enough that the trouble seemed to have stopped, that there were no further fears about the power supply and the efficiency of the emergency generator. She could get on with her work in peace.

But Theo told her she was far too sanguine when she said as much to him.

"My dear, just because the local characters have got bored with the situation without Ben to put firecrackers behind them, it doesn't mean that the situation doesn't exist any more. It certainly doesn't mean that other agitators aren't still beavering away in their usual fashion."

There was a silence, while he concentrated on the delicate tying of a couple of veins deep in the abdomen of the monkey he was operating on, and then he said, "Give a little more muscle relaxant, please, Harriet. It's getting a bit tight."

She gave the injection, and checked the anesthetic apparatus again, and Theo, his big square fingers seeming larger than ever against the small body on which they were working, began to stitch the muscles in layers.

"There's your specimen, John," he said. "One mesenteric node, and I don't much like the look of it. Don't start to section it till I'm through. I want to take a look first—what was I saying, Harriet?"

He looked at her sideways over the top of his mask, while his fingers continued the busy and elegant tying of knots in the catgut.

263

"Ah, yes. I don't suppose Sydenham offered you any more information in exchange for—er—the help you gave him over Ben?"

"Certainly not," she said, stiffly. "I haven't exactly been in close contact with him apart from that one interview I told you about. I'm going to stop the anesthetic now."

"Fine. Just skin ties to do. Now why are you so edgy with me? Because I mentioned Sydenham? Or because I mentioned Ben and, by implication, Patty? I would have thought that after the years I've known you and your children I could talk about such matters without irritating you?"

"Oh, do stop nagging me, Theo!" She pushed the anesthetic trolley away and began to undo the restrainers on the monkey's wrists, as Theo finished tying the last stitch and reached for the spray of mastic to cover the neatly puckered wound. "I'm not in the mood for family chatter."

"But you surely haven't broken off contact with Patty, have you? That doesn't sound like—" he persisted.

"No, of course not! But . . ." she shrugged. "Damn you! If you must talk about it then, she has to work out her own relationships. I think she knows what I know. That Ben won't last. He'll be away one day, discarding her the way he—well, he'll move on and leave her behind. And she'll come back to England and we'll pick up where we left off, she and I. We're civilized people, and she isn't a child, after all. I can't do more, even if I wanted to."

"Oh, you want to. You'd like to scoop her up and bring her back to the cottage and look after her as though she were six years old again. Poor Hattie—"

"Stop being so damned patronizing, Theo! It's none of—"

"You're absolutely right. It isn't. John!"

Caister came hurrying from the far side of the room.

"Take this one, will you? It'll be around in about ten minutes, I'd say." He picked up the monkey, holding its head delicately in one hand so that it didn't loll, and John took it from him carefully. "And watch it doesn't pick at the wound too much. It's one of the most active ones, isn't it, as I recall? Yes—watch him. Lunch, Harriet?"

264

"If you'll stop nagging me, perhaps. But if all you're going to do is natter at me, then I'll lunch alone."

"Such acidity! Of course I'm going to natter at you, and of course you'll have lunch with me. And well you know it. Do come on—I'm extremely hungry."

He talked only of work, however, as they ate, since young Rodney Ackermann and Geoffrey Cooper shared their table in the canteen, but afterward, he insisted that they take a walk about the grounds before going back to the animal rooms.

"We've got a grueling afternoon ahead of us—there's nine of those animals to work on—and I need air and exercise to fit me for it if you don't."

And she had to admit she needed the air, hoary and wintry though it was, and she thrust her hands deep into the pockets of her coat and stepped out beside him, along the damp gray paths between the odd patches of garden and untidy sprawls of buildings.

"Seriously, Harriet, I do want to persuade you to give a little more thought to matters other than work," he said after a while. "I know there's a lot for you to do, with extra staff to control and the experiments to plan and set up, quite apart from monitoring Ferris. But all the same, you can't just put things into abeyance as you have."

"What things?"

"Stop being deliberately evasive! You know damned well what I mean! Are you still going to leave Brookbank? Are you going to Whyborne? And if so, when?"

"Theo, please. I won't be bullied about this! You know perfectly well that I can't make any definite plans at the moment. George isn't fit to be moved for a few days anyway and—for heaven's sake, how could I? Do I take myself and three hundred monkeys and Mr. Ferris careering across country to Whyborne? Do be your age!"

"It could be arranged, I imagine. It wouldn't be easy, but those animals aren't any use to Brookbank without you, so if you go, they'll sell them to your new employer without too much—"

She stood still, and he stopped too, and turned to look at her, his head sunk into his coat collar so that he looked like a bad-tempered penguin.

"Theo, I won't discuss this or anything else any further. I'm going back to the unit right now. I want to see Mr. Ferris's results before I do anything else this afternoon. I'll be over to start the lists with you by two o'clock. I'll see you then."

And she turned on her heel and went marching back along the path, knowing full well that she had probably sounded and looked like a petulant child, and that Theo was standing there behind her, almost certainly amused.

She was still angrily simmering a little as she walked into the main administrative building to collect her afternoon mail before going over to the unit. She was walking with her head down, staring at the ground as she went, so that it wasn't until she was so close to him that she could have touched him that she realized he was there, and his quiet, "Good afternoon, Dr. Berry," made her actually jump.

"I'm sorry! Did I startle you? I didn't intend to, but you were so sunk in thought, it was unavoidable. Quite the absent-minded professor pose, though it looks a little incongruous on a woman as handsome as yourself."

"Good afternoon, Sir Daniel," she said warily, and she knew her consternation showed, and could do nothing about it. Had he heard about what had happened, somehow, and come to tell her he no longer wanted her at Whyborne, as Oscar had warned her he might?

"I do hope you don't mind my coming so unexpectedly." He stood there in his neat dark-gray overcoat, holding his hat and gloves in one hand, she thought with a moment's amusement, like an advertisement for a dress hire firm. "But I felt it necessary to waste no time. Is there somewhere we could talk? I promise you I won't take up too much of your time, but I know you'll agree that what I have to say is important, once you hear it."

"Er—Oscar—Professor Bell's away. We might be able to use his office," she said, and led the way across the hall toward it.

"I know," he said. "That's one of the reasons I'm here. No,

don't look so alarmed. You will, I promise you, understand. Ah, yes. Miss Manton, isn't it?"

Miss Manton had surged to her feet, and was standing in front of Oscar's office door in an obviously protective fashion, but Sir Daniel smiled at her and said easily, "Dr. Berry wants to talk to me in here for a little while. We won't require anything, thank you." And although he didn't touch her, it was as though he had physically brushed her aside as he opened the office door, and held it invitingly for Harriet.

"Do let me take your coat," he said, and obediently she let him remove it from her shoulders and watched him as he hung it, and then his own, on Oscar's coat rack.

"Now, do let's be comfortable, shall we?" He looked around the room. "As comfortable as possible, that is. This armchair for you, I think, and I'll be content here on the corner of the desk."

She sat and looked at him, feeling slightly stunned, and he stared back at her for a long moment, and then said rather solemnly, "Dr. Berry, I owe you an apology."

"Oh? Do you? I hadn't thought so."

"Then you are indeed a very charming lady. Very. I have been feeling—well, if I say I behaved as I did because I was so anxious to secure your services, perhaps you'll forgive me."

"Really, Sir Daniel, you'll have to be a great deal more explicit if you're not to lose me entirely," she said, and let some of her irritation creep into her voice.

"I do understand. Briefly, then. I apologize to you for behaving in so cavalier a fashion about your father-in-law, Mr. Berry. I could and, of course, should have stretched a point and found a way to circumnavigate those rules. It can be done, and it shall be done. I have come today to tell you that there is a bed for your father-in-law at Whyborne, in Dr. Ross-Craigie's unit, as soon as he is fit enough to travel there."

"You—but—what about the costs?" Harriet said, knowing she sounded stupid, but not knowing how to seem otherwise. "My financial circumstances remain unchanged. I can't possibly—"

He raised both hands in gentle rebuke. "Please, my dear, I hope

I don't seem to you to be so—no, no! Do please forget the question of costs. Mr. Berry will be treated completely free of any charge. There will be no problem on that score."

"Why?" She leaned back in her chair, beginning to feel a little less bewildered. His urbanity was so much in evidence, his pleasure in the conversation so apparent, that she felt less vulnerable. He's wheeling and dealing again, she thought, and he thinks he's going to win this, whatever it is.

"You wouldn't believe that it was due to a bad conscience? That I knew I'd attempted to—ah—use a form of blackmail on you, and felt guilty about it?"

"No, I wouldn't believe that. And you don't expect me to, either. Do you?"

He laughed with real enjoyment. "No. No, indeed. I'd be most disappointed in you if you did. You are in many ways a gentle person, Dr. Berry, not at all the stereotype of the successful hard-hitting top-of-her-tree lady. You told me you were no business-woman, and you were absolutely right. But under the gentleness, there's obviously a very shrewd mind."

"You still haven't answered my question."

"No, I haven't, have I? Well, if it's not sheer guilt, or sheer altruism—"

"That I could never believe in."

"No? Then you misjudge me. I *am* capable of it. But this time it isn't altruism—not obviously so, though it will be in the long run. I'm quite determined that you shall come and work for Whyborne, in order that your considerable scientific mind be given the research possibilities it deserves, and thus the world be given the vitally important fruits of that mind—"

"Sir Daniel, please, this is—"

"—so I intend to use every possible—ah—lever I can to get you out of here."

"And you think that definitely accepting my father-in-law as a patient will make me come?"

"Oh, no!" he said cheerfully. "That's almost immaterial, now.

268

Your father-in-law will very soon achieve the status of a staff member's relation, I have not the least doubt, because I'm quite certain, now, that you'll agree to accept my offer. And when I tell you why, you will also see why I came in the sure knowledge that Professor Bell is away."

"Well?"

He looked at her, suddenly serious and put his head on one side so that the light from the window shone on the sleekness of his hair.

"This may be a little painful for you, in one way. You're a very loyal person, as I well know, and I'm afraid I must tell you that you've been badly let down. But better to know now than later. Well, Dr. Berry, yesterday I met Professor Bell in London. We were both attending a Department of Science meeting. I have some small—ah—influence in those particular corridors of power. And he was at some pains to tell me that you had failed. That some of your animals had died of an unexpected very virulent recurrence of their disease, and that at this very moment James Ferris is here under observation, because you expect his disease to recur, also. Professor Bell pointed out that I would hardly want to maintain my offer to you under these circumstances, and assured me that he would be happy to tell you, on his return from London tomorrow, that my invitation had been withdrawn."

20

HER FIRST REACTION was to call him a liar. He sat there, so
smooth, so rich in style, so altogether hateful, telling her lies. And
she almost opened her mouth to say so.

But she did not, for somewhere deep in the recesses of her mind
she could see the whole little scene, exactly as it must have been.
Oscar, as elegant in his way as Sir Daniel, standing close enough to
him for his greater height to give him some advantage, but not
quite achieving it; the general chat on apparently unimportant
matters that was really a jockeying for position, and then, Oscar,
choosing his moment as skillfully as he could, dropping the news so
gently, so sadly, so affectionately, even. And Sir Daniel, nodding
and smiling and deciding how he would use the information, already weighing in his mind the pros and cons of Harriet Berry, that
prime piece of stock in the meat market. Not quite as prime as she
had been perhaps, not now, but still worth keeping a finger on, in
case some other shopper got there.

"Stupid Oscar!" she thought, staring dumbly at the man sitting
so tidily on the corner of the desk. "Stupid to play such games with
a man so far out of his class."

Sefton smiled at her, very kindly. "I'm truly sorry to have to tell
you so . . . unpleasant a piece of news. It's never agreeable to be
told that a person to whom one has given one's loyalty values it so
little. I hope you won't hate me for being the source of such
knowledge. It happens that way sometimes."

"No. I don't hate you. I don't hate people very easily. It's not
one of my skills." She paused, watching him thoughtfully. "Sir
Daniel, why should you—I'm a little puzzled. You've been told
I've failed. That my treatment is not as effective as we'd hoped.
And no one's likely to pay a great deal of money for the privilege of
being a research patient in a project that might leave them no

better off than they were before. Yet you're not withdrawing your offer to me? Why not?"

"But you haven't failed, have you? Nothing like it! You've had a setback, perhaps, but that isn't anything to make me panic—whatever effect it may have on other people. Actually, it hasn't really worried Professor Bell, I suspect, for all he used such emotive terms in telling me of what had happened. He was the one to use words like failure, and dead-end research—"

"He said that?" she asked softly.

"I'm sorry, but yes, he did. I'm afraid so. But, you know, I don't think he really meant it. That is, he meant me to *believe* he did, but for himself—he believes your treatment is basically successful, that you're on the right track. I'm sure of that."

"Because he tried so hard to persuade you to stop trying to get me at Whyborne?"

"Partly that. And partly because he's managed to convince his masters in Whitehall that your work is good. They'd never have agreed to what they have unless he'd been *very* persuasive. And even Professor Bell couldn't coax money of that order out of those hard-headed bureaucrats without having a very passionate belief in what he was saying."

"It is a great deal, isn't it?" she said carefully.

He laughed. "Oh, dear, Dr. Berry, I shouldn't be amused, but I am I'm afraid. You really aren't very good at this, are you? You knew nothing whatsoever about the extra money Bell has managed to get out of Blumer and his boys. Did you?"

"I—I had heard that—I knew that Professor Bell had spent a lot of time in London lately. And it's been pretty general knowledge around the Establishment that he's probably managed to get an increase in resources. He's allowed me more, certainly."

"But you, personally—are you going to get any more out of it?" he asked softly. "Not just for your work?"

"Why should I? If I were just interested in my own pocket, I would have come to you as soon as you held out your lure, wouldn't I? I'm not interested—"

271

"No?" He raised one eyebrow. "Perhaps you will be when you hear that Professor Bell will gain from it, then, even if you won't. His own salary has been increased to match the stature of the new financial structure of the Establishment."

"You have been listening to a lot of private conversations, haven't you? It really is remarkable how many facts of this sort one person can pick up with a little judicious prying!"

"Now, I know you're upset, my dear Dr. Berry, but you really mustn't be spiteful. It doesn't suit you! And I do want to be able to enjoy a happy working relationship with you at Whyborne. It is half the battle, don't you agree? Well, now—" He stood up, and straightened his jacket carefully before going to the coatstand and collecting his property. "I must leave you. Professor Bell will be back tomorrow and I'm sure you'll want to talk to him immediately. I'll be waiting at Whyborne to hear from you, and I know what it is you'll be calling to tell me, hmm? How could it be otherwise, now? Goodbye, Dr. Berry—" And he held out his hand.

She didn't move, but sat staring up at him, consideringly. Then after a moment she smiled a little, and said, "Before you leave—I'd like you to come to the ward to meet Sam Lemesurier. He's looking after my father-in-law at present. You can make direct arrangements with him about the transfer. I think he'll be fit to be moved fairly soon."

"Now, that really is unworthy of you, my dear! You don't have to make any attempts to force me to keep my promise! I said Mr. Berry would be treated—"

"Free of charge."

"Free of charge, and so he will be. I'll gladly meet your Mr. Lemesurier, but there's no need. The arrangements can be put in hand as soon as you choose. The admissions people at Whyborne are expecting a call from you, and they will do the rest. It's out of my hands now."

"And my present research—the failed work. I'd be able to complete it at Whyborne? You'd agree to buy my animals from Brookbank? You'd agree to my continuing with Mr. Ferris?"

"Of course! As I say, I have no fears about the progress of your work, none at all. If these monkeys die, if Mr. Ferris dies, the next will survive. As long as you're able to continue your research. That's the important thing."

"Yes," she said, and stood up. "That's the important thing. Very well, Sir Daniel. I'll contact you—after I've spoken to Oscar, of course. Goodbye."

"Naturally after you've spoken to Professor Bell! Goodbye, Dr. Berry." He took her hand and held it between both of his. "This will, I know, be the beginning of a long and fruitful relationship—working relationship—for all of us, I'm quite sure. We'll be able to forget the—um—unpleasantnesses that went before, and start out new and fresh. I for one am looking forward to it immensely."

Theo looked at her sharply over the top of his mask when she arrived at the animal rooms and began to scrub up, ready to cope with her own list.

"You *were* held up, weren't you? I called in to the ward to see you, but you didn't go to see Mr. Ferris."

"No, I couldn't manage it after all. I'll go as soon as we're finished here. Catherine, you can start the anesthetic on my first one, please. Which is that, Theo? Second case?"

He grunted an assent, and returned to his work, and she thrust her arms into the gown the new young assistant technician was holding ready for her, feeling a certain wry pleasure. Theo knew perfectly well that Sir Daniel had been here, she was quite certain, for Theo was as gifted as Sir Daniel himself in digging out information. And now he was consumed with curiosity, and she found herself enjoying the knowledge of that with what was almost malice. She smiled into her mask, and began to put on her gloves.

It was past six by the time they had finished the day's operations on the animals, and the collection of lymph nodes, mesenteric biopsies and blood samples were neatly stacked and refrigerated for the next day's work on them. She went round the pens, checking on all the animals that had undergone surgery that day, making sure they had all recovered fully from their anesthetics before leaving them to the care of John Caister and his assistant (and she was amused to see how much dignity John had developed, now that he was no longer the most junior member of the unit's staff) to go over to the ward.

Mr. Ferris was sitting up in an armchair, watching a television play, his supper tray on the table beside him, and he got up and switched it off as she came in.

"No need for that!" she said cheerfully. "I won't be here long. I just wanted to see how you were, and to tell you about tomorrow's investigations."

"That's all right," he said listlessly. "I wasn't watching it, any'ow. Load of old codswallop, all of it. Some bird in this play, looks like she's never 'ad so much as a cold in the 'ead, and she's supposed to 'ave three months left to live, so she's rushin' around doing good to other people. I ask you! Did you ever 'ear of such a load of old crap? If you'll forgive the expression."

"I'll forgive it. And you're right—it usually is. How are you? Bored out of your mind yet?"

He grinned, but it was a lackluster effort. "Bloody near. It's the most—well, I don't see no one but all you lot, all day, do I? And 'ow much time have you got to spare? Sweet fanny adams, that's 'ow much."

"I know, it must be pretty hellish for you, and I'm sorry. But I'll tell you one thing—it does mean you're fit. Ill people don't have the energy to feel bored."

He brightened. "There's a thought. All right—I'll go on bein' bored and I won't complain about it. But don't expect no miracles in the way of the old cheerful chappie style. I don't seem to be quite so much of a Polly as I was, one way and another."

"You're not doing badly," she said, and began to check through the pile of reports waiting for her in his notes. So far he seemed perfectly fit, certainly; there was no evidence of any disease anywhere, yet. But looking at him, she felt a momentary stab of real fear. He was sitting in the armchair again, his head resting on the back and his eyes closed, and there was a waxen look about him, a thickening of the skin that looked wrong, unhealthy.

But that was merely subjective, an emotional response that had nothing of science in it, and she was annoyed with herself for producing it; it was getting more and more difficult to separate the scientific part of her from the rest of her personality, and what she was coming to know of the rest of her personality she disliked. Watching him, lying there with his eyes moving slightly below the thin stretched lids, she thought bleakly, I wish I'd stayed a G.P. I wish I'd never started any of this. I wish I were a different sort of person—and then almost physically shook herself.

"I must be more tired than I thought," she said aloud. "I'm sitting here and wandering in my mind. Tomorrow, we'll be taking specimens for the first vaccine preparation, Mr. Ferris. Do you remember that drill? You were pretty ill when we did it last time, but—"

He opened his eyes sharply. "Then you've found something? You're going to have to start treatment again?"

"No, no," she said soothingly. "This is just an in-case measure, I assure you. Just in case—" But he looked at her with his eyes wide with anxiety, and she knew he didn't believe her.

"I'm doing my best!" she cried sharply. "I'm doing my best! I can't do more—don't look at me like that!" And then she rubbed her face, embarrassed and furious with herself.

"I really am very tired . . ." she muttered. "I'll see to it that Sister gives you a sedative tonight, Mr. Ferris—good night." And she went, closing the door behind her with intense relief.

Theo was sitting in Sister's office when she went in, and he looked up at her a little anxiously and said, "I thought I'd wait to come back with you to the cottage. I'm too lazy to cook my own dinner, and I couldn't face the Brookbank mush tonight. Could you provide me with a little sustenance, do you suppose?"

"Yes, I suppose so," she said shortly, and then was ashamed of her bad temper and smiled at him. "I think I may have a piece of steak. A little elderly, perhaps, but—"

"I like my beef well hung," he said. "Well matured, like a really interesting woman, eh, Sister?" And he leered heavily at Sister Hornett who looked at him with an expression compounded of affront and amusement.

"Sister, I'll write Mr. Ferris up for some Mogadon, I think. He's getting depressed, and I want to be sure he sleeps," Harriet said quickly. Theo's bonhomie was to her so obviously strained and artificial that she was embarrassed; surely Sister Hornett had recognized the falsity of it?

"I'm not surprised he's getting depressed. No other patients to talk to—only Mr. Cooper's obesity patients, and they're all women, and not of much interest to him. Of course, there's the heart patients, but they're mostly in no condition to sit up and chat. Your father-in-law's getting a good deal chirpier, mind—"

"My dear Sister Hornett, unless you want to plunge poor old Ferris right into a slough of despond, you'll keep him well out of reach of old George. I know him, and believe me, he's like a plague looking for somewhere to decimate."

"Theo, dear, did you say you were hungry? Because if you're going to sit here boring Sister out of her mind with your chatter for much longer—"

"All right, all right! I'm coming." He stood up and patted Sister Hornett affectionately on her rump, and went to the door.

"I'll meet you in the car park, Theo," Harriet said. "I'm going to say good night to George before I go. Sister—?"

The old man was asleep, and she was grateful for that, and after telling Sister Hornett that he would be transferred to Whyborne as soon as he was fit enough for the journey, she made a last visit to the unit to say good night to Catherine, who was still busily working on her graphs.

She looked up as Harriet came in, and said gruffly, "You look tired out. Going home?"

"Yes. I am a bit past it. You too—how much more have you to do before you can leave?"

"Just these chromatography strips. Then I'll be off. Half an hour or so, no more."

She looked down at her cluttered desk again, and then looked up at Harriet, smiling. "It's good to be busy again, isn't it? I missed it all—the pushing, you know. The importance of it all. It was all so . . . flat. Boring. Once we'd got there." She looked anxious for a moment, "Not that I'm not as furious as anyone that this has happened. I wouldn't have wanted such a thing for the world. But—"

"I know what you mean." Harriet was putting on her coat, and digging into her pockets for her car keys. "I'm enjoying it too"— she stopped suddenly and stood there with her hands in her coat pockets, looking somberly at Catherine hunched in the pool of light over her desk—"until Ferris looks at me, and I know it isn't just an intellectual exercise but more important than anything has any right to be. It was so easy before, when he was so ill. Now he isn't, and I hate him for it." She grimaced. "Does that sound sick? It does to me. But it's true, all the same."

"It is going to be all right, though," Catherine said. "You know that, don't you? It may take a few months yet, to get it right, but you're on the right lines, and it's as inevitable as—as tomorrow that you've got the answer. Breakthrough, isn't that what they call it, the cheap papers and the commentators on TV? Breakthrough. Well, you have. It's perfectly clear—you've just got to iron out the details."

"I know. I—that's the trouble, with Ferris I mean. His details are so personal to him, and I mightn't get them ironed out in time. And he sits and looks at me and—Catherine, it's time I went home. I'm getting maudlin. Good night. I'll see you in the morning."

He was sitting hunched into his coat collar in the passenger seat of her car when she got in.

"I'll spend the night at the cottage, if that's not going to discommode you too much. I can have George's room, I imagine."

"By all means. Why? You don't usually—"

"I know. I usually prefer my own company in the dark watches. But—" He shrugged in the darkness. "I'm feeling lonely, Hattie.

Very lonely. I want to be—oh, I don't know. I must be getting old."

She had switched on the ignition, but now she stopped the engine, and turned awkwardly in her seat to look at him, sitting there staring ahead into the night, at the misshapen Establishment buildings bulking grayly against the heavier flat darkness of the sky.

"Theo, I'm sorry," she said. "I've upset you. Haven't I? And it's unfair of me. I run to you when it suits me, and then hold my counsel out of sheer bitchery—"

"Yes." He looked at her now. "You have been bitchy this afternoon. You've been walking about wrapped in your own private thoughts, obviously highly pleased with yourself, and yet—"

"Pleased with myself? No—no, I'm not! Why should you—"

"Well, maybe not pleased. But something happened with Sefton this afternoon, something made you feel . . . different. You've certainly been behaving differently. Why? *What* happened? When you shut me out, you—" He settled himself more deeply in his seat. "I feel so bloody inadequate. A worn-out old queer—there's a thought! The only use I've been for—oh, years—is as your crutch. And this afternoon you chucked the crutch away. Not very enjoyable, dear heart."

"Only for the afternoon. Just to see how I got on without it," she said. "But I knew before I started I'd have to pick it up again."

He peered closely at her in the dimness. "You've definitely made up your mind, then. You know what you're going to do. You *are* going to Whyborne?"

She smiled. "That's what Sir Daniel thinks. Oscar, however, thinks he's withdrawn the invitation. Oscar told Sir Daniel yesterday that my research had failed. Was dead-end."

"He did *what?*"

"Yes, you heard me properly. But poor Oscar—Sir Daniel saw what he was up to, and came here hotfoot to repeat the offer." She laughed softly. "He started by agreeing to take George into Whyborne. I agreed to that, too. Whatever I do, George's treatment is assured."

278

"And he'll get better and you'll go on looking after him as he gets more and more senile. I suppose you had thought of that?"

"Of course I have. But what else could I do? You know how it—"

"I know the sort of woman you are. So I know how it has to be for *you*."

"So, that's how it is. But for the rest . . ."

"Well? You will go? You'll tell Oscar once and for all that—"

"That I'm staying with him, Theo. I'm not leaving Brookbank."

There was a silence, and then he said furiously, "Christ all bloody mighty! You make me *puke!* How much longer are you going to let that bloody ram use you as—"

"You're jealous," she said, almost wonderingly.

"Stupid bloody word! What does jealous mean? That I want what he's got? The drives of some lousy farmyard animal that makes him use a woman like a—like a—Christ, the man doesn't know what love *is*, what caring about people is all about, and you think I'm *jealous*? If you can't—"

"I know what I mean. And so do you." She almost shouted it.

He drew a heavy uneven breath, and then there was silence in the stuffy little car. "Yes," he said eventually. "Yes. You're right. Of course you're right."

They sat side by side in the darkness for a long time, not talking, and then he stirred and turned his head to look at her.

"Why, Hattie? You haven't said why."

"Because I'm—oh, I don't know. Yes I do. I'm tired of decisions, and problems and wheeling and dealing, and people jumping up and down and making great polemical statements about me and my work. I'm more than tired of it. I'm frightened of it."

She frowned a little, screwing up her eyes against the dimness outside, and then her face smoothed out and she laughed softly. "I think I've discovered something new about myself, Theo. I'm frightened—I've always known that, but I don't think I knew what I was frightened of. I do now."

"You're frightened of change," he said heavily.

279

"What?" she turned and looked at him. "You know that? Then why did you—?"

"Try to persuade you to go away?"

"Yes."

"Because as long as you didn't know what it was you were so desperately trying to avoid, there was a possibility of getting you out of here, and away from Oscar, who's going to destroy you if he can, and somewhere that you could really develop yourself—use your brain the way it's supposed to be used. But now you know—"

"Now I know. So I'm staying here."

"You're a bloody fool, Hattie. A brilliant scientist, a charming woman, a dear friend and the biggest bloody fool I've ever known. Can't you see that it just isn't possible? You'll never do what you're trying to do. You can't just dig yourself in here and stop change from happening just because you don't want to look at it! Every moment of your working day is devoted to changing things. You're changing the whole bloody world with what you're doing, can't you see that? When people stop dying because of the work you've done, you'll have made one of the profoundest alterations in human life that's ever been made! Yet you won't face up to it for yourself. You won't go out and make the changes—the inevitable changes—work *for* you instead of against you. You'll sit here, clinging to the comfort of things known while they quietly change and change and change under your stupid blind eyes, and then the whole thing'll explode in your face, and what will you do then?"

"I don't *know*, Theo! Stop nagging me, for Christ's sake stop nagging me! I just don't *know*."

"You *must* know. You must! In a few months, a year—I don't know how long, but it's measurable time—you'll know that your treatment really works. You'll have a dozen Ferrises to prove it for good and all. And by then, the Ben Shoemans and the Daniel Seftons will have had time to really get ready for you. They'll have a system all set up to make use of you and what you've done, and Oscar—your precious bloody Oscar—he'll be there too, all ready to join in and batten on you, and what will *you* do? Sit there in that cottage with that senile old man with your eyes closed and cowering away from change as though it were going to kill you?"

"I don't know and I don't *care!*" she cried at him. "Can't you understand that? I don't *care!* There's now, there's this minute, there's all the minutes I have to go on living with myself, as I am, with all the hatefulnesses that are part of me. The things I need, and want, and have to have—peace, and security, and people to care about, and Oscar—yes, *Oscar.* Without all those I couldn't go on, can't you see that? It's like *you*—you're part of me and my life that I can't bear to live without. I—this afternoon, I walked by myself, I didn't talk to you, I didn't share with you, I didn't use you, and look at the way you felt! Inadequate? Old? How do you suppose I would be if I shed almost everything I know and care about, except for work? What sort of work would I be able to do? Don't you know me at all, Theo? God Almighty, don't you have *any* understanding?"

Once again there was a heavy silence in the car, but it was underlined by the sound of their uneven breathing, as the car windows misted and shimmered, and the darkness pressed in on them.

"Yes. I understand, Hattie," he said at length and turned his head to look at her. "Dear Hattie. I understand all too well. That's why I get so angry. One always is most angered by the inevitable. I'm like Mr. Ferris, enraged at the disease that's waiting to come back and destroy him. I know it's pointless, but I can't help feeling it. All right, my love. You hide away here from hateful change, but when tomorrow comes and change sits gibbering at you, promise me something. Make sure I'm around, will you? You'll need me then almost as much as I'll need to be there."

"Tomorrow?" she said, switching on the engine, and putting the car into gear. "Tomorrow—there's work to do. That's all I'm interested in. I've got work to do. We'll deal with the rest of it if it happens."

The car moved forward, its lights cutting a narrow swathe into the darkness, and as she swung out into the driveway she said it again, contentedly, "Tomorrow, I've got work to do."

281